Death of an Entrepreneur

Geoff Olds >

Publisher – Godsforge. www.godsforge.com

Title: Death of an Entrepreneur

Author: Olds, Geoff (1978—)

ISBNs: 978-0-6483679-7-0 (paperback)

            978-0-6483679-4-9 (epub)

            978-0-6483679-5-6 (mobi)

Subjects: Fiction: Thrillers – Suspense

Cover by Leanne Larson at http://www.canetoadstudios.com/

Photo of author (page 275) copyright © Tony Jong.

He who fights with monsters might take care
lest he thereby becomes a monster.
And if you gaze for long into an abyss,
the abyss gazes also into you.

Friedrich Nietzsche

Mental Health Warning

If this story raises issues for you
please call one of the following numbers –

Lifeline – 13 11 14 (Australia)

Emergency Services – 999 (UK)

Mental Health America – 1800 273 8255 (US)

For other regions and countries
check online for free services.

With all my love and more …

Q	U	C	O	M	D	N	E	R	B	I	R	F	Y	S	R	A	D	F	S	F
A	L	T	Z	A	G	O	I	U	U	L	H	N	M	E	E	U	E	N	A	W
G	C	E	A	E	F	T	G	O	E	G	T	N	Y	B	L	G	D	L	A	E
W	E	B	G	L	L	T	T	E	S	E	E	S	C	H	P	L	R	F	R	
H	R	L	B	M	A	Y	H	O	E	M	N	R	I	C	T	S	I	E	O	J
R	H	H	N	E	L	E	H	R	S	V	E	E	G	G	T	E	I	U	V	U
I	C	T	T	C	H	I	D	D	N	V	J	R	E	R	L	N	R	U	O	N
M	A	A	G	O	Z	S	T	A	I	J	E	P	E	R	D	N	E	T	L	T
E	R	P	T	G	C	I	W	L	T	T	O	N	I	C	W	Y	I	E	A	E
E	E	K	R	J	L	I	B	E	N	M	Y	Y	T	L	O	R	T	D	V	R
D	T	A	Y	W	L	L	E	A	H	C	I	M	V	A	F	W	E	I	O	S
A	E	B	T	O	H	H	E	P	L	I	E	A	R	M	R	L	N	A	G	L
N	P	G	G	N	A	Z	O	L	E	D	R	O	L	E	L	H	U	D	W	R
L	O	U	Z	E	Q	W	P	J	H	R	Y	B	X	E	A	N	E	O	H	P
R	A	P	T	U	D	D	O	B	C	F	S	A	X	I	D	Y	A	N	T	S
H	T	G	R	Y	S	I	L	V	A	Y	A	M	F	M	D	O	T	C	H	S
K	E	N	E	L	E	A	R	E	E	N	N	O	W	N	O	T	E	R	S	H
F	N	I	N	Y	H	E	B	D	R	R	F	E	L	E	V	E	N	I	A	I
W	O	G	C	T	O	O	L	I	C	T	H	R	E	L	S	R	B	L	K	M
F	F	D	H	L	N	Y	C	H	N	A	M	O	F	O	I	U	N	V	N	O
U	E	O	E	D	N	E	A	V	I	R	D	R	O	Y	N	I	O	T	R	W
K	T	X	Y	T	C	A	B	E	L	F	O	N	K	W	E	U	G	S	Y	K
Q	N	I	T	E	T	I	O	L	D	A	L	L	A	O	D	F	Q	L	O	C
X	T	E	R	N	R	Z	A	H	C	A	G	H	F	M	O	D	R	B	J	I
A	B	R	U	Y	A	M	F	R	A	W	D	E	M	T	A	T	E	O	S	T

Carnegie

The gun felt heavy in his hand. And slippery. James Andrew Carnegie had thought a lot about suicide in the last two years but in this slightly upmarket Hong Kong hotel he had decided to go out blazing. Well either the gun or the bottle of sleeping pills. He wasn't convinced he had the balls to blow his brains out, so his insurance policy was the jumbo size sleeping pills and a bottle of decent Scotch.

The gun was heavy and slippery. His palms were sweaty, a function of his body ever since he could remember. A pain really. When under pressure his back and palms always sweated early. Carnegie fiddled with the gun and remembered the Russian that had sold him the illegal firearm down in a small and dingy Hong Kong bar. Ilyan Lechov had been good to his word in providing the Colt M19 and the magazine of 10 rounds.

Not only was he good for his word but he didn't ask too many questions and looked the other way when he saw the growing madness in Carnegie's eyes.

If Carnegie had been around later on that night he would have seen Ilyan shrug multiple times, swig vodka and mutter to himself in his heavy Russian accent, 'What does it matter if another crazy person kills himself ...' Pragmatic was Ilyan, a heavily pragmatic man. Pragmatism was his religion. And vodka. One mustn't forget Vodka.

1

Carnegie hardly remembered the blurry night when he acquired the gun into his backpack and hightailed it back to the hotel hoping he wouldn't be stopped or held up by the police or some foreign security outfit from a foreign country investigating illegal firearm smuggling.

This had been a strange feeling for Carnegie. For whatever reason he also felt a heightened sense of alert and alarm when dealing with security and the law. He didn't know why but he was always tense around police officers, customs agents and security personnel. It was like he had committed a million crimes and was awaiting them to grab him but, of course, he was innocent and had nothing to worry about, but why worry?

In this case, however, he had committed a crime and was carrying around an illegal handgun from the World War 2 era. Did he feel tense and worried? No. Excited. Carnegie felt excited.

Later on, he would ponder this. Was he secretly born for a life of crime?

His shrink would tell him the feeling was normal and most people felt tense in these situations. In fact, he had given Carnegie a fancy name for the syndrome, but Carnegie could never remember the name of the syndrome except that he had it. There was probably a syndrome describing people who forgot the name of the syndromes. There was a name or a label for everything under the sun these days, Carnegie mused.

The night was muggy. It was a typical Hong Kong night. No rain. Just humidity. And the city throbbed and bounced away as if the giant city was an organism with a heartbeat. Below Carnegie people hurried through the night on their way to homes, carefully avoiding the prostitutes and the drunken tourists stumbling through the streets.

The delivery vans rumbled away, stopping to drop off much needed seafood and beer to keep the hungry minds and thirsty souls from starvation, dehydration and condemnation. Not far from Carnegie's hotel, a small woman rocked back and forth singing softly under the solitary tree in a greenish park surrounded by giant constructs. The buildings reached up into the heavens, the glass and glamour, heeding no attention to the busy streets below and the coughing masses.

Carnegie stared down from his balcony, gun in hand, watching the ants move about on their purpose. He sighed heavily and threw the gun onto the balcony chair. The ants below had more purpose than he did. They were richer than him on ground floor despite his wealth and his height.

Carnegie lit a cigarette and inhaled deeply. A moment of guilt as he inhaled and then it was gone. He leaned over the balcony again and felt the familiar tingling in his feet. The sky was dark, but you almost wouldn't have noticed in the city of lights. Hong Kong was lit up like a Christmas tree, buildings glowing away like giant lanterns.

His mind drifted. He felt nothing as he stood there numb and exhausted. Alive but Dead. Asleep but Awake. He smoked heavily, unconsciously staring at his smart watch every now and again. It was an old habit that died hard. The watch and the smoking. It was like some sort of tick born from his stressful life as a businessman. A twitch that worked through his head and body to distract him from other thoughts and anxieties.

Carnegie finished off the cigarette, crushing it slowly in the glass ashtray on the balcony. He stood sadly for a while, rubbing his hands through his greying hair. Shaking his head sadly and muttering, Carnegie slumped into the chair and toyed with the gun.

He slowly released the safety catch and stuck the gun deliberately into his mouth. His hands shook. His finger hovered over the trigger.

Time stopped.

Moments passed, and tears involuntarily rolled out of his eyes and down his exhausted face.

'Arghhhhhhh!'

Carnegie cried in frustration and put the gun on the floor. He swore and punched the side of the chair, ignoring the blinding pain that sprung from freshly bruised knuckles.

He couldn't do it. His lack of courage infuriated him.

He had not lacked courage. He did not lack courage. Carnegie was a man to face his fears. Build his dreams. Rise above negativity. Take on the world. Step in front of the punch aimed for another. Swim into the waves. Find a solution in the most of complex of problems. Cut business deals that defied opinion. Follow his dreams and ideas.

But this was testing everything in him. And he couldn't rise above it. He couldn't take his depression and hollow existence and end it.

Where had a life so rosy ended up so thorny?

How did, at the end of the pathway of success, lie the gates of failure?

When did getting everything leave you with nothing?

The thoughts plagued Carnegie day and night. His head throbbed away and through his tears he laughed sardonically and lit another cigarette.

Right at that moment he could have done with someone to drink or smoke with.

At that time, he would have done everything to have Kennedy there. Oh Kennedy, can you just walk through the doors and maybe all will be well.

But the chairs remained absent and empty. Just how he had wanted it, but not how he needed it. He often drove people far away, so he could be by himself. After all, it was lonely at the top. He felt he should suffer for everyone and suffer alone. Carnegie believed in inverting the pyramid; particularly in business. He should be at the bottom holding everyone up. Not the other way. He despised organisations that had a puffed-up CEO with a full bank balance and an empty head. How many of these so-called Presidents would be out of the trenches and first to take the bullets for his team? How many would be willing to take the blame for the largest faults of the smallest people in the company?

Company. A group of people. Not an individual. He had always felt a lead singer in a band. A captain on a football side. Carnegie sighed. Where had it got him. Stuck in a faraway city where the lights burned brightly everywhere but the light inside him had gone out.

He thought about his friends and colleagues. What seemed so glamorous to begin with was now a fucking chore! A chore of epic proportions. He missed his wife. He missed his kids. He missed the Waitress with the Kind Eyes. Most of all, he missed his innocence and would give anything to have it back.

He remembered the time he was walking quietly and sadly in Darling Harbour. The sun was shining brightly. The tourists were glowing with cameras flashing. The suits were busy chatting on their phones and going about their business. The buildings gleamed in the sun and water rippled away, beautifully and seductively.

And then it hit him. All it took was a moment and a small child licking an ice cream.

It had gone.

The hope.

The dreams.

The true happiness.

The wishful thinking.

The childish wisdom.

It had gone.

Innocence had perished.

Carnegie had stopped. Stunned. Tears poured down his face. He wiped at them angrily. Innocence had gone. It had long gone. He didn't even know when he had crossed the threshold.

Gone was cricket matches in the front yard. Bickering with his brothers. Teasing his sister. Excitedly playing video games. Listening to music for the first time. Lying on the beach. Looking at Sarah across the schoolyard. Drinking from the bubbler. One dollar of mixed lollies. Sausage rolls with sauce. Eating with abandon. The joy of McDonalds. Playing board games. Staying up late. Reading the Hobbit for the first time. The first plane trip. Clumsily taking a bra off for the first time. Ripping the head of a beer for the first time. The first gig. That first kiss. Collecting football cards. The first bicycle kick scored. That genuine moment of falling in love.

It had gone.

The robes of white had been replaced with the suit of metallic grey.

It was alarm clocks. Boozy nights. Spreadsheets. Frequent flyers. Duty-free gifts. 12-hour days. Mortgage payments. Netflix subscriptions. Domestic duties. Mechanical sex. Board meetings. Doing deals. 5-star hotels. Betrayals. Repetitive music. Credit cards. Interest rates. 24-hour news. Political correctness. Terrorism. Reality TV. Kardashians.

Carnegie was exceedingly melancholy. The water lay below him. And in that moment, he wanted to hurl himself into the harbour and transform into a dolphin. A turtle. A small fish with wide innocent eyes. But instead he sat there numb, crying. Choking on nostalgia.

He loved that movie with Jim Carrey. The Eternal Sunshine of the Spotless Mind. The concept of wiping away memories and coming back as a new man was just peachy. The seduction of life had dragged Carnegie a long way from his humble beginnings.

He was a simple but very ambitious business man who had made it out of the little pond in his suburban existence and was on his way upwards in the world of Marketing and Design. Carnegie was in his mid-thirties and looked perpetually tired. He dressed immacutely and was good at most things and extremely charming, especially with the ladies. His risk-taking behaviour left him constantly exposed and depressive, despite enormous gains and success on the outward side. He kept his depression on the inside and hid it from everyone; especially his closest friends who he constantly revved up by engaging in cards, drinking games and the clubbing scene.

He stood amongst the drunken crowds. Hands aloft, jumping up and down. A permanent smile frozen on his face. And the more he did it, the less he felt. The more he piled things into his life; the more the gaping hole opened inside him. The more money he made, the more transactions his business did; the more he felt poorer and devoid of the richness of the good in the world.

Carnegie remembered The Shrink he secretly sought out to deal with his depression. A mild Mexican gentleman with a fine goatee and a most pleasant accent. But all he seemed to get back was more questions.

'How do you feel about that?'

'What do you think that means?'

'When did you feel like this last?'

'Why do you think that is the case?'

'Who suggested that to you?'

Carnegie kept sadly responding with the same message. 'I don't fucking know.' And he didn't.

He didn't know much at all. But he could add up quickly. He could read someone in a heartbeat. He had an outrageously high IQ for someone with little education. And he had to keep visiting The Shrink because of a budding bromance and the fact he got to ask questions back and cry from time to time, which made him feel a little bit better and in a better place to cure his disease or at least make the leap to suicide.

The Shrink's consulting room was a perfect environment to lay back and feel the disease in his body and soul. With its comfortable couch and reasonable climate, Carnegie wondered what it was that made him feel so at ease. Perhaps it was because he could be alone but with someone? Or perhaps it was the raw nakedness of his mind and soul being exposed to a complete stranger.

A siren broke his reverie and he realised he had the gun in his hand again. It was a cold metallic object. A picture of his daughter came into his mind and, in sharp guilt, he launched the gun through the balcony doors, where it crashed into floor and slid into the wall. Tears started to form again, and he went on the hunt for alcohol. The perfect temporary cure for his ailment.

'Faark!' He swore to no one in particular as no one indeed was there. It was fitting that he was alone because that was the truest feeling at the end of the day for Carnegie. No matter the occasion he felt alone. He felt that no one really knew him and no one really could reach him, except perhaps for the Waitress with the Kind Eyes and the Shrink with the Gentle Tones.

This feeling of alone …

A roast dinner at his mother's house surrounded by all of his family. Alone.

A train packed with strangers that he would randomly converse with. Alone.

A packed nightclub. Alone

An intimate love making session with his beautiful wife. Alone.

A gospel meeting soaring with hymns. Alone.

A playground giggling with his two children. Alone.

A business meeting in which he inspired others. Alone.

A roaring football game. Alone.

Alone. Alone. Alone.

Hauntingly, Carnegie remember a quote he once read;

'I used to think the worst thing in life was to end up all alone. It's not. The worst thing in life is to end up with people who make you feel all alone.'

It wasn't until days later he remembered; it was something Robin Williams said.

< Sydney

Carnegie was ecstatic. A moment of utter euphoria. He stood on a packed Sydney downtown street. He felt like dancing on the spot. The suits walked past, unaware of the true joy he was feeling. The cars drove slowly past on their way to repetitive destinations. It was a warm autumn afternoon and the streets buzzed with commerce and creativity.

He had just closed the biggest deal in his life and was set to make millions. He smiled and rubbed his flat stomach over his crisp business shirt. It was great to be alive and all of his struggles had finally amounted to something. He fiddled with his iPhone, excitedly wondering who he should call and talk to. His parents? His wife? His business colleagues? The excitement pulsed through his hands and he randomly called Hammond; one of his first colleagues. It dialled out. Carnegie swore. Trust Hammond to be too busy doing real work.

He left a random voicemail.

Halfway through his gibberish Hammond called back. 'Carnegie. Sorry, I was on the phone to a client.'

'No problem Hams. You won't believe what just happened. My meeting with the corporate just finished and we got the deal mate!'

'Fantastic. What did we get?'

Carnegie proceeded with the details and knew the inevitable response.

'Sounds like a lot of work ...' Hammond left it hanging.

Carnegie groaned 'Trust you to take a big deal and focus on the negative.'

Hammond responded with the standard reply, 'Well I'm just a realist at the end of the day.'

And Hammond was a fine realist. So fine, he dressed up negativity as reality and almost got away with it on a daily basis. Carnegie used to joke that Hammond could be surrounded by a shitload of gold and still complain he needed a way to transport it to the bank.

Hammond was just a simple man that thought the worst in everything and was presently surprised when the earth didn't crash down on him every minute of every day. Carnegie admired him greatly for his ironic negativity and decided from time to time he would much like to try this tactic. Unfortunately, every time he did it made him more depressed and he struggled to get out of bed each day.

One thing Hammond wasn't negative about was food. He always had an appetite and, amazingly, was a stick figure despite the number of calories he consumed. Perhaps it was the diet coke he drank with every large meal he ordered. Or perhaps it was due to the fact he was sex crazy and never got anything apart from the many times he flew solo.

Carnegie admired this as well. In fact, there was a lot about Hammond that was admirable, and Carnegie liked to listen for tips from Hammond and his simple life. He didn't seem to have a care in the world despite 12-hour work days six days a week in order to keep their marketing business surviving and growing in the challenging market times. The business that had started just before the Global Financial Crisis was a good one. Carnegie had dreamed up a great name and a great business model providing creative marketing solutions to the many businesses in Australia and Asia Pacific. Carnegie liked to tell everyone about the business and remind them that those who made money sold to those who were building businesses selling to the masses. It was some insurance policy that Carnegie like to espouse. Just like those who sold buckets and picks to the ones digging for gold in the gold rush.

Unfortunately for Carnegie, Hammond and Co. along came the GFC. The Global Finance Crisis. Or the Global Fuck Companies.

And they were nearly fucked well and truly. In a matter of a few months they went from a nicely padded position to a bucket of red ink poured all over their accounts. In one day, five of their customers went belly up, taking with them thousands of dollars in unpaid fees with no hope of recovery.

Carnegie sweated in this period. He was chased by everyone for money. Staff, Suppliers, Charities, The Tax Man and just about everyone else who had a hand and a wallet. The worst of this, of course, wasn't anyone else but his own alter ego that wrestled him day and night reminding him often of his impending doom.

But, for some strange reason, Carnegie felt riveted during this period. Well, for the most part. It felt like a war scenario where you were under fire and the challenge was constant to stay alive. It felt like start-up days where everything was on the up and your balls were on the line every day.

Carnegie knew he was fucked in the head during this experience but somehow put it off until he met the Shrink with the Kindly Tones. Besides, the GFC was a great conversation starter with potential and existing clients.

'How are you coping with the GFC?' To which the reply was always 'It's killing us James. We've felt nothing like it.'

The other one that was useful was suppliers chasing for payment. 'Well you know the GFC has hurt us a lot. We need more time.'

But now he had this deal it was like it was all going to be good. Carnegie looked around for a cab to hail. He had to get back to the office. He hoped he didn't get a chatty taxi driver who would rob him of his buzz or another buzz killer like that son of a bitch Hammond.

A Sikh with an Amazonian beard finally let him into a taxi after Carnegie stood around hailing down cabs. He always forgot to check the lights on the roof of the cabs to see which ones were vacant. When in a reverie he always became very poor in observation; that and, of course, when he was very drunk. Which was weird because he became more alive and observant when he was drunk.

In fact, arguably Carnegie was a very observant man in all.

He observed the small coffee stain on the waiter's collar.

He observed the sadness in the child's eyes while being led away from school by his parent.

He observed the light bouncing off the water in a hotel lagoon.

He observed hollowness in the street preacher's voice.

And he observed the Sikh's hostility as he climbed into the taxi cab.

'Where to sir?' The driver said disguising his own contempt. Carnegie didn't hear 'Sir' he heard 'Shithead.' He wondered if everyone was slightly racist. He wondered if it was his skin colour. Perhaps it was his neat suit or expensive glasses that he took pride in wearing, as it made him look more intelligent. Carnegie only thought this because of the collective wisdom. The collective wisdom of the crowd who commented when he wore spectacles as opposed to when he mostly wore contact lenses because they were more comfortable.

Looks over Comfort?

The ladies thought so, especially when they strapped on their impossibly large stiletto high heels. They didn't improve intelligence but apparently 'the calves got a work out' and the 'ass looked better.'

Carnegie was doubtful about this but the collective wisdom won out.

He gave instructions to the driver and sat back, deliberately not putting on his seat belt. Carnegie took great pleasure in not putting his seat belt on. He enjoyed the liberty when drove around in Asia and secretly hoped he would be in a great accident that would kill him instantly because sometimes he wasn't sure life was worth living. Sometimes it was better to leave it up to fate and give it a nudge every now and again.

The angry Sikh took off through the crowded streets and Carnegie popped on his headset, thinking he could find a track that would celebrate his success and give him an anthem to hum to. Randomly the first song popped up. It was Queen's Radio Gaga. He quickly changed tracks because it reminded him of the Masseuse with the enormous fake breasts and desirable ass. For a moment Carnegie was lost in memories. Provocative memories; but he decided now wasn't the time for fantasises. So, he hit next on the long play list.

The next to play was a random Cold Chisel song that made him want to catch the last plane out of Sydney, so he settled on a German dance track that was upbeat. No Lyrics. Just crushing beats designed to surge the adrenaline and give middle aged men on the dancefloor heart attacks.

Music was a lover and a hater to Carnegie. It swore and spat at him from time to time reminding him of people and places that ultimately left him feeling sad and depressed and living in the swirling memories of better times.

He had a shocking memory that could recall emotions and feelings at a drop of a hat and he wished he lived in a music free place. Or at least a music memory free place. He vastly admired the DJ and the way he could listen to music all day and not think of anything at all. How did people do this? Carnegie often wondered.

The music hurt him. The music stabbed at him. It dragged him all over the world and reminded him of successes and failures and promised him outrageous desires. At times, he would be caught up in the rhythm and the mood and start dancing in his office with the door closed. He wasn't drunk, but he might have been because there was nothing like dancing on the office desk to MC Hammer's

You Can't Touch This. Luckily his staff were accustomed to the strange sounds coming from Carnegie's office. They would often smile at each other with that knowing 'the boss is mad' look and return to their daily dose of emails, design work and social media.

Except for Hammond. He was too busy with this data to pay any care to social media. He despised it with great passion and would have loved to have a filter block all social media from Facebook to Twitter to Instagram. LinkedIn may have been allowed for 15 minutes at lunch. Ah, such was the world that Hammond lived in.

He was glad to exit the cab paying a generous tip, so he could turn his mind to better things and the drive back to the office. After all, why the fuck should he be so down? Hadn't he just closed the deal of his lifetime? Carnegie shrugged off the self-sabotage and promised himself a long night on the town for good measure.

Hong Kong >

Carnegie stopped thinking. At least he stopped thinking about the past and started thinking about the present.

He stood staring at the ground, leaning out the balcony, lightly gripping the metal railings. The ground beckoned to him below like the call of the siren. Little ant-like creatures milled about and disappeared into the shadows. Toy cars drifted through the streets, straining against the speed limits and congestion of Hong Kong. The night was warm, but his heart was cold. Suddenly he felt like he could just thrust out and let go. Drift gently to the ground like a snow-white feather. Carnegie felt tired and exhilarated at the same time.

He knew the gun and the pills lay behind him in the neat hotel room with its spasmodic air conditioning. Hot to Cold, Cold to Hot.

He was terribly attracted to the idea of leaping off a building in this moment, but his fear of heights was overpowering. The thought of a snow-white leaf instantly dissipated replaced by a physical reaction of great strength. His fear was a horrible one. His legs went numb and he felt nauseous as leaned out on the balcony. His body and reality overrode his mind and he stepped back sharply, thankful for the feeling of horror melting from his body.

Carnegie stood there rubbing his eyes and cursing his weakness. Before he could curse any longer he was distracted by the off-tune voice of an old man singing in Mandarin. He turned to have a look and a few stories below, in a much older building, stood an ancient Chinese man completed with balding pate and old grey singlet. He was a sight to behold as he stumbled about singing, practising Tai Chi and attempting to put up the laundry.

The old man was clearly intoxicated as he sang away, oblivious to the world and its problems.

Carnegie was envious.

But moments later not so much.

A sharp noise sounded. And a little head appeared out of an adjacent door. Something must have been important because the little old man suddenly sobered up and started to pin the laundry up with great efficiency.

Carnegie was amazed. And then he realised.

A little old lady with a fierce disposition stood in a doorway, hands on hips.

He chuckled to himself. And there it was. Marriage. Partnerships. Couples.

As INXS sang, 'They could never tear us apart.' Perhaps.

But we could tear each other apart, Carnegie mused sadly.

Hate

Sometime in his early thirties, Carnegie realised he was a hater. Which was a strange revelation because he was a very loving man. He loved his family and friends and was charitable whenever he could afford to be. He enjoyed old people's company and was a big fan of animals.

But secretly he despised and hated many things, many emotions, and many feelings.

What was this hate? Where did it come from? Why did it burn so coldly in him at moments he could not understand? It took all the strength inside him to hold the fury breaking forth and spilling over. The hounds of hell were struggling and straining against their psychological bonds. The violence of the flood was held back by the equal violence of the embankment straining against the swollen water.

How we hated at times ...

He hated the fact that nights always ended with day.

He hated the way that he wept at funerals; and hated the fact that the Man Who Couldn't Die ended up dying on him, leaving him weeping in secret.

He hated the fact that his wife loved him, and she deserved a better man.

He hated the fact that people were so simple in a world so complex. He wondered if in some drunken haze that he had taken the wrong pill like Neo and discovered the Matrix.

He hated the fact that the more he drank, the soberer he got.

He hated criminals, stupid laws and tariffs, corrupt politicians, lying sales people, pretenders and the word hate itself.

He hated feelings and emotions and wished that he could be more like the man from Jann Arden's song Insensitive, who had a chill in his embrace and vagueness of face.

He hated the fact he ever listened to Jann Arden in the first place.

In fact, while he was at it, he hated music in general. It was a time waster and generally a head fuck. Why anyone would bother tuning in and then tuning out of life, he couldn't understand at all.

He hated that someone had invented pornography and he had discovered it.

He hated that life spat out more questions than it did answers.

He hated that Kennedy left. He hated that he had to witness Kennedy leaving.

He hated that he remembered Kennedy leaving.

He hated that dark days brought out the finest of creativity and that love was a poison.

He wondered why he hated so much but was never angry about any of it. He was suspicious of road rage, angry drunks, violent people and lawyers. He was desperate to be detached like Heyloon. Who was always angry but never seemed to have any form of hate within himself.

When he asked Heyloon, he would mostly give confusing responses such as 'I am Zen like the fat man on the hill.' Or 'Buddhism is a calling.' Or 'Stop hating, start participating.' Which Carnegie knew was a Vince Vaughan line from a movie. But he was still confused as to why Heyloon would offer up such a cheesy line when he was so inquisitive as to why a man could be so detached.

Heyloon breezed through life like a man on a mission; although Carnegie was always suspicious of his motives. His unemotional oriental face caused Carnegie alarm, especially when they were talking about the deep things in life. Topics like God always made Carnegie uneasy especially when Heyloon, with his ever-present poker face would say 'God has many faces. It's up to us to recognise them.' Carnegie was spun out. 'What faces?' 'Where?' But Heyloon kept coming up with the perfect mysterious responses, such as 'If a dragon becomes a mouse then surely a mortal won't recognise the beast within.'

Carnegie hated these conversations and Heyloon's bloody stupid responses, but the way he consistently lined them up sowed the seed of doubt in his mind. He wondered that perhaps to know such great spiritual things sent you off the end, as Heyloon clearly had gone a long time ago.

That brought on another pet hate for Carnegie. He wondered why he was so sane. Other people had gladly yielded to madness before him such as accountancy, 9 to 5 jobs, knitting and many other pursuits. Why couldn't he reach the clouds and be touched in the head. Instead he sat contemplating suicide in a small Hong Kong hotel, listening to the revelry down on the street as women of dubious career choices made off with the hearts and minds of old ex-pats looking desperately for their libido and their youth.

Carnegie wondered briefly about the Waitress with the Kind Eyes and realised that she was off taking care of her child and he was not going to get any care from her tonight.

He sat for a while, counting out the sleeping pills and arranging them into small piles of three buildings. They were small artistic arrays that made words link together like 'Hate = Love'; 'Gain = Pain'; 'Fear = Near'; 'Hope = Nope'. He began to cry as it brought back memories of him playing with his toys as a child and teaching his eldest child to count by arranging smarties on their glass table. Carnegie wiped away his tears in a slow painstaking way. Now was not the time to be emotional. He was on a mission to terminate himself and the pain that dwelt inside his body like a pulsing cancer. No sorrow was allowed, because it always held him back from finishing the deed.

He got up and drank another scotch, pausing to look in the mirror. The dark eyes stared back at him; furious that he had denied them so much desperately-needed sleep. The greying hair spoke out at him, reminding him about his lost youth and the life that was half over. The lines in his forehead jumped out at him accusingly, like thick trenches dug into the soft sand of a war-torn Egypt. Carnegie sighed and stared more. Age. A number. A curse on humanity. A balancing act to the wildest of egos. A number out of 100 and beyond … Why not round it up now and get to the finishing line faster?

Suddenly the air in the room was too cold. Freezing cold. Carnegie shivered and rubbed his hands together. He knew the air conditioning was a beast in itself but the fever that raged through him had taken hold again. Deep down, he felt his immune system slowly dying and his body struggling against the ravage of his desperate lifestyle.

He stood up and paced for a while before switching off the air conditioner. He coughed and gasped for air, furious at the state of his lungs and chest. Carnegie swore violently, more violently than the coughs that shattered across his chest. He swallowed lukewarm water and, for good measure, he swallowed his favourite pills provided to him by the Pharmacist. Cold and Flu tablets had a wonderful number of benefits for the sick and sorrowful. For the tired and the terrible. In no time his fever would be gone and another burst of energy would come along.

For whatever reason, Carnegie decided he should start exercising, so he pummelled himself with crunches, sit ups, planking, squats and push ups. Soon he was sweating and red faced and coughing away like an unprotected chemical factory worker in his sixtieth decade.

Carnegie walked into the pristine bathroom and washed his face and wiped off the water and sweat combined. Once again, his face stared back at him. He stared back defiantly as if to try and change his visage from the aging that had beset him. But the same face came back in spades. He was no longer in his prime. The scales of time had tipped. The lines were coming. What was handsome in a youthful way was disappearing.

He was lost to the world. Father time had stretched out and put his firm hand on Carnegie's back.

Oh the vanity. The balloon had burst and was beginning to come down.

< Sydney

'Amazing darling. You have your hair and not a single grey one, despite your family being bald and grey at an early age.' Carnegie's wife smiled at him in bed whilst rubbing his messy hair gently.

Carnegie smiled. He was lucky. He didn't want to go grey. He didn't want to go bald. He wanted to stay handsome forever. He reminded himself this wasn't vanity but purely a desire to stay charismatic in order to pursue his life's visions.

After all it was easier to get things done if you had the looks …

But he knew the Mystic was right when wrote those lyrics:

At the beginning,
It will seem like,
There will be no ending.

But as the sun fades,
And so, does your beauty,
Then you will know truthfully
That all things will pass.

He had been young and skilful in the art of self-deception.

Carnegie had learnt the lessons of business. Rationalise it all. Anything could become anything good. Junk could be marketed. Everything could be spun.

Debt – Enablement
Millions – Freedom
Staff – Team
Mistakes – Learnings
Public Apologies – PR Wins
Client Dinners – Building Rapport
Drinks at Strip Clubs – Building Rapport
Flirting with Clients – Building Rapport

And the list went on.

Before you can truly deceive. You must truly believe.

They didn't call it the Kool Aid for nothing. And he freely drank. And he freely gave to drink. And so, in their handsome faces and bodies, enhanced by handsome clothes and designer accessories, they danced like free creatures under the mystical corporate bubble. Kissing Air. Kissing Ass. Swearing never ending fealty. Loyalty until the death while casually looking over their shoulders – looking for the next target to intoxicate their souls with.

The young and handsome Carnegie kissed his wife and then arched his arms behind his head. It would be a good day. He smiled smugly to himself, wondering which one of his many suits he would wear today.

< Sydney

Carnegie was feeling very much the Rockstar businessman while he was getting ready for another day at the office. Their ensuite was immaculate as usual, thanks to his industrious wife. Even the mirrors were without stain. Like a movie in HD they brought every vivid colour, bump and wrinkle into clarity for viewing pleasure.

Carnegie stared in the mirror and exclaimed, 'Oh no a grey hair!' He pulled at it furiously, finally dislodging it. *Dear God, I'm only 31*, he thought. Maybe dye was an option when they came out in force. After a few short seconds he dismissed that idea very quickly because he was too proud to use hair dye.

He reconciled his annoyance quickly as he remembered George Clooney was exceedingly handsome and had grey hair.

Maybe he could be the Australian version.

Rationalise.

Find the good in the bad. Find the rage in age. Maturing like a fine wine.

Just another day getting ready for the world of business. The entrepreneur takes the hits and turns them into hits.

Hong Kong >

Carnegie's memories faded, and he was back staring at his aging face.

The hate rose up again and he lost himself in his list of hates.

Like his pet hate of electrical appliances running out of battery and never being able to charge them.

Or

His hate for those that kept pushing into queues with blank expressions on their faces.

Or

His hate for the media always stirring up hate.

Or

His hate for the day he was born.

But the thing about hates in the business world, is the entrepreneur learns to deal with hate. He learns to deal with the hate, the same way he deals with pain. To bear it. To endure it. To let it lie unconsciously below and never reveal itself. To never show rage. To only express the positive and with passion. Game face, game face. Keep wearing the mask. Even though the list of hates spun inside Carnegie, the same way the devil dances on the hex, outside his face was unemotional – crafted in a way that an angel would sip honey from the nectar of gods.

What is inside must not come out.

Carnegie even hated, with great hate, the reality of self-control and self-discipline in the business world. So what if he wanted to tell the arrogant customer to go fuck himself?

Or take a stick to a slothful staff member.

Or chase down a wicked and cheating former partner.

Was this not healthy emotion?

So, to cover it up ... it was self-control.

Which leads to hatred.

The worst of all hate.

Self-hatred.

And eventually his list of hates dried up and he sat down to smoke another cigarette and review the time. 3.33am. Early, he mused to himself. Another few hours to see the sunrise if he was going to last that long. He searched through his tracks and put on his favourite trance compilation: In Search of Sunrise. It was a great mix of sadness and joy. Hope and despair. And it seemed fitting that the songs seemed to take him in circles and spin him around in thought.

And then he realised his mistake. He hadn't written a suicide note. That seemed like a monumental screw up. He should at least explain in brief why he had exited stage left. It didn't seem right to leave behind any sense of mystery along with tragedy. Mystery and tragedy made terrible bedfellows. Carnegie was also reminded about the quote he once read about not being fired from life but quitting. On this basis, this seemed like the perfect place to start an explanation or at least a goodbye note.

It seemed appropriate to drink a bottle of wine at this stage, so he cracked open a bottle of dubious hotel Sauvignon Blanc. How many dubious wines existed on the planet, and how many more dubious wines existed in expensive restaurants and expansive mini-bars, Carnegie mused to himself. It was cold and bitter, which was a great metaphor for life to Carnegie at such times. He drained his glass and flinched. A second glass followed quickly. Unsurprisingly, it didn't do any better than its predecessor. Carnegie sighed. Alcohol was a great example of the Law of Diminishing returns.

He sat down in front of one of the complimentary hotel notepads and pens. Picking up the plastic pen, that clearly hadn't been touched for some time, he started.

Dear beloved friends and family.

But that didn't seem right, so he crossed it out neatly and wrote:

Lovers, Mothers, Fathers and Others.

He stared at this for a while, pleased. But then realised that perhaps it was a little corny. He crossed this out too and wrote in capitals:

TO WHOM IT MAY CONCERN.

That seemed to capture things broadly, so he wrote underneath slowly and carefully as to not make a mistake. This was, of course, a titanic effort for Carnegie as his hands shook from the nicotine, alcohol, lack of sleep and elevated blood pressure. But he did his best.

If you are reading this note I send you my thanks and love. It's not easy writing your own suicide note. I would much rather have someone write it for me and make it less personal but here I am and this is now.

It seems foolish with everything going for me that I would want to stop the world and get off. However there are so many questions and too little answers, so perhaps in death I will find what I am looking for or at least the questions will not stop flying at me.

Carnegie stopped there and felt pleased so far, he was on track to writing something meaningful.

My family and friends and indeed everyone I love so much; you are the best and I will miss you deeply. I know some of you will miss me but take courage as time heals everything and hopefully you can remember all the good days and forget the bad days, like the day you are reading this message.

Carnegie stopped. A chill ran through his spine. The hairs on his arms rose and quivered like antennas in a strong breeze. Was he really doing this? It seemed surreal, but it seemed like his destiny, so he continued.

One day we will all meet on the other side. I will be waiting.
With all my love.
JAC

He was tempted to draw a little love heart but realised just in time this would be a little pathetic and totally unnecessary, like a lot of drunken emojis. The girlish thought made him curiously angry. He was often irritated at the cute supposedly feminine side that popped out at the worst of times.

He folded the note and laid it on the table, putting a scotch glass on the top to hold it down as if some mysterious wind would blow it in and under the couch where a diligent house cleaner would find it many days later and many days too late.

With a note done it was time to get on with it.

Carnegie grabbed the gun and looked at the pile of sleeping pills lined up nicely. Perhaps fate would help him choose his method of departure. He grabbed a random coin out of his pocket. 'Heads is guns. Tails is pills.' He said to no one in particular.

He spun the coin on the table and watched for what seemed an eternity.

And then something strange happened.

The coin stopped spinning but neither did it land heads up or tails up. It just stood there erect, mocking him in the bitterness of night. The lighting from the apartment cast a small but significant shadow on the cluttered table.

'Fuck!'

Was this a sign, Carnegie wondered? He quickly dismissed it. He was not a fatalist or superstitious and didn't believe in all of that nonsense.

There were a lot of significant unbeliefs he held on to. There was no such thing as star crossed lovers. The Zodiac was a joke. Fate was for the weak. Re-incarnation belonged to a whole group of wishful thinkers. There was nothing beyond life. The devil was the biggest cop out under the sun. And there was most certainly nothing that could destroy his mission.

Carnegie scowled and drank more wine. He had met all of the morons and fools in his life, he mused bitterly. The snake oil salesmen. The palm readers. Those that look into symbols and signs to see the future. He had come across them all. What a place or space to be in. Where you take leave of your senses and every little sign becomes a major reason for a decision to turn left or right, to invest or divest, to love somebody or not ... Throw logic to the wolves and howl at the moon with the witch doctors.

Carnegie sighed and rubbed his temples that were thudding away.

He laughed madly in the empty apartment when the thought appeared in his head: *Heads are guns. Tails are pills. If you land on the edge again I will jump off the balcony.* Carnegie smiled grimly. Maybe he would find Kennedy on the way down.

'Fuck you and your randomness, coin. I will beat you!'

He plucked the coin off the table and flicked it. It spun and spun and just as it began to topple the fire alarm spat out. A wretchedly mind jarring and screaming noise enough to wake the dead and bring on the four horsemen of the Apocalypse.

Carnegie jumped up alarmed and ran out of the apartment with great haste, spilling the wine on the way out.

After all he didn't want to burn to death.

Fire in the Hole

< Adelaide

That wasn't the first time Carnegie had felt the panic of the fire alarm. He sat in Adelaide airport waiting for his plane and drinking hot chocolate when the place erupted in alarm. The café was immaculate and dressed up to replicate a beautiful chocolate themed shop in modern downtown Geneva.

The plush seats cushioned many a plump set of buttocks who had over-indulged in chocolate goodness in the well fit-out shop. The tables were varnished within an inch of their lives with a colour that only a true craftsman could concoct. The waitresses buzzed around contented and unconcerned with the humdrum of the airport. They held a self-confident demeanour and upright approach that only the smell of honeyed cocoa could give and the sense of fulfilling many of humanity's needs. After all it was chocolate.

The music that played chimed out in pleasant tones enough to make the most disgruntled and tired traveller feel at ease for a moment. This was a haven inside a busy and monotone structure. A sanctuary against the squashed airline seats, batteries running out and abrupt voices that echoed around the terminal.

And despite the alarm ringing out loud enough to wake the dead, the liquid goodness and squares of sweets kept flowing and growing. Carnegie didn't know what to think. He was alarmed at the thought of hellfire and brimstone ready to erupt and destroy them. His imaginative mind leaped to many conclusions. A bomb? A burning Jet? A villainous nicotine addict sneaking a coffin nail in the back of the male toilers? He was alert, he was alarmed.

What was more alarming was that nobody seemed to take notice. He looked left and there was the dear old Grandma feeding rocky road to the toddlers in her care. On his right a Businessman looked up annoyed while bashing out a tonne of emails on his overused Blackberry. A pale faced student with the beginnings of a beard bopped away to some racket through dirty headphones, but took no notice of the hubbub that bounced around scratchy speakers through the airport

Ahead of him stood a security guard chewing gum and waving people away who mildly questioned the ear-splitting siren.

Carnegie's legs tensed up and he began to sweat. Why the hell wasn't there mayhem going on?! Surely they were all going to die with the place burning down or a bomb going off.

The thought of the bomb made him calm. A glorious death inside an exploding airport would be perfect. Unfortunately, he stopped mid-thought because he realised no one in their right mind would blow up Adelaide airport. After all, what would be the point? Adelaide was one of the most docile places in the world. Probably the biggest sleepy hollow in the world. The ass end of Australia. A clean and nice ass end, but still quite possibly the ass end of Australia.

His colleague and friend, Bruce, broke up his reverie. 'How's the hot chocolate? Mine tastes like muddy water.' Bruce was a fine food connoisseur and absolute whinger about the quality of coffee and assorted beverages, at pretty much every place in Australia.

But this time Carnegie was too intrigued with the events to listen to Bruce carry on. 'Bloody hell Bruce. You'd complain at a three hat Michelin restaurant,' he stated, still looking around the airport.

Bruce tilted his head and arched his eyes disapprovingly. 'Well some of us have to have taste! So, what's this alarm all about then?' he said, almost as a complete afterthought.

Carnegie's exploding airport wasn't going to happen, as the sirens halted, just as Bruce got interested. The feeling of mild silence made Carnegie feel both glum and normal at the same time. Ho Hum. Nothing to see here. Move on.

He vowed to gobble down some vodka on the plane trip home just to lift his spirits.

His spirits almost always lifted when he drank spirits.

A trip with Bruce complaining about the airline food wasn't going to do that. About the only thing that would shut Bruce up about airline food was the oversupply of alcohol and an argument about some irrelevant fact or facet of some facetious prat.

They were silent for some time as the smooth brown liquid seeped down their throats. Carnegie sighed when he stared at the bottom of his elegant cup. Hot chocolate and its deliciousness had a great way of running out before its time in the same vein good times always ended before their time was up.

In the end, it was time to get moving, so they ambled to the airport gate back on the topic of bad coffee and alarm systems. And Carnegie always thought that the airport systems were alarming. Why they were shuffled off in an orderly fashion into a tubular flying coffin, he could not figure out. He also struggled to figure out why fat people always came late to the gate sweating and puffing. And equally alarming was the way they inadvertently squeezed their fat bottoms in between two impatient passengers while simultaneously losing their seatbelts down the sides of their neighbour's thighs.

Carnegie had no problem with fat people. He always found them troubling though. He couldn't understand why they chose to be fat. He couldn't understand why the diet Pepsis and 97% fat free snacks didn't work. He never thought he was one of the lucky ones because he spent so many human minutes on a good diet and plenty of gym sessions in assorted five-star hotels. Of course, as an intensely driven entrepreneur with a history of achievement, he did not factor in any genetics, medicine, age or other criteria as to why poor souls carried extra weight around. Carnegie was the centre of the universe and in his still forming mind and psyche, he abandoned all sense of thought from other perspectives. As his good friend Hammond would say on occasion, 'That was just loser talk.'

Bruce couldn't understand it either but smugly added, 'If the world's quality of food was better then perhaps they wouldn't be on the upper end of the scales.' This amused Carnegie to no end because Bruce was always a borderline fatty himself. Of course, Bruce didn't think that way and you dare not make any comment on his largesse. He always said, 'If you could look down and see your appendage popping out then you weren't fat.' Lord knows how that worked for women, but it satisfied Carnegie enough to be distracted with the thought of obese people lining up at a diet store being asked to strip naked and look down in search for their old fellas. Carnegie smirked at the term 'old fellas.' Bruce looked at him slyly. 'Yup, old fellas.'

'What a silly name.' Carnegie mused. 'Mine is certainly not an old fella. In fact, I would proffer that it isn't a fella at all.'

Bruce grinned and giggled. An odd combination. 'Well, what do you call yours then?' He asked with distaste. 'Mine is the old fella or, if I am in the mood for it, it's a Brewski.'

Carnegie wondered what sort of bogan red neck sheila would be turned on by a Brewski bouncing up and down trying to stab her; but shuddered at the thought and quickly tried to dismiss it.

It certainly was time to change the topic, so Carnegie talked about the first thing that came to his mind.

'Bruce, shut up for a second. Remember that deal we cut for two million dollars?'

'Haha of course,' Bruce chuckled to himself.

'You never told me how you found that lead. Maybe it's time to fess up?'

Bruce giggled to himself. He couldn't help himself.

'Maybe one day I will tell you Carnegie but trust me you would rather not know.' He looked a cross between a smug gambler and a shifty street seller. 'Put it this way, there might have been some back scratching along the way.' He winked at Carnegie.

Carnegie groaned. He had figured some shady dealings with Bruce had occurred. Some sort of greasing of the palms. Carnegie did not like this at all. He did not want any part of this as all. Of course, as a businessman he had been accused of all types of things. Foolish, naïve, ignorant and the list went on. He just didn't believe in bribery and 'payments' of any type at all. Most of all, he did not want to 'owe' anyone anything. Sure, he had plenty of debts, but he did not transact in the nefarious product called favours.

He shook his head. In the end he would rather know. Carnegie sighed. 'Ok Bruce, come on, tell me what you got us into.'

Bruce grinned. It was a sharkish grin that said a million things and yet nothing was said at all. This was the art of Bruce. The ability to use facial expressions and body language to tell a million tales, most of which were dubious, and at the same time come across as an Angel to the right people.

'Remember Albert?' He said.

Carnegie nodded. Of course, he remembered Albert. Albert was an old school business man with troves of land, property and business. They had stumbled on him at a function for the National Mining Association. He was an odd-looking fish. Sitting by himself. Tall, skinny, pale, grey with razor sharp eyes. He was wearing a 3-piece black pin striped suit without a crease in it. Immaculately. He was a combination of funeral director and the grand admiral ready to fire the main weapon on the Death Star.

He was a compelling and odd sight at the same time and Carnegie couldn't help but introduce himself and Bruce. Albert had regarded them frostily but over time he had come to tolerate their monthly appearance on his table with the association. In the end, they had come to do quite some business with Albert as he grudgingly gave them cold praise for their efforts in building his new company a digital marketing and communications strategy.

He was a hard man. He was a fair man. He was a frightening man.

And this puzzled Carnegie. What possible insidious business could Bruce get up to with Albert. He mentally kicked himself. Bruce was well loved by all, but he was hardly one to double check and review terms in agreements. What chunk of their soul had he sold for the Xyros transaction?

Bruce smiled again. 'Well Albert called me, and I remember this clearly. He said 'I have a problem laddie. One I need your help with.''

'What could we possibly help Albert with?' Carnegie frowned.

'Not we, me.' Bruce chortled.

'What do you mean, me?'

'He needed me to help him with a little matter on the side. Remember Linda. Well she had some property of Albert's and he wanted it back.'

Carnegie's jaw dropped.

'What …'

'Easy James.' Bruce softened his overt expression. 'It was nothing. I had some old country contacts that I called on to take care of this. Albert got his goods. Linda has no clue who has what. All's well that ends well.' Bruce patted him on the back and gave him a rakish wink.

'Goddamit Bruce. I didn't authorise you to pull this shit. You are going to get us all caught and thrown in jail.'

'Wanna bet?'

Carnegie was pissed. This was the last thing he needed hanging over his head. Trust Bruce to get involved with something he never should have. It was okay to be roguish but not a rogue. It was okay to be rakish but not a rake.

Carnegie sighed and expelled a large amount of air.

'This is going to hurt us.' He said grimly.

'Wanna bet?'

'Now's not the time for your wagers Bruce!'

'Wanna bet?'

Carnegie groaned. Bruce had a one-track mind when he refused to budge. He was always calling for a wager.

Bruce was criminal in creating wagers and cheating people out of money. He had an uncanny way of reading people and calling their bluff. 'Look I'm not playing into one of your stupid games and I am really really angry.'

Bruce grinned mischievously. 'I knew it,' he said matter of factly.

Carnegie hated himself for asking. 'Knew what?'

'Clearly you don't have the balls.'

And there he had him. Carnegie had a mental weakness and had done everything with his mates, family, friends, strangers and enemies just to prove 'he had balls'.

He had eaten whole chillies. To prove he had balls.

He had swum 100 laps of the pool non-stop. To prove he had balls.

He had drunk a litre of tequila. To prove he had balls.

He swum with the sharks. To prove he had balls.

He had punched a heavily tattooed pest in an Indian nightclub. Just to prove he had balls.

He had downed shots with many topless strippers. Just to prove he had balls.

And the list of his testicular body of evidence went on and on. Never did it occur to Carnegie that it might be easier and less dangerous to not have balls at all. If only he had learned the Marty McFly Chicken lesson from Back to the Future. But he had been too busy knocking on doors to make sales, to pay attention to the subtle and not too subtle messages from Hollywood, the great moral guide of our times.

'Okay,' Carnegie said. 'I will wager that you are in serious shit by the time the year ends.' It was a safe bet in Carnegie's head, but he was not thinking straight. This was Bruce.

And sure enough, the matter stayed buried. And at the turn of the year he had received the usual torrid of messages wishing him well for the new year and beyond.

And one drunken voicemail, that woke his wife up at 5.23.

'You owe me Carnegie.'

Bruce never missed the opportunity to have the last word on a matter.

Carnegie rushed down with the other residents of the hotel, stopping to bum a cigarette off a German tourist in an exquisite set of pyjamas and with a tiny Filipina girl as a companion.

'Danke, Danke,' he said as he bent down for the young lady to light the cigarette with a worn zippo lighter embossed with the flag of the Philippines. 'Salamat,' he said inhaling heavily.

'For fuck's sake!' Carnegie coughed and choked at the same time. Carnegie couldn't believe what these Europeans smoke. The toxic fumes nearly caused him to suffocate.

The German smiled plumping up rosy cheeks developed with years of investment in schnapps. 'Strong Yah.' He sucked in his own cigarette and patted Carnegie's shoulder and his girl's ass at the same time. No mean feat for a man who had clearly tried to drink a few pubs dry a few hours ago.

'Yah.' Carnegie coughed again and nodded. He ran his hand through his hair and disappeared into the crowd, feeling the girl's eyes burning a hole in his back.

He stood out on the road and smoked the German cigarette cautiously. The crowd buzzed away in a state of tiredness and drunkenness. The weather was warm and as usual Hong Kong throbbed away, humming like a gigantic steampunk futuristic landmark of future dystopia.

All of a sudden Carnegie felt tired. He felt drained. He leaned up against a concrete pylon and tossed away the foreign cigarette, desperately feeling alone and at the end of the world. His numbness need combined with fatigue and he felt like he could sleep for an age. If only he could get the mind to stop replaying the past. Reminding him of his fall from grace. Reminding him of his mistakes, slip ups, foolishness and self-destruction.

Carnegie slowly looked up to see if his fortunes were changing and a miraculous fireball would erupt giving him some excitement and a reason to temporarily part ways with his depression and self-pity. Yet no fireball happened, and nothing took his depression away – not even the hot backpacker with the cute butt and a black G String poking out of her mini pyjama shorts.

Carnegie had a real fucking problem. Lust he got. Sex he understood. But for some time, it had been just oblivious to him like a chore. Not even the Pharmacist had a pill for that. Oh, the Pharmacist had a pill for everything with a few wise words thrown in; but this was something else. Carnegie thought that perhaps he had burned out as a result of too much pornography or something. After all, from the age of 13 he had been mercilessly flogging himself and staring at women's bodies in all sorts of carnal form. It seemed wicked and forbidden and a bit dirty but that was also part of the pleasure.

Taboo. Ta Do. Taboo. To Do.

For some people anyway.

What makes us look behind the curtain, Carnegie mused sadly. The curse of the entrepreneur. Never satisfied. Always looking. Always searching. Always solving. Always looking. Always wanting to do more. Never stopping. Never ending. Never pausing. Always consuming. Raging away tirelessly 24/7 looking for the cure for the world's diseases. Dressed up as the quest. Presented as the only plausible plan of action. A 24/7 McDonalds mind always looking for new items on the menu and fresh ways to deliver to the masses. Regressive Progress.

Chasing the dream. Dreaming the Chase.

Unreasonable.

Carnegie had once been sent that quote about the world's development being based on unreasonable men. It was bittersweet and was scant comfort for the fury of an entrepreneur's mind.

He turned his mind back to the backpacker's back.

Baby got back. He smiled briefly when he thought of all of the asses he had seen in his lifetime. They were all the same but when you saw them the first time around you always had the same reaction. There was no immunity to the female form. In whatever form it was in, it was always in form. Red blooded men couldn't resist the urge. Blue blooded men couldn't resist the urge. They were all were wired for procreation; but Carnegie did not accept this. His heart was the Perfect Knight; but his head was configured as Rockstar, Porn star, Shooting Star.

The Shrink with the Gentle Tones told him something about Narcissist Syndrome and Carnegie loved this. It explained exactly why he always felt that his consciousness was the centre of the universe and all other life forms orbited around him. It also explained why he liked spending time in the mirror in the morning ensuring he was at the best. It also explained why he spent time at the gym, wore expensive suits, brushed his teeth 3 times a day and ensured he had a delicate layer of moisturiser on. It didn't explain other things, however, so Carnegie was annoyed. It was one thing to be told that you gaze into the Pond. It's another thing to be told why you want to gaze into the Pond. You stare at the abyss long enough, you become the abyss.

The entrepreneur's curse. Great knowledge. Little meaning. Great quests. Little understanding.

The Shrink, however, couldn't tell him any meditations or chants or breathing exercises to get rid of it, so he went away disappointed. Well he did give him a lot of exercises, but Carnegie scoffed at all the kooky nonsense. Meditations. Pffff. Breathing exercises. Pfff.

Sadly, the Shrink had no cure all. No magic potion. No fabulous shiny package of pills that wiped away all the misery and explained all the mysteries of the universe.

Carnegie felt eternally sad that while everything orbited his being, he had no control over his inner being. He wondered if the sun ever felt the same. A great gigantic, powerful, explosive, godlike orb providing power to all but secretly crying meteors of loneliness.

The thought made Carnegie stop in his tracks.

He had gone to see the Pharmacist but even the Pharmacist didn't have a pill for this prescribed syndrome, although he tried prescribing Carnegie some miserable pills that made Carnegie feel like the Stay Puffed Man without the fun of killing humans, destroying buildings or chasing Ghostbusters around.

So, he had gone back to medicating himself on a stable of grog, smokes and women. They didn't cure the illness, but they sure brought relief, even if it was for a small measure of time.

< Melbourne

The fire exploded dramatically from the installed pyrotechnic towers outside the Crown Casino in Melbourne. A small South American tourist jumped violently while a baby quietly shat itself in the shadows. 'Awwww,' cried the tourists and flashed their digital cameras, capturing the extravagance of the exterior of the Casino.

'Strewth,' Bruce called out. 'Enough to take your eyebrows off.'

The friends looked up at the fire spurting and exploding from columns outside the Casino. They were both majestic and vulgar at the same time. Like a lot of the features that Casinos love to parade.

Like a lot of Casinos, the Crown Casino was a vast shiny building, built seductively for those who desired to escape the poorness of life and the dullness of day. It sat on the banks of the Yarra River in the heart of Melbourne, the City of Events. It lit up at night and glowed in the day, inviting all to come in and partake of its pleasures.

The Pharmacist was not impressed by the building. Not much impressed the Pharmacist, but especially not buildings that were built on the sorrows of mankind. It was enough to give him indigestion and he would much rather be at home watching his new collection of Blue Rays. But, as a loyal friend, he went where the group went. Like all good supporting actors and cast members in general he knew his place. Not front and centre but centre of the front.

The Pharmacist smiled to himself at the thought of the crew and his role. He popped a pill for acid reflux and dry swallowed with the grace of a professional pill popper. He was a balding middle-aged man with a nervous shoulder twitch and a knapsack filled with prescription medicines.

'After all, you can't be too careful right?' It was his catch cry he loved to tell anyone and everyone. Carnegie and friends were almost always annoyed at the Pharmacist's suggestions and his dorky appearance and knapsack. But secretly they had all been on the receiving end of the Pharmacist's good will – especially with the many bugs and health issues they all seemed to track down as they pursued the tried and tested philosophy of Work Hard, Play Hard.

The Pharmacist was loyal. He was also annoyed. He often prescribed the prevention but found nobody listened to him, so he was left to hand out the cure. This was frustrating beyond belief for the Pharmacist. He had the solution before there was a problem.

He had tried often to argue his cause, but it had fallen on deaf ears. He even tried to repeat the complaints that Hammond, Carnegie and Bruce often made about customers not listening.

Carnegie hated bugs. It was a slower way to die and besides it made him feel miserable and want to go to bed early and waste a good night. The Pharmacist was useful, so they put up with him despite his amazing ability to reduce the group's overall sex appeal without even trying.

In truth, the Pharmacist was not a pharmacist at all, he was a Business Analyst (someone who does something with numbers or something like that) by trade and worked for Carnegie's technology firm. He was thoroughly brilliant in analysing almost any business case and presenting it on paper with the necessary solution. Carnegie admired the pharmacist deeply for his discipline, because Carnegie hated details and long-winded documents. He would simply skim through them with his very capable mind searching for key words and expressions before passing them off to an underling to put his ass on line to make sure it was right.

The Pharmacist could also sit rooted to his chair for six hours on the trot, which was something that Carnegie had no chance in hell of doing. He had to lurch out of his chair every twenty minutes almost like he had restless leg syndrome, or he was possessed by the spirit of a school boy with a bad case of ADD.

The Pharmacist had some medication for restless leg syndrome, which worked for some time until Carnegie found out it was also used for the shaky people's disease and then he stopped taking it in case he developed the shaky people's disease. From what Carnegie had researched on WebMD this was also a long way to die and he didn't like the concept of shaking to death anyway. There had to be a better way.

The Pharmacist had some pretty interesting ideas on how to exit stage left quickly but he was offended when Carnegie asked him in a round-about way; referencing 'The Friend'. The Friend was a very useful person in Carnegie's life. The Friend always stepped in to preserve Carnegie's dignity and protect his identity.

'Pharmacist …' Carnegie had asked one day.

'Yes Carnegie,' said the Pharmacist, looking up from a complex diagram on a hot summer's afternoon. He wiped away a bead of sweat building on his forehead.

'I have a Friend who has a terrible illness.'

'Ah.' The Pharmacist was very interested. 'This sounds interesting. What illness does he/she have?'

'Well.' Carnegie thought carefully. 'Well, it's like this. My Friend has a fatal disease and he is thinking about other options.'

'Options?' The Pharmacists was very intrigued. 'What sort of options?'

Carnegie whispered in the Pharmacist's ear, looking around the office floor furtively. 'You know, options. Other options. You know, as opposed to getting better, well, getting off.'

The Pharmacist looked puzzled. 'Getting off. How does that help at all? Does he, assuming it is a he, have you known functional issues?'

It was Carnegie's turn to look puzzled. 'What do you mean functional issues?'

The Pharmacist stood up and looked around like an eastern European spy, then hissed into Carnegies ear. 'You know, like non-functions, ummmmmm, and dysfunction?' He dangled his hand in front of his genitals and gave it a fan like wave wriggling his fingers back and forth.

'What?!' Exclaimed Carnegie. 'Are you talking about the Friend having erectile dysfunction? Never!' He thought for a quick moment and then added, 'Well not that he mentioned.' He looked away.

'Oh,' said the Pharmacist. 'Well what do you mean options?' He looked terribly disappointed.

'Well other options for getting off, I mean getting out. I mean, you know, exit stage left.'

The Pharmacist was confused. And then it dawned on him. 'You don't mean ...'

Carnegie took a back step. The Pharmacist was starting to look angry. 'Well, you know, compassion and all of that.' Carnegie put his hand on his chest hoping to pacify his friend.

The Pharmacist stuck his finger in Carnegie's face. 'You tell the Friend that there is none of that from here. We have a code. Do no wrong. We're here to help etc etc. What do you take me as? A hack? A German death doctor? A Swiss life transporter? I'm here to make people better!!'

Carnegie began to beat a hasty retreat. He had never seen this side of the Pharmacist before. 'Well what about something for sleeping. Say in higher bulk volumes?'

The Pharmacist stopped. 'Well in that case.'

Carnegie smiled at the memory. The 'Friend' had been useful. Everyone needed a 'Friend' to have to deal with awkward situations, questions and situations in general.

All in!

Like every other half decent Casino in the world, if such a thing exists, the smell was exotically perfumed and a delight to most of the senses. The music was played at the perfectly right volume with the right melodies to inspire such great heroic acts on the tables and the machines. The colours blended harmoniously and brilliantly disguised the sun rising and setting, as the punters burned away their life savings and inherited debt at nose bleed volumes.

But all was peaceful and well. The House burned down others while at the same time collecting souls and feeding them to the ashtrays of the high rollers, who in turn burned down their own houses to feed the souls of the Casino Lords. Somewhere at the top of the global gambling trade lay an Arch Daemon with erectile dysfunction who had nothing better to do than torture the poor and whip the rich. Carnegie suspected this and wisely avoided all forms of gambling, except living on Earth and doing business in Asia.

He was both repulsed and excited by Casino and Gambling Dens. There was something pungent and exotic about it while at the same time being akin to the insides of an animated corpse.

He watched the proud little robots do the master's bidding while the All-Seeing

Eye above scanned the life forms for malcontents and the skerrick of anyone getting lucky. He wondered once about how the All-Seeing Eye in the star-lit-ceiling tracked all beings and then began to draw a technology diagram on the back of a beer coaster instinctively. He wondered how long he could look up at the ceiling before being escorted out of the building. Carnegie set the stop watch on his smartphone and waited.

It took six minutes and fifty-two seconds precisely before two burly security guards muscled up to him.

'Sir, could you step aside for a moment?' The one with the barely disguised neck tattoo asked in an overtly passive aggressive manner.

Carnegie was intrigued. He spun slowly towards the guards while tucking the beer coaster furtively into his jacket pocket. 'Err does there seem to be a problem?' Carnegie sprouted a naïve looking face.

The whiter of the two security guards flushed. Was it embarrassment, awkwardness or a warning sign his skull was to be crushed in? Carnegie wondered.

Neck Tattoo spoke up. 'Loitering. We don't like loitering.'

Ah! There it was, Carnegie smiled to himself. Loitering. A heinous crime; Loitering. Carnegie always found loitering an interesting crime to be charged with. A strange crime. A strange name. It's like somebody didn't like the term waiting, hanging around, standing or something else. You couldn't charge someone with waiting, could you? Loitering was, however, quite plausible. Like someone looked up the dictionary of crimes and threw together littering and looting and came up with the word loitering.

'Oh, I am most certainly not loitering,' said Carnegie in a matter of fact way with a thin smile. 'I am merely puzzling over the next wager I intend to make.' Perhaps he had over egged it because the security guards looked confused. Carnegie decided to have some fun. 'Peradventure upon deciding to exchange some currency for the purpose of taking a hedge, I was scanning the forum for a likely wit to extrapolate on the rule set of an afore presented game. To which I was to receive a chance encounter with a duo of mercenaries for the purpose of exchanging pleasantries. And in thus I bid you adieu.'

With an extravagant flourish, Carnegie left the two looking blankly at each other and gesturing to where he had been standing. Perhaps he had better stick his two-bob in. He had already attracted enough attention.

< Sydney

Carnegie, as a young man, had the misfortune to meet beginner's luck and not have the foggiest on what to do with it. It was a drunken night at a club and he had managed to sneak in with two of his mates. Carnegie was enchanted. Lights flashed and noises rang out. 'Just do this,' his friend showed him how to insert money into the poker machine. The young Carnegie, like a lamb led to slaughter, was sucked into the world of gambling after beginner's luck shined his foul beacon well and truly on him. But what was to come was years of pain and depression as the young Carnegie funnelled his hard earned into the bowels of the house leaving him penniless from pay-day to pay-day.

And it didn't matter what method of distribution he chose. He punted on the dogs. He wagered on the football. He gambled on the horses. It didn't matter how he hedged his money; he found a way to lose it almost the moment he received it.

But the young man experienced a cycle of hype and depression every fortnight as he chased his dream; or was it his nightmare? And every time he got to his limits end he was somehow sucked back into the system with a cheeky win or two; just enough to keep him believing.

Just thinking about it gave Carnegie pain. The memories were burned into his skull … They were deeply etched in the tablets of his heart.

The long bus ride home after losing thousands on cards.

Chain smoking on the back steps of the local club staring at his last fifty dollar bill.

Sipping on bourbon wondering how he was going to pay his long list of mounting debts.

Staring grimly at the spinning wheel bargaining with God to grant him one miraculous final victory.

But, eventually, the inherent cunning in Carnegie came out when he subtly realised he couldn't win and was being played as a fool. And almost without a conscious plan he began to plot a way to exit this vicious cycle. He patiently applied his remaining funds in a disciplined way; waiting for the next win that would suck him back into the cycle and when it came he cashed in his chips and walked away forever.

Well not quite forever.

But never again did Carnegie chase the dream. He became physically ill at the prospect of being hooked again and forcefully dragged himself from away from all forms of gambling until one fateful night in a Melbourne casino.

< Melbourne

Shortly after Carnegie left the two guards gaping he found himself parked at a black jack table with Bruce and the Pharmacist. Bruce was looking amused, sipping away on his aged scotch of some unpronounceable Scottish name. The Pharmacist was in Business Analyst mode, intently staring at a gambling chit with a myriad of numbers and arrows drawn on it. For a moment Carnegie thought he looked like the Rain Man combined with a serial killer from the movie Se7en.

He sat down with bare acknowledgement from his friends. After watching a number of cards being played, he flourished a crisp hundred dollar bill, insisting on his favoured purple chips.

Bruce chuckled. 'Think it makes any difference?' He gestured to the small pile of chips in front of Carnegie.

Carnegie responded, 'Of course not, but it's a matter of preference.'

'You know what the colour purple stands for right?' Bruce grinned. 'Sexual frustration.' He made sure he said that loud enough so the dealer and other punters at the table could hear. A flicker of amusement crossed the pretty female dealer's face.

Bruce was on the micro expression in a heartbeat. 'Sexual frustration.' He gave the dealer a vulgar wink.

Carnegie chose to ignore the dig and started to strip the label off his beer bottle with his finger nails. The dealer smiled at Carnegie sympathetically and hinted at something to come. Carnegie was aroused. The perfect cocktail for stupid decision making. Adrenalin, Alcohol and Arousal.

He dumped the whole hundred on the first hand and lost.

He dumped two hundred on the next and lost.

He put down five hundred on the next one and lost.

He stripped out the last thousand dollars from his Armani wallet and promptly lost it as the dealer managed to meet his twenty with a twenty-one.

Carnegie's heart raced. He forgot about being hooked. He forgot about being a fool. There was something about this beauty and the odds of losing three in a row. The streak must come to an end and when it did he was out.

The Pharmacist shook his head and started pointing at his messy notes and diagrams with an explanation. Bruce chuckled evilly and self-consciously draped his arm around his pile of chips.

But Carnegie didn't hear or see them. He was off in a haze searching for the nearest cash machine. Out of four accounts he managed to withdraw four thousand dollars and half an hour later he was withdrawing eight thousand out of a separate number of accounts he had set up for precisely not this purpose. But it would suffice.

Carnegie was over joyed. For a short period of time he was alive and feeling every nerve ending flickering. The dopamine was pumping vigorously, and he didn't feel the scotch he was downing. He heard the crowd vaguely behind him cheering, or jeering, him on.

He could beat the system. He was all in.

But he couldn't, and he didn't. And when the excitement died down he was fifteen thousand dollars poorer for the experience.

The Pharmacist was ropable because Carnegie had ignored every fail-safe strategy he had proffered. He was almost apoplectic. 'Don't you trust my judgment?' He slurred from the combination of scotch and caffeine pills he had been consuming on the late-night bender.

Bruce rubbed his belly and chose the moment to let out a bourbon fuelled belch.

Carnegie rubbed his eyes. The money didn't bother him. He had plenty more. He could make plenty more. The tiredness didn't bother him nor the half-eaten kebab he was holding in his hand. The chill Melbourne wind didn't bother him either.

What bothered him was the look the pretty dealer gave him as she left the shift earlier on the night. He hadn't known it then, but he knew it now. It was pity.

Hong Kong >

Carnegie jumped up the stairs two at a time after the fire alarm had been stopped and the way had cleared to go back to his room. He pitied those who couldn't match his exuberance up the stairs, especially the plump German and his Filipino friend. He took pride in flying upstairs and was terribly impatient behind people who took one stair at a time. Carnegie figured it was a waste of efficiency to be stuffing around with one stair at a time. He had a theory that it was more efficient and less tiring to get upstairs in the quickest possible time.

It was the same theory he applied to his driving. Heyloon didn't appreciate his driving at all and made the same damn stupid comments all the time. 'What's the rush big boy?' Or another personal favourite, 'Michael Schumacher eh?' He would say it in his Malaysian private school educated accent.

Carnegie never understood why Heyloon didn't appreciate efficiencies. He was almost always driven crazy by the way that Heyloon would eat a meal. Every bite was carefully chewed and dissected, then analysed, followed with a statement of claim. 'Best noodles in KL,' he would say or something of similar nature. Carnegie was nearly driven around the bend when Bruce and Heyloon would eat together. They were so fucking elitist trying to constantly outdo each other. It was like an episode of Masterchef on weed.

'Heyloon. Have you ever had squid like this?' Bruce would hold his piece of squid up to the light and then look intently at Heyloon.

'This squid is good,' Heyloon said, allowing a lengthy pause. 'But you just have to try Century Dragon in Shanghai. It is squid to die for.'

Bruce would bristle and contemptuously counter Heyloon's argument with something else equally wanky. And so, it would go on. The two would spend the better part of the evening jousting over seafood, salads, wines, cigars and the list would go on.

Carnegie's modest upbringing and total lack of interest in food would let his mind wander in these arguments. He liked to think about the Waitress with the Kind Eyes, or do the analysis on how profitable the restaurant was.

That was a Carnegie thing. He couldn't help himself. He had to do the analysis on every business he set his foot in.

Analyse This

< Sydney

It was just innate. He couldn't help it. Carnegie was born a business man and didn't know how to do anything else. His mind was constantly buying X and selling it for Y. He couldn't look at an object without wondering about its manufactured price, imported price, distributed price, wholesale price and retail price. And then he wondered about the equivalent online price.

Then he wondered what the supply chain looked like. Sometimes he would be lost in his head for 15 minutes or more building a virtual map of a business. His wife would often snap him out of it by making casual remarks or grabbing him affectionately on the cheek.

It was a blessing and a curse. It gave him great joy in understanding and predicting a business model but robbed him of all the joy in eating at restaurants, shopping for clothes or purchasing gifts. Carnegie always suspected he chose the wrong pill somewhere along his life. Oh, why hadn't he taken the blue one and just been living in blissful ignorance? He sure as hell didn't want to be Neo from the Matrix.

This was a long conversation with Kennedy. Kennedy was the master of inserting his favourite conspiracy theories into the mix at any possible opening in a sentence. His pale skin would flush and his tired eyes would flare immediately at the opportunity to discuss the Matrix, the Moon Landing, Mars and the greatest conspiracy of all: The Masons. That's how good he was; he could drop conspiracy theories out by a code, a category, a number or alphabetically.

Al Gore. Artificial Intelligence. Aliens. Area 51.
Banks. Barack Obama. Brady Bunch. Bush.
Catfish. Crypto Currency. Cannibalism. Camelot.

And the list went on. Kennedy really was an encyclopedia of conspiracy theories. He hardly got excited about anything. But he made things really interesting and always had a history lesson tucked away which everyone, even the biggest jock in the room, would lean in and listen to.

The only time he couldn't deliver a powerful lecture on the Illuminati, 9-11 or The Templars was when a lady was present. He would just clam up and look sideways. They had always wondered if he was gay but were too polite to ask him until he got into the subject one day on the matter of the Porn Industry and how it was being funded by the East to corrupt the West.

'What sort of pornography?' Bruce asked delicately.

There was silence and the group of friends leaned in.

Kennedy looked at them. He opened his mouth and then closed it. 'All right, I get it,' he muttered under his breath.

'Yes, I watch porn. I jerk off. You happy.' He didn't look happy at all.

'You do realise that 90 percent of men jerk off and the other 10 percent are liars right?'

The friends remain unmoved.

Hammond coughed. 'Umm what sort of porn Kennedy?'

'What do you mean what sort of porn?' Kennedy was cross and irritated. 'What sort of porn is rumoured to be funded by the east? Or the sort of porn that I watch?'

Heyloon looked away furtively 'Um, you?' He spoke with his inscrutable face.

Kennedy shook his head. This was just boys being boys. 'Anything to do with girls ...'

Ah. Their faces said. But no one said anything verbally apart from sideways cast long glances. Such were the ways of boys to men, or rather men to boys as it would turn out.

Carnegie talked about this to the Shrink with the Kindly Tones. Which inevitably led back to his depression and the dark days.

The Shrink with the Kindly Tones offered up a suggestion, 'Why don't you just live life one day at a time and try to just enjoy the moment? Smell the roses. You know that sort of thing?'

But this didn't work, as Carnegie's hay fever almost always went off as he stopped to enjoy the moment and smell the roses.

The roses of course were fresh. $38 dollars for a dozen. Procured by the local florist through a buyers' group for approximately $18 per unit including delivery fees. The average unit moved every 3.5 hours with enough room on the floor space to hold fifteen units. The rental space cost didn't justify the number of units, so when Carnegie helpfully suggested an online channel and a second delivery run in the event of more sales, the large breasted elderly lady running the shop flung herself into Carnegies arms and sobbed.

'Where have you been all my life?' She exclaimed.

Carnegie was conscious of the lady's large bosom pressing up against his sternum and felt strangely aroused. Was it the presence of the large bosom or being genuinely appreciated? Or perhaps it had something to do with the Shrink's prescribed narcissist syndrome.

That afternoon he asked his assistant to cancel his meetings, so he could spend the afternoon with the florist working on her business plan. Within no time Carnegie was smiling to himself as he flourished a concise 10-page document complete with spreadsheets showing cashflow analysis, profit and loss and balance sheet movement. The Florist fussed about him, organising coffees and showing him pictures of her adult children and their children.

Carnegie politely nodded and smiled throughout the show and tell; trying his best to explain the business plan to the Florist but giving up after the Florist's husband, Pete, turned up in tradesman overalls with a large rag sticking out of his back pocket.

'Are you trying to stick it to my wife?' He growled at Carnegie and poked him in the chest.

'What?' Carnegie didn't know what was more frightening: a fight with a senior man mountain or sticking it to the elderly florist. 'Of course not. I was merely helping her out with her business plan.'

'So fancy pants. You think we can't fend for ourselves. We have no idea on how to run a business?' Pete poked Carnegie again.

Carnegie began to protest and then decided to beat an easy retreat before he took a beating.

'Call me …' The Florist waved to him as Pete glowered at his retreating back.

Carnegie got a few shops away and then stopped scurrying on. 'For fuck's sake!' he exclaimed. The thought of a brutal beating over a grandma florist brought a shudder to him and then he laughed. What a story to tell. He giggled all the way back to the office at the thought of the elderly florist. He only stopped when he drove past home feeling a twinge of guilt at not stopping for dinner. But there was work to be done. Well at least that's what he told himself.

Hong Kong >

The door slammed behind him and once again Carnegie was alone in his Hong Kong hotel room. The fire alarm was just a distant memory. And the memory of the elderly florist was fading just as fast as the dehydrated hydrangeas that sat on her shop floor, because she hadn't followed his articulate business plan that covered stock rotation.

He stood at the doorway for some time before spotting the scotch bottle and helping himself to a generous tote. Carnegie felt the depression seep in again as he realised he was facing the task of offing himself. Pills, Gun or something else? The scotch wasn't helping. Nor was the time as it patiently ticked away to dawn – its little stick figures glowing in angry red. The room was dead silent apart from the muffled sounds of downtown Hong Kong finding their way through the glass balcony doors.

Carnegie coughed. The European cigarette still felt raw on his throat and his choice of cleanser didn't improve matters. For some random reason Carnegie went and brushed his teeth, contenting himself with the sound of the electric brush rubbing up and down his gums. The figure in the basin mirror stared back at him accusingly. Carnegie leaned into the mirror and looked at his reflection. Whether it was a trick of light or not he looked both tired and energised at the same time. The light brown eyes looking both dead and alive at the same time.

Maybe that was the problem, Carnegie mused. He was trapped between the land of the living and the land of the dead. Perhaps this was all just a dream and he would wake up to find his name was actually Alan and he was a pet shop keeper with an incontinent pet weasel called Alice.

Carnegie pinched himself, but he didn't wake up as Alan; nor did he find a urinating stoat companion at his feet. Carnegie sighed and looked back at the blinking clock on his smartphone. It was 3.33. It felt surreal to see the three numbers lined up perfectly like a parade of well-orchestrated soldiers. Was there something lucky in Asia about three threes? Somehow, he knew somewhere an Asian was getting married, engaged, being born or more likely gambling on the number three. He didn't understand the Eastern obsession on numbers.

He decided to Wiki the numbers again on his tablet computer. It took him several minutes to get past the emails alerting and more minutes again to untangle himself from the news pages. By the time he had found the articles on Wikipedia an alert sent him jumping from the couch. His nerves were tingling. It was a calendar reminder to email some documents to Hammond. It was 4am Hong Kong time. He looked at the article again. Four! The number of Death in China.

It was all too spooky for Carnegie. He fired off the tablet and left to find the nearest open club.

< Melbourne

Numbers came easily to Carnegie but not mathematics. He hated maths and all of its theoretical nonsense. He loved numbers and he loved making them sing and dance. Not like a chartered accountant, mind you. But the entrepreneur type who could show numbers growing miraculously without a single piece of evidence. The famous J Curve graph was his favourite. A massive swoosh like the Nike symbol that started at the bottom of the spreadsheet before magically jumping into the high heavens of orgasmic proportions. Oh, the investors loved his numbers and his spreadsheets. Just do it!

Of course, it was all hocus pocus and bullshit, but you had to play the game. It was dead clear to Carnegie that the success of a venture was one simply formula:

Work Hard. Work Smart.
One plus One equalled Three.
$1 + 1 = 3$

He loved this thought and often told people when they asked him about his successes. But strangely they didn't like the saying and went away discontent.

Carnegie had a sneaking suspicion they didn't like the work hard part. He didn't mind it at all because the work made his mind focus on getting things done and this satisfied him. When he wasn't working hard he often thought about why he was born and that made him depressed and wanting to go to sleep for a long time.

Numbers couldn't make sense of life, but they could attract money. And money was useful in making life busy and when life was busy Carnegie didn't have to think. It's also why he loved loud music pumping through his head phones, intriguing movies, long books and two-hour strong massages.

Especially when the masseuse with the large breasts looked after him. She too was interested in numbers but in the form of currency. She was a clever shark that Carnegie read through immediately but enjoyed the game of barter.

If he paid her good tips she took to his body as if it was a crash test dummy. If he didn't pay her good tips, she worked his body harder than a freshly divorced sergeant-of-arms. Carnegie nearly fainted with the pain, but he loved the pain as his mind was taken off any depressive thoughts.

Not that Carnegie was interested in pain fetishes or anything like that. People into that stuff were sick fucks. He couldn't understand the thought of hot wax, whips or the other weird things that people got into.

His bondage thoughts were broken up by the masseuse. 'You are a bad boy, aren't you?'

What an odd question, thought Carnegie. He felt he was neither bad nor a boy. In fact, most women that he had been intimate with often called him a good man.

The masseuse with the large breasts often talked in riddles. She also had a large range of names she gave herself that amused Carnegie. One day it was Kyla, the next time it was Sasha, then it was Selena. She clearly didn't store her memory in her mammaries, because she had a short-term memory like a gold fish.

Carnegie enjoyed the masseuse because the game was to work out her story in life while groaning and gritting through the pain. He had worked out some simple facts. She was from Taiwan. Her breasts were definitely designed by a skilful surgeon. During the day she did topless modelling and during the night she worked as a masseuse; not for the money but to torture men. This led to the assumption that she had definitely had Daddy issues. Carnegie never raised this for the sake of getting on the wrong side of the masseuse and not finding out the final story behind the masseuse. And the fact she might ditch him as a client.

He was scared of turning up at the spa only to find the pale African girl with the small breasts who was too gentle and smelt like Thai food and mint. Plus, she often cried when she massaged Carnegie, which made Carnegie feel ashamed and want to go home.

'Do you like bad boys?' Carnegie asked suggestively.

The masseuse laughed an exotic throaty laugh. 'I do. Have you been a bad boy?' She pointed her elbow onto his back and pushed down with force. Carnegie's follow up was quashed by the shrieking pain emanating from his shoulder and upper back. His eyes popped out and sweat moistly appeared on his brow.

'What makes you think I have been a bad boy?' Carnegie managed.

'I know the type. I know you all. The inquisitive type that keeps asking questions, so you can get my clothes off and make me suck you.'

Carnegie's eyebrows shot up. Where had that come from? The masseuse always kept her clothes on and Carnegie was way too classy to let his fantasies out. That being said he did feel exceptionally aroused at the thought of the masseuse disrobing.

'Interesting thought Selena but no that's not what I had in mind. I am just interested in people.' Carnegie attempted a face down shrug.

'So you don't want me to take my clothes off?' Carnegie could feel her pout at the back of his head.

Carnegie wasn't going to play the game. Ten years of business negotiations had taught him to handle these types of setups.

'Babe. I'm sure you have an amazing body under those clothes, but I come here to experience your amazing massage skills.' Carnegie smirked. Rejection and a compliment in one simple sentence.

The masseuse was lost for words. Carnegie could hear the gears in her brain working away.

'Thanks hon.' The masseuse caressed his lower back and slid one hand down his Calvin Kleins and played with his buttocks. 'You sure you don't want to see anything?' She prodded him again.

Carnegie groaned. She was persistent. And the hand moving on his ass gave him a serious erection, so much so he almost levitated off the massage table. 'For fucks sake,' he mumbled.

He was in deep conflict when he heard the sound of the masseuse's top being unbuttoned. Carnegie's imagination ran high. He wondered what this would cost him. Out of sheer instinct he lifted his body and slid the masseuse off his back. He rolled on his side and propped himself up on his elbow. The masseuse had let her hair down and her top was undone to below her belly. A fancy bra barely restrained her epic breasts that leaped of her chest like the tallest Himalayan peaks.

Carnegie was blatantly aware of his own state of undress and the large erection poking from his underwear. The masseuse wrenched off her top and slid off the accompanying skirt. Carnegie resisted the male urge to reach down and touch the throbbing.

The masseuse looked at him squarely and glowered. She posed for him and waved her hands down her body. She looked down at his groin. 'I thought you didn't want to see my body?' she asked accusingly.

Carnegie smiled. 'Only a gay man wouldn't want to see your body. Of course I do. And I am glad.' The masseuse was placated, and she forced Carnegie to lie down so she could hop on top of him. Carnegie felt the walls come down around him. The animal instinct was taking over, especially as Selena or whatever her name was started to rub his chest. He was blatantly aware of the bare cheeks of her ass touching his groin. He started breathing heavily.

And when she unclasped her bra and the twins popped out to stare at him proudly he nearly stopped breathing at all. His wife's face flickered in his mind for a Nano-second. He deleted it, as well as the following guilty thought.

Like a man possessed, his reached up his hands to gently caress the finest pair he had ever seen. Millimetres from their erect destination, his digits were enfolded in the masseuse's strong hands.

'It will cost you.'

'Ah,' said Carnegie.

< Brisbane

Strippers. Hookers. Ladies of Pleasure. Insurance sales people. They were all admired and loathed by Carnegie at the same time. He loathed them as, somehow, they managed to skirt around the moral pillars of justice that weighed heavily on him. He loathed himself for being in their company. At the same time, he was amazed at their sales ability and their incredible ability to get over rejection and play the numbers game. Ten 'no's led to one 'yes'.

One drunken night at a client function in a strip club, Heyloon and Carnegie came up with a great idea to recruit these ladies as their sales force for a new business they were launching.

'Imagine that Carnegie. We cherry pick the best strippers and dancers from all over the world as our international sales force. They would be able to sell anything. They are perfectly equipped for the sales role. They work in high heels; and sexy outfits would be an upgrade for them. They don't complain about working long hours. They can turn it on for every client. Men would just melt into their arms. We could be heroes rescuing these girls from the underbelly of cities around the world.'

Heyloon was very excited by the idea.

Carnegie, in his state of inebriation, nodded sagely at every sentence and added his own feedback.

He and Carnegie spent the next hour working on the back of beer coasters and paying strippers to leave them in peace. The beer coaster was one of Carnegie's favourite templates for developing business ideas. It represented freedom of thought and liberty of mind. No boardrooms. No Word documents. No templates or forms to fill out. No indexes.

Just a slightly stained and wet square with a logo to write around.

Heyloon summoned over an exotic Southern Indian girl wearing a black sheer dress with white lingerie underneath. They proceeded to pitch the idea to the dancer.

Heyloon and Carnegie looked up awaiting her feedback.

'Fuck you and fuck your idea,' she said rather too pleasantly and spun around, disappearing to the final chorus of George Michael's *I Want Your Sex*.

And that was that.

A Capital Idea

< Sydney

Carnegie always found it hard to deal with disappointment when his ideas weren't readily accepted and given mountains of praise. They were so clear in his head. He could see the idea working. He also had the supporting documents and the killer spreadsheet in his arsenal. Perhaps that is why their idea for employing strippers failed miserably. Not enough supporting documentation.

Carnegie had a lot of ideas. And a lot of visions. This was the formula for his successes and the key source of his depression. Or so said the Shrink with the Gentle Tones.

'You think too much. In fact, you think too far ahead. What's wrong with today hmmm?' His Shrink never finished a sentence without asking a question or suggesting something to him.

He followed it up with another. 'So when you think of the future, what do you think of?'

Carnegie thought a lot about the future. He loathed the future. He hated his daydreams and visions and the way his mind would wander. Where once, as a young man, it was an exciting place to dwell, it was now a desolate land equivalent to Sarah Connors coming of Skynet.

He thought of his wrinkled face.

He thought of wheezing up the stairs.

He thought of waking up next to an old woman.

He thought of not being able to get an erection.

He thought about no longer being relevant and exciting.

He thought about incontinence.

He thought about losing his memory.

He thought of dying alone in an old, but fancy, nursing home with the sound of beeping machines and the open back of a ward gown with his life force slowly leaking out of him combined with urine and faeces.

He thought so much about it that he drank six bourbons and drove for an hour at neck-break speeds, silently hoping for an errant truck to run into him or for him to hit an oil patch and gloriously sail off the edge of the cliff in his black Audi RS4.

But no such luck happened. And his consciousness pulled him up at a droopy truck stop where he succeeded in drinking coffee and chain smoking until dawn.

The truck stop manager was a dark-skinned African with a smile that probably saved his life. She patiently served him coffee and chided him gently over his drunken state and the fact that smoking gave people cancer.

Carnegie cleverly turned the conversation away from himself and listened with interest to the manager's story. He loved the fact that she was from Ghana and her name was Tazhee. She was a distant cousin to one of the tribal queens. And she had bought the truck stop to help pay for her family to slowly migrate to Australia.

He learned a lot about Ghana that night. He learned a lot about Africa and he learned something about himself. But he didn't realise it until much later on.

He rose wearily from the balcony he had been sitting on and gave Tazhee a long hug.

'I love what you are doing.' He wanted to say he loved her as well and thought she was an angel. He withdrew $1000 in cash from the ATM and tried to give her the money for the sake of her family and the village in Africa. She refused his charity on no less than five occasions.

Carnegie was frustrated. He wanted to do something for this angel that was meaningful.

'Take it. Please take it.' He pressed the money into her hands.

'James,' she said sternly. 'I cannot take your money.'

'If you don't take it I will make you take approximately 35 percent of it!'

'What?' Tazhee was clearly confused. 'I'm not going to take your money,' she reiterated, holding her head high in an impossibly glorious expression of African pride.

'Fine.' Carnegie stormed out of the truck stop and filled up his car with premium fuel. He strode back into the shop and proceeded to fill up baskets of goods. Tazhee looked on helplessly. It took Carnegie 45 minutes to buy $987.00 of goods and pay in cash pocketing the $13 left over.

He smiled at the dark-skinned angel as she helped him stuff lollies, cigarettes, engine oil, beverages, bread and assorted goods into every nook and cranny in his car.

'You are freakin' crazy man.' Tazhee laughed as she hugged him again. 'Thank you so much.'

Carnegie felt much happier as he drove off and was glad that Tazhee didn't see the tears streaming down his cheeks.

Carnegie regularly had crazy ideas to spend money. His best ideas, however, came in the form of getting money into his assorted businesses. Carnegie leveraged his contacts, told amazing stories and showed his killer spreadsheets. The combination of sharp suits, Ray-Ban glasses and his greying hair painted a picture of confidence, intellectualism and hope.

Carnegie had never forgotten the first time he had raised finance for his first business. Prior to the dot com bubble bursting, he started a technology real estate firm while still at university. The concept was simple; he would contact website owners and sell their ad space for them. He would take a piece of the action on the way through. One owner. One advertiser. One plus One equalled Three.

$1 + 1 = 3$

Unfortunately, before he could get the business humming he needed money to build his own website and e-business – because he was damned if he was going to do administration. Let the friggin computers do it! Besides, there were more interesting pursuits to follow such as beer, women and football. But not necessarily in that order.

So his idea needed money. Well it needed more money than Carnegie had. He wasn't from a well-off family with rich uncles to bankroll his ventures.

He drew up a spectacular business plan with a spreadsheet that was off the charts. Carnegie then spent the next month socialising with his university cohorts pitching the idea to see if he could find a money man. Or a money woman for that matter.

Scott Townsend was interested. He came from a business family of great pedigree but Scotty boy, as he was referred to by his classmates, was incapable of a single original thought or idea. But he had ambition burning in his body with no talent. Carnegie represented the opportunity for him to get in the good books with the Townsend family.

The Townsend's had made their money from agriculture and mining and their fortune was developed by the 'uncles' as they were referred to. Old Man Townsend came out from England generations ago with nothing but the clothes on his back, a pocket knife and a few pounds, which he promptly drank away in the local pubs in Perth.

Bereft of resources and not much of a clue, Old Man Townsend spent the majority of his life breaking his back out in the mining and farming lands of Western Australia. He gave up the grog and saved every piece of money; only investing it in land and mining rights. He was ably assisted by a mouse-like lady whom he married named Pearl. Pearl was quiet, unassuming and a wonderful cook. Old Man Townsend loved her to bits, especially when she produced him five strapping boys who worked the land and helped build the family fortune.

When Old Man Townsend quietly retired to his outback cottage, the Townsend rags to riches story was famous. When Old Man Townsend was asked about his success he used to drawl the same thing over and over again: 'Nothing beats 'ard work!'

And so, the next generation built the wealth that Old Man Townsend kicked off, finally establishing a foothold in the East Coast when one of the 'uncles' moved to Sydney to build an investment bank. The 'uncles' met every four months to discuss the Townsend business interests and their family pursuits. When it came to Scott Townsend, the topic became grim.

'The boy's a no hoper.'

'Brainless nincompoop.'

'He's half the man of Jack.'

'Old Man Townsend will be turning in his grave.'

Scott's father shook his head sadly. He knew his boy wasn't much chop. He had tried everything to get Scott interested in the family business or get creative and build something for his own. But instead, Scott wound up at university doing

Arts and spent the majority of six years repeating subjects, owning the bar and perfecting his pool skills.

'So, James. The idea is fantastic and the numbers look good.' Scotty boy peered at the numbers again, not sure what to make of them. But the graph sure looked good.

'Scotty boy, it's a solid plan. We'll rip it.' The young Carnegie was full of optimism and hope.

'Let me line up a meeting with my dad. He'll be keen on investing I'm sure. What's my share?'

Carnegie wasn't so sure about having a business partner like Scotty boy. He was lazy and dense. But he had a source to money, so that had to be worth something.

He offered 30 percent reconciling the thought that the business would be worth millions, so he could live with a payout of seven million dollars when the business was sold to a big corporate or private equity firm.

Scotty boy took the idea home and his father was pleased. This was the first time his son had shown significant initiative and interest in the business world. The plan was amateur and the numbers were cock-eyed, but the required capital was low at one hundred thousand, so he agreed to meet James Carnegie.

Carnegie was thrilled. An opportunity to get things moving. He borrowed the money to buy a new suit and spent hours rehearsing the meeting in his head. Carnegie's parents weren't so thrilled when they got wind of the venture. 'Shouldn't he be studying?' Carnegie's mum asked his father one Saturday morning as they lay in bed thinking about their family.

Carnegie's dad mumbled something about ill-discipline and left the conversation at that.

The meeting was set up at the Townsend offices in the city. Carnegie met Scotty boy at the station. Carnegie was early and sat down at the café he had pre-arranged to meet Scotty. Carnegie was nervous. What would Mr Townsend be like? He felt he could prove his passion and his idea but didn't know what to expect.

Scotty boy turned up to the café late and ordered a café latte. 'You ready James?' Carnegie nodded and sipped his mocha, his third coffee for the morning.

'So, what's the plan Scotty boy?'

'Okay, we are meeting at Dad's office. Don't worry, it is a cinch.' Scotty took his latte and sat down with a bump, accidentally spilling some of the coffee on his expensive polo. 'Shit.'

The young men strode off to the Townsend's office after finishing their coffees.

Soon, they were sitting in the comfortable reception lounges overlooking Sydney Harbour.

'What a view!' Carnegie was amazed at the view from the office. The Harbour Bridge, the Opera house. You could almost get the Sydney Tower in the view.

Scotty looked bored and flicked through a random magazine.

The receptionist smiled at Carnegie. She was a plain-looking girl with a smile worth a million volts. Carnegie kept taking long glances at her, wondering what her story was, what her ambitions were.

His thoughts on the receptionist with the smile were interrupted when an attractive, middle-aged women came to the door of reception. Her hair was neatly done, and she wore an official-looking pants suit. She held an expensive-looking diary in her hand.

'Mr Townsend will see you now gentlemen,' she said in a clipped tone. 'Follow me.'

They walked through the office and were ushered into a beautiful boardroom filled with memoirs. Carnegie looked around at the pictures, awards and was pulled up at a stern-looking man gazing down at them. He had a neatly trimmed beard and was dressed in a tailored suit. Carnegie felt a level of solemness creep into the room and into him.

'Yes, that is my father. Fondly known as Old Man Townsend.' The voice came from behind Carnegie. A firm voice with a hint of baritone. Carnegie turned around and shook hands with Scotty boy's father. He was a tall man with a brilliant moustache. The suit was tan with a soft blue tie and stark white shirt to match. The shoes were polished.

'Thanks for meeting with us sir.' Carnegie smiled at Mr Townsend.

'Hi Dad.' Scotty boy flung himself into a boardroom chair.

'Pleasure to meet you James. Scott has told me a lot about you and your idea. Please sit down and tell me more.'

For the next thirty minutes, James walked Mr Townsend through the business plan and numbers. He felt he was very unprepared, especially when Mr Townsend made comments and he didn't have the answers. But he answered everything honestly and made careful notes. He had a sense this meeting would have some profound effect on him, so he squeezed every moment out of the meeting.

Scotty boy sat back and occasionally interrupted. For the most part, he poured himself water and scrawled on his own notebook. He hoped that his father would think well of him in this situation.

And then the meeting was over. Mr Townsend flicked through the proposal again. Carnegie waited anxiously. Scotty boy looked on, imploring his father to say yes.

After what seemed like an eternity, Mr Townsend looked up. 'Gents, there are gaps here in this proposal.' Carnegie tried not to look down. 'But …'

Carnegie eyes widened ever so slightly.

'… I'd be happy to invest the money into the venture.' Carnegie let a small smile out. 'However …'

Carnegie's breath came out slowly.

'I expect 50 percent of the company. And I want the plan re-submitted before the money is issued. You need to fix these areas.' He produced a copy of the plan filled with notes and questions.

Carnegie smiled. He could manage that.

A while later, Scotty boy and Carnegie were celebrating over a beer or ten. Carnegie's heart was beating fast. He was off and running. His folks would be so proud. 'Fuck yeah!' He high fived Scotty boy. They would be tech millionaires in no time.

And thus, the entrepreneur jumps off the cliff believing they can fly.

Hong Kong >

Carnegie staggered through the downtown streets of Hong Kong, looking for a pub that would suit his dangerously dark mood. It needed to be gloomy enough to sit in the corner and drink himself to sleep but alive enough to be open and without any strange apparitions. His skin was crawling. The number 4 followed him everywhere. As did the numbers 3.33. Why was the fucking time always 3.33am when he woke up? Why not 3.31? Why not 3.34? Something was not right.

Was he dreaming? Was he really in the Matrix? What was the whole point of his entrepreneurial actions and his life's work if he was just a digital marionette dancing to the architect's string code?

He kept walking along, stooped. The humidity bringing a sheet to his pale face. The masked men and women of Hong Kong kept wandering next to him – their impenetrable eyes seemingly staring into his withered soul. Like No Face from Spirited Away they glided along the streets going somewhere, going anywhere. While he, James Andrew Carnegie, was going nowhere.

He coughed and hacked away before reaching for his cigarettes. Soon he was gliding back along.

The cigarette hung limply from his lips; noxious smoke trailing behind him as he strode through the streets contemplating his own weakness and failure. He had not only bailed on life, but he had also bailed on bailing.

Carnegie smiled grimly at that thought. 'What a fuckup.'

Somewhere in his head he missed his kids, he missed his wife and he missed his peaceful little patch of land a world away. The lights flickered in front on him. The cars drove past. The night drizzled with rain. It was just prior to dawn. A tired hooker walked past him managing a cursory smile. She wore tight shorts that barely covered her private bits. A crop top revealed a rock-hard stomach with some Asian characters tattooed over her midriff.

The tattoos look vaguely like Cassandra's. Out of reflex he turned his head as the woman walked past. Nothing like Cassandra.

Cassandra

< Sydney

To most people, Cassandra was 110 percent bitch. Carnegie knew better though. He had been fortunate or unfortunate enough to peel back the many veils that beneath her skin. The tattoos across the sides of her body were enough to shout bitch to everyone. One in Mandarin, the other in Hindi. The one on the left shouted 'Take No' and on the other side it yelled 'Prisoners'.

'Fucking weird,' Carnegie muttered to himself when Cassandra first showed him the tattoos on the beach in New Zealand.

Many months later he found out why the tattoos, why the attitude and why Cassandra.

He first met her at a social function for business. It was an awards night celebrating entrepreneurial spirit. She sat at his table across from him and they spent the whole night taking furtive glances and asking questions like:

'So, who is she?'

'Where is he from?'

'What does she do?'

'How well is business going?'

Eventually, after the wine dripped through the systems, Carnegie seized the opportunity to slide into the chair next to Cassandra and introduce himself.

It was a bizarre feeling. He felt no attraction to her at all, despite the fact she was clearly a beautiful and remarkable woman. But there was something mysterious and enchanting about Cassandra that he just had to explore.

It took Carnegie a long time to figure out what it was. It was her eyes. Those startling green eyes revealed so much and said so little.

They shouted suspicion.

They wept sadness.

They held hardness.

They hinted at tenderness.

They cried mercy.

The eyes had it all.

But most of all, there was a layer of ice over a layer of enigmatic vulnerability. Was that what his mind screamed at? Vulnerability? Really?

'Hi, I'm James Carnegie,' Carnegie said and extended his hand. Whatever chaotic thoughts were tearing his head asunder would have to wait.

'Cassandra Kirk.' Cassandra firmly shook his hand and her eyes narrowed slightly under her designer hat. Her body shifted away from him in her chair.

'What do you do?' Carnegie asked, feeling a little silly. He had already found out a tonne of information about this remarkable lady, such as she ran The Other CK design agency – founding it and building it from scratch. She had 8 amazing staff and had developed some high-profile client accounts. She took no shit from anyone and developed a fierce reputation as a tough negotiator and a workaholic.

Carnegie had always wondered if Cassandra was the female version of himself. Or perhaps he was the male version of Cassandra, his politically correct self-conscience reminded himself.

'I run a little agency.' Cassandra took a sip from her glass and spun slowly towards Carnegie. 'And what do you do, James?' She asked in a somewhat per functionary tone with more than a hint of annoyance and suspicion.

Carnegie talked a little about himself and his ventures. They sat oblivious to the crowd and the function in front of them, mentally fencing with one another, sizing each other up and working out their next moves.

The wine went down, both matching glass for glass, and neither of them flinched. The conversation was quite stilted and one way. Carnegie was very aware he was talking too much but then silence was the other option.

He had wrapped up another well trotted out line, beginning to feel the effects of the wine. A mental note said to him: time to move away. He turned back to the table in an attempt to find a reason to disappear. But, before he could say anything, he detected movement in his peripheral vision.

Cassandra then reached for her designer bag. 'Care to join me for a cigarette, Mr Carnegie?' She spoke it in a mocking tone, which Carnegie couldn't quite grasp.

At the time he didn't smoke, and he didn't want to smoke. He also didn't want to say he didn't smoke. So, with a sinking feeling, he joined her outside with poker face well and truly attached.

They continued their stuttering conversation on the balcony, exhaling grey smoke.

Cassandra seemed to open up away from the social scene and after a cheeky second cigarette. Like all default entrepreneur resting positions, they got onto business and started to build each other's social network, trying to work out how to position each other.

And then everything that could be said had been said.

They stubbed out their third cigarettes and went back to glancing at each other across the table, still blatantly conscious of each other in such short distance.

Carnegie pretended to be interested in what his dinner companion was talking about, but it felt awkward as he felt Cassandra eyes burn into the side of his head.

'And the winner is, for business of the year ...' The room went silent.

Carnegie wondered who had won the award. He generally viewed awards with a little disgust but would have been quite happy to win one.

'... The Other CK!'

The room applauded, and Cassandra smiled that hard smile that a socialite would have paid to have burned on their faces.

Cassandra shuffled past Carnegie and let one finger touch him ever so slightly on the shoulder – leaving him feeling like a battering ram.

Carnegie was intrigued. Carnegie was mystified. At that stage though, he didn't understand that it was all about the game that Cassandra played. And at that time, he was just another contestant.

Hong Kong >

'Are you ok?'

Carnegie's eyes snapped open. It was daylight and he had dropped off to sleep on the steps of an old office building. He blinked a few times and realised it was a young Chinese man dressed for work and off to the office. He didn't remember how he got to the steps from the pub. Did he even make it to the pub?

The blackouts were regular and made for some adrenaline, excitement and anything but the same boring routine that was on the menu for Carnegie. After all, if his days were up, what did it matter if he woke up somewhere he couldn't remember?

'Yeah I'm fine. Thanks.' Carnegie got to his feet, rubbing his stiff legs. He smiled half-heartedly at the young man and embarrassingly turned away to check his smartphone. The iPhone's screen popped on and told him in a menacing tone that it was 7.15.

'Farkkkkkk.' Carnegie exhaled. What happened again? He didn't remember sitting down. He checked his pockets and then sank down wearily on a park bench. A crumpled packet of Marlboro's lay snug in his jacket. He shook one out and sucked at it hungrily. The smoke caused him to cough. I'd better give these things up, Carnegie mused out of habit and then coughed once more as he sucked in more fumes.

The phone beeped at him accusingly. He looked at it again. Messages.

There were a lot of work messages that he hurriedly filed away. Fuck them. They can wait.

But one took his interest. Cassandra. He opened it.

'RUOK.'

Carnegie wondered what it meant and then realised it was an initiative for mental health. He laughed ironically.

He typed out a blasé comment and then deleted it. After what she had gone through she deserved more from him.

< Sydney

A casual coffee meeting with Cassandra after the awards dinner turned into a boozy lunch, which turned into afternoon drinks, which turned into a wine-filled evening meal, which turned into shots; and then finally a strip club with both of them teasing and daring each other to do all sorts of things.

Carnegie wondered if Cassandra was a lesbian or bi-sexual. He felt extremely aroused seeing her slip strippers' dollars and get into the gist of the place like any man. In fact, she looked like she was more at home in the strip club than at the awards function or any business function.

And she could drink. Good heavens she could drink.

Carnegie fancied himself as a good old-fashioned brawler when it came to downing the liquor having once burned through 80 standard drinks in one session, leaving all in his wake.

But he knew it would be a contest if Cassandra ever got stuck in.

Cassandra teased him wickedly that evening. It was all a great game to her. She danced sexually to the pumping beats and rubbed up and down against Carnegie, daring him to abandon his scotch and join her.

The men in the club were in a trance.

The strippers were glaring at Cassandra, especially when she squeezed out of her top revealing a Victoria's Secret black bra and two striking tattoos – one on each side.

Carnegie smiled at her and beckoned her over. She slowly writhed her way over to him, almost reluctantly.

'Shy, James?' she purred at him, casually tossing her top on the vacant chair next to Carnegie.

'Shy? Really?'

He grabbed her and pulled her onto his lap. The smell of tobacco and exotic perfume closed the walls in for Carnegie.

He whispered into her ear. 'Let's get out of this place.'

She looked at him wickedly and shrugged her top back on. 'What do you have in mind?'

Carnegie could feel all eyes were on him and Cassandra.

'Come on. I'll show you.' Carnegie slid her off his knees and pulled her to the door.

A large shape appeared in front of them. He was a six-foot five football player with a chiselled jaw and enormous biceps. 'So why don't you guys join us for a drink?' They looked at the footballer's companions. They were all muscle-bound members of a local football team out on the piss. They leered at Cassandra and smirked at Carnegie.

'We're just off mate.' Carnegie felt short at five eleven.

'Maybe ask the lady if she would rather a real man,' Footballer said loud enough for his companions to here. They roared with laughter. Footballer crossed his arms and tempted Carnegie to respond.

It was all so tiresome.

Carnegie didn't do fights. Sure, he had been in a few of them. He'd won some and he'd lost some. The worst being when he was beaten resoundingly by five charming Middle Eastern gentlemen just because he had been in the wrong place at the wrong time.

Carnegie looked left and right. Somehow all the tough bouncers were nowhere to be seen.

His pride being at stake he did what all men do in front of charming, attractive women. He squared up to the footballer and said, 'Mate. We are leaving.'

Footballer smiled. Violence was at hand. He just didn't realise from where.

'Boofhead!'

Footballer turned to his left. 'Yes, you fuckwit.' Cassandra's eyes sparkled. 'Get out of the way.'

Footballer looked surprised. His companions laughed.

'Shut your mouth slut. This is between me and your man.'

'He's not my man, dickhead. And who are you calling slut?' Cassandra eyeballed the footballer with a dangerous glint.

Carnegie felt a little impotent with Cassandra standing up to the footballer. But it all happened so quickly.

The footballer was enraged. Perhaps the steroids kicked him in his raisin nuts, but he raised a drunken hand to slap Cassandra. An unfortunate mistake.

Cassandra's left arm moved impossibly quick to block the raised forearm with her other arm slicing at his throat while her stilettoed foot slipped in behind to knock footballer over.

Footballer hit the ground with a thud and Cassandra stood over him. 'Tough guy …' She spat at him and dared the companions to get up. They either enjoyed it or feared more humiliation as they clapped and raised their hands.

Carnegie was still a little stunned when Cassandra grabbed him and said, 'Let's go.'

Hong Kong >

Carnegie stared back at the text. RUOK. Did Cassandra know something about him? Perhaps she judged below the sunny exterior that Carnegie was wallowing in self-pity, depression and a general malaise. He texted back. 'Fighting on.'

He felt that was an appropriate comment given Cassandra's martial arts background.

He didn't have to wait too long for her response;

'I hope you're winning, and don't forget this: It is better to conquer yourself than win a thousand battles. Keeping fighting. :)'

The smiley face said a lot. The quote said more.

He wanted to text back and say he was winning. But he knew she would know he was lying.

< Sydney

'Wow, where did that come from?' Carnegie asked.

'Well that's what you get when you mess with a black belt, third dan.' Cassandra smiled, made a fist and waved it under Carnegie's nose.

'Impressive.' Carnegie wasn't lying. It was very impressive how Cassandra dispatched the footballer. Somehow, he felt emasculated through the whole process.

They walked the streets of Sydney. It was a late evening and the booze had hit both of them quite hard; not to mention the adrenaline of the fight that had just occurred. It was over very quickly but they both felt the effects.

Cassandra was an impressive woman. They sat down at a late-night café and ordered coffee. They were in no state to make their way home. As they chatted about random events and stories, Carnegie noticed something in her eyes and demeaner – a vulnerable side to a strong woman. He wondered where it stemmed from.

Cassandra drank her coffee with relish. She was a hard woman with a hard edge. She looked it too. But Carnegie saw something through the act. He probed subtly, not wanting to upset this woman who he was beginning to respect with great admiration.

'So, tell me about these tattoos ...' He said playfully, hoping he wasn't opening a can of worms.

Cassandra stiffened. Why was she going to tell this guy all about the back story of something very personal about herself? She just didn't want to. But something had to give. She had this feeling that perhaps she could just let go.

'It's a long story. Do you really have time for it? Besides it isn't that inter-esting,'' she lied through her teeth.

'You aren't going to get away that easy.' Carnegie chuckled.

Cassandra sighed and took a long sip of her coffee. 'Well I suppose if you are interested then …'

She told him a story. But she didn't tell him the story. And he knew it.

So, a few weeks later, when they were back drinking whiskey, he probed again. She told him another story. But she didn't tell him *the* story. His curiosity surged.

But this was the cat and mouse game that played out for some time.

There was clearly a connection between the two of them; but not a sexual one despite the undeniable beauty shared between them. Cassandra was the 'Red Sonja' of the world. And Carnegie the 'Neo' – the intense, intelligent, charismatic business leader.

People gossiped away, and Carnegie got more than his fair share of sidelong glances from the Good Wife. There was just something magnetic about Cassandra. And of course, there was business to be done. But that wasn't good enough for Carnegie. There was something else. Something that Cassandra was avoiding. Something she was dodging. And it clawed at him. Annoyed him. Attracted him. Pulled at him.

And just as he was going to give up unearthing what those beautiful orbs were hiding, Cassandra called. It was 3.33am in the morning. He was staying at a hotel in the city, feeling utterly exhausted after 3 long days of conference. His feet ached, and the social drinks were beginning to stack up.

There was only one appropriate response to a call at that time of the morning. 'Fuck.'

He rubbed his eyes and reached out to silence the phone. Probably some shitty automated system from somewhere in the world trying to sell him website design services or cheaper phone services.

But he stopped. It was Cassandra.

Instantly, he was awake. Cassandra was independent and strong. She had a network of people around her and had taken to talking at length with his old friend Kennedy. God knows what they talked about, but they seemed to enjoy perennial conversation.

He answered the call. 'Cassandra, what's up?'

'James.' The voice was small and soft. Not like Cassandra's usual husky and direct tones.

'Cassandra, you okay?'

'No James, I'm not. I need to talk to you.'

'Um okay. Hang on. I'll stick my head under some water and get a tea.' Carnegie needed a pause in proceedings. To gather his strength. This was not good. 'I'll call you back.'

'You still in town?' Cassandra asked quietly.

'Yes, still in town,' Carnegie answered scratching his matted scalp.

'I'm at the casino,' she said with a hint of a slur. 'Can you come please?' The voice came through the phone passively but with an iron underlay.

'Okay. Give me 20 minutes.' He walked to the bathroom, phone against the ear.

'Thanks James. I really am thankful,' she responded quietly. Carnegie could hear the click of a lighter. Cassandra didn't smoke all that much but, intuitively, he knew she was in one of those modes. Booze, cigarettes, caffeine, chemicals in the blood stream. When the entrepreneur lets go, they really let go. Whether to celebrate the conquest or numb the pain or stave off boredom, the entrepreneur ferrets out whatever gets them through. There is the good. There is the bad. There is the ugly.

Thirty minutes later, Carnegie lit up a cigarette, sipped away at the Glenmorangie lying around a large ice cube and stared at Cassandra. She was nothing like he had seen before. The makeup was smudged. The eyes were looking down. The hands trembled a bit. She was puffing away like a chimney stack and her eyes were red.

He began to speak. But checked himself. What was he going to say to his friend?

Finally, he said, 'Rough night?' He tried a little levity.

She gave him half a smile, coughed and stubbed out her cigarette – completely unaware of the noise and lights flashing around her at the Star casino.

'Yes,' she said huskily and quietly, self-consciously sniffing. 'I know I'm a mess.'

Carnegie shrugged. 'Your down days are much better than mine. At least you are upright.' He smiled and dragged on his cigarette.

Cassandra gave that half smile again. 'I need to tell you something. I don't want to go into the details, but I got into a fight tonight. My date tried something that opened up a lot of demons that had been previously locked away.'

'Oh.' Carnegie leaned forward and held her hand briefly. 'What did the asshole do? Or perhaps I shouldn't ask?'

'No. You shouldn't ask. Nothing I couldn't handle. To be honest, I just need to talk to someone and my master isn't available or my counsellor.'

Carnegie felt vaguely disappointed. Without thought he said, 'Kennedy?' regretting the flicker of jealousy he felt.

If Cassandra detected it, she chose to ignore the meaning of the question. 'Yes, he is a good listener. But he is dealing with his own demons. You seem to have your shit together, so I just need an outlet where I can get it off my chest. And, I'm sure you know, I have been avoiding telling you my whole story.'

Carnegie twitched at the comment. He was far from together. But he felt it wasn't the time to tell her about the demons he was wrestling with. And it wasn't about him. He had to remind himself that.

At last, she told him the story.

Cassandra's life was one of sorrow and more sorrow. She was born out of wedlock and left with a single father after her mother disappeared. Her father did his best, but Cassandra knew each day that the burdens of responsibility were catching up with him. Then tragedy happened. She was twelve years old, waiting for her father to come home from the office. The next thing she knew she was taking a call from a police officer oddly named Cody DeCody.

'You know, I'll never forget that name or that man,' Cassandra said to Carnegie. 'He had such a strange accent.'

Cody DeCody had some terrible news. On his way home from work, Cassandra's father fell asleep at the wheel and hurtled straight into an oncoming truck, killing himself instantly. Little Cassandra didn't know what to say. Her daddy wasn't coming home. Shortly after, Cassandra was moved to live with her ill grandparents and never felt more trapped or more alone. She worried her teachers with her spectacular art and poetry as it mostly depicted anger and violence.

By the time she was sixteen, she was regularly in trouble at school and had to shift schools. To make matters worse, her counsellor was sent away after systematic abuse and sexual harassment. Cassandra continued to implode, getting mixed up in the wrong crowd.

By eighteen, she had left school and ended up as the youngest fully paid up member of the local Alcoholics Anonymous. Her poor grandparents had no control over her and were struggling with poor health.

And then Cassandra's darkest hour came. She had started hanging out in Kings

Cross with her posse of rebellious teenagers. Under the influence of alcohol and crystal meth, Cassandra found herself alone with three bikers down a dark alleyway.

Her mouth constantly got her into trouble.

'You're a pretty little one, aren't you?' The leader of the gang had a giant red goatee and a large paunch. 'Have a swig of this.'

He threw a bottle of Bundaberg rum at Cassandra.

Cassandra's head was already spinning, but out of her stubbornness and pride she took a long draught and fought the urge to gag.

The little weevil of the gang, a gaunt man with a thin moustache, reached and grabbed at Cassandra's left breast.

'Fuck off you dick!' Cassandra slapped his hand away.

'Oh, pretty and feisty.'' Weevil chuckled and leaned in towards Cassandra. 'Plant one here bitch.' Weevil leered at Cassandra and pointed to his mouth.

'Sure.' Cassandra whacked Weevil in the face with the back of her hand. She nearly fell over as the drugs and booze swung her around.

Weevil grimaced and swore. 'Fucking little bitch. She needs a lesson. Grab her Chops.'

Chops was the third companion and had an enormous chopper moustache that stood out on his otherwise hairless body.

Chops struggled with Cassandra who tried to fight him off among the swirling sky and the neon lights. Red watched on impassively before joining in. He spun the bottle of rum around in his hand and smashed it against the back of Cassandra's skull.

Cassandra nearly fainted with the pain and gave way to Chops grapple; blood leaking through Cassandra's dyed hair and dripping down the sides of her neck and back.

Cassandra paused in her tale and said, 'I still have the scars.' She parted the back of her sweaty hair and showed Carnegie. Carnegie was glad to look at the back of her head as it allowed him the chance to wipe away newly formed tears. The bastards! Carnegie thought about those animals doing it to his daughter and he felt despair well up inside of him.

Cassandra vomited and felt her head spin on its axis. She was in an alleyway with her head wedged up against a garage door that crudely stated in red paint 'NO PARKING IN DOORWAY. FUCK OFF AND DIE.'

She was on her knees moaning in pain. The events that occurred next could not be recalled, however the police report stated that she had been violated in many ways. Cassandra passed in and out of consciousness. She only came to when the rape was interrupted by a slightly built Persian man.

The Zen Master.

'The Zen what?' asked Carnegie, at this stage openly weeping at Cassandra's story.

Cassandra smiled through tears. 'My saviour. Hamid Irzai or, as I affectionately call him, the Zen Master.'

Carnegie found some napkins on the table and passed them to Cassandra, then went to her side of the table and plonked down. He held her hand under the table and hooked his arm around her shoulders. Cassandra looked at him gratefully.

The Zen Master by chance was out rescuing a student from a lifetime in jail, after a pack of red necks descended on his student and their friends. He strode through the streets confidently and intuitively his ears pricked up for danger.

His skin tingled.

This was not a good place. Subconsciously, the Zen Master moved his neck back and forth hearing a slight crack.

The sound of clattering and something being rammed into a garage door took the Zen Master's attention as he strode past an alleyway. A bikie stood in front of the commotion, half on watch and the other half watching the abuse.

The Zen Master's skin crawled. This was not right.

He turned and walked down the alleyway.

Chops saw the slightly built Persian walking hurriedly towards him.

'Fuck off Arab,' he drawled touching the scratches on his face.

The Zen Master had no intention of stopping. This one wouldn't communicate in words, the Zen Master's mind told him quietly.

Chop's cry was cut off in mid-sentence as the Zen Master, feinting to his head, smashed his palm in Chop's solar plexus – knocking the wind straight from him. Chops lay groaning, feeling the devastated blow across his entire torso along with the feeling of suffocation.

The Zen Master calmly turned the corner and, for a moment, he was caught aback. He had witnessed some hideous crimes in his time back in his native land. Torture. Rape. Terrorism. But to see two savages molesting this youngster; it was another sight.

The Zen Master's keen senses repelled.

He smelt the vomit that Cassandra's face was grinding against.

He felt the anguish and crime against humanity.

He heard the young girl moaning.

He saw the blood and the shards of glass.

And he channelled his basic instinct of anger.

Red came at him first while Weevil was desperately pulling at his trousers. The bottle in his hand, Red stabbed at the Zen Master's face – a quick blow that would have ended many a man's sight, if not his life. But the Zen Master was a master of multiple disciplines and had read the move seconds beforehand.

He lifted his right hand impossibly quick and impossibly accurate. The blow was diverted to the right of the Zen Master's head. As Red followed the bottle past the Zen Master's blurring body, the Zen Master tap danced and stuck out a foot, before tapping Red firmly on the face. The big man slammed into the ground.

The Zen Master was one fluid motion. Not turning to Red, he took two quick steps and landed an arcing foot straight into Weevils groin. The man groaned and sunk to his knees. The Zen Master altered his stance and brought up a knee straight into Weevil's jaw, fracturing it in five places.

The Zen Master stopped. The sight of Cassandra lying next to the screaming Weevil made him take pause. She had faded mercifully into unconsciousness. He bent his knee and felt for a pulse. She was still alive. He wiped away the blood from her face and eyes.

Whipping off his light grey sweater he balled it up and quickly stemmed the blood at the back of Cassandra's skull.

'Fucking Arab.'

Danger.

The Zen Master spun in an instant, crouching. Red and Chops were on their feet and closing in. Chops was holding an evil looking blade while Red clenched a menacing set of knuckle dusters.

The Zen Master sighed. Why didn't people just stay down?

Like a choreographed movie, the Zen Master blocked Red's swipe, moving him into the direction of Chops. Chops plunged his army disposal knife into the side of Red. A scream of pain filled the alleyway.

'Shit.'

Chops looked frightened. He quickly pulled the knife out of his comrade and took a step back. Perhaps this freak was not going to be bettered.

Before anything further could happen, a baritone voiced called out. 'Drop the knife!' Chops spun to see two police officers pointing standard issued revolvers at him. The gig was up. The knife clattered to the floor.

The Zen Master wasn't taking any instructions from anyone at that point. He was kneeling down at Cassandra's prone body.

Hong Kong >

Carnegie stared at his smartphone. He had been sitting there for a while thinking, of what he could write back to Cassandra.

Nothing he could come up with would be an adequate response. Bitterly, he looked away in disgust. He was a self-centred fuck. Here people had gone through nightmarish lives and survived. They were the happiest. He wasn't happy because he was bloated with self-pity and toxic thoughts.

He wanted to cry but he couldn't.

He thought about the Man Who Couldn't Die. What a champion! And then he had to go and die.

It was just another reason to off himself.

The Man Who Couldn't Die

< Auckland

The Man Who Couldn't Die was a modern marvel of the scientific world. He was born into the world a screaming premature infant with every major defect. A weak heart. A soft brain. A stunted arm. The doctors on duty wondered if the parents weren't better off letting the invalid just die.

The parents, however, were made of sterner stuff and loved the little tacker despite all his failures. The doctors warned them the little one probably wouldn't survive and if he did he wouldn't be expected to have a long life. They were half right.

The baby who couldn't die hung on to grim life, glowing unhealthy under the premature lights. His stunted arm jerked repeatedly, waking him up from time to time. But he didn't cry. He was a tough little bastard who just happened to have a legitimate father.

And slowly by the degree, the stunted baby grew and grew 'til the adoring parents could take the infant home. People marvelled and took courage from the little baby. He became quite an unattractive attraction to all and sundry.

Carnegie wept to think of the pictures of the little baby struggling against the call of nature. If he was a dog, the bitch would have given him a nip behind the ear.

But the nipper would have no such thing. He struggled over the years to keep up with everyone else. What he lacked in natural rights he made up with a sharp brain and more importantly a drive that was unparalleled.

Despite the mounting sick days, he placed well in every class. And every time an emergency trip beckoned the boy who couldn't die he came back stronger than ever. He devoured books and information. And when everyone else was jerking off to internet porn, he was reading Wikis on all matters and studying the markets.

Through university, he qualified for accountancy and promptly went into business for himself. He always had his laptop with him, so that he could always be productive whether from the hospital, emergency ward or at home in his bed.

The man who couldn't die received a number of grants which he put to good use. He always tracked Carnegie down via phone, email or mysteriously turning up at airport lounges.

Carnegie always asked the most stupid question whenever he saw him. 'How are you?'

The Man Who Couldn't Die always smiled brightly. 'Pumping it mate!' For good measure, he would always pump his stunted arm up and down and give a 'I don't give a shit about my disabilities' cackle.

Carnegie laughed at his own foolish. Of course he was going well. Even when he was on death's door he always found a way of expressing a dark form of humour.

'You know, Carnegie. The doctors pumped me full of cockroach blood.' He grinned. 'Yep I'm a survivor. When the Russians decide to blow up the world you pricks will be wasted and I will be humping along quite nicely.'

Carnegie smiled at the joke and quietly wondered if cockroaches had blood. They squished and cracked when he stood on them but what came out look more like ooze. Carnegie left that thought to himself.

Carnegie gave the accountant who couldn't die all the work he could. Not because of sympathy but because he was a damn good accountant. He had an amazing analytical brain that could spot a trend and build a model. He was irreplaceable. In fact, he was so good he predicted the Global Financial Crisis. Of course no one listened to him.

'Carnegie my man.' The Man Who Couldn't Die looked up from his dialysis machine. 'Look at this analysis I have done over the last 50 years.' He pointed to a series of graphs and charts on his spreadsheet.

'Bam! Bubble bursting.' He looked very pleased with himself.

Carnegie spent the next four hours poring over the analysis. He was good, but he was nowhere near his mate's capability. The analysis made enormous sense, but Carnegie couldn't see it. Surely all the experts around the world would have picked up on this.

The machines whirred and beeped while the two friends sat talking and discussing financial markets.

Carnegie was through a detailed explanation of a theory when he turned to the man who couldn't die. His head was tilted back and eyes closed. His stunted arm lay calmly wrapped across his chest. He was at peace.

Carnegie looked carefully.

His friend's chest rose and fell in rhythm with the machines he was plugged in to. Carnegie laughed in spite of himself. For a moment he was alarmed. But this was the Man Who Couldn't Die.

He rose and put aside the laptop they had been poring over.

He didn't know why, but he kissed his friend on the forehead. 'Good night sweet prince.'

Hong Kong >

Carnegie choked on the memory as the people of Hong Kong bustled past him, unaware of the demon's he faced within. Carnegie hated his farewell to the Man Who Couldn't Die. It was the last words he had said to his friend.

Carnegie pushed his greying hair back from his forehead and silently pleaded to someone to stop and talk to him. Anyone would do. The old lady washing the red taxi cab. The skinny delivery man with a box of suspicious smelling goods. The lady with the impossibly short denim skirt. The bellboy labouring down the streets with bags.

But they didn't stop and talk to him.

Carnegie looked around miserably and wished he was somewhere else. The hollow feeling of being alone shook him like a wave. He prayed that the Waitress with the Kind Eyes would walk around the corner, but she was somewhere else on the planet, probably in her own little village reading her sweet daughter a bedtime story.

The thought made him think of his own kids. What the fuck was he doing across the ocean when they needed him? Just like Cassandra needed her dad. Just like he needed his father when he was growing up.

But Carnegie felt a failure. He was an almighty fuckup in the great sense of the meaning. He was a terrible husband. A poor excuse of a father. He rationalised that the kids would be in a much better space without him. The thought sounded bitter, felt bitter and tasted bitter.

He reached into the pocket of his cotton Country Road shirt and pulled out a cigarette. Bitter thoughts, bitter smoke.

He didn't know what he despised more: his wretched self-pity or his wretched former clueless self. A dreamer. A visionary. An optimist who had no time for the present iteration of himself. Carnegie imagined a vision of his former self striding along purposely with a new satchel and a swanky suit. Neatly groomed with a perfect shave.

The past Carnegie would have looked upon with a cocktail of condescension and disgust. Oh he knew that former self. Wrapped up in his own plans for world domination. An empire builder. The man with a plan.

He didn't know whether it was daydream or hallucination from a lack of sleep and a long weekend of alcoholic abuse, but Past Carnegie sat down next to Present Carnegie.

Past Carnegie looked at him with a frown. 'Get yourself up and do something positive. You are your own worst enemy.' Past Carnegie had that striped pin suit on with the skinny pink tie on that Present Carnegie had liked so much.

Present Carnegie just stared at him. It was him all right. Less grey hair. More weight. No dark rings around the eyes. Crossed legs. Polished Aqua shoes and the aged satchel.

Past Carnegie stared back at him. 'Well don't just stare. Get up and make something happen. It's all in your head.'

Present Carnegie snarled. 'Fuck you Carnegie. You can't possibly know what's in my head.'

Past Carnegie smiled. 'I know mate.' He patted his shoulder. 'I know. It's a lot of bad stuff in there. You need to clean up, sleep up and get home.' He checked his Rolex watch. Impatience.

Present Carnegie knew all about that. Past or Present. They were both impatient but only one of them could move on.

His lips twisted into a bitter shape and he laughed. 'You know Carnegie. You become me. Thought about that? Look at me. See where your optimism and fucking visions got you? Royally fucked up.'

Past Carnegie frowned. The present version of himself had a very good point but the optimism naturally flowed from within. 'But it doesn't have to be the end. We move on right?'

He continued. 'Look around. Which one are you?' He gestured at the multiple versions of Future Carnegie walked around.

A smiling Future Carnegie nursed a third baby and held hands with a little girl while his wife cradled the middle child.

A chain-smoking Future Carnegie bent his back to shovel asphalt into an opening in the road.

A casual Future Carnegie walked past talking markets with his companion who was another Future Carnegie trying to get the stain of his hot dog off his burgeoning stomach.

A Future Carnegie sat on a piece of cardboard begging for change and glaring at the back of non-contributors.

A Future Carnegie cycled past decked out in lycra.

But Present Carnegie wanted none of the future versions, for his version of the future didn't include a future Carnegie.

He took a drag from his cigarette and rubbed his eyes. He turned to the Past version of himself but there was no one perched beside him cradling a new satchel and sporting pin stripes.

He looked around and no Future Carnegies walked, cycled, cradled or begged. They were just normal folk going about their day.

Carnegie inwardly groaned. Now he was seeing things. Time to move on. He rose to his feet wearily and headed back to his hotel.

< Mumbai

Carnegie woke up from his luxurious bed in Mumbai. The phone was blinking and vibrating. Carnegie didn't feel refreshed and for some reason he was in a heightened state. A manic state in some ways.

He was in Mumbai to close a large deal and he was weary from flying all night. The eight vodkas surprisingly hadn't helped.

He rolled over and grabbed the phone. There was a string of text messages from his friends.

The first one mysteriously said 'OMG. Did you hear? He is gone.'

The second was less subtle. It was Agro. Or Aguero as his proper name was.

Everyone called him Agro because he was always going on a rant about something.

It said. 'Fuck sake. The Man Who Couldn't Die just died.'

Carnegie sat bolt upright. His heart raced and sank at the same time like a fancy yacht trying to break the Sydney to Hobart race record.

A sense of despair filled Carnegie. A cloud of black smoke filled his soul. The black dog climbed firmly on his back. The straw dog that broke Carnegie's back.

Replying to texts and making calls didn't help and made no sense of it all. He stumbled to the balcony and sucked on an early smoke. That didn't help either.

He was dead. A tiny mysterious bug got into his blood stream as he was doing a regular health check-up. *Hospitals*, swore Carnegie. *Clean and deadly*.

It was perfectly ironic.

His stunted birth didn't kill the Man Who Couldn't Die.

His liver and kidney transplants didn't kill him either.

Pneumonia hadn't taken him off either.

Nor glandular fever.

Nor a strange blood mutation that the doctors couldn't explain.

A little bug got into the cockroach and had nuclear ramifications.

Carnegie wanted to cry but he couldn't. Nothing would come. The little man's picture filled his mind. It smiled and told a joke. But it didn't help Carnegie.

Why now? he asked himself futilely.

Only one thing could help. He rang his first and second assistant and finally got hold of his assistant's manager.

'Hi Doris. Cancel all my meetings. I'm going on annual leave.' Carnegie was in no mood for small talk.

'But Sir. You mean the Shahib deal as well?' Doris sounded anxious.

'Especially the Shahib deal. Tell them we've had a death to deal with.' Carnegie knew he sounded irritable and impatient to the lovely Doris. But he didn't care.

'Okay Sir. Do you want me to book you flights back for the funeral?' Doris asked taking notes in the background.

Carnegie paused. He didn't know what to say. It was the last place he wanted to go. But it was the right thing to do. The words didn't come out.

'Sir, you still there. Hello?' Doris leaned into the phone.

'Yes, I'm still here. No that won't be necessary Doris. I won't be going.'

'But …'

'No buts Doris. I'll take care of my plans.'

'Okay chief.' Doris sounded clipped and a bit let down.

Carnegie hung up. No more talking. He poured himself some coffee and sat back down to light up another Marlboro. The combination of nicotine and caffeine made Carnegie feel superficially better. A few hours later he was standing at Mumbai International airport. 'Where to?' he mused.

The phone vibrated in his pocket. He reached for it. Ah good. His wife was calling.

'Hi Hon,' Carnegie said somewhat brightly.

'Hi Babe. How are you feeling? You would have heard the news.' His wife sounded her usual gentle, caring, calm self.

Carnegie hated his wife's gentleness and caring. It made him feel like a selfish prick. Which he knew he was.

'I'm fine but I have to go away for a few days to deal with things.'

'Okay sweetie, I understand. Will you be back for the funeral? I don't know when it will be, but some are saying Friday.'

Carnegie glanced at his phone and made a quick calculation. *That's just great. Friday the thirteenth. Perfect timing.* He sighed. 'Darling I know you will understand but I won't be back. I can't handle it right now. Everything is collapsing on my head.'

Carnegie's wife paused, clearly not agreeing with his call. 'Okay that's fine. Where will you be going?'

'I don't know but it will be somewhere warm. I need to just put my feet up. I'm sure I will be back soon.'

Carnegie listened to his wife for a few more moments and exchanged more domestic administrative discussions.

He was about to hang up when his oldest child came on the phone.

'Dadda, when are you coming home?'

Carnegie felt terrible. He loved his kids. He just found it hard right now to love anyone, especially himself. 'Sweetie. Dad's very busy. I will be back soon.' Carnegie paused. 'I'll bring you back something really cool.'

His daughter spent some time detailing a shortlist of toys she was after before Carnegie said goodbye.

He looked at the international departures board. And then it hit him. He knew where he had to go. He would talk to someone who really understood him and would make the pain go away. With a spring in his step he took off towards the Cathay Pacific sales desk. He was going to Hong Kong. Its hustle and bustle, and more importantly the Waitress with the Kind Eyes, could nurse his spirits back.

The Waitress with the Kind Eyes

As it turned out, the only nursing of spirits that was done was the copious amount of booze that Carnegie downed as he finally gave up his search for the Waitress with the Kind Eyes. A wall of despair and pain hit Carnegie when he realised his hope of consolation was far far far away. He was very very here.

Like every self-respecting man who has given up on life; he went on a bender lasting a week. Days blurred into nights, nights blurred into days. He only stopped to pass out in his room, eat enough to say alive and provide the most rudimentary of messages back to the homeland.

The exhaustion was staved off by caffeine, alcohol, sugar and anything he could force down his neck. Even through his mission to obliterate brain cells and his already taxed liver, Carnegie had a cunning plan. For every signal his brain received from his clapped-out body he had a remedy to stay in an inebriated state. He had the Pharmacist to thank for that.

Hunger equated to energy drinks and chocolate bars.

Reflux was quelled by taking anti-acid pills.

Red and dry eyes were cleared with solution.

Sore throats from chain-smoking were resolved with sucking down on menthol cough lollies occasionally mixed with the odd cigarette.

Fevers and chills were cured drinking sitting down.

Sleep deprivation was cured by drinking standing up and loud music

Headaches were pounced on quickly with a range of varying painkillers. He found Aspirin in the strongest dose – best washed down with Red Bulls.

The Pharmacist would have been proud. Of course, prevention was better than the cure but like all good pharmacists the cure was more compelling.

For the purposes of making life easy, he slicked back his hair with a nasty looking gel and let his beard grow.

He traversed the bars and clubs across Hong Kong generously tipping taxi cabs and paying women to pour him drinks and go away unless he wanted to dance; and then he was up on the floor with at least three women at a time.

Carnegie was lucky. He had learned the secret of dancing for white men. The DJ had been very quick to let him in on an age-old secret. If you are a white male; MOVE LESS! Carnegie always smiled when he saw drunk middle-aged Caucasians on the dancefloor. They were a mix of flailing arms and legs like a rotating water sprinkler on full motion.

And so, when he hit the dancefloor, he gyrated and bounced ever so slightly letting the girls rub up and down him. He looked around arrogantly when he was on the dancefloor and told himself he could have any girl in any club he wanted. Narcissistic wanker, Carnegie told himself.

But, in truth, during his act of physical self-terrorism there was only one girl he wanted to be with.

< Hong Kong

He had met the Waitress with the Kind Eyes in a Hong Kong bar. It was impossibly late for Carnegie. He had lost his friends and his phone was dead. He was physically ill from the night's festivities and his stomach was plaguing him. Down in the dumps he had staggered into a random bar and propped himself up, ordering the mandatory beer to appease the bar tender who was an acne-scarred middle-aged woman who had seen better times.

He wasn't sure how long he sat at the bar with the ceiling spinning and the floor doing a synchronised dance with the beat to the trance music the club was playing.

'Are you okay?'

Carnegie wearily stopped thinking about the wold of financial pain his businesses was in and turned to look at the voice.

She was a Portuguese woman of rural up-bringing looking impossibly out of place in the seedy bar. Clearly, she had chosen a career of hardship given her uniform. But her face was unmarred by time or place and she looked at Carnegie with concern.

'I'm fine,' Carnegie snapped and turned back to his contemplations and his lukewarm beer. The last thing he needed right now was to be propositioned by another woman.

A minute passed and for some reason he felt sorry for the girl. He had no right to judge anyone and he had no right to be rude to some random stranger that asked him a simple question.

Another minute passed as Carnegie contemplated his guilt. He took a sip of his Heineken and turned back to the woman.

'Look, I'm sorry. I didn't mean to be rude. I just have a lot on mind and clearly I have had way too many drinks.' Carnegie had to focus on each word to avoid slurring like a drunken idiot, which he clearly was.

'That's okay.' The Waitress with the Kind Eyes had dealt with and seen a lot worse. Every inch of her body could write a TV episode of the experiences it had endured.

She smiled at him. Carnegie was nearly knocked of his stool by the smile. It wasn't a Colgate smile by any means, but the teeth were pearly white. The lips were full and it came from her heart. The smile shouted loudly at Carnegie. In the Nano seconds that ticked away, Carnegie's brain rapidly computed a mixture of words and emotions in one simple expression.

Care

Love!

Nurture

Compassion

Empathy

Pity

Magic

Desire

Escape

And the brain spat signals to Carnegie. He resisted the urge to fall out of his chair and fall into her arms.

In his drunken state, and it had nothing to do with alcohol, he only managed one word.

'Hi.'

Carnegie was instantly angry with himself, as he prided himself in being a great communicator. He enjoyed Shakespeare and was well read. He picked up foreign languages fairly quickly and had an array of facial expressions that rapidly conveyed his message. In one particularly boardroom he had spent an hour sharing the micro components of what made up a datacentre.

And yet all he could manage was 'Hi.'

It didn't seem to worry the Waitress with the Kind Eyes as she said hello and turned back to her sparkling water.

'Let me buy you a drink.' Carnegie shifted stools and sat next to her.

She looked confused for a second, looking at Carnegie and then at her nearly full glass. Carnegie felt like a fool, but she covered for him.

'Sure. I will have tequila.'

Carnegie liked the way she pronounced tequila. He very much disliked the fact that she ordered tequila.

He motioned over the aging bartender and ordered two tequilas. Don Julio. If he had to drink tequila in this wretched state it might as well be a decent one.

'Orange and Cinnamon,' she said to him.

Carnegie wasn't sure what she meant and wasn't sure if she meant a brand of tequila. He tried to adjust to the statement (or was it a question?). In the end he gave up and asked her again with a quizzical look.

'Sorry?'

'Orange and Cinnamon. You know. For the tequila …' She looked at him with another smile.

'Ah.' He hadn't heard of that. *It must be a Hong Kong thing.*

The bartender computed his order fairly simply leaving Carnegie feeling terribly ignorant.

The tequila tasted good with orange slices dipped in cinnamon. In fact, it was so good he ordered another.

He realised he had been sitting there for some time. 'I'm James,' he said, awkwardly offering his hand. She took it and an electric shock went through his body. The hands were both incredibly strong and soft.

She told him her name. It was something that Carnegie lived to regret. A name that perfectly framed her in every way and burrowed its way into his brain for an eternity.

Hong Kong >

Carnegie stood in the hotel lobby waiting for the elevator to come down. He was thoroughly miserable thinking about the hooker with the kind eyes. He was even more miserable recollecting her name. Why couldn't she have just stayed as the Waitress with the Kind Eyes.

Or even better ...

Just 'the Waitress' would have been fine.

< Hong Kong

The Waitress with the Kind Eyes dropped back the second shot of tequila like a pro. Carnegie followed suit looking, feeling and being anything but a pro.

'Are you here for long?' She asked him, sipping on her water.

'No just passing through. I've lost track of my friends and am just heading back to the hotel. I've got a plane to catch in twelve hours.'

She smiled again at him. That perfect smile. 'So, you look like you've had a good time.' She turned ever so slightly but gave him her full attention.

And then it hit Carnegie like a bolt out of the blue. Those eyes.

Holy fucking shit!

The dark round pupils floated perfectly on the purest of milky orbs perfectly framed by incredible eyebrows. There was no hardness. There was no corruption. No streaky tangents of red. Just perfect eyes that spoke volumes. They promised better times. They promised everything would be okay. They offered hope and faith and care and a future worth living.

They were the kind of eyes you saw in your mother.

They were kind eyes.

Hong Kong >

Carnegie rode the elevator back to his room wiping the tears out of his eyes. What he would give to see those eyes again. The door to his apartment opened again. The room expanded in front of him. Alone. Empty. Desolate.

He reached for the sleeping pills. Maybe in my death those beautiful eyes will come to me.

< Hong Kong

Carnegie looked away in embarrassment. He knew he had been staring at her entranced. For how long he did not know. She didn't seem to mind. And something inexplicable happened.

She slid gracefully off her stool and wrapped her arms around him. 'It will be okay,' she said to him, somehow knowing the mountain of stress and pressure swamping him.

Carnegie's last zephyr of dignity and pride disappeared. He sobbed and held onto her tightly, never wanting to let go. He drank a recipe of two parts relief and one part of hope with a sprinkling of guilt.

'It will be okay,' she said again, giving him a kiss on the cheek that left a slight outline of lipstick that Carnegie didn't want to scrub off.

An eternity seemed to pass and then he let her go, grateful for the embrace. They climbed back up on their adjacent bar stools and silence followed. Carnegie didn't know what to say.

So, he just said, 'Thank you, sweetheart.' It didn't seem adequate but that was all he was capable of saying.

'It's no problem,' she replied with a smile that gave Carnegie no clue as to what she was thinking.

And so, they that sat there and had another drink. And then Carnegie found words he never could find for anyone in his life. He just poured out his heart and soul to this woman that sat there.

She was a wonderful listener sitting there and taking it all in; occasionally patting his knee and nodding when he told her all of his woes. There was no judgement. There was no criticism. There was no condescension.

Carnegie's intoxication took another form. Like a starving man before a feast he set to his confession with relish, leaving no stone unturned. And in that time those kind eyes looked on.

He tried not to stare but the dark orbs just kept dragging him in.

And when the sun came up he talked some more and then walked her back to her hotel. It was a long walk, but it felt like no more than two blocks when finally he stood outside her three-star hotel, not wanting her to go.

She brought him out of his daze with a sentence that felt more like a death sentence.

'Sweetie, your plane has to go in a few hours? Your friends will be waiting.' She said it while holding his hand.

Carnegie's mind stopped to register the thought. She was right. His friends would be packing up and ready to go soon. And then he thought, *Maybe she's just trying to get rid of me?*

He put away that childish thought and sighed.

'Yes, you are right. I must go but thank you so much. You are a very special person.' He wanted to say something foolish like I Love You but he managed to hold in dangerous words. They embraced for what Carnegie honestly thought would be the last time. Turning around lithely, the Waitress with the Kind Eyes disappeared into the hotel – leaving Carnegie feeling joyous and sorrowful at the same time.

Six Million Ways to Die

Hong Kong >

Loud banging then dull thudding. Carnegie didn't know where he was or what was happening. He managing to open one eye with a titan effort. A fog appeared in front of him with some hazy objects in the background. The effort exhausted him, so he let the eye shut. In the blackness of his mind he wondered where he was and what was going on. It must be part of a strange dream.

But it wasn't, and the banging continued. He tried to open his mouth and say something, but his mouth and tonsils were like sandpaper with a dust storm blowing through.

He tried again, panic starting to flow through him. His heart started beating faster.

And then the banging stopped. In his semi-comatose state, he listened to his heart beat through his chest; his thinning body vibrating with every beat. The fog settled lower and he felt himself drift off.

And then he heard a voice.

A distinctively female voice. 'Get up Jamie.' He tried to groan but only managing a hoarse croak. It was a voice that came clear. 'Wake up my sweet Jamie.'

Through the mist a face came. In his mind he reached out to touch it. But his invisible digits grasped up thin air.

'Get up Jamie.'

The voice spoke louder. The face came nearer.

And then Carnegie knew the face. It was his wife's beautiful face, which he had loved so much and still loved so much.

'Wake up Jamie.'

'We need you Jamie.'

The faces of his children appeared in his heads. They were frozen in time except for crystal clear tears running down their cherubic faces. Their expressions mixed between love and accusation.

'Wake up Jamie.'

But he couldn't wake up. He wanted to sleep. He felt himself drift back. It felt like slowly sinking in to a warm bath.

'Get up Jamie.'

And the faces began to fade. His wife's face turned from determination to sorrow. A single tear dropped. It traced through the air clearing acrid smoke.

Carnegie followed the path of the tear through the air. It grew bigger and then he realised the faces had been above him. But they were gone. Despair.

The tear crashed into his face and shattered into a million shards.

'Arrrrrrrrrrrrrrrrrrrrrrrrgggggggggggggggggggggggghhhhhhhhhhhhhhhhhhh.'

Carnegie screamed as he fell off the couch he'd been asleep on and his smashed straight into his scotch glass. The pain was intense and over rode the nearly lethal dose of sleeping pills he had taken.

His eyes shot open and his hand grasped at the gash on the side of his head. Blood spat from his head like a water cannon. The drugs he had taken had thinned the blood and his heart pumped it out in large doses.

He screamed again as he realised where he was and what had happened. Glass pieces stung his hand and bit into his fingers. He managed to get to his knees. Carnegie was partially blinded by the blood spurting everywhere. Somehow, he found his discarded shirt and wadded it against the wound. The adrenaline pumped through his body naturally helping him through the emergency.

Carnegie groaned. His left eye was somewhat clearer and he quickly surveyed his room. It was a diabolical mess. A knocked over bottle of pills spilt everywhere. An empty scotch bottle. His shoes and socks lying against the hotel world. A designer vase lying randomly on the grey carpet.

'Sir?' Two knocks.

'Fuck.' Carnegie swore. Terrible timing. He lurched towards the door and then realised his state. He was also suddenly aware of an illegal firearm sitting on the wooden panelled coffee table.

'Fuck!!' He dragged himself to the coffee and awkwardly shoved the gun down the back of his jeans.

'Hello Sir?' Two more knocks.

'Yes.' It hurt to call out, but he knew if he didn't get his shit together he was in some serious trouble. He zombied his way over to the door, painfully aware of glass fragments lodged in the sole of his bare feet.

He gazed through the door's peep hole. The duty manager was looking somewhat concerned but a small measure of relief came when he realised it was Hung or 'Barry' as he was referred to. Barry was an excellent duty manager. A man of inscrutable face. He had been on the door at the Hong Kong hotel and seen it all. Celebrity deaths. Smuggled pets. Copious amounts of drugs. And a bizarre number of requests.

Wax candles from Austria.
Inflatable dolls.
Venezuelan cigars.
Sugar free sugar.
Powdered Coca Cola.
Room temperature ice.
100% organic bird seed.
One thousand blue M&Ms.
Pink edible g-strings.
Tiger's blood.

And the list went on. But as a consummate professional Barry would nod and take down the request. If ever he wanted to laugh out loud at the crazy demands he never showed it. Barry did not do humour.

And there he was knocking on Carnegie's door with his usual inscrutable face.

'Barry, it is Carnegie,' he called through the door, propping himself up against the wall.

'Are you okay Sir?'

There it was again. Fuck off! Stop asking me if I am okay. I am perfectly fucking amazingly doing not well. But I wouldn't tell you because I just can't. Carnegie's mind was spinning.

'I'm okay Barry. Just had an accident. I fell off my couch when sleeping and broke a glass.'

There was silence.

'I'll send housekeeping up to clean up for you Mr Carnegie.'

'No need Barry. I've already cleaned up most of it.' Carnegie lied too easily, very aware of the firearm tucked into his jeans. He hoped that was enough to get rid of Barry.

But Barry knew more than he let on. 'Sir, I am going to come in and check. I hope you don't mind.' He said in his polite Hong Kong accent.

Carnegie wiped his mouth to clear the blood running on his lips. It tasted salty and intriguing at the same time. The adrenaline was pumping and his body was in a state of alarm. Was this it? The end to his journey? A million foggy thoughts floated through Carnegie's mind. Jail. Hospital. Mental Hospital. More time with the Shrink with the Gentle Tones?

The thought both emancipated him and drove terror through his soul.

'Okay Barry. Can you give me five minutes to get my clothes on?' He slurred the last part of the sentence and grasped his makeshift bandage.

'Of course, Sir. I will wait for you.'

'Don't worry Barry. I have also cut myself, would you mind bringing the first aid kit?' Carnegie knew he needed to be patched up and at least it bought him some extra time.

Barry left to fetch the first aid kit. Somehow, he knew this was going to be a strange one.

< Sydney

The Shrink with the Gentle Tones knew his client was suffering from a malaise. But he felt he couldn't reach his patient. It made him feel impotent and worthless. After all, he had worked hard to reach this role, slaving away in Mexico City before succumbing to the wiles of travel and ending up in Australia with his partner and four kids.

He was a homely looking man. Plump, with round spectacles and a classic little Mexican moustache sitting above his thin lips. He knew in terms of moustaches it wasn't much of a specimen, however he liked to have a little bit of facial hair that hopefully dressed up his youthful face.

Why couldn't he reach this patient?

He was a young business man with all the trappings of success. The house. The wife. The kids. The companies. The burgeoning profile. But he was more depressed than anyone he had ever met. And worse still, he refused to take his anti-depressants.

He had always argued logically with his patient, but his patient always came back to something that made perfect sense.

'Drugs are not the answer. Something else is. And I need my wits about me. Besides there are some serious side effects like ending up like a fucking leering zombie.'

This upset the Shrink with the Gentle Tones. He wasn't in the business of creating zombies. He was in the business of restoring mental health.

He remembered the first day he met his patient. He had come into his consulting room and cynically tore apart everything in his profession and left. He had shrugged it off and thought he would never see this one again.

But for some strange reason his patient turned up against his own accord.

'Why did you come back?' He had asked.

The patient shifted uncomfortably in his chair. 'I wanted to give this a second chance. My friend told me that counselling brought her a lot of relief. Personally, I don't see it but what the fuck.'

'So, your friend got help for something. And you need help for something. How do you think I can help you?'

The patient paused and thought for a while. 'Look doc. I'm suffering. Everything about me is successful except I am dead inside. I want to get out of this life but I can't.'

The shrink was taken aback. He hadn't thought this one might have suicidal tendencies. He looked far too sensible and together to be taking things to the extreme.

'Two questions. Why do you think you want to get out of this life? And why can't you?' He was gambling with this line of question. He was more comfortable steering clients towards happier places.

The patient looked sad and stared away for minutes. 'All I can see is a forlorn hope. A future of death. A future of aging. A future of dying in bed in a pile of your own faeces and urine. A future of impotence. A future of assisted showers. A future of journeys ending and no more journeys to take. No more mountains to climb. A future where innocence is lost. A future where my children don't love me anymore. A future where my wife wakes up next to a sad old man.'

'And for all of those reasons, I want to stop this train and I can't.' The patient rubbed his tired eyes.

The shrink gently smiled at the patient as he scratched out some notes with his biro. He wanted to ask the second question again. But he knew he shouldn't.

However, the patient proffered his own answer. 'I can't get out of this life. Hell waits should I take that route. Plus, I can't subject my wife and kids to that tragedy.'

Ah, hell, thought the shrink. Something that came up from time to time and something he knew a fair bit about having been brought up in a strict Catholic household. For a lot of people, hell was here on earth. This one was clearing burning up in nine shades.

'So, you believe in God?'

'Ah the God question. That didn't take you long.' The patient looked angry as if he had ventured onto taboo ground. 'Are you planning on talking me into wearing a crucifix and whipping myself ten time a day?'

The shrink was aghast. How could he get that idea?

'No. No. Not at all; it's just a question because you mentioned hell.'

The patient looked dubious. 'You head ringers are all the same? Just questions, questions, questions. Where are the answers?'

The shrink nodded. This was a common one. He smiled gently and looked across at his patient. 'The answers are within. I just help you find them. I'm a fellow traveller on this journey you are on. But before we find the answers together we first need to know what the questions are.'

Hong Kong >

Carnegie sat on his flight and wondered about the questions. Maybe the shrink was right. What were the questions? He swigged the last of his scotch and dry and folded up his travel tray. Carnegie was used to working in the confined space of economy class. He was occasionally tempted to fly business class but every time he considered the cost he thought of the poor African kids and how much food it would by them. First world problems were just that; first world problems.

Carnegie would always donate 10 percent of his flights to his favourite charities because he felt compelled to do something about the world's problems; and it made him feel good.

He reached into his bag and pulled out his notebook. It was a tired old notebook with a picture of Einstein emblazoned on the front cover. It was his source of pride and pain and could tell a million stories. Sighing, he turned it open to a blank dog-eared page.

He wrote in bold.

WHAT ARE THE QUESTIONS?

He wasn't sure how to start so he wrote the obvious.

Why are humans trying to stay alive and he wanted to die?

He followed it up with another question.

Why are humans?

And then just one word. The most dangerous word that Carnegie had ever come across.

Why?

Why indeed. Why him? Why here? Why now? Why do people fall in love? Why do men and women marry when the contract is totally against nature? Why do babies make everyone smile? Why does everyone want babies to smile back?

Why does the moon effect the tide and some people? Why did he feel alone the most when he was surrounded by many people? Why did he wake up at the same time some nights? Why 3.33am? Why not 4.44 am? Why is 13 unlucky?

Carnegie kept feverishly writing the questions – scribbling them down like a mad man flipping the pages on his notebook rapidly.

Why did he see failure in every success? Why did he see success in every failure? Why was he most alive when things were not going well? Why was he constantly sabotaging himself? Why did his visions of the future turn sour?

Why?

Why did God not reveal himself? Why was dog the opposite to God? Why was the opposite of golf flog? Why did he punish himself? Why did he feel so guilty? Why did he drink himself sober? Why didn't he think of himself as an alcoholic?

Why?

Why had Kennedy had to leave? Why did he have to leave? Why Kennedy? Why?

Why?

It felt good letting all the questions out on paper and suddenly he had a man crush on the Shrink with Gentle Tones. He promised himself that next time he met with the shrink he would not be rude or cynical.

Hong Kong >

Barry knocked on the door and Carnegie meekly let him in. His head was throbbing but at least he had hidden the gun and managed to clean up somewhat – especially the sleeping pills, which he flushed down the toilet after painstakingly picking up every single last pill. Thankfully the gash had missed his vital components and it looked a lot worse than it really was.

'You are very lucky Sir. You could have lost an eye or cut a main vein,' Barry said as he dabbed at the wound, which stung like a giant sting ray.

Lucky, thought Carnegie grimly. If he was lucky he would have done the job properly and be on the other side of this wretched world.

But he simply said, 'Yes, very lucky. Maybe I should sleep more and drink less?' He asked rhetorically.

Barry nodded, which didn't say anything to Carnegie at all.

With the wound holding together with clever pieces of plaster, Barry ordered a taxi for Carnegie on the vanilla room phone.

Carnegie's only thought, as he groggily made it down the elevator, was that he hoped he had hidden the gun well enough.

Smoking Gun

It was meant to be another night. Another night of depression. Another night of drinking. Another night of sitting in a random bar in Hong Kong drinking away the pain. Another night when the music went on and happy and unhappy souls left and entered in altered states. Another night where Carnegie wanted to be somewhere else but at the same time was in the only place he knew to be.

He had sadly rose from his bed with all the energy he had in him. Mental. Physical. Whatever. It was everything in him to climb out, one leg at a time, out of his soft comfortable bed. He ordered room service, no appetite, but purely out of habit. He lay on the floor and whatever transpired next he did not care, nor did he care to remember it. He just knew that it was after 12 and in some far transcendental universe it was okay to find somewhere to find a bar and drink himself senseless. And so, he made it to some named, but nameless to Carnegie, bar in Lan Kwai Fong.

He couldn't remember what day it was and thank God he left his mobile phone at the hotel because he couldn't give a flying fuck what was going on his world, whether it be personal, business or otherwise. Of course, he was guilty as hell about the thoughtlessness, the carelessness and the callousness but after three beers, four shots of tequila and three vodkas the guilt went away, replaced by bleakness, blackness and the emptiness of life itself.

He had made his money, why couldn't he do whatever he wanted. He was successful. He had outlived the odds. He had defied the economic poison and the failure of others. So, he could do whatever he wanted. Only on this night, what he wanted was nothing.

And in that single thought, he realised.

He thought he was successful. But in life he was a failure.

From white; he was black.

The pot of gold at the end of the rainbow came with conditions. Some irrelevant but one main condition. The condition he was in.

Carnegie groaned in himself. The noise faded. The music dulled. The liquor burned in his soul. Like a devilish scene from a horror movie, he felt like he was trapped on stage, and humans had become ghouls; only to realise he was king of them all.

So, this is the inheritance of the rich. A vacant playground of lost souls. A faraway land filled with the emptiness of the unrighteous and the lost.

He scratched at the slick wooden table and quickly swallowed down the rest of his booze. Dizzy from the effects of chemicals, Carnegie rose from his stool nearly wiping out the pair of Poms boozing boisterously behind him. With a mumbled apology, he strode to the bar with a dark intensity that even the devils would have been proud of.

The bar was packed as the night was peak time for the sozzling of souls. The wait was agony for Carnegie. He desperately wanted to smoke. He desperately wanted to inhale something. He desperately wanted to leave. Anywhere but here.

But he had to wait his turn.

The air was thick with riotous living. The football on a fuzzy screen buzzed away above Carnegie's head and he hardly knew whether it was one nil, fourteen seven or in extra time with one apiece. But five angry Austrians sat yelling at one another and at the screen simultaneously, which confused him to no end and made him angrier. What right did they have to be so passionate about punting a pigskin around when life was shit. Worse than shit.

Carnegie's black cloud lifted momentarily replaced with black rage. 'Fucking zombies,' he muttered under his breath, belching at the same time. He fantasised about kicking their table down. Drowning them in their Eastern European beer. Anything to shut these people up.

But instead he stood there impotently.

The anger turned inward. Somewhere in the back of his mind a voice shouted at him. He should get out. Get home. Get good. Get right. Get on with life.

But like all lost souls, the voice faded to the background replaced by immediate needs. The need to be lost. The need to stay lost.

Carnegie turned his attention to the bar trying desperately to gain some semblance of control. There was two people behind the bar. A large tattooed Maori with a broad smile and a thin female of some sort of South American descent. They couldn't have been more different except for the pouring of intoxicants to the willing.

Maori Man made conversation and seemed to have something funny to say. People willingly or unwillingly smiled and laugh. He had been packaged in a size where all jokes were funny. The bar was wooden and soaked. Colourful flags hung from the narrow roof representing all nations and their unfortunate citizens that ended up dancing to the tune of grog and gargantuan nights in Hong Kong. The natives were restless but the visitors took this to a new level. And Mr Maori was more than a capable curator on a night like this. Not only was he amicable, he was a real mover. He jiggled with the music and made his partner look like a salt statue staring back at Sodom.

In spite of the fog and depression, Carnegie couldn't help but to manage a bleak smile. Whatever he is on, I want a life supply of it, his mind unconsciously said with no little hint of bitterness. Sadly, Carnegie wasn't served by the friendly New Zealander – he ended up getting the short stick again.

Self-pity does a wonderful job in the fog.

She was thin. Thin as a rake, who had rusted away for a while and been on a 'no leaf diet' for a year. Gaunt and somehow looking pale, despite coffee coloured skin, Ms Bartender stared dangerously at Carnegie. For a while Carnegie was stunned. Animosity wasn't a new thing nor was indifference, but this was something else. This was a fog of hatred and the air was poisonous.

Suddenly he was sober. Or at least he thought he was.

'Double vodka, lime, soda and two shots of tequila,' he croaked; somehow managing to make eye contact with the darkest eyes known to mankind.

She moved away, not appearing to register anything nor asking him what brand of vodka or tequila he wished. Carnegie preferred the finer versions of his drinks but somehow his tongue clave to the roof of his mouth.

He watched her stick-like body move away with no apparent rush or desire to provide service. Her body was clad head to toe in black unlike the usual bartenders who at times were clad very colourfully and with not much clothing to speak of.

'She's a fucking bitch that one,' came a voice next to Carnegie.

Carnegie turned to see a tall thin man leaning over the bar. He nodded and was about to turn back to the bar with his fog and curiosity when his observant and vocal neighbour grabbed his arm.

'Drugs it is,' he leaned in to Carnegie, showing his yellow teeth, carefully cultivated from years of smoking and neglect.

'Oh,' said Carnegie not thinking of what else to say nor caring to make conversation.

'Yeah. Bitch on the bad gear. I told her many times cheap shit is cheap shit,'' the man said in a heavy accent.

'That's no good.' Carnegie nodded hoping that the dialogue was done.

Unfortunately, it wasn't.

'You want something. I can get,' he said bluntly, pressing Carnegie's shoulder in an overtly aggressive manner.

Carnegie wasn't a violent or aggressive man. Nor was he a push over. Years in the commercial pool swimming with all types of sharks had developed his foundation. And right now this jerk was up in his face at a very inconvenient time.

He spun slowly and drunkenly towards the over enthusiastic neighbour.

'Mate,' he said in a deathly quiet tone. 'Back off.'

The offender was tall and covered in strange tattoos with a hollowed-out face that could have been perfect for any gangster film on the planet.

Neighbour gave him a look that stopped Carnegie in his tracks. It was a dangerous glower designed to ward away evil spirits and enemy combatants.

'Okay.' He paused. 'Ilyan will back off. But Ilyan will remember unfriendly man from Britain.'

Carnegie was suddenly sober. This Ilyan character looked like an extra from Eastern Promises and he had perhaps unwisely poked a Russian bear.

'Sorry mate,' he said diplomatically. 'I'm just tired.'

Something flickered in Ilyan's eyes. And then he somehow smiled. 'Okay, you tired. Here take these and come and see me later for a drink.' He handed a silver slip with some white pills in them to Carnegie in a surreptitious manner, forcing Carnegie to instantly and unconsciously reach for them and stuff them into his pants pocket. It all happened too quickly among the fog and dim of the bar around him.

'Ah.' Carnegie said and then his mouth slammed shut faster than a toll gate at any international airport car park.

Ilyan looked at him and smiled. 'Just come and see me later okay.' And with that he turned back to the bar.

Carnegie thought for a while and then turned around to see his drinks waiting for him and the bartender looking at him with narrowed eyes.

'Sorry,' he mumbled again wondering if it was a night of apologies.

He paid for the drinks and, just before the transaction concluded, stopped arm over the bar.

'Could you please send two Greygoose vodkas straight to that man there,' he said pointing over to Ilyan who was now laughing with Mr Maori.

Ms Bartender was about to argue; however Carnegie slid an extra wad of notes into her hand.

'Just do it okay,' he said before slamming down the tequila shot, grimacing at the strength and taste of the booze.

The bartender looked at him and then counted the notes carefully. She nodded and said something uncomplimentary under her breath in a foreign language before jaunting off to the cash register, still muttering. Carnegie sighed, swore and did another shot, thankful that the drunken fog was coming back. He staggered back to his spot and searched for a cigarette. He needed one.

Two hours later, Carnegie was back in the pit of despair. The alcohol was doing nothing for him, nor was the bar or the atmosphere. He was trapped. There was only blackness ahead of him. He wanted to leave and sleep. Or sleep and leave.

And at that point he realised there was a way out.

And end to it all. Somehow the idea resonated in a triumphantly bitter manner that made him shiver and smile cynically at no one and nothing in particular. There was no sadness at the answer. Nor was there any questioning. Just a solid resolution that bubbled in the surface of his consciousness.

He had come this far, to come this far.

But all thoughts were shattered when Ilyan pulled up a chair in front of him and sat down without permission or any form of diplomacy.

The figure loomed in front of Carnegie forcing him to snap out of his bleak reverie.

'Still tired?' Ilyan asked, drinking and smiling at the same time like a Cheshire cat.

'What?' Carnegie responded grimacing. 'Oh. Yeah somewhat.' He slurred stupidly, regretting ever stepping into this damnable pub.

'That's no good. I have more. Ilyan will give to you at a good price.' The tall Russian smiled again and leaned forward. 'Anything you want, Ilyan can get.' He leaned back and somehow his tattooed arms rippled supernaturally.

'Anything?' Carnegie asked fumbling his attempt to drink casually as an idea formed in the back of his mind.

Ilyan pursed his lips and smirked. 'Anything. It's what I do,' he said firmly leaning back in a defensive position.

'Okay,' Carnegie said with a hint of smile. 'Get me a gun.'

Whether it was originally an idea to get rid of Ilyan or to get the tool of his departure, Carnegie couldn't exactly distinguish.

The Russian laughed. 'Good joke.' He drained his glass and chuckled to himself in a gurgling manner.

Carnegie was not put off so easy. 'You said anything. I want a gun.' He said this firmly, pushing home his advantage.

Ilyan's eyebrows went up slightly and then he grinned. 'You're crazy.'

'Crazy maybe,' Carnegie shrugged. 'But I want a gun.' He spun his hand into a gun symbol and cocked it. 'A gun. I don't care the type, but a gun.'

Ilyan looked around at the scene. The drunks and happy heads were too busy in conversation, arguments or trying to get laid.

He leaned forward. 'A gun is hard. Why you want it?' He stared at Carnegie intently.

Carnegie shrugged. 'My business not yours.' He put his hands on the table and gestured at Ilyan drunkenly. 'You said anything,' he repeated.

The Russian stared for a while. 'Okay, I'll be back.' He stood up and strode to the bar.

Carnegie smiled to himself in a silly manner. There would be no gun, he said to himself. And I can drink in peace. But somehow, he felt disappointed.

And he didn't drink in peace. Because the Russian came back. How long he was away Carnegie did not know but it seemed such a short time. And as he watched the tall tattooed man walk towards him in a surreal manner, his heart beat faster and his pulse quickened.

Carnegie tensed up as Ilyan sat down smugly. 'Okay, Ilyan will get but will cost big money.' *There was the out*, Carnegie thought to himself. An eternity seemed to past as the subconscious wrestle between survival and pride took place – and, as usual, pride won out.

'No problem,' Carnegie said, almost not believing what he was saying.

'No, I mean big big money,' Ilyan said sternly. He rubbed his fingers in Carnegie's face overtly.

'Yes, I know,' Carnegie replied, shrugging in what he hoped was a nonchalant manner. 'It's not a problem if you can get me the gun.' His voice firmed up in superficial strength.

Ilyan smiled. 'Okay. We have a shot and we go. Okay.'

Three shots later Carnegie followed the Russian out onto the cluttered streets of Lan Kwai Fong. The air hit him like the wind from a NASA test turbine and he clung onto his consciousness as he walked. Tourists and ex pats walked past talking and stumbling – oblivious to the mission they were on.

And then there was black.

Or at least that is all Carnegie could remember.

He awoke some time the next day. Blood shot eyes. Heading pounding. With a strange dream about a tattooed Russian man and the purchase of a gun. Carnegie looked around, sighing slightly. He knew where he was. He was back in his hotel lying face down on the tiles of the balcony that overlooked the streets of Hong Kong Central. He closed his eyes and tried to ignore the smell that was causing him to want to throw up.

Something hurt like hell from his abdomen. With his eyes still closed he reached down and felt something plastic. What the fuck?

Gingerly he rose – shivering and then gagging when he realised he was face down in a pool of vomit.

Argh.

It wasn't his first outing to have ended up in an outing. But it was painfully new and fresh. Carnegie wiped the dried vomit off his face and stumbled naked into the shower. He was about to turn on the blessed holy water to cleanse himself of his sins but realised there was a foreign object wrapped around his body. Looking down blearily, he saw what looked like cling wrap, wrapped around his torso.

Suddenly he was soberer than hungover.

With heart pounding afresh, he gently unwrapped the plastic wrap with trembling hands to reveal a bandage.

Oh God, his mind screamed at him.

He stopped at the bandage. The plastic wrap gently floated to the floor of the bathroom.

'No' is all he could say to himself. It wasn't a dream. It was a waking nightmare.

It took all of his mental strength to shut off the noise in his head and open up the bandage. It came away easily revealing a red patch and the tattoo of a gun pointing towards his left leg.

Carnegie took a moment and closed his eyes. He sank down deflated on to the edge of the toilet, his bare ass reacting to the chill of the seat.

Relief slowly made its way to his consciousness.

Like all good entrepreneurs, Carnegie always found a way to remind himself of worse scenarios that could happen.

After some time, Carnegie dragged himself out of the bathroom, head spinning, but somewhat closer to a functioning human than the corpse that he had been. He had no idea about tattoos but knew Cassandra would know what to do.

He walked into the bedroom, water dripping from his wet hair.

Before he could even think about looking for his phone his eyes settled on a rough black bag that lay lazily on the corner of the untouched bed.

Carnegie froze. What was it?

Gingerly he moved towards the bed; clinging on to the towel that was loosely tied around his waist.

Closely he inspected the bad. It was a rough old black bag that resembled a satchel. It had strange markings on it in Russian script and some sort of naval symbol. It smelt like a combination of diesel and fuel and was well worn around the edges.

Sitting down to nurse his pounding head, Carnegie picked up the bag. It weighed a little and two items made a small thud when they connected together in the bag.

Stranger and stranger, murmured Carnegie to himself.

He opened the draw string at the top of the bag and the nightmare awakened completely. It was a dark old handgun and a clip of bullets.

Carnegie swore and put the bag down. It was all true and now he had become a gun owner.

DJ

< Goa

The last time Carnegie felt his head hurt as much it did now was when his drink got spiked in Goa, listening to trance with DJ. Sure, they all laughed about it now, but it was a nasty affair.

DJ giggled. 'You should have seen yourself man. You were lying on a beach chair riding a bicycle for at least an hour.'

Carnegie laughed in spite of himself. It certainly sounded hilarious and explained why he woke up in the morning aching all over with the worst hangover he had ever experienced.

'Did you find out who spiked my drink in the end?' Carnegie asked almost knowing the answer.

DJ shook his head. 'Nope but you nearly dragged me into the ocean. Nearly took my bloody iPhone out man. You were seriously fucked up dude.'

Carnegie nodded. He had an almost guilty pleasure when he thought about that experience. It was the first time he had thought about death.

They had gone to Goa with the DJ, as they had to be in India anyway and, at the time, it seemed like a good idea to check out where DJ was planning on doing a series of gigs. They landed on a steamy Saturday afternoon. Goa airport was in the process of renovation, so they walked through almost a construction site. It was a musty smelling old airport that did nothing to please the friends when they were in the mood for good smells and good times.

Carnegie had a very sensitive sniffer. It was the one sense that he wished he had an off button for. His nostrils picked up on the most micro of scents, whether it was the smell of a woman who had just had sex or a single drop of eucalyptus. Every smell floated through the air and reached Carnegie and instantly conveyed so many emotions. Sadness. Disgust. Loneliness. Pain. Weariness.

And so, the companions ended up on Curley's famous beach house on Anjuna beach. The trance music pumped out, offering solace from life's problems even if for just one night. The beach house looked out over the ocean and a number of dancing Eastern Europeans who had bunkered down away from the icy freezing temperatures of Prague, Vladivostock, Warsaw and Tiblisi. They were a rag tag bunch dressed in dirty shirts and loose singlets. Their skin was burned to brown and the men sported rough stubble while the women carried unwashed dreadlocks and rough tattoos.

Carnegie listened to them speak in drunken tones and tried to pick up the languages they were speaking to each other. He figured it was mostly Russian or something similar. They were a motley crew on the hamster wheel, constantly drinking and dancing but going nowhere in a hurry.

Carnegie realised that he was no different. He too was running fast and going nowhere. There was no end in sight; only the next foot forward on this impossible and ironic life. The thought made him sad and a tear emerged from his eye. He wiped at it and hoped his friends wouldn't notice.

The DJ bounced over to Carnegie with a fresh beer. 'Listen to this mate. Listen. Just listen.' He was bouncing on one foot while balancing a full beer in his hand above his head. 'This is the shit. Listen to this. This is real trance. It's definitely not the commercial house crap that is everywhere. David Guetta. I spit on him.'

The DJ was excitable. He had an incredible ear for music and a library in his head on all types, sub-types, sub-sub-types of trance. Carnegie had no idea. Yes, he picked out the speed of the beats but that was it. His definition for the strain of music was slow trance or fast trance. He liked it all the same.

'So, what is this about David Guetta?' he asked the DJ, not sure why he would hate someone who was popular and that Carnegie only knew about vaguely. And the only reason he knew about him was he liked to keep abreast of the latest and greatest via general news.

'You don't know?' The DJ looked slightly insulted. 'Come and sit over here and get an education.'

The DJ dragged a plastic beach seat over next to him. He was dressed in jean shorts and sported a plain black shirt that stated loudly on the front 'en-tranced!'

Carnegie sat down and took a swig from his Corona. This could take some time.

The DJ proceeded to give them the history of trance, starting in Goa where it apparently all began. After an hour and another three beers he finally made it to Guetta.

'So, you know the song Titanium.'

'Sure,' said Carnegie. Who hadn't? It was one of the most popular songs sung by the beautiful Sia. He made the mistake of telling DJ that he liked the song.

DJ looked at him in horror. 'You can't be serious. Guetta completed screwed up Sia's voice on that track.' Carnegie didn't look convinced.

The DJ whipped out his iPhone and magically conjured a set of tiny headphones that played the music impossibly loud and impossibly clear. 'Now listen to Sia by herself.' The first track was called The Fight. It started with an almost garbled song before Sia kicked it off after a nice drum beat.

'Can you hear her voice?' Carnegie nodded.

The DJ stopped him with a hand. 'No, can you really hear it?'

Carnegie nodded and said yes again. He wasn't sure what answer he should provide to confirm that there was a voice coming out of the headset and he definitely heard it.

'Listen to that amazing voice. It conveys so much meaning and the tones are beautiful.' Carnegie nodded again.

'Now listen to the other crap.' The DJ ripped the headphones out of the socket and gave them to Carnegie. 'Come on, I know you would have that shit on your phone,' he said insultingly.

But Carnegie wasn't insulted. It was just a track.

So, he listened to the music again. 'I'm bullet proof, nothing to lose ...' The DJ stared at him accusingly as he listened to the track.

'Ok I get it. The voice is different.'

The DJ was angry. 'Not just different. He has warped her fucking voice man. What a sell out.'

Carnegie rocked back and forth to the music in background. He was in the mood to play the devil's advocate, so he proffered his commercial wisdom.

'Well David Guetta must be doing something right. He is popular. And he must be good at what he does. He also makes a lot of coin. They can't be all wrong, right?'

The DJ stopped and opened his mouth in protest. 'But art, true art is not commercial. Most artists go south when they go commercial. Guetta is a sell-out. It's quite clear.'

It wasn't clear to Carnegie.

'But what he offers as a product has market. If it didn't he wouldn't sell his music?'

The DJ turned up his nose at that idea. 'See business and music. It's not a business. It's fucking music mannnn! Do you think the Beatles or the Stones were talking products and markets when they were making music?' He sniffed and wrinkled his nose before taking another long pull at his beer.

Carnegie had to concede that point. 'True, but if there wasn't a commercial system would we have heard of the Beatles or Stones? In fact, I would argue you wouldn't have Dylan, Hendrix, Springsteen, U2 or Chisel.' Carnegie added Cold Chisel to the mix of some of his favourites because he thought they were a great act and *Khe Sanh* had a special place in his heart.

'You wouldn't have Britney Spears or Miley Cyrus either,' the DJ retorted.

They both laughed at that thought.

'Very true. But the point remains markets exists all over the world and on balance it gives people choice.'

The DJ was stubborn. 'People are idiots.'

'But people make choices. People make the industry. If there wasn't a bunch of school kids wanting to sing to *Baby One More Time* then there wouldn't be the Britney Spears of the world. And furthermore, I dare say your favourite artists wouldn't exist if the market didn't give them distribute. You are just a niche market.'

DJ was genuinely shocked and his brain stewed over the concept of suddenly being labelled a niche market. He wasn't sure if he was more annoyed at being referred to as a niche market or that someone had dared label him. Artists were not to be labelled. Music should not be labelled. It was poetry for the soul. A business had no place in his world of soaring music and ripping beats.

'Music comes from the heart. It comes from the soul. It comes from the mind.' The DJ was genuinely passionate.

'Money comes from the wallet.' Carnegie instantly felt like a smart ass.

'You don't say,' DJ said sarcastically. 'Cigarette?'

They mixed the classic combination of beer and tobacco and mulled on the conversation.

'What I am saying is that music begins in the right way and then gets corrupted due to greed.' DJ continued, 'The music starts with the soul not with a business plan or a mission statement.'

Carnegie countered, 'But a lot of artists choose music as a career choice and become successful. They choose it as a career choice. That's like a business plan. They have a style and whether they express it or not they have a mission statement subconsciously written.'

And so, the conversation went back and forth as a ping pong match with neither side able to hit the killer blow.

Their conversation was interrupted by the waiter. 'Chicken or Egg?' he said in a usual accent with a lisp.

Carnegie and the DJ looked up at him and then looked at each other and laughed. 'Yep that about covers it.' Carnegie said smiling.

'No. Chicken or Egg?' The waiter pointed to the menu.

'Oh.' They said in unison.

Hong Kong >

Carnegie found himself sporting a nifty bandage and sitting outside his hotel, pondering life in general. His head felt like cotton wool. He had been given some serious horsepower painkillers. Under Barry's watchful eye, the clinic staff had taken care of him and administered a small portion of additional drugs to take away.

Barry had spoken quietly to the staff on the side in Cantonese: 'Don't give him any more painkillers than what he really needs. He already takes too many.'

Barry had smiled to Carnegie when he spoke to the staff and Carnegie had no clue what they were saying. It might as well have been 'Puff the magic dragon is coming back in Autumn.' Or 'Kung Pao noodles are best on the sauce.' Or even 'I'm big bad Barry ready to go bonking.'

Ignorance can be bliss, thought Carnegie, staring blissfully at the people wandering through the streets. The night was warm. The drugs were running through his system.

He could feel his body shaking. There was only one option when he was like this. It was to hear the music. Any music. Something to take his mind off his head. Off his heart.

He hit 'random' on his playlist and plugged into the music and tuned out. At least that is what he tried to do.

David Gray started singing Babylon on a playlist named Chemical Streams. He couldn't believe how appropriate the music. It hit him with all its might and he started to cry. He cuffed away his tears as a default response, but he couldn't stop. He just couldn't let go. So, he let the music do the work, holding on to each word, as if it was the cure to all his ills.

Time seemed to stand still.

Carnegie was openly weeping on the streets of Hong Kong, looking like a madman to all that passed him. But he didn't care. He just pushed repeat on the track, wishing the music could affect his head and his heart.

Not just his heart.

'Fucking music,' he sighed bitterly, after he was forced to get up and head back to the hotel.

Like all good drugs it helped but it also hurt. And the hurt usually came at the end.

< Goa

Far away from his home, and before Carnegie found himself riding an imaginary bicycle on a beach deck chair, he was lying on the beach, semi-drunk, listening to the music and taking solace in the sounds of the waves and twinkling of the stars. *They sit high up in the sky, merrily doing their thing*, thought Carnegie. Why couldn't he be like a star – just a simple, content existence that fades away to nothing.

The thought brought instant despair to Carnegie's heart.

He couldn't go on.

He couldn't simply live on the hamster wheel anymore.

In his madness, he took solace in a dangerous number of shots; topping it off with tangerine mixture that he hadn't seen before.

The night blurred.

The trance flooded his senses and he cackled like a madman – high fiving everyone on the sandy dancefloor. Before he knew it, he was sweating up a fever and had ripped off his shirt. Chest bumping with the DJ, they started shuffling their way down to the edge of water.

They splashed each other, kicking up water in a fury. To the casual observer they looked like a pair of loonies. The full moon bore down on them and Carnegie howled like a wolf. The senses were in over drive.

And then, as he moved to the beat of the music, the water captured Carnegie's imagination. It sat there, gently rippling away; lapping at the edge of terra firma. The water was warm. The ocean hid a million mysteries. The moon bounced up at him off the water – a kaleidoscopic reflection that dizzied Carnegie.

His depression compounded by the sights, the music and the alcohol; Carnegie felt the call.

'It is time,' he said to no one in particular. Emersion would take him. There was no sadness as he walked to the water. He smiled benignly and accepted his fate. Grabbing DJ, he wrapped his arms around him and set a foot into the water. And another. And another.

The music pumped loudly matching the beat of his own pounding heart. He kept walking, grasping onto DJ.

Up to his waist in the water, he reached out and DJ was nowhere to be found. He took another step.

Suddenly the sand gave way to a hidden shelf and Carnegie plunged into the water. He flapped his arms and treaded water. A dark shape moved towards him. He looked closer.

The Waitress with the Kind Eyes appeared through the murky water in the shape of a mermaid. She smiled at him. He reached to take her hand, but she swam by gracefully.

'No!' shouted Carnegie. He tried to turn but realised he was choking on water. In a state of total panic, he flapped his hands and kicked his legs; propelling him to the surface.

His head burst from the water and he desperately breathed in the air. His whole body shook violently as he managed to climb from the water.

Then suddenly DJ was grabbing him.

'She's a mermaid DJ!' Carnegie shouted, spitting up water.

'Who is?' asked DJ, as he helped his soaking friend out of the water.

'The waitress,' Carnegie said excitedly. 'She is a mermaid.' He wanted to go back and look for her, but his legs lay rooted to the beach floor.

DJ didn't let on that his friend was a little bonkers right now. Instead, he helped him into a deck seat on the beach and gave him a towel. He lay there and then the night disappeared on him.

Flying High

Carnegie sat on the plane with a head full of painkillers. Drugs. The Pharmacist had given him a decent amount of strong painkillers for this recent trip. Because he needed it. He needed it badly. It was a case of headaches and desperate heartaches.

Carnegie had just been through the worst betrayal of his life and he had to make a choice.

Choice 1 – Give up, admit defeat, lose everything, become a failure. It was the nuclear option. The end of days. The opening of the gates of hell.

OR

Choice 2 – Focus on the positive. Work three full time jobs. Put everything on hold in his life and do the 16-hour days, 7 days a week and refuse to buckle. Put on the mask. Turn up to work. Get on with the task. Ensure that everyone was taken care of. Make sure nothing collapsed.

Of course, he had chosen to take the only choice an entrepreneur could take. Death or Glory! The red pill. The jump off the cliff and hope to God you somehow discover how to invent wings on the way down.

As Joseph Campbell once said:

'If you are falling; dive!'

And Carnegie dived. He clenched his jaw. He turned up before 6am every day and left well after midnight; allowing himself only the luxury of 7 hours sleep on the weekend, so he could focus on some play time with the kids and to be well enough do it all again the next week.

His wife, being the Good Wife, just accepted the choice and backed him all the way. She would smile at him, put her hand around his shoulders from time to time, rough his hair or rub his neck on the rare occasion when they were in the same proximity and one of them wasn't asleep or holding a child.

Sitting in economy class, waiting for the pills to give him some relief, he sat – numbly scrolling through his emails. His father had sent him an email. When he read it, he could have wept. Thank God for his father and his number one fan. His dad had nothing but encouragement for him, even from Day 1 when everyone else thought he was too young, too dumb or too full of come.

It was Rudyard Kipling's famous poem and one that Carnegie had often read. His father had put a little note at the top ...

Son, feeling for you. I believe in you. Please take care. Mum and I love you heaps.

If you can keep your head when all about you
*   Are losing theirs and blaming it on you,*
If you can trust yourself when all men doubt you,
*   But make allowance for their doubting too;*
If you can wait and not be tired by waiting,
*   Or being lied about, don't deal in lies,*
Or being hated, don't give way to hating,
*   And yet don't look too good, nor talk too wise:*

If you can dream—and not make dreams your master;
*   If you can think—and not make thoughts your aim;*
If you can meet with Triumph and Disaster
*   And treat those two impostors just the same;*
If you can bear to hear the truth you've spoken
*   Twisted by knaves to make a trap for fools,*
Or watch the things you gave your life to, broken,
*   And stoop and build 'em up with worn-out tools:*

If you can make one heap of all your winnings
  And risk it on one turn of pitch-and-toss,
And lose, and start again at your beginnings
  And never breathe a word about your loss;
If you can force your heart and nerve and sinew
  To serve your turn long after they are gone,
And so hold on when there is nothing in you
  Except the Will which says to them: 'Hold on!'

If you can talk with crowds and keep your virtue,
  Or walk with Kings—nor lose the common touch,
If neither foes nor loving friends can hurt you,
  If all men count with you, but none too much;
If you can fill the unforgiving minute
  With sixty seconds' worth of distance run,
Yours is the Earth and everything that's in it,
  And—which is more—you'll be a Man, my son!

He was glad that the man next to him was quietly snoring and the cabin was dark. He wiped away the tears. For the most part he felt a failure. And he knew that he tried hard and did have a measure of success but felt he fell short of the standard that many had set before him.

Carnegie roughly, angrily wiped away the tears.

There you go, you fucking loser, he cursed under his breath.

Self-pity again. He clenched his fists and wished he could smoke; but then he was on a flight and he couldn't. He needed something more numbing than the four codeine he had swallowed. He looked around anxiously in the dim lit cabin and figured he might try and charm his way into a few more whiskey bottles that he had already chugged away.

If he couldn't escape the work. If he couldn't escape the challenge. He could numb the pain; he could escape through other means.

Carnegie had learned all about escapism in the early days of school and university and was very familiar with experimental drugs. It was all casual. Unfortunately, casual ties with drugs ended up with casualties. Well the war on drugs left a few casualties in any case.

Not all, except a few seriously ill people who had some wiring problems (at least that's the excuse they made). The fact was everyone was getting high and everyone was escaping. For Carnegie it was always sex, nicotine, porn and pot.

It wasn't until he entered the Capitalists Club that he discovered the pursuit of harder substances. But before he became a regularly high flyer, he spent a lot of time escaping the mundane by flying high.

Sex. Oh sex. What a great escape from the rules of the past. *Hate the Sin not the Sinner,* he used to console himself when visions of hell would appear over the pale body of some university graduate he was making love to. Those moments pre-guilt when interlocked legs and thighs rubbed up against each other, tongues caressed like frolicking eels and noises echoed through the backseat of the old Holden Kingswood Carnegie used to drive. Sex. One of the greatest drugs and addictions.

Of course, what came after the sticky panting mess was an awkward inexperienced exit and the guilt of pre-marital sex and the wondering about whether casual sex could lead to something more than just a string of casualties on both sides.

Carnegie found that sex was an opportunistic drug that could be taken to escape the cold hard daylight of a life misunderstood and the grey days of wondering what, where, how, why and when for his pre-entrepreneurial pursuits.

A more convenient guilt-lite escapism was pornography. There were no casual ties or casualties in the pursuit of that moment of pleasure and letting go. And everything and everyone was available. No need to fear repercussions for not wearing an umbrella in the shower; in that moment you would be bare backing a lithe minx with not a scar, flaw or wobble in site.

A few clicks and despite the slowing grinding of gears of the then clunky internet, all was available, like an international harem on a lazy Sunday afternoon.

Carnegie never understood porn. He never wanted to understand it. He wanted to use it, so he could abuse himself and never bother to worry about any interaction or connection. That was the downside to sex for a modern narcissistic male brought up with ever growing anxieties around body image, what it meant to be a man, what it meant to be a gentleman and what it meant to be a SNAG (Sensitive New Age Guy).

Before he discovered the serious pursuit of business, Carnegie always felt introverted and out of place despite his growing good looks, sporting prowess and extroverted charm. So, in the passage of time and the limbo he lamed around in, he retreated to the safe haven of porn. It was the drug of choice at university and the guys regularly threw out the insensitive remark:

Had plenty of bad roots. Never had a bad wank.

The drug of porn was intoxicating and never failed to deliver. However, there was an ever growing level of sadness and dependency building for Carnegie. At first (like all good drugs) there was the thrill and high of seeing something never done before. And then being whisked away into fantasy land where he was in charge and suddenly, the director, horn firmly grasped in hand, was barking orders and the minions danced and thrusted to his demands. But inevitably, he would slump post orgasm to the floor or bed, sore between the legs with a growing level of sadness and shame that he couldn't shake.

Strangely enough, that's where drug number two made its serious entry. To get over the post porno-graphic slump, Carnegie would roll up the dorm window and surreptitiously light a cigarette, blowing smoke out the window while trying to let the shame of self-indulgence drift away and be buried among the ever-growing stack of Kleenex in the paper tray.

The dorm room often smelt like smoke or body spray. Carnegie preferred it that way because, occasionally, the smell of smeg would waft away making Carnegie even more embarrassed – especially when ladies popped into the room for a kiss, cuddle or to rarely study notes.

Cigarettes will kill you, sang Ben Lee, and he was right according to the science, but Carnegie and his alumni were all invincible and liked to stick their fingers at the establishment especially the do-gooders (mostly do goaders) and health nuts who spent much of their time trying to stay on planet Earth. But Carnegie in university was part of the left.

They were Left in many ways. Left behind. Left alone. Left of Centre. Left to their own devices.

Left enough to be Socialists but not quite enough to join the solitary guy with the hammer, sickle and tired old trench coat.

So, they Left their classes early and drifted about talking about chicks, making stupid jokes, coming up with scams to make more money, bumming smokes and trying to muster up enough pot to be able to sit around in the local park, getting stoned and solving the world's problems, forgetting to write the plans, because no one could remember to keep notes.

Carnegie had a love-hate affair with marijuana. It was the best of friends at the right time and the worst of enemies at other times. It helped him escape on a regular basis and stopped the mind at night long enough to get a decent rest. It was also useful with the right dose of alcohol, in connecting with his lover on a night, because suddenly everything else disappeared and the mad train of thoughts and anxieties drifted away long enough for Carnegie to stare into his lover's eyes and see the soul behind the windows.

And then the sex coupled with the pot was good. Damn good. But these moments were like lining up the lottery numbers. Jackpot! Then when he and his lover looked to repeat it the very next night or the following week, it failed. Leaving the sex perfunctory and repetitive and both looking at each other, clinging onto their naked bodies, bed sheets strewn, moonlight coming in, with all the right ingredients, but a look of disappointment and sadness.

Expectations were the enemy and destroyer of many well-laid plans, particularly when intoxicants and escapisms were involved.

Carnegie stirred in his seat, snapping out of his reverie. Goddamn drugs. Goddamn pot. He could do with some green stuff right now. It might help him to sleep; somehow the codeine and the sleeping pills couldn't do it for him. Beads of sweat appeared on his head. The whiskey hadn't helped and the anxious mind was winding up. Carnegie closed his mind and thought about sex and pot again and shuddered.

Suddenly Aeni came to his mind. She was the epitome of the black and white nature of sex and pot.

He had met Aeni on a beach in Goa, India. She was beautiful, defiant, flippant as fuck and well-endowed with a tiny waist and an ass that belonged to Brazil.

He was there on a break with business and very much losing his shit. Business was breaking up. He was avoiding home and his wife. He had developed a new crave for thrills and had long arguments with God. Carnegie was looking for an escape and Aeni was his perfect muse.

He always sighed when he thought about Aeni. Two fucked up people do not make a perfect pair. It was a torrid affair that was never anything other than two anxious, stressed out people trying to use each other during the whirlwind of life and strife. And there was pot thrown in just to make sure it made less sense.

It was always fresh and painful in his mind. There was no excuses for it and it replayed in his mind like a slow-moving car crash. Over and over and over again.

She slinked up to him with the sex appeal of a goddess and Carnegie had responded like the sex-starved man that he was. Ten cocktails and pumping tunes had not helped his cause. But the kicker was the two joints that they sucked down together before making out in the water with pure abandonment.

She was maddening and dangerous. He went to her like a lamb to its slaughter.

And for a brief moment, under the cloud of drugs and alcohol, he crossed a line that he could never uncross.

He touched her gently all over her body and she stiffened at his touch and then let herself into his embrace. Drunk and stoned, they played lovers and danced all over the beach before Carnegie excused himself from the party to the knowing looks of his posse.

It was a familiar look.

What goes on tour stays on tour.

Under the haze of chemicals and the emptiness in his existence, he clung onto Aeni as if she was an angel from above. And she clung onto him. Their empty existence was momentarily filled with something tangible, forbidden and exciting.

Thou Shalt Not.

But Carnegie had not learned Why Thou Shalt Not.

The Capitalist Club didn't teach that. They preached a different message. Thou Shalt because Thou Can.

The chemicals drove the godly guilt away from Carnegie and, for a brief moment in time, it was like he was back in university, lost in lust and hunger, craving the interaction with another starved female.

But like all sin. And like all pleasure. Time has its measure.

They parted ways in sorrow for there was not to be a tomorrow. There was just two married people parting ways and returning to their unhappy existence, made unhappier after tasting the forbidden fruit.

Carnegie had covered his tracks well, thanks to the Capitalist Club and the winking of eyes. But the connection with another soul always leaves another disconnection in place and it wasn't long before he was off in another city doing business, waiting for Aeni to arrive in his suite. This time it was a little more exciting and a little more dangerous.

This was playing up right under the nose of the authorities and the family. But like all thrill seeking, hollow, unconscious people, they had played their game. But the rules were different. He should have learned from his university days about drugs and expectations, but he was a fool with a fool's heart chasing fool's gold.

The anxiety of the situation led to too much alcohol and Aeni, with her superhuman ability to do business under the bong on a daily basis, laid Carnegie on his back. Frozen, all he could do was try and reach out at the angry undressing woman. The failure was of epic proportions.

She had tried to stir him to some point of passion but, the chemicals, the jet lag, the stress and the morals of it all had led him to lay limp, unable to speak, or do anything to resolve the situation. The hero had fallen.

In sadness that night, he lay facing his demons; stoned out of his brains; watching the ceiling spin; alone with a bitter Aeni who left him with a few choice curse words about his weak prowess.

And like all ego-driven proud men, he rose again in the morning, made an appointment with his protesting lover and drove her to the point of exhaustion. Though his pride was satiated, his soul shrivelled once more. A crime of passion left no traces outside but scars inside.

Carnegie could have cried. His anger at himself was palpable. These memories wouldn't go away. Why did he betray his wife? Why did he betray his children? Why did he betray his honour?

And then he understood why he had been betrayed. Karma was a bitch.

On the plane he slumped. Whiskey. Painkillers. Sleeping Pills. Stress. Anxiety. Depression.

And then a lightbulb. He deserved what he was getting.

His choices led him there.

Betrayal

< Sydney

The conspirators were clever. And through their cunning deeds they drilled a hole in Carnegie's business. But that was nothing compared to the hole they punched in his heart. Unfortunately, Carnegie was romantic, naïve and saw the best in everyone. These were fatal flaws within an entrepreneur.

While Carnegie was away securing some business and acting the goat in Goa, they struck with fear-some efficiency that surprised everyone. When Carnegie arrived back with Agro, the DJ and Heyloon, he was confounded by mass resignations. Half of his business was gone along with clients, ideas, contracts and morale dropped to an all-time low.

The dominoes had been neatly laid out and, with a casual flick, they knocked them over within a matter of a week. Carnegie was horrified, hurt and ready to commit Hari Kari. Then he saw the look on the faces of those loyal to him and his team. It was that look that made him grow a backbone and face up to the music.

He worked on an action plan and set the remaining folks into play, reminding himself daily of the word passion. Suffering for something. He knew absolutely he was at fault. His burnout, marital problems, loss of faith and everything else stacked up against him. But he was no quitter. In the face of all of the odds against him, he knew he had to fight.

That week he hardly slept and as soon as he could he went to see the Godfather.

The Godfather was a long-term advisor to Carnegie and was called the Godfather for his appearance, stature and respect. The Godfather was the perfect person to talk to in a time of crisis. The iron-grey hair matched the iron-grey will. His forefathers had endured generations of war and hell and the Godfather was more than a match for any matter that came his way.

A lawyer by trade, the Godfather had spent most of his life representing clients at the smaller end of town. He was not a passionate fan of big corporates. It had a lot to do with how he was raised and the issues he had faced with big government and big corporates screwing the little man.

He was, like Gandhi, a fan of production of the masses, not mass production. Within reason. As he always liked to say; concluding any profound statement in his gravelly voice.

'Come in James,' he said when the Godfather's pretty secretary led him to his office. Carnegie was led like a lamb to the slaughter. Empty. Like a zombie he walked through a small maze of cubicles filled with zombies.

'Hi Godfather,' Carnegie said and shook his hand warmly. He felt less prepared than ever for a visit with this discerning character. In fact, he felt like a fool.

A fool and his money will soon be parted. The words rang through his head. That and the many uses of the word fuck.

He sat down in the pristine office also known as the Godfather's Den. 'Well I fucked up,' was his opening line, tensing up, ready to deliver an impassioned monologue, the fallen businessman's version of What About Me but before he could get in another word, the Godfather lifted up his hand and leaned forward over the polished desk.

'Not another word James.' He frowned. 'I will be honest. If you have come here awash with self-pity and ready to quit, you can get up and walk out.' He pointed a heavily tanned finger at him. 'You didn't fuck up. They fucked up. You are taking responsibility. But this is silly. You trusted in people and while you were off on your early mid-life crises, you left the door open for the predators to take a shot. The chicken coop was left open for the wolves to slip in.'

Carnegie scowled. This wasn't how the script was meant to play out. In his bitterness and hurting state, surely, he was allowed some sort of Hari Kiri, some sort of noble martyr's way out. He had planned to walk the plank, he planned to walk, to fall on his sword and start again. To take responsibility for the losses and business collapsing around him.

'But ...' He looked dangerously away from the Godfather's gaze.

'No buts. Any more and you can bugger off mate. Like this you might as well be back over in Hong Kong or Bangkok or whether you have been trekking around doing God knows what.'

Carnegie flushed. He had fucked up royally. In his misery and mindless state, he had abandoned his family and his business. Now he was paying the price. He was also swallowing the bitter irony that he was complaining about being betrayed when he was also the betrayer. His mind flashed with the images of the naked princess climbing on top of him.

The hidden lust pulsing through his veins making him grasp for just one more second onto his youth that had slipped through his fingers.

He had hurt people and he was here complaining about how others he had trusted had hurt him. Fucking hypocrite.

'James.' The Godfather came around the desk and sat next to him. He put a hand on his leg, in a way that only a father or mentor could do. 'I know what you are going through. It is tough, but you have to go through the suffering in the right way and do not quit. Do not give up.' He patted Carnegie on his slumped shoulders.

'I ...' Carnegie coughed. 'I ...' He slumped over and started spontaneously crying.

The Godfather sat by his side. Yoda to Luke. Observing, caring, understanding. Waiting.

Like all good mentors do. When the student is ready the master will appear.

Eventually Carnegie got through the emotions and he started to see the light. The little pinprick of light that comes with vision. He also found something else. Humility.

And it came in the following words.

'Okay Godfather. What do you want me to do?'

This was Carnegie. The man who always had the plan. This was the guy who had the skills to pay the bills that ended up buying pills to give them all thrills.

But he knew this was beyond himself.

And at that point, he heard his father's words:

Humble yourself or be humbled.

Carnegie sighed. His dad was right. His glorious chart of rising through crisis and challenge after challenge, he was now stumped.

The Round Table had been shattered and his romantic view of a Commercial Camelot had been crushed.

But the Godfather had a plan. He had lived a career of dealing with adversaries, especially those who had limited scruples, and it was Money or Nothing. It was when dire straits began to play out.

The first part of the plan was to analyse the damage done. The second part of the plan was to stop further damage from happening. The third part was to understand the lesson from the failure. The fourth part was to ensure failure would not happen again.

The four parts were simple to understand and plan out. The part that wasn't easy was the three years of staying on top of it all and allowing the parts to all play out. A greying, suicidal Carnegie would later reflect on those three years in Hong Kong. They were struggles but they were triumphant days. There was a clear adversary. There was a clear requirement to survive and then thrive. There was clarity.

But then you 'win'. And then you have 'wealth'. And then the chicken coop is never opened again. The Round Table is repaired and those gathered again serve to build Camelot.

And so, the quest is complete and then the same question comes back to haunt. What does it all mean? And how does one purge of the guilt and burden of the buried secrets that have sunk well below the surface when one is very busy on the superficial and the external?

Carnegie knew no answer.

But like Cold Chisel sang; he kept going back to South East Asia. Even though he knew no answer lay there.

Hong Kong Hangover

< Sydney

Carnegie sat on the Cathay Pacific flight with his friends; hours after he'd met the Waitress with the Kind Eyes. He drifted in and out of sleep, not aided by the vodkas and the airline food he had consumed. Carnegie made a habit of skipping the food on airlines. He wasn't an elitist, but the food violently disagreed with him. In fact, he had a bad romance with most things on an airline and wandered frequently whether he should walk away from this part of his business that he hated to love and loved to hate.

Carnegie stuck in his headphones and chose a random playlist. It was Supertramp. The random tunes rang in his ears as he desperately tried to fall asleep and get his mind to sleep. But he couldn't. Every time he tried, he kept drifting back to the Waitress with the Kind Eyes. He thought he would never see her again. Never take solace in her presence. Never be able to get everything off his chest.

After days of monotony, he fled to the Shrink with the Gentle Tones.

'I'm hollow, doc.' Carnegie laid back in the couch and folded his hands over his chest.

'What do you mean by hollow?' The shrink rubbed his moustache.

'Empty. Deleted. Carved out. Sucked dry. Dried up. Poked through. You know?' Carnegie felt faint. He had lost a number of kilos after the Goa incident. The cocktail of drugs he had unwittingly taken, and the attempted drowning, had serious health consequences.

His lovely wife had kept pushing food and drinks at him but all he could manage was the bare essentials to keep him going. In fact, he preferred to eat his meals through a fruit smoothie. It soothed his sore throat and gave him an energy boost. It didn't stop his hands shaking though. Nor did the cigarettes he smoked every couple of hours.

'I see. You clearly don't have the best of physical health. It affects our mental health. Are you taking enough vitamins?'

'Ah.' Carnegie smiled. This was one area he had down pat. Thanks to the Pharmacist, he had a solid routine that he followed religiously.

Vitamins A, B, C, D and E.

Vitamin X. Carnegie didn't know what this was, but the Pharmacist had told him it was good for males over thirty.

Magnesium.

Wild Krill Oil.

A teaspoon of olive oil.

Supplements B and D.

St John's Wort stirred into his coffee and tea.

'Now that's quite a collection.' The shrink made a mental note to check out what Vitamin X and Supplements B and D were.

And then, explicably, Carnegie started crying. He hadn't cried for years; but something just hit rock bottom. 'Can I hug you?' he asked the shrink.

'Come here.' The shrink held his patient tight. Maybe he was making progress.

Carnegie finally pulled away feeling a lot better. 'I'm sorry doc,' he said, flushing with embarrassment.

'Don't apologise James.' The shrink dabbed at the wet patches on his shirt which made Carnegie flush again and push at his greying hair awkwardly.

'I have to tell you about the waitress,' Carnegie said matter-of-factly leaning forward.

'Do tell.' The shrink grabbed his notepad.

'Well it all happened ...'

Carnegie told his sorrowful tale and felt an enormous amount of pressure lift of his chest.

Compulsively, he flourished his iPhone and strode around the Shrink's desk.

Before the Shrink could ask what, he was doing; he had docked his iPhone and was playing a piece of trance music he couldn't get out of his mind. The Shrink sat back intuitively, knowing he was getting involved in something that would test him.

The Mystic knew how to write them and how to smash them up for maximum impact.

The beats flew out of the mini dock along with the husky voice of his … The track was perfectly titled *Who Am I?*

This question buzzes through my brain,
It causes me so much pain
It's a blot on my mind, a great stain

I want to know.

Am I a work of fiction?
A creature from someone's diction.
Designed to live and cause friction.

I want to know.

A human app, a living software,
A piece of AI, advanced science to share
Just a piece of code running aware.

I want to know.

A puppet dressed and in mask,
An automated servant on task,
A floating spectre, a ghost, aghast.

I want to know.

I lack purpose because of ignorance
I lose my rhythm and can't dance
I am stuck and by chance I'm in trance

The question remains.

I lie awake at night and sigh,
I've lost the buzz and the high,
It's because I don't know who am I.

The question remains.

Where is the answer, where is the solution,
Where is the key to generate fusion
Soul searching only leads to confusion

The question remains

It's maddening, the mirror stares back,
But you don't know what's fiction or fact
And everything is grey, no white or black

Who am I?

I hurt, I feel I walk, and I reel,
Is this pain or is it just surreal?
Is there a quest or is the enveloped sealed?

Who am I?

I lash out in anger and rage.
I swear and blame it on a phase,
Deep down I know I am locked in this cage.

Ohhhhhhhhhhhhhhhh

Carnegie sang along with the song and grabbed the Shrink for a dance. The Shrink helplessly submitted to the manic fellow's movements. He wasn't sure this was positive progress. But he had remembered stranger stuff happening in his college days back in Mexico City.

He sang holding the Shrink and then he lost it again. He sobbed his heart out.

The Shrink didn't know what to think. Every now and again a case of a lifetime comes along. The Shrink feared that this was one that would go down to the wire.

Hong Kong >

A couple of days later, Carnegie got rid of the wretched bandage and let the head wound heal. He had spent the last 48 hours laying in a malaise; ordering room service and dreaming in a drug-fuelled state about his children, his wife, his business and the Waitress with the Kind Eyes.

Like spectres, they floated through his room of a day and night. Chiding him, comforting him, caring for him and whispering to him. He tried to chase the ghosts away but then they cried out at him loudly. Carnegie breathed heavily and blocked his ears. He rocked back and forth in his bed and swore vehemently.

'It's my fucking imagination. It's my fucking imagination.' He banged his head against the back of his bed. The intense pain gave him temporary relief, but the voices came again.

'You betrayed me James.'

'Where's my Dadda?'

'Look at you, you self-serving wretch.'

'Read me a bed time story Daddy. Pleeeassseee read me a bedtime storrrryyyyyy.'

'Why don't you love me husband?'

'Death is an easy way out and then the gates of hell open up.'

'Come home Daddy. Come home.'

'You think you have problems. I have debts to pay and children to feed ...'

Carnegie sobbed. 'Go away, go away,' he cried, waving helplessly in front of his face.

The spectres didn't go away. They floated above his head and cried in unison, 'Don't send us away. Don't send us away.'

Carnegie couldn't take it anymore. He fell out of his bed, crashing a night stand. He opened up his suitcase and pulled out the gun he had hidden.

'GO THE FUCK AWAY!' He screamed and pulled the safety catch of the gun.

The ghosts floated towards him looking angry.

'You want to shoot me el diablo!' The waitress's kind eyes flashed in anger.

'Do it, you miserable excuse for a husband!' spat his wife.

His children said nothing but floated closer.

He sank to the floor and crawled backwards up against the wall; aiming the gun at the spectres until they were impossibly close. And in his utter misery and psychotic state, he jammed the gun into his mouth. The metal tasted cool and he bit down. He closed his eyes and his heart raced.

Then silence.

He flashed his eyes open. The spectres were gone. He looked around suspiciously, but the apparitions did not float out of the walls.

And then he was suddenly aware he had an illegal Colt 1911 stuck in his mouth and he felt a little stupid. He threw the gun into the closet and breathed heavily. He wasn't sure how much more of this he could take.

< Sydney

The Hong Kong hangover started to ease for a while for Carnegie. He set about distracting himself with the matters of the real world and stayed clear away from booze, trance music and sorrowful memories. The days grumbled past and Carnegie slowly and steadily lifted himself out of the funk. He smashed the gym every day, slowly building up some more body mass and the will to walk in a straight line again.

The shrink was proud of his progress. 'Confession is good for the soul,' he said subconsciously – instantly regretting the religious context. But Carnegie was in a cheerful mood, so he simply said, 'Si Padre.'

They had some wonderful visits together. Carnegie wondered why he was still interested in visiting the shrink when he felt quite normal and non-depressive. He lost the will to die and began taking pleasure in the simple things again. Cradling his children, embracing his wife, closing deals, the feeling of a buzz after exercise and the smell of a well-cooked meal.

He even stopped hating his greying hair.

The Good Wife

< Sydney

She was the Good Wife in every way possible. Carnegie had fallen in love with her from day one. She was everything that an unconscious, ambitious, hell-bent man would want to have in his life. The looks, the career, the background, the challenge, the innocence, the proportions, the desire that sat just behind a thin curtain that she wore around in the shape of professional clothing. The demeanour was the perfect combination of go away and come get me and Carnegie fell straight down the trapdoor.

The madness overtook him and the entrepreneur's mindset gripped him immediately.

She was not in his circle, church, culture or community. His family and friends would all be doubters, no doubt. PERFECT. The challenge seized him immediately.

His skin was white. Her skin was the perfect coffee colour. His personal dislike for his whiteness sat bubbling below in his subconscious; driving his unconscious desire to find something far, far away from the Celtic paleness that was handed down to him from generations of others living far from the sun.

The strict ruleset of discipline and purity clashed with her naughtiness and playfulness. His defaulted dualism slammed into her pluralism. Black and white stared hatefully at fifty shades of grey and the rainbow that danced around her soul.

Her anxious flurry of work to survive in a foreign country aroused his desire to play the white knight and gain a maiden on his hero's journey.

The entrepreneur knew it was a jump of the cliff, but the pulse quickened as they met, the heart raced, the mind deleted objectivity and his drive began to objectify her as the perfect challenge to win. The perfect romance to dance to.

A young Carnegie barrelled right in. Ignorance was marketed as innocence. There is none more blinded than the unconscious and all of his drivers launched him head first into a perfectly imperfect match.

But she was the Good Wife.

And it all started as the Good Girlfriend.

Carnegie still remembered the thrall he had been in. It all started with a casual conversation. About something he cannot remember. But he would always be able to recall the white teeth. The long, black, curling hair tossed over her shoulder in an act of rebellion. The look of subtle amusement in her eyes.

Carnegie felt awkward, stunned and engaged all at once. His swagger instantly abandoned him and the thing he hated most about offices and corporations – the office cubicle – instantly became his saviour, as he could duck down and disappear behind its beige and inoffensive tones. That didn't stop the good girlfriend from coming around and visiting him with a range of activities in the office that he was not sure about.

Carnegie was more interested in his fledgling business; and the social activities; and keeping the day job on an even keel as he built up his network and spruiked his ideas. But as soon as the Good Girlfriend came along, things went lopsided for a short while.

He was not sure why, but for once he decided that getting smashed was a good idea. Perhaps it was because the Good Girlfriend was there that night and seemed to be talking to all the other guys from the office. Carnegie was decidedly put off and decided to drink his way through the night ...

Why did she invite me?! He cursed in his head.

This was followed with ...

Why the fuck did I accept the invitation?! He angrily chastised himself in-between warding off the local bar inhabitants with their small talk and slurring voices.

Eight tequila shots later, he got the shock of his life. The Good Girlfriend came up and asked him to dance. Carnegie always laughed when he told this story later on – he always liked to let his ego out and talk about the pretty girl coming up to the guy and asking him to dance … The Good Wife always made him feel wanted.

'Hey you, Mr Snob,' Good Girlfriend said.

'Who me?' Carnegie said with as much bravado as he could muster, looking around dramatically.

She laughed prettily and gave his shoulder a playful push. 'You must be the most boring guy in the office.'

'Who me?' Carnegie was outraged. 'Boring. You must have the wrong guy. You mean Ed over there?' Carnegie gestured over to Ed who was busy recalling the last time he converted his … (aw who cares, it was a boring story anyway).

She laughed again and then took a serious face. 'Don't tease poor Ed. He's really a helpful guy and he has a crush on someone.' She immediately had a conspirator look and gave him a large wink and another touch.

'Uh,' the young Carnegie managed; very aware of her presence. All of a sudden, the booze and the too much booze was a huge mistake. He shifted awkwardly in his chair and then curiosity got the better of him. 'Who has he got a crush on?'

'Me to know and you to find out,' she giggled and pulled him all of a sudden – managing to hold her glass of Sauvignon Blanc perfectly level. 'Come on, let's dance snobby guy.'

Before he knew it, Carnegie was on the dancefloor, dancing awkwardly (can white guys dance any other way?) to Samantha Mumba and Ronan Keating. Where the night ended up, Carnegie had no idea at all. He just remembered, brown skin, curly dark hair, green eyes, kissing under the park trees, sharing cigarettes out the back of a dubiously named night club and then madly ripping each other's clothes off in a dirty upstairs motel room.

Then he woke up with a raging headache and a note.

And that's where it all started.

Unconscious to unconscious with alcohol, awkward human interaction, bad pop music and cigarettes somewhere in between.

But the Good Girlfriend was to become the Good Wife. And Good Wives know how to be Good Girlfriends whether they are with Hopeless Boyfriends or Bad Husbands.

So, the Good Girlfriend summoned him kindly for a coffee on Monday morning to share a smoke and to chat. Young Carnegie was expecting someone of this quality to use the usual excuses to justify their behaviour and be polite. But the Good Girlfriend was having none of it.

'Look,' she smiled …

Carnegie narrowed his eyes and dramatically turned away blowing smoke. He was never good at being vulnerable or dealing with let downs.

'I really enjoyed the evening and there is more for me. I'm a girl and forgive the expression, but when I open my legs it's because my heart is open already.' She smiled again, almost shyly.

Carnegie didn't know what to say.

'So, in other words, last night was not how I am usually am. I …' The Good Girlfriend looked into the horizon for a while. 'Well, let's just say it was out of character. Maybe something to do with the tequila.' She laughed with a hint of nervousness.

Carnegie still didn't know what to say. He was more than puzzled and a little bit out of his depth. There was a strange feeling in his chest. He wanted to say something stupid. Something really, really stupid so he bit his tongue.

They were silent for a while. 'Well,' the Good Girlfriend said, staring at him in an unsettling way. 'I'm guessing you are like a lot of other guys, and it was just a one-night stand.' She chewed at her nails,

The Good Girlfriend prompted him. 'You can say something you know.' She smiled, and he was instantly comforted. It wasn't quite the words but the open space and the open channel and a strange connection.

'It was a great night. And I feel something too,' he admitted; feeling all shy and virginal. 'It's different from the usual girls and fun nights if you know what I mean …'

She arched her eyebrows for a moment. Young Carnegie was horrified. Was he saying the wrong thing. He was about to stutter something out and then she laughed.

'Usual girls eh.' She laughed again. Carnegie smiled awkwardly and smoked again. He was thankful at that time to have something in his hands and some nicotine into his system. God knows how much more nervous he would have been without the nasty habit he had picked up.

'Um. Not really. Well I mean I'm not really a player if you think of it like that. It's just I'm focused on business and work and stuff.' He mumbled, looking at her shyly.

'I get it. Anyway, I gotta go back upstairs.' She motioned with her coffee. 'Nice chatting.'

Carnegie smiled and nodded. As the Good Girlfriend stepped away, something in him blurted out: 'Can I ask you out?'

She turned quickly and smiled. 'Sure.'

'Great.' He smiled and stubbed out his cigarette.

He started to make a move back to the office, but she teasingly pushed him. 'Well?'

'Well what?' He was confused.

'Ask me out.'

'Oh.'

He felt stupid. Awkward. Like a teenager. There was only one way to man up and get the courage, so he lit another cigarette and pretended to be cool.

'Would you like to go out on a date with me?' The words felt alien to Carnegie. It had been almost seven years since he had uttered those words in high school to a beautiful blonde girl. They'd only dated for two days when they realised the whole excitement was the catch and not the keep.

'Sure. Where and when?' She smiled again, almost blinding Carnegie. 'God,' he muttered under his breath, instantly hoping she would hear him.

'Tonight?' he said hopefully. 'Movies, dinner?'

She smiled. 'Easy tiger.' The accent made him dizzy a little bit more. 'I am studying tonight and working the next three nights.'

Carnegie was disappointed. It would seem a lifetime before he could be with this girl again.

'But I can see you on Friday. I'm free then?' she asked inquisitively.

'Great, great,' he repeated unnecessarily. 'Ah where should we meet?'

'We'll figure it out – there's time ...' She touched him playfully on the shoulder. 'I'll let you finish that thing.' Pointing to the cigarette, she walked off. Carnegie watched her go.

And all that the strangers saw, who bothered to look, was a skinny young guy holding a cigarette with a dopey dreamy smile on his face. Looking off into the distance. And if they bothered to ask him what he was looking at he wouldn't have been able to answer.

Young Carnegie had fallen into love. And as dear Plato said; Love is Blind. And as dear Plato did not say; Love strikes like lightning when you least expect it to.

And from that moment on she became the Good Girlfriend. Carnegie was comforted and reassured with her around. It was a beautiful thing to be in love.

They held hands and laughed at each other's jokes. They stole kisses and sent love notes at work.

She sometimes cried lying down on his lap, telling him her background and her tough upbringing. He held her tightly and wiped tears from his own eyes.

They went to see movies but missed a lot of the plot by locking faces and putting hands in places that were best discovered in the dark.

They met respective families and behaved very well while thinking about each naked and doing dirty things to each other in the backseat of Carnegies car.

They were lovers!

They missed each other and sent each other silly text messages and teased the hell out of each other. When Carnegie was away or with friends he became a social pest. All of his friends told him he was a dork, under the thumb and wasting his valuable screwing around time. But he didn't care. He just stole away from their presence to give her little calls with his finger stuck in his ear, so he couldn't hear the clanking of beer, the sounds of music and the noise of society. It was so he could hear her clearer. The voice that lit him up like a Christmas tree.

And she thought of little things to do for him. Like make him coffees. Buy him cigarettes. And when she went to her cupboard, she thought about him. About the event. Sometimes, despite her conservative heritage, she would delight and surprise him by not wearing underwear. And at the most inappropriate times, she would whisper in his ear. Then she would giggle when he went red in the face and was distracted while socialising with business colleagues.

Of course, when they turned to her, she was nothing but the face of an innocent angel. But not long after, she would find his face in the crowd and point to her body and wink.

She drove Carnegie crazy.

But behind the playfulness she was the Good Girlfriend and strengthened Carnegie and nurtured him.

He gained new purpose and social comfort. It felt good to have a beautiful amazing girl on his arm and allowed him to focus on his business and other ventures without being distracted by other feminine shapes or desires floating through the air.

It made sense that there was someone to turn to and in his height of uncertainty, stress, weariness and inner conflict; there was someone to rest upon. To smile at him and make him feel at peace.

Carnegie went from strength to strength. He and the Good Girlfriend got stuck into life and a great routine that went on to last thirteen more years. Two years as the Good Girlfriend. Eleven years as the Good Wife. Five years as the Great Mother.

Their magic art was that they mastered the art of doing, getting and achieving. Their empire began in love and was built on ambition. The neck and the head perfectly in alignment.

Hong Kong >

Carnegie lay in bed covered in sweat and crying his eyes out. He lay reminiscing about his wife and how he missed her so much. But more than miss her, he missed those days. Those magical beautiful wonderful days where everything was so simple. When he saw the sparkle in her eyes. Where every slightly romantic song brought bursts of joy into his heart.

Where his achievements were not achieved; but ahead of him in a magical pathway that led to the end of the rainbow. He missed the challenge of chasing her, making plans with her, missed feeling young and on a quest with the perfect partner.

His self-pity was interrupted by his phone pinging.

'Fuck,' Carnegie groaned.

He slid across the bed, dripping in sweat. With as much energy as he could muster, he flung his arm out and grasped at the vibrating and beeping phone.

He wrenched it out of the socket and pulled it up in front of his face. Cursing again, the screen grimly said 112 messages with an unlock screen and the familiar names of well-meaning people. Carnegie had no energy or willpower to respond. He closed his eyes and wiped his forehead with the edge of the bed sheet. It was wet – it was all wet and soaking. Soaking with shame, guilt and fear. Suddenly he shivered and collapsed in the bed; letting go of the phone with a dull groan.

He wanted to cry.

He wanted to die.

The misery was a horror.

How the mighty do fall.

From the wings of youth with the Joie de Vivre. A joyful radiant beautiful hopeful butterfly.

To the crisis of a caterpillar in a cocoon of chaos.

< Sydney

The young handsome Carnegie stared in the mirror with controlled nerves and a smile that he had used all of his life to mask the awkwardness of social appearance; and to mask the bullshit negativity that he kept at bay with all of his might. The suit was rented, but it fit him like a glove. His longish black hair was freshly cut and perfectly combed. The dimple was on display and the skin showed nothing of the bucks' night that he had the night before. Luckily the family and friends could see nothing of the ripping headache that pounded his head. He felt like a cigarette, but his throat was sore from the night before and he had learned that there were times to smoke and this was not one of them.

Today was his wedding day. He was young. And he was on a pathway and this was the perfect next step. He smiled again, ignoring the little voices that said otherwise. The Good Girlfriend was becoming the Good Wife. He felt exultant. This was all happening, and they would set out and do all of the great things that they (he) had talked and dreamed about. The Good Girlfriend was absolutely amazing.

And short moments later, Carnegie was wiping away tears. This beautiful woman with that curling hair and the wide smile was walking down towards him across the green grass with the sun shining across the tops of groomed trees.

Then, short moments later, when the wine was finished, and the cake was cut, he was holding her naked wet body in intimate embrace, staring deeply into her eyes. It was everything he had imagined and more. The champagne flowed freely as two innocent and ignorant people collided into each other, merging and mashing together their dreams and hopes and wishes.

And so, the Good Girlfriend transformed into the Good Wife.

She somehow understood Carnegie even in the moments of madness and sheer terror at the horror of his ambition and drive.

Carnegie built the empire with her and without her. Days at the office started to blend into nights at the office. Days at home transformed into trips overseas. Hugs, cuddles and moments of intimacy were upgraded to text messages and then the amazing, all seeing, all doing Facebook and its messenger.

Despite children and momentary per functionary intimacy, one ship sailed out of harbour only to return as two. And like ships passed at night, something was there – but there was no fellowship, no relationship. Before they knew it and were aware of it, somewhere, some way, some time, the ship had sailed.

Hong Kong >

Carnegie awoke from a feverish dream where he was choking his wife. His hand and wrist hurt hard. He was exhausted and the realistic images in his head brought on sheer terror. He could feel his heart racing. And then all he could hear in his head was lines from the Mystic's latest track.

Because I stumbled,
I have been humbled.
But not matter how hard I work at it,
Life's still trying to smash and hit.
How do I get back to the start?
How do I re-discover my heart?
How do I come home at night?
How do I make things right?
Questions, questions, questions.

But I want,

Answers, answers, answers.

And no matter what he tried. No matter what he did he couldn't let go of those words.

It was Agro who stopped him screaming and summoning up the strength to leap off the balcony, days later. He turned up in Hong Kong, armed with love, reports from the homeland, a business opportunity and some care.

The fever didn't leave him, but nor did Agro.

Strangely enough talking business, and gently medicating himself saved him from the psychotic collapse long enough to feel normal again whatever normal was. It was typical of Agro to turn up and know how to handle things so that he could emerge out of the bubble of pain.

Carnegie hated that he loved Agro. But right now, he loved that he didn't hate Agro.

A familiar face. A familiar place. A familiar race.

Agro had seen one jump. He lived through it. It wasn't going to happen again.

Agro

< Johannesburg

Ignatious Constantine Pepe Aguero, or 'Agro' to his friends, was a passionate man. He had often expressed an opinion on life and everything around him. He was apt to talk to strangers and swear at beggars.

In short, Carnegie found his company very welcome. Not to mention their combined business ventures. And every trip and meeting they did together.

Carnegie became quite facetious at times, throwing in the latest opinion piece and then watching Agro explode on the verbal hand grade.

'These fucking politicians should go fuck themselves.' Agro was fond of that saying. Anything he didn't like had to go and fuck itself.

'That cab driver can go fuck himself,' cried Agro as he jumped out of the way of a swerving South African driver.

They were in South Africa to close a new distribution deal. Agro had discovered a small Cape Town telecommunications provider who had a voice application that could be sold into the Asia Pacific markets. He needed Carnegie's network and contacts, so he agreed to split the deal down the middle – casually adding at the end of the negotiations that if Carnegie didn't like it he could go and fuck himself.

Carnegie had laughed all the way from Perth to Johannesburg. Agro was in a particularly fired up mood and was grandstanding the whole way to their destination; particularly when the pretty flight attendant leaned over to serve them.

'She is fucking hot man.' Agro opened his eyes wide. 'Would you do her?'

Carnegie smiled. Of course he would. After all, he was a red-blooded male.

'Hey Carnegie.' Agro stretched over and whispered hoarsely in a loud voice. 'Have you joined the mile-high club?'

Carnegie had come close a couple of times; but the desire to squeeze into a small box and acrobatically please a woman hadn't really crossed the threshold between maybe one day to let's get it on right now!

'I haven't,' Carnegie said honestly. His male pride wanted to say 'absolutely!'

'I have.' Agro looked smug.

'Really. Tell me.' *This will be interesting*, thought Carnegie.

'I was on a Singapore Airlines flight and sat opposite the flight hostess in the exit row. She was exotic, man, and had this killer smile and serious tits.' Agro raised his hands in front of his chest to emphasise how big the mammaries were.

'Shit.' Carnegie wondered if this was a fishing story where the size of the fish inevitably grew in every telling of the story.

'Yes massive. Anyway, I spent the whole fucking trip with a boner, man. Eleven hours. By the end I was ready to root the cup holder. So, I snuck down the back and rubbed one out. I nearly came all over the mirror and basin.'

Carnegie laughed. 'Agro that doesn't count mate. You know it.'

'Bullshit. It definitely counts. Flying solo counts.'

'Yeah right. If that was the case more than sixty percent of the male population would be members of the mile-high club.'

Agro looked annoyed. He subconsciously rubbed his crotch. 'It definitely counts,' he said stubbornly.

They took an opinion poll sometime later.

Hammond: 'Technically it counts but it is a little bit of a negative tactic.'

The Pharmacist: 'Was it chemically enhanced?'

Heyloon: 'No way. That's cheating.'

Bruce: 'Fucking lame dude.'

Cassandra: 'Pffttttttt. I've done that before, but I also qualified the real way.'

And she had their undivided attention. Cassandra had laughed and told the attentive men a couple of detailed stories, revelling in their joy and interwoven discomfort.

But she had stopped abruptly when she saw Kennedy looking away. They didn't notice it. But Carnegie did. It was his job – the entrepreneur's job to notice the room, pick up on the slightest of changes. Entrepreneurs needed the sixth sense of networking, charisma, psychology and the ability to understand what was being said without it being said.

It was mastering the dark arts of seeing what art was done in the darkness.

Agro and Carnegie touched down in Johannesburg. They called it the Home of the Fookin' Prawns having both been inspired by the surprise smash hit movie set in Johannesburg titled District 9. It was a terribly grey city, stricken by poverty everywhere and the smattering of wealth. Carnegie felt very depressed when people drove around in Mercedes and Audis while other people quite literally died on the streets. Did that make him a communist? Or perhaps a modern socialist?

Carnegie didn't know, because he had always thought of himself as a passionate capitalist with a social conscience.

It reminded him of a time when he was in Mumbai and had just visited one of the most amazing hotels.

The Taj was the famous hotel that was subjected to the terror attacks in 2008 by members of the Pakistani militant organisation Lashkar-e-Taiba. The terrorist had killed a lot of members and injured many more. Carnegie loved the architecture and enjoyed the visit to the neighbouring Gate of India: a famous Mumbai icon.

What Carnegie didn't love was walking a single block away and nearly treading on two dead bodies of street beggars that had either been dumped in the street or had passed away overnight. Carnegie had nightmares of turning that street corner and seeing the swarm of thousands of flies lifting off the bodies.

He had hurdled the bodies in a state of shock. And nearly walked on as if it was just another part of walking the streets of a foreign city.

But he had stopped and looked around. People walked past on their daily travels, seemingly unaware of the stench and the dead bodies.

He motioned to one of the men nearby.

'Yes Sir?' said the elderly Indian man mopping his sweaty brow.

'Ummmm. Do you see these men?' Carnegie's brow wrinkled.

'No Sir. Don't get involved. It's a matter for the authorities.' His face was impassive.

'But has anyone alerted the authorities?' Carnegie asked.

'No Sir. Really. It is a matter for the authorities.' He walked away.

Carnegie was angry. 'So it's a matter for the authorities to see these bodies and then alert the authorities?' He turned away in disgust.

He finally summoned a police officer handling the tourists, vendors and beggars alike. He reluctantly came and then officiously handled the process writing neatly in his notebook in Hindi.

Carnegie hadn't slept that night.

And his first night in Johannesburg he hadn't slept either. Somehow the water supply to the five-star hotel was cut off, so he contented himself with washing himself with a number of bottled waters.

Agro was cheesed off in the morning and gave both barrels to the hotel staff.

The large Afrikaaner behind the hotel service counter wasn't a bit phased with Agro's finger waving and ranting.

'You call this a five-star hotel. Even a one-star hotel has running water.' Agro was scratching at his two-day growth.

The Afrikaaner just shrugged. 'Thees ees efricaa.'

'Well perhaps they should put that in the fucking tourist brochure and information packs eh?' Agro slammed his fist in the counter. 'What are you going to do about it?'

The hotel staff swarmed to the counter.

Agro pointed at the large gentleman. 'Where is your manager?'

'I am the manager. Can you please keep the noise down Mr Aguero?'

'Fuck no. I'll only get louder. And you call yourself a manager. Why don't you manage the fuck out of this situation?'

The manager's face went a dangerous red and his low brow became even lower. He scowled at Agro. 'What do you want me to do? Turn on the water myself?'

'How about we start with some goddamn politeness. Then maybe you can tell me where I can get some extra bottled water.'

And the argument went on for some time. Carnegie sighed wearily. It would be a long trip!

One thing Agro didn't argue about was the quality of food in South Africa. The selections of meats were incredible, and Carnegie guiltily ate springbok. He wasn't sure how he felt about eating the national icon.

Agro told him to stop being a pussy. 'These buggers would come over to our country and hammer the kangaroo and emu. I'm pretty sure they would even try to throw a koala on a spit.'

Carnegie was horrified. Koala bears were so cute and sometimes cuddly.

'Besides,' added Agro. 'They have no qualms at biting chunks out of our rugby players.'

Carnegie laughed.

But his laughter didn't last long. In truth, Carnegie was miserable. He was miserable because of the abject poverty. He was miserable seeing the shanty towns. He was miserable when eating enough food to feed a whole family for a month. He was miserable seeing a rake thin baby look at him with hollowed eyes.

It reminded him horribly of the Angeline Jolie and Clive Owen film he saw recently called Open Borders. He had wept openly, and his wife had held him while he bawled his eyes out at the desperate poverty depicted in the film.

He swore an oath to get involved with the UN and do something about changing lives. Agro thought he was mad. And told him so, in no uncertain terms, but that was the old Agro.

But days later caught up in his business affairs, Carnegie forgot all about the starving African babies. He forgot about abject poverty. He forgot about stalking vultures picking the flesh of dying babies.

The road to hell was paved with good intentions and there is no convenient time for Agape to set in.

Hong Kong >

Eventually Carnegie got tired of Agro hanging around or Agro got tired of Carnegie hanging around Hong Kong.

Either way, Agro left, promising to stay in touch and bring the Honourable Shing back with him.

Carnegie admired the new Agro.

Caring had replaced Consumption.

Agape had replaced Anger.

Mindfulness had replaced Medication.

Parenting had replaced Pride.

Self-Love had replaced Selfishness.

The new Agro was a good man. Transformation had replaced tragedy.

Was there hope for himself? Carnegie mused, staring out into the horizon vaguely, after Agro had left.

He had tried to meditate – practising the techniques that Honourable Shing had tried to teach him through Agro's introduction.

But then, when he couldn't meditate, he had to medicate.

Carnegie was alone in his Hong Kong hotel with his Hong Kong habits. Stumbling, mumbling, grumbling and rumbling around the streets searching for answers that didn't lie in the Asian metropo-lis. There was nothing there but bad memories, tired souls and vacant eyes wandering around, prop-ping up an economic system that was not propping them up.

God really is dead, Carnegie said to himself, remembering Nietzsche briefly during a small sober spell. Those moments were the worst. Where the depression held him until he broke the back of the hoard ever so briefly with his drugs and alcohol and the arms of a street girl – who for a moment in time could heal him by showing him so much more pain and suffering than he had ever gone through.

In this state, the rapidly aging entrepreneur wished Nietzsche would spring up and pronounce him dead. After all, this life in between, the pause in purgatory, was no life at all.

Sex Slavery

Eventually, Carnegie overdid it and spent three nights in the local hospital. Barry had seen to the delivery of his fever-riddled body to an immaculately built hospital, where a bunch of wonderfully joyous angels took care to the restoration of his body and somewhat his soul. They washed him of his sweat, fed him slowly and slowly weaned him off his dependencies. For the most part, they were master medicine managers, keeping him on a steady stream of antibiotics and heavy, heavy sleeping pills that were also used for tranquilising wild life.

It was heaven for Carnegie. He was surrounded by purposeful people and, because of his status, he had no right to have a purpose for the moment, so he relaxed. Maybe, he mused to himself, you do nothing when there is nothing to do. Or perhaps because there is nothing to do, you do nothing.

Carnegie weakly rose up from his coma, to write these wandering words on the notepad next to the clean white bed. The whispering spidery words waited for him in the morning, but it was a riddle he couldn't figure out. And then he feared he was finally going mad, because a small Chinese doctor sprung out of the side of his bed with a comical smile on this face and all the motivation of Anthony Robbins on mushrooms.

He scrunched up the paper and hid it under his pillow while trying to make sense of the doctor and his antics.

And then, finally, he got the boot from the hospital and Barry took him back to the room, smiling and pointing out that his face had colour and he had put a little weight on.

If only he knew about my shrivelled soul, Carnegie said to himself wistfully. He may not be smiling so much. He looked back at the departing white building among the colourful dirty apartments that shrouded its being. An oasis in the desert of the dead.

Not long after the recovery, he got sick of his hotel room and its emptiness – so he began to wander again. The lights of Hong Kong twinkled and beckoned him onwards one street at a time. He walked past the alleyways where itinerant workers sat smoking strange Asian brands of cigarettes.

They looked at him mutely as he walked past; headphones singing into his ears.

He kept repeating the same song from the Mystic, listening to the chorus over and over again.

Give me time, give me rhyme.
From a crawler, cocooned.
Let me fly to divine.

The music lifted his spirits and he felt his morale turn upwards.

He even felt positive enough to look for The Waitress with The Kind Eyes. He smiled his bitter sweet smile that he often wore on his face. He knew his mission was impossible, but it didn't stop him trying. The answer sure wasn't here but it didn't stop him looking.

The chickens hung upside down in the windows; their bony carcasses a stark reminder of the brevity of life. The happy hour signs hung everywhere; tempting Carnegie to go on a serious pub crawl. He didn't understand the concept of happy hour. Was it that you would be happy after drowning in a well of cheap beer? Or was it because you could be happy paying less to support raving alcoholism?

Either way, Carnegie kept away from the temptation of drowning his underlying sorrows. Besides, he didn't want to get into a discussion about the latest football scores with a bunch of British drunks.

He stopped outside a Lexus dealership and perched on a concrete bench. His thinning frame stared back at him accusingly, crying out abuse. He stared back at the reflection, hoping that Past Carnegie wasn't going to come back to speak to him.

The luxury car dealership housed a range of the elite brand of Toyotas. The workers buzzed around the showroom despite the late hour. Carnegie was amazed at the work rate of the Hong Kong workers. All they seemed to do was work and sleep. He wished he had that motivation, but right now motivation was just a word from his past.

His reverie was rudely interrupted from a big breasted African 'lady'.

'Hi stranger.' She sat down next to him. 'Watcha doin' here all by yourself handsome?'

Carnegie groaned inwardly. Hookers. They turned up at the most inappropriate of times.

< Auckland

Carnegie was a naïve young businessman when he first encountered a lady of dubious career choice. He was at a high flyers' function in New Zealand; invited by the Man who Couldn't Die. Unfortunately, his host couldn't turn up due to a mild dose of the runs coupled with some serious heart flutters.

So, Carnegie was stuck in Auckland, the city of sails. The night poured with rain and Carnegie had half a mind to cancel as he sat banging out some work on his laptop. His Hugo Boss suit felt uncomfortable and he decided that no matter what, he was going to lose the tie that grabbed at his neck like a live noose. He tossed it against the wall and let it slip behind the leather couch. He made a mental note to fetch it in the morning but promptly forgot about it in his rush to get home.

Carnegie was tremendous at leaving things behind. He had gone through a number of iPhone chargers, toiletries, jackets, clothing in general and the worst was when his passport went missing. That caused a right cock-up with the airport staff, the hotel staff and his staff.

Carnegie sighed and closed his laptop. It shut with the self-satisfying click of a well-crafted machine. He got up and drained a scotch and then organised a cab. The foyer of the hotel was abuzz with other socialisers. Carnegie felt terribly left out and cursed the Man who Couldn't Die for being ill. He had specifically made the flight across the Tasman to be with the little rascal and here he was feeling lonely and depressed.

He spent the night making small talk and drinking Greygoose vodka straight.

The first few tickled his tonsils and went to his head. Eventually, in the early hours of the morning, he made his way to the bar. He had spent the previous hour with a bunch of randoms talking up their businesses. They were drunk as skunks and doing blow off the hotel toilet seats and they didn't seem to care who knew about it.

The slightest beat from the DJ had them jumping up and down and slapping each other. A chubby little man in a purple velvet jacket had even grabbed Carnegie from behind and begun to dry hump him. Carnegie did know whether he should head butt him or ask him to butt out. Either way his butt was going to be left out of the writhing.

So, he sat at the bar and downed his final drink. Before he could get the final drink down his neck a pair of arms grabbed him around the waist and then slid a hand down his back.

'What are you doing here by yourself?' The somewhat feminine voice sounded like a mixture of honey, booze and cigarettes.

Carnegie spun around to find a very attractive middle-aged Maori girl smiling at him. She wore a stunning flowing gown that finished strapless above her pushed-up cleavage.

Carnegie was disarmed. 'Just having a drink love.' He hoped he sounded casual and suave at the same time.

'Mind if I join you?' She didn't stop for an answer and slipped into the bar stool next to Carnegie.

She was haughty and inviting at the same time; and could drink like a fish. After a few hours had passed of them making drunken conversation, she asked him a leading question that Carnegie followed up with an innocent reply.

'Where are you staying?'

He mentioned the hotel he was staying at down near the viaduct in Auckland CBD.

'Cool hotel,' she said to him, narrowing her eyes. 'Looking for company?'

Carnegie was either to stupid, drunk or naïve or all of the above. So, he answered, 'Isn't this company?'

She snorted and smiled at the same. 'Oh, the company I have in mind will blow this out of the water!'

She wrote on the back of a beer coaster and slid it across to him. Carnegie spun it over and read it.

'You can do anything you want to my body. $1000.'

Carnegie's eyes instinctively widened when he realised that he had spent the last two hours with a high-class escort.

He couldn't make it out of the bar fast enough.

Hong Kong >

So, Carnegie found himself in the presence of another hooker. Unfortunately, every city had its underbelly, which both excited and terrified Carnegie. The African looked at him harshly and raised her top showing large breasts that had drooped with age.

It disgusted Carnegie in ways he couldn't explain. In truth, it wasn't the ugly aesthetics but the vulgar manner in which someone chose to behave. The hooker clearly read the expression on his face and slapped him across the face hard. Carnegie was so surprised he nearly went flying of his seat.

'You don't like me eh?' She looked angry and something else that might have been guilt and sadness.

Carnegie rose to his feet, fists balled. He was never going to hit her but hopefully he could run her out of there. Unfortunately, that didn't have the desired effect.

'You want to beat me? Take me back to your room and beat me!'

Carnegie took a step back repulsed. 'Of course I don't want to beat you. Please just go away,' he said, wearily smelling the rum on her for the first time.

'You don't want me baby?' She writhed in front of him vulgarly and pumped her hips at him, rubbing her groin.

Carnegie groaned in despair. He felt embarrassed by the sight of this woman behaving in such manner to him. He didn't understand at what point these women transferred from angelic children into such adult demons.

< Brisbane

Carnegie sat in a bar in Brisbane's Treasury Casino. He had no intention of gambling, but it seemed like a useful place to meet someone – so he sat sipping on vodka and cranberry juice, watching people come and go. The punters were busy spending their hard-earned money on the tables and slot machines. Some were already drunk at 6pm and mindlessly blowing a small fortune. *The house always wins*, chuckled Carnegie, glad that he had reformed from his gambling addiction.

A voice interrupted him.

'Have you ever paid for sex?'

Carnegie was shocked. He spun around to see a petite Asian girl with large glasses looking at him nervously.

'Umm no.' Carnegie was still trying to register where this figure had come from and why she was asking him such an affronting question.

'Oh, I'm sorry, I didn't mean to be rude. I have a habit of blurting out things,' she said, grabbing his hand and shaking it feverishly. 'I'm Jennifer Chu. Mind if I sit with you?'

'Sure.' Carnegie motioned for her to sit down next to him. *This has got to be interesting*, he thought to himself.

She was a bright little thing with a shy smile and a quick wit. She was brash and prone to speak her mind. She wore a summer dress with a billowing skirt. Her glasses were oversized wayfarers that gave her a distinctively intelligent look and made her eyes magnify like the moon through a telescope.

'I'm sorry again for the question. I didn't mean to be rude. It's just it is on my mind and I am working on my thesis,' she continued, sipping on some lemon water. 'A friend of mine just committed suicide. We had no idea, but she was brought to Australia as a prostitute and forced to work long hours in appalling conditions.'

Carnegie was intrigued and terribly depressed at the same time.

'Surely not in Australia though?' he asked, feeling immediately naïve.

'Oh yes, in every country. These poor women are exploited everywhere. They are sold the dream of building a lifestyle through partying and entertainment and, in the end, they just give up their bodies for abuse.' Jennifer looked terribly sad and Carnegie started to feel an unusual sense of anger. He didn't get angry often but when he did …

'Take a look at these pictures.' Jennifer flashed the pictures in front of Carnegie.

A gorgeous smiling school girl holding onto her father's hand.

A uniformed girl looking concentrated while playing volleyball.

A vibrant girl posing for a modelling picture.

And the pictures rolled out. Carnegie had a growing sense of anger and shame at the same time for not thinking about these poor souls.

And then the next pictures. A dead body lying on the crushed boot of the car. Pictures of a bruised and battered face and beaten body.

Carnegie wept. He thought of his own daughter ending up like this and he couldn't bear the thought.

Jennifer just laid a hand on his arm. She looked a little surprised that Carnegie would have a deep re-action to the pictures and story of her friend.

And when Carnegie stopped weeping, he got angry. He leapt to his feet and resisted the urge to punch the concrete pillar that they sat next to.

He angrily gestured at the pictures. 'What the fuck are we going to do about this!?' He followed up with, 'Excuse my language, I am just very angry.'

Jennifer nodded and smiled. 'Raising awareness is really important, which is why I approached you to start with. We can change things if we get enough people to know about what goes on.'

'So, what happened to the monster who did this?' said Carnegie, shaking with rage.

'Fled the county with his wife, the asshole! The authorities didn't move quickly enough but hopefully the international law enforcement will catch him.'

'But what about the people that organise this?' Carnegie was thinking about the root of the problem.

'They are numerous. They are everywhere. Especially South-East Asia. And as I said, the families are below the poverty line, so they tolerate the practice with the thought of the money taking care of their families.' Jennifer looked sad and determined at the same time.

'So, poverty is the cause?'

'That is part of my thesis. How education and taking people out of poverty helps eradicate these scumbags. I want to do a documentary in sex slavery and get the message out there through YouTube, so that many people can see the truth of these matters. Sweet Gloria didn't have to take her own life.' Jennifer was talking excitedly, her bright eyes sparkling.

'We are going to make a difference. High Five!' She stuck her small hand out and Carnegie laughed and smacked her hand. Her enthusiasm lifted his spirits.

But he was waiting for the punchline. He had been pitched to many times before and was waiting for the eventual request for money or resources. He didn't mind contributing but hated scammers.

He decided to cut to the chase.

'Jennifer. Thanks for bringing this to my attention. I really appreciate it. Now how much do you want from me?' He instinctively narrowed his eyes.

'Don't be silly!' Jennifer scowled her impish face at him. 'I don't want money, I want to raise awareness. And every person that I speak to gives me courage to finish my thesis and start to do something about this serious social problem.'

Carnegie was taken aback. *Not after money?* He was puzzled.

'Well that's odd. Most people come to me for causes and want money.'

'Is that right? Really?' Jennifer shrugged. 'I have to finish my thesis and I don't need money for that.'

'Well, what can I do to help you?' quizzed Carnegie.

'Nothing. Just being nice and talking to me helps!' Jennifer opened the palms of her hands to show her feelings on the subject.

'Okay, here is my card. If you think of anything that I can do to help, let me know.' Carnegie handed over one of his business cards.

'Thanks,' said Jennifer and tucked it into her compendium.

She finished her drink with a long and loud slurp through the green plastic straw.

'See ya.' She bounced away, leaving Carnegie feeling flat. He hated himself for being a man and for not being able to do something to stop this barbaric behaviour.

That night, he lay in his cool air-conditioned hotel room, angry and depressed. When sleep came it was accompanied with the sinister imagery of his daughter being dragged off by men in black suits with gorilla masks.

When James Carnegie woke up, he was covered in sweat and his bed sheets lay all over the place. Only an hour of scrolling through pictures of his daughter on his iPhone could help mediate the Sandman's meddling.

Streets of Wan Chai

Hong Kong >

The streets of Wan Chai represented Carnegie's purgatory. Like a trapped soul, he desperately wanted to leave the neon light district but couldn't find the way out. The non-stop activity bounced through the day and night, leaving Carnegie feeling exalted and thoroughly depressed at the same time. Where evil men come to live and good men come to die. What did that make him? He sure wasn't living but he wasn't able to die and leave this place either.

Every time his ticket came for him to exit, he used every excuse there was to stay in the same place. The excuses ranged from a tropical cyclone warning through to illness and a lack of desire. Carnegie knew exactly what he was doing but the guilt of being a selfish person only compounded each time he rang the airlines, desperately hoping to speak to someone new after calling each time and pushing back his ticket.

Each new day or night when Carnegie's emaciated frame walked through the streets, silently puffing away on cigarettes, something new happened to him – whether it was being accosted by African hookers or getting scammed by Indian so-called fortune tellers.

'I look in your forehead and see pain,' said one fellow with a busy black beard and matching gold earrings.

Carnegie stopped. 'Sorry?'

'I know the pain you are going through.' He pointed a long finger at Carnegie's forehead, which felt intensively intrusive.

He went on. 'You sleep at night, but your mind doesn't sleep. You worry about your business and you worry about your family.'

Carnegie lifted his eyebrows and drew heavily on his cigarette.

'Yes, I see you in pain. But from next month your pain will go away. It is the willing of my holy teacher.' The Indian flashed a picture of an old Indian priest sitting on a hill in the Himalayas. 'The future has been seen for you and your luck is about to change.'

Carnegie smiled; at the same time entranced by the surreal experience.

'I will write your lucky number.' He took a thin piece of yellow paper out of a purse, wrote a number on it and scrunched it up. 'Blow on it,' insisted the Indian.

Carnegie felt a bit silly, but he blew on the paper anyway. However, before he could find out what the lucky number was meant to be, Bert charged out of the local pub with a rolled-up newspaper.

'FUCK OFF!' He shouted, brandishing the newspaper.

Bert was the local manager of a collection of pubs. He was part of the furniture in Wan Chai and took a very dim view on hookers, scam artists and suspicious looking individuals. He was a tall thin man sporting a florid face that was forever coated in a sheen from the humidity. A navy tattoo had faded into his large forearms. Someone once made the mistake of calling him Popeye because of his forearms.

They had spent a cold night in one of the local cellars enjoying the company of rats, roaches and a humblingly sore jaw.

Carnegie smiled.

Bert said to him, 'Watch out for those scammers son. They're a bunch whoresons. Innit?'

Innit! One of the favourite British words of all time. Akin to Australia's 'G'day mate.' And New Zealand's 'Aye.'

Carnegie nodded to Bert and thanked him. He was still curious about this lucky number but wasn't curious at all about how much money was going to slink out of his pocket.

So, he walked artfully – dodging the reaching arms of the local line-up of madams. They all had the same hard faces of being exposed to the elements twelve hours a day and being exposed to Wan Chai for longer.

'Want massage darlingggggggg?'

'You over come here big boy.'

'What the matter handsome?'

They were the less offensive ones that started around midday. By 4am in the morning they were closer to:

'You like fucky fucky?'

'You used your cock today baby?'

'Look at Crystal here. She bends over good.'

But he wasn't interested in how flexible Crystal was and he found his mood crashing when he saw Crystal's uncomfortable stance grasped in the madam's claw-like hands. And then, when the pictures of Gloria's body smashed up against the car flooded his mind, he felt he could hardly move.

'Dammit.' He shuffled over to the train station and jumped on the waiting carriage after flashing his Octopus card up against the scanner.

The Octopus card system was totally brilliant and Carnegie wished the system was everywhere. It was as simple as loading money onto a card and flashing it over the terminals that were located all over the city. Highly efficient. Carnegie couldn't wait for a version for the smartphone to come out.

Carnegie was genuinely surprised at these odd and random thoughts that sprang from his mind like a plucked fish on a line. Only he wasn't fishing, but someone was …

He found himself slumped on a train bench with his mind wandering. He wished desperately that the Waitress with the Kind Eyes was with him but she was not here. He was alone with his memories and his weakened condition. Somewhere in his brain a signal was desperately trying to get through to him – imploring him to eat and put some wait back on. Sixty-five kilograms was not nearly enough for his 5'11' frame. His eyes were hollow and raccoon dark. His hands shook occasionally, so from time to time he produced a small metallic flask that Kennedy had given him before the tragedy. Carnegie forced himself as penance to drink from the flask at least once a day to remember the guilt and never forget it.

They were all morons. Drunken idiots sipping deeply from the cup of foolishness. They slapped each other on the back and danced about telling tall tales about their epic lives and the future that burned so bright.

They feasted well and played poker to the early hours of the morning before they went out on the hunt for female company. It was always booze, drugs, gambling and women but not necessarily in that order. They all hated the hangovers that eventually came, so they dosed themselves up with H2O and multi-vitamins; crying like children when they eventually woke only to get stuck into fatty food and strong lattes.

Eventually one of the morons would crack open the beer, brandishing it as a symbol of triumph over the forces of nature. And so, they cheered again and high fived each – whipping towels at each other and playing drinking games.

They were intoxicated on the apparition of their immortality and taunted by the demons that woke them up each morning. And each day the ribaldry continued. The fools failed to notice the state of one of their comrades that pushed him further and further.

Alas, Kennedy was a tragedy that was always going to happen. They would comfort him but Carnegie refused to believe that, so he drank from the flash of guilt daily, remembering the sadness of Kennedy's face and hating himself for not knowing about it.

In fact, his sadness crept into his heart each day, as the memories of Kennedy did not fade away but seemed to solidify – grasping at him further and stabbing him repeatedly. From time to time, as the emaciated Carnegie lay in his bed at night, Kennedy would come and visit him.

He stood sadly at the end of Carnegie's bed and just watched on. Carnegie tried to wake up. He tried to go asleep. He tried to shoot himself. But the apparition took no notice of his guilt and just maintained his vigilance; silently mouthing the same words over and over again.

'Why me Carnegie? Why me?'

But Carnegie had no answers to Kennedy's question and nor did the Shrink with the Gentle Tones. He comforted Carnegie by telling him that it wasn't his fault and he should find a way to let go. He was tempted to tell Carnegie to go to confession, but he knew Carnegie would explode. He was a very anti-Christian Christian.

The typhoon struck Hong Kong with a vengeance and Carnegie was miserably happy. He sat at Pacific Coffee House drinking coffee and engaging in small talk. He drank his third Grande cappuccino and twitched nervously, reading through every magazine and pumping his legs to the sounds of Bryan Adams rasping in his ears.

The trees blew into silly shapes and open-top buses flooded. A small dog stood rooted against the wind before giving into the forces of natures and retreating into the shadowy alcove to do a sad wee. It was a good day for signage companies, as they rubbed their hands gleefully to see signs swing to and through, eventually shattering on the soaked asphalt.

Locals looked at their smartphones nervously and wondered whether to pack up and go home. The tourists looked at their Wi-Fi-enabled tablets and searched in hope for a way out of the disaster.

Carnegie was cheerful. Hopefully the whole island would blow away and take him away from the Colt 911 sitting in his apartment, Kennedy's apparition and the terrible weight that sat on his chest and wouldn't go away. There was no cure for Carnegie's malaise.

He sat staring out the window of the coffee shop, smiling from time to time. The Typhoon bar ironically closed as somewhere a bar thudded deep base through the walls of the block as an act of defiance to the inclement weather.

The flags above the building flapped away in time with Carnegie's twitching legs. Their icons of beer and honour stood out against the grey day. They worked in tune with the wind, fluttering in hope of eventual liberty.

A plump Chinese woman skittered across the road, her umbrella blown inside out. Her choice of a tight white blouse and light cream pants seemed entirely inappropriate as the layers of fat jiggled up and down like a kid's bouncing castle.

Carnegie's observation was cut short when the harsh words of Tagalog were thrown across the room. Eight Filipino girls, Two Aunties and One Mother pressed inside with a foolishly grinning old man. They arranged themselves into neat pairs of two with the Mother ordering the old man to pay the bill and cuddle up to one of the girls.

She was a sad little thing, probably no more than 18. Her teeth stuck out when she smiled wanly and she fought the uncomfortable feeling as the silly old duffer rubbed her thin thighs. The Mother looked on approvingly, her face permanently masked.

They gabbled away in impossibly fast tones, laughing sporadically and gesturing around. They had a matching outfit of tight tee shirts and little shorts that they must have squeezed into. Carnegie wondered if the old fella got eight for the price of one and someone that thought made Carnegie sad again.

The perverse scene meant Carnegie needed to leave the coffee shop and take a shot from Kennedy's flask. He decided to buy cigarettes.

'Marlboro light,' he said to the Chinese vendor whose shelves were half empty from frightened locals. The vendor shuffled over, speaking quietly in Mandarin and gesturing to the point of sale terminal. Carnegie pulled out a wad of Hong Kong dollars and paid for the tobacco.

Later that night, Carnegie inadvertently walked straight into the mother of all brawls. He had ducked around the corner straight into a couple of 'ladies' fighting. His gentlemanly instincts kicked in and he jumped in between them. Claws reached past him and scratched him, and legs extended between his legs, nearly kneeing him in the groin.

'Ladies, Ladies!' He called out, but then a cohort of companion women emerged out of the shadows; faces dark with anger.

'Uh oh.'

One of the females smashed her elbow into her victim's face while another lashed out, catching one of the women in the groin. She doubled over in agony.

Carnegie became a whirlwind of movement, his adrenaline pumped to the max. Like a drunken character from the Matrix, he swirled and dodged the flailing arms and legs. The shrieks were loud and clear and Carnegie panted with exertion. He copped a fist to the back of the head that stunned him for a second. He searched for an exit from the tornado of bodies but none appeared.

And then, just as soon as it began, it was over.

The 'ladies' had an innate sense of the law and when the long arm started to bend around the corner they fled like rats – leaving a sinking ship and leaving Carnegie breathless and clueless as to what just happened.

'Are you ok Sir?' The policeman was a young man with an unfortunate mole on the tip of his nose.

'Fine, fine.' Carnegie didn't feel fine but there was absolutely no point in making a big deal out of it. Besides he could hardly complain about being assaulted by a bunch of 'ladies'.

The policeman nodded and asked, 'So what happened?'

Carnegie proceeded to tell him the story of the encounter, feeling a bit silly and knowing he shouldn't have got involved. That was Carnegie's problem. He couldn't just not get involved. It was some supernatural reflex that washed over him. He had found the only way to resolve the instinct was to take a heavy dose of alcohol and look the other way. After all, why should he care what happens to others when he was on a mission to find a way out?

But he should have been more involved with Kennedy. The signs were there. They were all over him but, as one of the drunken fools, he overlooked Kennedy's problems and spent more time looking over the edge of a beer mug.

Kennedy was a quiet, tall man with a mournful look and hollowed eyes. He was brilliant to the point of eccentricity and he often sported a thin red goatee that he took flak for but wore as a badge of pride. He shaved his head regularly, arguing that hair was just an annoyance that didn't need to be bothered with.

He believed in UFOs and had a vast collection of conspiracy theories – particularly on America. His favourites ranged from Roswell through to JFK and especially, of late, he believed deeply in America's setup of 9-11.

Carnegie was not a convert but it made for interesting conversation as the tall man sadly depicted the 'real' events of September 11, 2001.

'Bush and Cheney are responsible James.' Kennedy took a pull from his beer and swirled it around in his mouth loudly. 'They manufactured the whole thing.'

'Really? They murdered their own citizens?' Carnegie was unconvinced.

'Oh yes my friend. Every dictator and empire clings to desperate power and in the end is willing to sacrifice anything to ensure it remains in control. You think the Americans are any better than any other regime?'

'No but they are more transparent. They are democratic, and no doubt face their fair share of corruption. But they are more open than others like the Russians and Chinese.' Carnegie was aware of the direction of the argument.

'Perhaps the Russians and Chinese are just more honest?' Countered Kennedy. 'They oppress and deceive their citizens like every other government but at least they are honest about it.'

Carnegie couldn't wrap his head around that statement, so he just drank more beer and responded incredulously.

'So, an advanced country like America allows planes to fly into buildings and, especially the pentagon, one of the most important buildings. What no scrambling of fighter jets, no ground to air missiles? I find it hard to believe.'

He looked up from his beer to see Kennedy's sad thin face flushed with fervour.

'And the buildings just collapse on themselves? Wasn't it closer to a demolition job? What about the plane coming down in Pennsylvania? Where were the parts in the photos? The hole in the pentagon – where were the tips of the planes and the debris?'

'I'm telling you James, the largest cover up.' He shook his head sadly.

Carnegie had seen it all before. He had watched the documentary In Plane Sight but there were more arguments against the arguments.

'How many people would have been in on the conspiracy? Hundreds? Thousands? What about the families of the dead? Why wouldn't they have been rising up in the masses and decrying the government? I don't buy it. Look Bush appears to be a bit of a dope but, in the end, the president is simply a figurehead of the government.'

'Exactly!' Kennedy seized on that point. 'Because Bush is such a dunderhead it was easier to have him sit as a puppet while the government machine ran his course. It's why JFK was shot. The CIA, the FBI, the NSA and the apparatchiks never allow one man to control their destiny.'

Carnegie smiled. He knew all roads would lead to JFK.

'You love conspiracies, don't you? You sure you aren't doing too much of that gunja?'

Kennedy stared back at him indignantly. 'I don't use too much herbal medicine, thank you very much! Besides it's natural and grows in the ground. One in the morning, lunchtime and evening just helps relax things and helps me to see clearly.'

Carnegie snorted. He had a love-hate affair with pot smokers. They were a fun cruisy bunch in the right mode but at other times they were paranoid fuckers.

Kennedy must have read his mind. 'Well you smoke that cancerous combination.' He gestured at the packet of Dunhill's sitting on the bar table.

'Guilty as charged.' He lit one up. 'But only with alcohol. They go together like chalk and cheese. And besides I'm quitting at Christmas.'

'Haha. I've heard that one before.' Kennedy giggled his weird little giggle that made Carnegie think about serial killers.

Carnegie was the king of quitters. He had quit smoking no less than 20 times in his life and had jumped back onto the coffin nails at the drop of the hat.

A beer? A cigarette.

Stress? A cigarette.

Need to get creative? A cigarette.

Working late? A cigarette or ten.

Making the chip onto the ninth green? A cigarette.

Long drive into the country? A cigarette.

A detective novel at a French café? A cigarette.

Wanting to look like a detective in a French café? A cigarette.

Carnegie had thrown out hundreds of packets, swearing it was his last cigarette. But when the withdrawals came he was powerless to escape their octopus-like tentacles – forcing him into the nearest supermarket, petrol station, newsagency or wherever he could find a way of destroying his lungs.

He always remembered his first cigarette. A sixteen-year-old desperate not to be uncool, he had sucked down lucky strikes at the local pool hall before remembering to spray deodorant and take off his jersey on the way heading home.

He was a foolish kid that would live to regret having the balls to do things he should have had the balls not to.

Hong Kong >

That night, lying in bed, Carnegie saw the Waitress with Kind Eyes. It was a crowded bar. Through the smoky haze she leaned forward and smiled at him. Carnegie felt so happy. She propped the luxurious head of curls up with her hand. In the distance he could see the little tattoo of infinity on the beginning of her left wrist. He looked down and saw his matching tattoo that sat over the scar on his wrist from a past time.

He rose from the bar seat and stubbed out his cigarette. He wandered over in the moment of his lifetime.

Halfway across the floor with the music bumping and the lights oscillating, he looked at her. She reached her arms out with that beautiful smile on her face.

But her hands didn't reach for him.

They reached for another man. He was faceless with handsomely groomed long hair.

Carnegie screamed.

Lying and Cheating

When Carnegie was young, one of the greatest horrific acts he could imagine was the betrayal of a man towards his wife and family. It seemed the greatest sin he could think of. Far worse than murder; far worse than theft.

Adults talked about it in hushed tones and women had looks on their face when talking about Bob, Roger, Bill or Slaven, that could ward off the winter for 100 years.

A childish idea will be a childish idea, and eventually reality would backhand Carnegie in the face very quickly. When he realised these 'cheats', these 'villains', these 'criminals' were just men who were cast down from the moral high ground; and most were ruined for life and branded, by others, and worse, by themselves, well they could have been anyone! In fact, they were everywhere because, by creating measures so far high, not one single human could be measured up there as the perfect man. For some had not physically betrayed their love but they had done far worse in the heart and the soul.

All of this despaired Carnegie. It depressed him when on business trips – those he knew ducked off quietly and subtly, to emerge later looking relaxed and with a warm glow. (The experienced ones that was, others came half smiling and half grimacing with the guilt that replaced the fluids that had left their bodies.)

Raising his head slightly in the sweat-soaked bed, Carnegie tried to clear the vision of his raven-haired saviour reaching for another man, with better hair. He was strangely jealous and tied up in knots.

It didn't take him long though. He got it. The picture was very clear.

This was karma being revisited on him. And by God did it fucking hurt.

But then, when you cross the line, you are sucked into a dark vortex of lust, desire, guilt, sin and pleasure and the free falling with flailing arms.

Rules weren't meant to be broken. And those who say otherwise are simply just rule breakers. Better to have no rules. Have no vows. Make no promises. Create no computer program that is impossible to understand or operate particularly as it is written by human minds filled with brilliant viruses and impossible bugs.

The thoughts always came on Carnegie in a rush. The guilt. The shame. The black. The white. The wrong. The right.

Dare he go there, he said in his mind. Dare he go there? He didn't want to go there. But sometimes he could not fight the visions. They came on strong. And why did they visit him? Why couldn't he banish them forever and sweep his mind clean? He couldn't. Just like he couldn't not dream what he dreamed. He could abolish the time when he was Adam, Eve, Serpent and the Fruit all at once.

It started with a simple look. A look was all it took.

< Melbourne

Carnegie sat there with all of the guys. It was a celebration. A celebration of capitalism. A celebration of commerce. A celebration of closing the deal. They were all there and all there to give themselves to the night. To toast their businesses, their triumphs and their constant battle with the hardness of stresses, doubts, anxieties, madness, troublesome clients, supply chain dramas, legal stoushes and finding their way in an ever-growing suffocating market – only being freed from time to time with digital disruption if you had the courage to leap of the cliff and sacrifice the illusion of safety for the illusion of predicting the future.

But this was a night of triumph and not a night to be blown over by foolish thoughts of the morrow. So whatever triumphs small or large that they could command to the front of the mind, they did so; fuelled by the loving arms of alcohol and whatever other substances they could summon up and drop into their bloodstream subtly.

Hammond was there, surrounded by his favourite foods and chatting earnestly with some Asian stripper that he swore he knew from another life.

Bruce was leaning back against velvet cushions, a blonde on each arm, telling another tall tale and pounding back the beers.

Heyloon was giggling away, haggling for lap dances, with one of the managers. He would end up with her on the night. Both were up to no good and perhaps it was just one of those alien nights where two wrongs may make a right.

The Pharmacist sat there talking idly to Agro and Carnegie about the spirit molecule in DMT and about a range of other chemicals without making a lot of sense. He was slurring early in the night and might have just decided unwisely on self-diagnosis leading to self-medication. The pills didn't always sing the right notes when executed incorrectly by the conductor.

And then there was Kennedy. The reluctant participant that came alight because Cassandra was there and was the Goddess among the pretenders. She stood out among all of the scantily-clad women. And she knew it. And like all great muses and Amazonians she sucked in the attention with only a hint of a smile and minimal interaction. Carnegie admired that. She was not afraid to be one of the boys but wouldn't take shit from any of the boys.

The entrepreneur's club was filled with the rotting bones of the superior sex who thought they could rumble in the lesser halls of the male club. Women were far too sane to spend time in the swirling chaos of man's menial maudlin.

Carnegie took in the scene and smiled. These nights were rare. Most nights were in the home or at the office. There was no madness, no magic, no creative spark, no mountains to climb, or sliding cliffs to fall off; just the requirement to keep putting one step in front of the other and pretend that it was the life that you signed up for.

These were the nights.

The nights where anything was possible.

Where the air of uncertainty, comradery and wild abandon were more intoxicating than amphetamines and alcohol.

And then deep into the night, the look happened. It was one look.

Carnegie was sitting back, waiting for his friends to return from another round of drinks when a tall, tanned lady of South-Eastern descent looked at him across the room. With piercing green eyes.

Carnegie was stuck. Held in a trance. His kids and his wife slid from his consciousness, his subconscious, his unconscious in seconds. And there was only green eyes.

She came to him, eventually playing a well-practiced game of seduction. And she was no whore. She was a proper lady who happened to be of high intellect and status. She wove a web tightly around Carnegie and he sucked in the air because he felt being drawn into a dizzy vortex. Wherever he was, she was on the radar. Wherever she was, he was on the radar.

They went out for cigarettes. The piercing green eyes piercing into his mind and piercing through the stream of grey smoke that emitted from their Marlboros. Carnegie wanted to look further into their orbs. They reminded him desperately of his mother's eyes but not in a sexual way, a healing way.

They talked endlessly about all things in life and when it was appropriate, left the crowd in the early hours of the morning. There was no consciousness. Just a man following a pathway that many men had slid down across humanity's generations.

They touched. They kissed. It was a moment in time when pathways didn't matter. Egos were thrown out the door and marital status and morals were cast away. Their mouths grabbed hold of each other and drew thirstily from each other despite the night and its participants floating around.

Carnegie headed back to his hotel, holding her hands and her waist; punch drunk with sudden love and lust and, more importantly, a joie de vivre that sprung from his loins. His body was on fire and his youth restored. There was just an appetite to be human or animal but, more than that, a being on this planet, wedded to this rock, signed up for life, neither concerned for the thoughts that usually plagued him.

He was grounded firmly in now.

He refuted the past.

He rejected the future.

There was no afterlife. There were no rule books. There was no responsibility. There was no God with lightning bolts.

There was a green-eyed goddess and he worshipped at her alter.

They made love. In the stairwell. Arms in a dervish, shifting impatiently, ripping at each other's clothes and skins. Tearing away comfortably and uncomfortably. Grabbing each other's bodies, tasting each other's sweat and breathing loudly and heavily with whiskey and smoke-stained taste.

He gave himself to her. Because she gave himself to him. All of his sexual fantasies and desires came tumbling out and, with unconscious guidance, she let him go at it and gave herself to it. And finally, they were done as the sun rose from the balcony. They were undone not by orgasm but because their bodies could take no more. Dehydration and tiredness grabbed hold of them as they passed out, Carnegie still inside her. With a sigh, he laid on her bountiful breast and, hearing her softly sleep, he let go. Darkness came.

He woke up – head pounding on stained sheets. Legs cramping up and an emptiness next to him and a great emptiness in his heart.

Green eyes had gone. There was no note. There was no number. There was no evidence of his partner's existence or exit with exception to the brief hint of perfume in the air.

Carnegie groaned out loud and stumbled to the bathroom. Medication. Water. Urination. Berocca. Hot shower.

And then he was struck down with the thought.

He had cheated.

He had crossed the line. And it all started with one look.

The nights pleasures were a fantasy slideshow in his head. But the morning realisation was a fixed stone table carved into his soul. And it came with three faces.

Wife. Daughter. Daughter.

Carnegie sank to the bottom of the shower. He was an oath breaker. A law breaker. A vow breaker. He had become the man he despised.

No amount of scrubbing of his genitals or body would wash away the sins of his life.

She was the praying mantis that struck off his head in the moments of lust explosion. Not his physical or sexual head but the godhead.

And then suddenly, Carnegie remember the Old Testament bible verses.

He didn't want to hear them. He didn't want to listen to them. He didn't want to remember them.

But these words spat at him like bullets.

Drink waters out of thine own cistern,
And running waters out of thine own well.
Should thy springs be dispersed abroad?
And streams of water in the streets.

Let them be for thyself alone,
And not strangers with thee.
Let they fountain be blessed;
And rejoice in the wife of thy youth.

As a loving hind and a pleasant doe,
Let her breasts satisfy thee at all times;
And be thou ravished always with her love.

For why shouldest, thou my son, be ravished with a strange woman,
And embrace the bosom of a foreigner?

For the ways of man are before the eyes of Jehovah;
And he maketh level all his paths.
His own iniquities shall take the wicked,
And he shall be holden with the cords of his sin.
He shall die for lack of instruction;
And in the greatness of his folly he shall go astray.

The words were in his head. He cried in the shower. Sad, pathetic, foolish, sinful, naked, stained, shrivelled – and water could not wash all of his filth away.

He never saw green eyes again. But she never left his mind. Those eyes, those eyes.

And like most men, he lied. But women are not fools. Their heart beats in rhythm with their partner's and the Good Wife knew something had happened.

Carnegie disappeared from his family home using the usual excuses of business and battles. The guilt was all too painful.

And the sadness compounded. Because of the eyes.

It was no longer the green eyes of seduction.

But the sad brown eyes of the Good Wife.

> Hong Kong

Carnegie yearned for the God of his youth. The one where you just had to follow the rules. And you had no choice but to follow the rules. There was a simplicity in it. If only you could stave off doubt, reason and logic.

He sighed and climbed out of the bed. His search for God after he broke away from his traditions and community lead to nowhere. He knew there was a search if only he could figure out where to start looking or perhaps even why he wanted to look.

If only those fucking nightmares of hell would go away, perhaps he could sleep and find some peace, he reasoned with himself, smoking on the porch.

Oh God, oh God, why have you forsaken me? He cried out, echoing the words of Christ on the cross.

But he knew the answer. He had forsaken God.

The God Dilemma

< Hong Kong

Who is God? And why is he invisible? Where did he come from? Is he a male God? Or does it have a sex at all?

Did we invent him as a way of making up for our natural despair in our own mortality? Had we really killed God, as Nietzsche claimed? Was the entity's blood dripping on our hands and nothing could cleanse us for all time?

Why were there so many goddamn religions? And Holy Books? And symbols?

Why the hell was there a hell anyway? Or was there? And if so, what power sustained it? Was there an opposite named heaven? Why would anyone create these states?

Why were little babies baptised in water when Jesus didn't baptise any babies in water? It seemed a very quick re-birth. Ye must be born again? Seemed a little rushed to Carnegie. Out of the womb and into a new one and then out again …

And why were women treated poorly in Islam as a whole? Being allowed to burn because of the lack of modest clothing in a building fire. Wasn't the great prophet's daughter one of the greatest icons of all time and even led a horde of warriors into battle?

And why did the Buddhist set himself on fire? Why couldn't the Dalai Lama go home?

And why were there all of these wars? These goddamn stupid wars over the same thing goddamn thing. The elephant looked different from every side.

And were we Gods? It seemed possible if there was so much power and reference to it. No?

Or were we making a God through technology? A new Sauron to keep an all-seeing blazing day and night; to watch us and 'protect' us from our pitiful lives. Big brother was watching, just make sure you don't give him a ring.

Carnegie fought these questions daily. His successes and failures in business did nothing to stave away the thoughts that smashed into his mind like acid-crazed lemmings.

He tried to hide.

He tried to run.

But they followed them everywhere.

Why did saying Allah Akbar make him feel guilty?

Surely God was great?

Why do we exist?

Why the fuck do we exist!

Carnegie was exhausted, and he knew he was on the edge of his own rationality.

It all started with a question from out of his head. Which went out of someone's mind, into their mouths, into his ears and then lodged firmly into his head.

What an annoyance.

He couldn't remember who asked him.

Maybe he deleted the person from his mind because of the nasty virus they had uploaded into his brain.

It was a seemingly simple and innocent question.

'So what?'

What miserable, horrifying words?!

What pain and torture!

He had been telling this wicked person his life story. He was a hero after all. He was the entrepreneur! The. Yes, The.

He was on an epic adventure. He was climbing out of his station. He was helping others. He was a leader. A changer. A visionary. A master. The one who was leading the way.

So what?

Well business can grow and we can all make money.

So what?

Well money means we can buy things and have families …

So what?

Well then we can have fun and drink and hang out.

So what?

Well you get older and then …

So what?

Fuck! It all ended at nowhere. His body of work was at best a miniscule blip on the universe. And he was going to die. Old. Alone. Crippled. Broken. Urinating and shitting all over himself.

And so. So what?!

Well then, the God Dilemma came in.

Was there life after death? And the quest began. The miserable fucking quest that destroyed Carnegie's desire for business and ventures. That destroyed his sleep. The quest that took him into another maze. From the frying pan of mindless purgatory into the burning fires of hell.

So Carnegie went looking. He knew where not to look. So he started there just to make sure. And when the hangover settled he bought tickets immediately to Hong Kong.

He sat staring at the giant golden Buddha. It was a terribly steamy morning and a drunken Carnegie sat hovering on a stone rock while looking at the rotund statue. He was covered in sweat. The tight black tee shirt he favoured clung to his thin frame like a sodden rag.

Each of the 268 steps he had climbed for a closer look at it felt like hell. He reached the top of the climb, breathless and terribly faint. When had he eaten last?

So, he sat and looked. Buddhism. An ancient practice that taught a very simple way of living. No highs and no lows. Carnegie could stand the thought of living on the plains. The emotional and mental highs of the mountains almost made the hurtling crashes of getting down worth it.

He wondered about the so called 'awakened one'. He never looked too awake. And the concept of meditation frightened the devil out of him. Sitting in one place and just left to his own mind was enough to send Carnegie over the edge. His mind was a hateful, horrible place that tortured him. He needed music. He needed his painkillers. He needed his alcohol. Most of all he needed to be with someone.

Someone who held him tight and someone who calmed his spirit. There was a terrible burning hole in his soul and no matter what he did he couldn't find a way to mend it.

He wiped away tears as they formed at the corners of eyes. He stared bitterly at the large immobile idol. Nothing. Where was there peace in spirit?

He watched bitterly as people stood around in seeming awe. What were they in awe about? Death that lurked at the end of every life? Old age? Seeing loved ones come and go?

Carnegie closed his eyes. The darkness jumped out at him. His wife's face appeared in a gentle smile. Right then he wanted to lay down with her and make sweet passionate love. He wanted to make another baby. He smiled as he thought of the beauty of his sweet innocent children. But the vision never stayed that way. It always twisted and turned. He saw two kids that were older; and they turned their backs on him. He saw his wife grow old in his mind and reject him.

He sighed deeply and shoved his headphones into his ears. AC/DC belted over the miraculous little cable and filled his ears with *Thunderstruck*. The energy from the music got him standing. Unconsciously, he started rocking his head back and forth. The sadness temporarily left him. The stress of life and his living drifted away.

He pumped the volume and started humming.

The great idol did not rock out with him.

He opened his knapsack up and sprayed himself with deodorant, ignoring the looks of those gathered around. Zombies, he said to himself, they were all zombies. The Walking Dead was not a work of fiction it was simply a reflection of the many lives that just staggered about seeking the next life to take, the next meal to make.

The thought of all of the pilgrims as zombies staggering about amused him and he was reminded of Michael Jackson's *Thriller*. He searched for it desperately on the iPhone, finally finding it filed under *Thryller*. Damn those downloads.

So he pumped MJ and his monster song. He resisted the urge to do the dance. He resisted the urge to howl at the moon. *The occult sure made for good music*, he mused to himself.

Carnegie skipped down the 268 stairs. No God. No hope. But music took his mind away for some time.

< Bangkok

Cassandra didn't have an answer for his lack of faith. She simply said, 'Find the calmness in your heart and mind. Meditate.' Carnegie could have screamed. Meditation was no medication for him. His mind attacked him when he tried to find a calm point. He wanted to switch his mind off. In his bitterness he uncrossed his legs, folded up his mat and buried himself neck-deep in a bottle of bourbon.

A dank smile emerged on his face. He needed a club. He needed mindless dancing bodies. He needed to suck in Nihilism for the night and sink to the bottom of this earthly plane with fellow writhing souls, covered in sweat and poisoned from the mind to the liver. He needed darkness. He needed flashing light. He needed to climb into the cage and open his ribs and skull, so that the succubi could cut out his heart and dull his mind.

He needed to sacrifice his body on the altar of hedonism.

Give me rain. Give me clouds. Give me music all aloud.
Give me rain.
Give me clouds.
Give me music all aloud.

His mind chanted as he walked up the alleyways of Bangkok.

Give me rain.
Give me clouds.
Give me music all aloud.

A club emerged on his horizon. Weird light emerged from it in shades of green and pink. An uninterested bouncer stood outside staring into the nightlife. Music crawled out of the club, writhing away and punching his ears. He hadn't been drinking. But he was high. He was drunk on his demise. He willingly sucked on Socrates' poison and gave up his soul searching. The music grabbed him and guided him. Their beautiful tendrils reached out and pulled on his ears. He stumbled down a sticky stairway. Stained. Soaked in the sweat of those worshipping to the great Three Goddesses of Debauchery.

He rocked back and forth. He bobbed. Unconsciously moving with the music. In a trance, he moved through the crowd and shoved a wad of Baht in the hand of the waitress – motioning to the VIP area. No words were exchanged, except two critical and somewhat cruel smiles. Self-destruction was a common practice here and was highly welcome, especially from the Farung.

Eight shots later he was writhing to the beats of P!nk on the underground dancefloor of the Bangkok nightclub. A multitude of small-breasted Thai women rubbed up against him – desperately trying to catch his eyes and glimpse a smile. Carnegie stared at the DJ, curiously named High Minded Low. He was a small Asian with an impressive gold chain and an old Slayer tee shirt. He moved his hands, juggling an oversized set of speakers. His Aviators were glued to his face as he pumped up and down and wriggled his hips in acid black jeans.

He caught Carnegie's eyes and a smile twisted on his face. He gave Carnegie a crude waist hump and shook his hands in a vulgar movement.

Carnegie looked around him, suddenly incredibly depressed. He didn't agree with P!nk's lyrics about trying to love. He was an empty man with money and all the trappings of success, but nothing felt successful right now.

He wandered through the maze of pumping bodies and grasping hands and slumped into a leather booth. He paid double for a Tiger beer and watched the dancefloor, careful not meet anyone's gaze. Behind him an innocent-looking student was being groped by two Thai girls. The sucking and kissing noises slid between the beats. The student's eyes were vague and Carnegie wondered where the poor kid would end up tonight. He resisted the urge to get involved and send the vultures away. Perhaps the poor fool needed a lesson.

The students haze was interrupted by an over-confident lady of the night and her companion. She was dressed in a strapless mini dress with large fake breasts and large hands that frightened the devil out of Carnegie. Her companion was a timid, miniature caricature of the leading lady.

She slid in beside Carnegie with a devil may care.

'Hi darlinnggggggg,' she said in a thick Thai accent. 'I'm Lily. This is Shelly. You look lonely.'

Her eyes narrowed around her dark mascara. Shelly plonked down next to Lily and gave Carnegie a nervous grin.

Carnegie inwardly groaned. Why did he always find himself in these situations?

'I'm Edward,' he lied. 'I'm just here by myself. You might want to find someone else?' He left his face perfectly passive.

It didn't work.

An excuse of a girlfriend didn't work either.

Sickness didn't work either.

Nor an early flight or any other reason.

In the end, he promised them a night's fun if they could go round for round with him.

He ordered 12 shots and smashed them all back. His head swimming, he ordered another 24 and slid them over to the girls. They managed four before they lost Shelly. Lily impressively got to 11 before excusing herself to the bathroom.

Carnegie resisted the urge to vomit and wandered out of the seedy nightclub – hurriedly looking behind him on the exit and grateful to see no apparition appearing. His legs were functioning like winding pieces of spaghetti dancing on their tips. The tequila went to his head and, before he collapsed drunkenly onto the floor of his hotel bathroom, he asked himself one sad question.

'Where is God now?'

< Vatican City

Carnegie stared at the ceiling of the Sistine Chapel. He had angrily left the monasteries of Thailand in a hungover state and caught the first flight to Rome via Dubai. He swore never to drink again until he climbed onto the flight and ordered three strong vodka and lemonades. The British Airways flight attendant smiled at him, hinting concern.

'Are you ok?' Carnegie asked sarcastically in his head. And she had hurried away.

But now he was staring at magnificent artwork. And that was just it. Magnificent artwork. The hawkers and gypsies that hung around the Vatican made him angry and cross. He was a terrible pilgrim and an even worse art admirer.

He did admire the great business model of the Catholic Church. Boy had it generated some serious funds in the past and wielded some political power, Carnegie mused. Carnegie often wondered deeply about their property portfolio and asset value. In fact, he wondered so much about it he spent the next four hours scribbling notes and drinking short blacks.

In the end, a trillion dollars sounded too little, so he counted pigeons instead and eavesdropped into conversations. He liked the sound of the Italian language.

He knew why George Clooney liked Italy – it had racy cars, racy women and racy coffee.

Alas! He could only afford the racy coffee.

In the end, he drifted off. Untouched by man's handiwork in the Vatican and terribly aware of the lack of God's handiwork on his life.

Sighing sometimes loudly and too dramatically, he wandered the streets of Rome, looking at the ancient architecture, sculptures and incredible work. Every picture of the Lord, sculptures of angels, tributes to the Divine only made him feel more glued to terra firma and soullessness.

With the sun setting, Carnegie gave up his search for another and contented himself with his stomach. The pasta cooked to perfection was perfectly accompanied with a full-bodied wine and a full-bodied waitress of Roman descent.

The night spun inwards and then outwards and when Carnegie slipped out of the waitress's small apartment he realised that he had spent a day in the Eternal City.

God, he breathed loudly, as he finally made his way back to the hotel on a pungent Rome bus filled with gypsies. He had the mother of headaches that only wine could give you and the lack of water that often accompanied it. Carnegie sighed. There were no more miracles, he mused, holding his head.

If only some of the wine had been turned back into water.

< Goa

The humidity of Goa was affecting him. He sweated through his cotton tee shirt and was aware of the smell it might have. Carnegie sneaked in some more deodorant and hoped that his cologne held up against the weather. He shouldn't have worried, he told himself; everyone was sweating like a crab in a boiling pot. But he was always self-conscious. Narcissistic moron, he would mutter to no one in particular.

He was there to explore the Cathedral of St Francis Xavier and witness the miracles of God. He did his level best not to be cynical and morose but the emptiness and void clung to him like shackles that he just couldn't shake off. A millstone of depression hung around his neck. He wanted more. He wanted true joy and happiness. But money couldn't provide that. Lust was vain and vaporous. Love was just another drug he couldn't get enough of. Even charitable works had a used by date.

And in the end, Carnegie knew he had surpassed his used by date.

But in this depressive mood he wandered up to the tour guide and asked for the full rundown on the old and new cathedrals. The tour guide, a darkly tanned Indian, smiled to him and pointed to a standard fee on an aging board outside the old Cathedral. Carnegie paid him double without thinking twice and hoped for even half of an experience.

There was no doubting the brilliance of the stained-glass windows and the ornate ceilings. This was some architecture. He wandered about the Vatican City and thought he might get there one day but in the meantime, this had to suffice.

They wandered through the churches respectfully and Carnegie found himself listening in curiously. It was a great tale of how the Saint had come to land in Goa and eventually return in a lesser state. He smiled ironically when he was told about the pope insisting on St Francis being interned in the Vatican and all he got was a hand. Talk about a five-fingered discount, Carnegie mused.

He knew he was terribly irreverent, but he couldn't imagine the Almighty One being so concerned with these things. And that night, lying on Anjuna beach, sipping on a Mojito, he looked at the setting sun and then the shining stars and he knew the magic of the Earth had to be forged by a greater power. How could such beauty be a result of a big bang? The only big bangs he knew about left dark smoking creators and a helluva noise. Carnegie suffered a deep sadness as he felt totally disconnected from the miracles of nature. He hated every cigarette he smoked and the poisons he subjected his body to on a daily basis. But because of the sadness within himself he just couldn't allow himself to have any sober moments. He silently willed the DJ to pump the music louder and force the melancholy thoughts out of his system. But they just sat there, reminding him of his loneliness.

He sat there on the beach, absent from the revellers and his friends and silently prayed that purpose and God would find him before he ran out of options.

< Kathmandu

The Hindu priest didn't like him. He knew that. He sat on the steps of ancient Kathmandu and mused at the passers-by. They seemed so busy or happy or happy and busy. Were they busy because they were happy or were they happy because they were busy? He asked the question to the priest that sat next to him, shaking his tin for some money.

The priest spat Hindi back at him and rattled the tin again.

Carnegie felt like rattling his cages. But he knew not all were like this one with his white painted face and terribly long nails.

He asked him a lot more questions, trying out his limited Hindi. Rattle. Rattle. Rattle.

Carnegie ran out of patience and stuffed a wad of Nepalese rupees into the man's tin and wandered off to find this living goddess he had heard about.

The living goddess was a legend of Nepal. Young girls were recruited to become the living goddess from a young age and were effectively ostracised from society after they hit puberty. No one wanted to marry a living goddess, so they were destined for a sad and lonely life after their short ceremonial stint.

Carnegie remember humping his knapsack through the crowded Patan Durbar Square, only to be railroaded by a long, large and loud procession. He stood aside and watched the procession of priests and hangers-on amble past.

A large carriage rolled past in the middle of the procession, rumbling along on wheels being pulled by a stream of reluctant oxen who looked bored and over-tired with their source of employment.

And then the moment hit him. High up in the carriage rode the painted face of the living goddess. She was no more than eight Carnegie figured. Her face was as white as a ghost and hung in the shadowy darkness above her coverings and robes.

Carnegie could not take his eyes from her. The sadness that poured from the large oval eyes bore down on him and hit him like a sledge hammer. He was transfixed and mournful. She rolled on, looking down on him in her immense sadness. A pale bird trapped in a dark cage.

Carnegie had sunk to the nearest dusty step in the square and tried desperately to stop the tears from coming – but they ran down his sunburned cheeks and into the four-day stubble of his greying beard. He covered his face in embarrassment and sorrow with his red paisley bandana.

That night he had sort to sleep in his Thamel tourist hotel; but the pale face of the living goddess kept jerking him away with her terribly sad eyes and lonely existence.

And so, on the next day, Carnegie left the irritable priest and sort out the living goddess. His Nepali was only basic, so he switched to his equally basic Hindi and then back again, realising it only made matters more confusing when he asked for directions to the goddess' chambers. After being led on a wild buffalo chase he finally managed to stop outside a large structure with signs everywhere in Nepali. Two large swastikas sat on either side of the fading door.

Carnegie had never gotten used to seeing the swastikas everywhere in Nepal. He, as a young man, had always loved the World War Two movies that saw the good allies conquer the nasty Nazis and their crooked cross.

But everywhere in modern society in Nepal was surrounding by this sign. He had to keep telling himself it was a good sign that the nutcase Hitler had corrupted for his evil and maniac schemes. The sign came from the Sanskrit, the old root language that many languages, including German, had stemmed from.

What made matters even more surreal was the red hammer and sickle painted everywhere in the streets of Kathmandu after the communists had just swept into power. The swastika and the hammer and sickle everywhere! Carnegie half expected to see Hitler and Stalin sitting around the corner having a coffee and dividing up the map of Poland.

It was bizarre and breathtaking.

He approached the doorway to the living goddess' chambers, crunching the hard dust and rocks under his Colorado boots. A band of Nepalese stood outside the doors extracting donations from those entering into the chambers. Crumpled up rupees were slapped into the guardians' hands as the superstitious Nepalese touched their heads and ducked under the low door frame.

'Sir!' A chubby guardian with a traditional Nepalese Topi perched curiously on his head stopped him as he reached for his stack of rupees.

'Eh?' Carnegie looked up.

'You cannot come in. You are a quiray. You are a foreigner. You may not see the living goddess,' he stated, puffing out his sinking chest.

'Sorry?' Carnegie was confused. He had found the temple. He had the money. What was going on?

'You are white. You are different religion. You may not come in,' he stated firmly with his fellow door keepers standing around in interest.

'Ahhh. I came all this way. Are you saying the colour of my skin precludes me from entering within?' Carnegie was irritated. It seemed ridiculous.

'You are white. You are Christian. You may not come in.' The man's tone became high pitched.

'So it is my skin colour?' Carnegie asked, pointing at his skin.

'Yes you are foreign. Quiray.' (The word for foreigner.) He shook his head.

'So the living goddess is for Nepalese only?' he asked, getting annoyed.

'For true Hindus,' he stated.

'What about Indian Hindus?' Carnegie asked, ready to pick a fight.

'Yes. Yes. You can go now.' He waved his hand dismissively.

Carnegie stuck in. 'Hang on. What about African Hindus?'

The man looked confused.

'What about European Hindus?' Carnegie opened his arms wide in mock disbelief, although he did disbelieve this sort of thing.

The man looked at his friends. A young man with oily, slicked-back hair ambled over, casually tossing his cigarette aside. 'You can't come in friend. You are not Hindu,' he said with a reptilian smile that Carnegie wanted to punch off his face.

'How do you know I am not Hindu?' Carnegie asked belligerently.

'Ahhhh. We know these things. The living goddess knows these things. It would be blasphemy for you to come in, Christian.'

'What if I was Muslim?' Carnegie scowled as he turned around and left.

The young man called out behind him. 'You can still leave a donation.'

Carnegie chuckled and climbed back up the tired and dusty slabs that served as stares. Something made him turn back. He turned around and, up in the ancient ornate temple, the pale little face stared at him. And in seconds it was gone, only to haunt him again that night in his sleep.

No God was here either, Carnegie mused. Only a system that locked him out and idols that stared stone-faced at his inner sadness.

In the morning, he crawled out of bed and prayed. But emptiness filled the room and alcohol seemed like a better idea – so he crawled into a vat of beer to swap the numbness for a slightly better numbness.

He hurried out of the hotel and suddenly needed to play something from Faith No More.

< Jerusalem

He wasn't a pilgrim, and he wasn't sure why on Earth he abandoned his business and family again, but he had to find out what was here and why so many people came. He paid through the nose for a religious tour guide and sat feeling terribly isolated as he rode through the streets of Jerusalem to visit the Mosques, Temples and Churches.

He had never felt more like an alien in a country. Everybody seemed to have a purpose, a vision, a goal. Even the tourists seemed driven and on a life plan. Carnegie, however, was a miserable visitor with a cynical view.

The heat was almost unbearable as he rode through the city in a clapped-out old Mercedes that had seen better days. Carnegie watched the people walk past on their way to prayers or commerce. Sadly, he wondered why the two mixed together so much on the globe.

It was a dangerous cocktail; money and religion.

How much was a soul worth? Carnegie wondered that a lot in a rich vein of bitterness.

He knew he was coming at his problem with faith from the wrong angles, but it wasn't hard to be a cynic when he was passed a credit card machine in a modern church in America. And when you saw the poverty around the world and the influence of religion on desperate people, you started to understand why people were so easily captivated by the promise of a better life next time around.

His depression building, he hardly paid attention to the spitting tour guide that pointed out pilgrim sites and other sites that were apparently significant to a saint or religious person of order. Soon the tourist guide realised that his customer was in a funk, so he avoided any further commentary for the rest of the trip. Carnegie just sat vaguely and looked into the heavens. Sadly no one looked back at him. No old wise face appeared with a floating white beard or grasping at lightning bolts.

Maybe God didn't exist at all. Maybe we were all just born to die. Maybe, just maybe, life had no meaning and they were all products of a random intergalactic phenomenon, which was also just a random result of another intergalactic cosmic coincidence, which miraculously and impossibly began as an accident that was simply a large alien rolling a couple of dice …

Dangerous thoughts James, he said to himself in his sadness.

He left Jerusalem in a desolate state, dragging his heels and slowly boarded his plane home. He desperately missed his friends and family. He desperately missed that peace of mind and peace of state. He desperately missed the absence of questions and the childlike innocence.

Hong Kong >

Carnegie sat at a Hong Kong bus station, absently rubbing at the scar on his head where he had come off second best in a fight with sleeping pills and a scotch glass. Buses came but he didn't catch any of them. He stubbed out his tenth cigarette and drained the last of the Gatorade that had sat lonely in the modern-formed plastic bottle.

His mind turned to his friends and family. Cassandra. The Good Wife. His Girls. Heyloon. Hammond. The Pharmacist. Agro. The Good Banker. Bruce. And Kennedy. Fucking Kennedy.

Why did he have to leave and where did he go!

Where were they all?

Where indeed.

Board and Bored

< Sydney

Carnegie sat back in his leather seat and stared off into the distance. Through the picture of Winston Churchill smoking a cigar. Through the wall. Out of the building and off into the grey skies. The boardroom and its contents, its agenda, its directors could not hold Carnegie's mind. He was day dreaming, as his mother would have said. Carnegie had a massive problem with day dreaming. In essence, he was a dreamer. He worked hard to achieve his dreams – to reach into the deep and grab hold of his visions and make them a reality.

And so here he was, with the board of directors he had appointed over his business. The business that he had dreamed up and made a reality.

But what happens if your dreams turn out to be nightmares?

The entrepreneurial James Andrew Carnegie worked so hard to develop something he was passionate about and had dreamed of achieving. And now, instead of being a motivated individual enjoying the fruits of his labour, he was listening to business risk studies and cost benefit analysis.

Instead of making exciting gut decisions and travelling to exotic locations to close deals, he was rooted in the tired boardroom within his office, working through complex business modelling. He was terribly bored. Terribly bored of a board. The boardroom. And everything around him. The walls were closing in.

So his head was in the clouds thinking about euphoria and how he missed it. How he missed the thrill of the chase. How he missed uncertainty and the risks it came with. He felt numb. He thought of his friends and wondered when he could round them up and get thoroughly plastered and talk silly nonsense until the sun came up. But they were all too busy with their existences – leaving Carnegie feeling guilty about the neglect of his family and the blatant excuses he was making to avoid the mundane existence in suburbia.

He greatly admired the citizens of suburbia. They were steadfast, stoic and hardy souls that were to be roundly congratulated for mowing their lawns every Saturday, cooking barbeques, dropping the kids to soccer, eating toast for breakfast, spring cleaning their McMansions, the annual car servicing, helping out at the school canteen, walking the dogs, buffing the car, talking about the next annual holiday and sitting on the balcony staring away into nothingness while the prim wives and partners baked lasagne and secretly read gossips magazines like Who, New Idea and Women's Weekly.

He wanted to take the other pill and slip quietly into the exact opposite of Neo's choice and join shoulder to shoulder the grand brigade of suburbia.

But 9 to 5 drove him crazy.

Long service leave made him shake.

Footy tipping competitions made him restless.

And he was allergic to baby seats in SUVs.

And so, he sat contemplating his existence.

'Mr Carnegie. What do you think of our assessment?' Carnegie sat bolt upright and concentrated. The speaker was a hard-faced, middle age woman with a pair of heavy purple plastic specs that sat on her incredible nose. Carnegie wondered how much of it was manufactured.

She had a complex spreadsheet projected onto the boardroom wall. It was the risk assessment of diversifying into the supply market. Vertical integration. Riveting stuff; and Carnegie felt the more complex the statements made, the higher the bill would be at the end of the day.

Carnegie was a little cheeky when he replied, 'I'd like to put it to the board.' He waved dramatically at the board members who sat concentrating on the consultant's presentation.

He looked around the room and the six other board members, including Chairman Saul, were seemingly riveted.

Chairman Saul was a splendid man with an excellent head of white hair and a shrewd outlook on life and business. When it came to business acquisitions, he always preached the three Ds in his drawling eastern European accent.

'Three Ds James. Dead, dumb or divorced,' he had told Carnegie.

Carnegie had an immediate thought. *Dead, dumb or divorced? What the fuck?*

'These are the best acquisitions.'

'Dead. Well the estate mostly doesn't give a ficky fick about the business, so they will sell it cheap.'

'Dumb. They always undervalue the opportunity and give up the business for peanuts.'

'Divorced. They most always have to sell the business and get rid of it cheap.'

And this acquisition was no different except, according to Chairman Saul ,it was the magical trifecta. John Doe was a dumb man who married the wrong woman and from the resulting divorce he had a nasty heart attack that took him off. Now the estate and the ex-wife were trying to flog off his electronic supplies business to get the cash that John Doe had busted his hump developing.

Carnegie felt sad for John Doe. And slightly envious. He wished desperately at times he could find the peace of John Doe; but he knew there was more to life and he really felt guilty about feeling like that. He thought of the starving African kids. He thought of the little twisted up man he met in Nepal. He thought of the Indian woman thrusting her baby into his arms.

And he felt guilty for ever thinking of offing himself.

Ms Bird's Nest was postulating on the presentation, so he forced himself to snap out of his reverie and focus on his sole female board member. She wore dangerously conservative pants suits everywhere and had her greying hair stacked layer upon layer on her small round face. She had all the features of a mother but there was nothing motherly about her personality. Yet Carnegie had a soft spot for Ms Birds Nest. She drew him near with her impenetrable gazes and her enigmatic personality. There was something awfully sexual about her, but Carnegie could not pinpoint why she aroused him. And besides, she was as cunning as a rake and a damn fine businesswoman who served as an exemplary board member. The company was in good hands with her on the board, even if she was an awesome distraction.

Carnegie gave all of his board members nick names. Chairman Saul, Ms Bird Nest, Ole Blue Eyes, Mr Monopoly, The Publican and Itchy. He found making up names for them based on their features and character traits made boardroom discussions slightly more interesting.

Ole Blue Eyes was a Sinatra lookalike who oozed old school charm and spent all of his time trying to impress Carnegie and Chairman Saul with old war stories on how he won deals and built up businesses. Carnegie was never seduced by Ole Blue Eyes but loved the entertainment of the stories and, one thing for sure, Ole Blue Eyes had the contacts that would see his business interests flourish. He always carried this large black book that contained carefully-pencilled contact details in capital letters. When asked about a Smartphone or an organiser of some sort, Ole Blue Eyes would always smile and say the same thing. 'This old dog can't learn new tricks but the ones he has are damn tremendous.'

Carnegie secretly thought Ole Blue Eyes wanted to be his mentor and father figure. He wondered if Ole Blue Eyes wanted to relive his glory through his humble achievements and the possibly of being great again. Carnegie didn't want to be great. He wanted to feel alive and excited again. He wanted to take desperate risks and win. He wanted to confront demons and scythe through them, wielding his golden sword of wit and his kite shield of determination. Instead, he found himself stuck in a fortress of micro growth and managed risk.

Mr Monopoly had no such charm. He looked like the iconic figure from the popular real estate game that Carnegie played to death as a child. Mr Monopoly had a 'take no prisoners' approach that Cassandra would have been proud of. His first thought was always about ambition and gain and how he could grow the company stock options and thus his own interests. He had a chief interest in acquiring other businesses rather than growing the business organically through marketing and sales. He was always harassing Carnegie to get more involved in the industry and pick off any competitors or emerging players. When he stopped harassing Carnegie, he harassed Old Blue Eyes for contacts, so he could propose more acquisitions. Carnegie had never met a more voracious empire builder.

Mr Monopoly was like his namesake. He seemed to have a real estate ownership of every street corner in Sydney or some property development emerging to block the sun from shedding its glorious rays on the humble Australian dirt. Mr Monopoly had no care about any such things like open space. His favourite word was 'Bullshit!' He used this frequently to the despair of Ms Birds Nest who thought such words were vulgar and unbecoming. Carnegie was mildly amused at their differences of opinions and enjoyed the entertainment.

Social responsibility. Environmental responsibility. Human rights. Occupational Health and Safety. They were all bullshit according to Mr Monopoly, but property rights were sacrosanct. Title deeds were his life, and nothing excited him more than to see a wad of paper stacked on the desk for the acquisition of some form of asset. Carnegie deeply admired his ambition and wondered if he could find his motivation on the back of this furiously capitalistic man.

The Publican just drank anything that came his way and sat in the boardroom with a shy smile on his weather-beaten and florid face. He always sat back a few extra inches from the boardroom table to allow his prodigious belly room to sit like the swollen pimple on a teenager's face.

Carnegie wasn't sure why he had appointed The Publican. Maybe it was the feel-good factor and the encouragement to find reasons to consume alcohol.

Itchy annoyed the shit out of everyone with constant scratching at his flaky skin and his irritable questioning. He was to business risk analysis as the Grim Reaper was to life insurance. Constantly scrabbling away and protecting the borders of the business like a demon-possessed guardian patrolling the tops of an ancient castle in the way of Rome's advance through Europe.

Despite being subscribed all sorts of medicine and seeking professional help, Itchy could not help scratching away. It drove everyone crazy; especially Ole Blue Eyes who hated any form of aesthetic imperfection. Every time Itchy scratched, Ole Blue Eyes would tense up and his mouth would twist away. Carnegie always smirked when he saw these little interactions. It was amazing how little things would drive people crazy. He too was driven crazy by little things, but he tried to maintain his poker face at all times.

He was driven crazy by men peeing in front of a urinal and getting it on the ground. How hard could it possibly be to piss into a sizeable trough?

He was driven crazy by how collars on shirts never seemed to sit right on top of a suit. They were either tucked in or hanging out over the top of his suit collar. How hard could it be!?

He was driven crazy by the amount of hair his wife shed in their ensuite. By now she should be as bald as a badger but somehow the hair remained thick and luxurious.

He was driven crazy wild by people who bought clapped-out old cars and then spent thousands of dollars on brand new epic sound systems.

He was driven crazy by people driven crazy by Apple products. Why, oh, why would they queue up for all hours of the night just to get a device that was in a different colour and had a headphone jack on the top of the phone with an extra megapixel?

Megapixels drove him crazy. And mega fans who rambled on about how many megapixels their camera had when they probably only used a fraction of the capacity.

Wrapping presents drove him crazy. Why some people could make presents look so neat and tidy and yet his presents always looked crap. How hard could it be?!

Just thinking these things drove him crazy.

And his thoughts drove him crazy. How could he stop his crazy mind driving him crazy?

Hong Kong >

Carnegie was driving himself crazy in Hong Kong. His wound on his forehead itched away and he clawed at it like a possessed man. No matter how much booze or painkillers he consumed, the damn thing sat their itchy and throbbing like a porn star's appendage after a dose of the clap and a three-day furlough.

He decided to do something crazy and get sober and quit the cigarettes. But after 24 hours he was starting to go crazy, so he booked himself into the front row at the local pub and knocked off three tequilas to take the edge off.

He pursued a flirtatious game with the barmaid, but she didn't have magic eyes or a welcoming smile. Only an outrageous wink that could possess a man's soul and shove it into a dark place in a dank closet.

He settled on a stool and watched sadly as his favourite football team took a spanking from a clearly better outfit. He was morose and swore quietly at his Carlsberg beer, which was sitting humbly in front of him on a soaking beer coaster.

He had nothing.

No morals. No Waitress with the Kind Eyes. No buzz. No family. No activities. No God. No purpose.

He was empty and sad but couldn't cry; and no matter how much he drank he couldn't be filled. His hands began to shake, so he lit a Marlboro and sucked away sadly – watching the passers-by wander on their journey home or wherever they were going.

Carnegie wished he was going somewhere but he couldn't find a reason to leave his bar stool. A shy tourist borrowed his lighter while a street dog shat in the gutter and looked away, interested in the next amusement and not even noticing his own defecation.

It amused Carnegie how innocent animals were about their own basic acts and why humans struggled so much. He remembered two monkeys in Bali humping away in the middle of the street. The furry little pink face sat watching the street walkers pass by with innocent eyes as he pumped away on his willing companion. It was funny to watch but, at the same time, reminded Carnegie how humans were so caught up with their own sense of morality and taboos. Perhaps the Bloodhound Gang were correct when they sang about doing it like they do it on the Discovery Channel.

< Sydney

Carnegie cast the deciding vote in the boardroom and the acquisition was approved. A neat 3 million dollars spent and straight out of the capital fund. Carnegie still couldn't grasp the concept of having over 100 million dollars available to do whatever the hell he pleased with as long as it made business sense!

It wasn't always like that. He didn't like to go down memory lane. There were too many dead bodies, rusting relics and ghosts that haunted him. But on occasion he would let his mind slip back to when he was a struggling entrepreneur with no money and enough expenses and demands that demanded an immediate heart attack and/or a mental breakdown.

Carnegie remembered one particular day when his enterprise was failing to many causes including:

The GFC, commonly known as the The Global Fucking Crisis.

Staff exhaustion.

Defaulting clients.

Dishonourable strategic partners.

Defeat was on the horizon. And what had he done to deserve it? Hard work. Hard work. Hard work. Striving always. He was not perfect, and he knew it, but he never made the same mistake again. Just mistakes in different ways. And each one was a lesson. An upgrade to the mind that ran 24/7.

And for what. To what end. For it all to unravel in a few months with no control over his destiny. What the hell? How was this the entrepreneur's game? Entrepreneurs were meant to be creative, invincible, rising above, finding new ways.

He could taste the dryness in his mouth. Each day was a new day of defeat. The dawn of defeat every morning followed by the nightmare that was each night staring at the ceiling. Lying next to the Good Wife who trusted him, loved him, cared for him and believed in him. He couldn't even tell her that demise was driving to their house and getting closer each hour.

And then the day of defeat came. It was a Saturday and Carnegie was in the office early. Bright and early. But not feeling so bright.

His computer sat there waiting to be switched on. Waiting for instructions to compute but all Carnegie could do was watch the car crash happening that was his pride and joy and his hard work.

He stared at the computer screen and no matter how many spreadsheets he did or how many times he went through the finances, it all said the same thing.

Doom.

There is nothing more frightening than when the most optimistic scenario doesn't meet the obligations owing. Carnegie had poured over the machine and then he had lost it. His heart was pumping, and his chest hurt. Was seven years of hard work going to end up here? Failure.

He had made himself a strong cup of coffee and proceeded to walk the corridors of the office; muttering under his breath and thinking through every possible scenario. Nothing came to him. One did not stretch into two. Four didn't somehow expand into ten. And so, the real spectre of failure sat on top of him cackling away like a drunk kookaburra.

It was a warm Saturday afternoon and he sat glumly on the pale threaded carpet that was less than two years old. He thought of all his friends who would have been out the previous night having fun and eating copious amounts of gourmet food washed down by European beers. They would be at the beach by now, viciously attacking their hangovers with greasy burgers and sick grins.

And yet he was here: facing the immediate shutdown of his enterprise and the trashing of seven years of hard work. Approximately two thousand days spent on this adventure. Ten percent of his life. He swallowed the bitter thought and flipped open his phone. Who could he call?

The phone didn't have any answers or miracle contacts. There was no Eddie McGuire asking him if he wanted to phone a friend. There was magical answer or call that came in that suddenly solved all of his problems and lifted him out of the pit of woe that clawed at his feet.

He sat down again at his laptop and sipped his now lukewarm coffee. Google flashed up on his browser. Maybe, just maybe, the internet had an answer. He typed in 'cashflow' and ended up on a dubious looking site looking at a dubious calculator. The numbers that spat back him were just compounding his woe while a topless Latin girl stared at him from the corner of the screen – tempting him to click once, just once, and enter a world of solo sexual self-satisfaction at just $9.99 per 15 minutes.

He sighed and closed the browser. The Latin girl offered him no real answers; nor would the damn internet. This was his frigging mess and he needed to find the frigging solution. Carnegie stood up and paced his room. This was his entire fault. He knew he was expanding his business at a risk but the opportunities all seemed great and he was terribly impatient.

He stared at his office door. It made sense to slam it, so he slammed it shut and locked it. There he was stuck in his office with his problems. It felt strangely uplifting. His shadow stared back at him from the back of the door as the afternoon sun crept through his office window behind him.

He grabbed a thick black marker and traced the shadow on the door. A shape that looked like a roadkill mark stared back at him ominously. Carnegie wrote in capitals on the shape's torso.

IF IT'S GOING TO BE, IT'S UP TO ME!

He felt enormously pleased with himself, so he sat cross-legged in front of the door and stared back at his handiwork. His mind spun for a while and suddenly the time blurred. He couldn't pull back from the odd form of meditation.

When he eventually snapped out of it, the sun had long disappeared, and he felt silly sitting there staring at the door. He realised he had not accomplished much.

Carnegie was hungry, so he decided to take a hike to get some form of nourishment. The Seven Eleven store was a stretch down the road, so he washed his face in the office kitchen sink and then took off. The warmed-up hot dog and can of Mother filled the hole in his stomach and gave him a quick burst of energy. The lovely Indian lady had not approved of his selection, but he was beyond caring about his health – especially when his brain was going to explode, and his reflux was out of control. Right now, eating well seemed about as important as collecting ant excrement.

He shuffled back to the office to fight once again. There had to be a way out.

The Dark Side

< Sydney

There is a dark side to entrepreneurship and the truest adventure of commerce. Perhaps this form of creation is more Sith than Jedi. Perhaps only Chaos can give birth to new ideas, as Order can only control and manage the ideas as they happen.

When an entrepreneur sets out on an adventure there is a level of excitement and the scent of hope in the air. But, like all adventures, there are dark chapters and most of them happen early on. The entrepreneur's spirit is destroyed, and our heroes are laid to death in the smoking ruin of debt, stress, disillusion and despair.

Carnegie knew the odds. He had failed before. Twice before. And the lesson was simply of one thing. Do not give up. Do not quit. Spend every second of every minute of every hour of every day of every week of every month of every year working and staying ahead of the burning bridge behind you.

The entrepreneurs' club is small but is filled with bike riders that are experts. Because, in business and in video games, if you don't keep running the bear gets you.

Behind the entrepreneur is the darkness of the four pale riders of the apocalypse. And they don't tire. Even when the entrepreneur is asleep, they whisper into his or her ear about their coming demise – frequently resulting in the recipient lying wide awake at 3 in the morning, listening to the anxiety engine that's consistently revving. Like a nightmarish cherry automobile waiting outside from a Stephen King novel.

Their partners, should they have them, sleep blissfully next to them or wake up confused and reaching out in gentle kindness, only to be hushed or rebutted by hard heads accepting the hands of hell on their hearts and determined to not lose the mind battle.

Then they lie back down, but no sleep comes. Just calculations about cashflow, debates about dealers, painful pondering over paperwork to be done, busy with thoughts of berating bankers and the fear of letting others down.

Such is the way of the entrepreneur.

Carnegie had failed twice before. But they were small failures and of his own making. His first business was successful from day one and, like the first-time lucky gambler, a laziness and naivety sets in. Well, good times last, right? So, you will find that the first-time punter sits back and revels at sticking to the boss; carving their own way through the wood and content to spend the evening hours socialising, sipping on spirits and smiling as they think of bountiful barns filling up in the future with the harvest from their clever commerce.

But of course, to his bitterness, Carnegie lived the good life and the first pale horseman caught him. Suddenly he couldn't afford to pay his tax. Then he realised he had to go and work. And then because he was working he couldn't run a business. And then the end came.

So, he licked the wounds and disappeared for a year into the world of study and corporations, slowly shredding his soul in a cubicle, forcing himself to study at night and then anxiously waiting for Friday to come along, so he could drink and dance and numb the pain of an existence fit for robots.

The next failure came along by, not the lack of work, but by the lack of wisdom as he went chasing after quick riches of the new world of the internet. But like a lot of entrepreneurs, he was before his time and was insufficiently capitalised to run the race to the end.

Instead, like a foolish marathon runner, who doesn't know the way, hasn't trained and hasn't stocked up on energy; he burst out of the gate only to shortly fall over. Bruised. Battered. Beaten. Broken.

This time, his ego shattered, he once again sojourned in the purgatory of corporate life with the only relief being the arrival of the Good Wife.

But Carnegie was not a quitter. And if the blood of the entrepreneur flows through your veins, like the moon calls the werewolf, and the blood calls the vampire; you heed the call of the adventure.

The siren sings clearly and loudly and the hairs on your arms go up as the music flows and forms and you cannot hide from it, nor resist it.

Each loving chord strikes.

And the entrepreneur listens.

They will wake up in the middle of the night as the music of the idea forms clearly. The pulse quick-ens. The blood flows. The skin shivers. The melody of the idea calls them. And in the middle of an organised and orderly life, chaos strikes a blow for life. The idea is formed.

The womb of the mind is impregnated with the seed of the idea.

And no matter what the entrepreneur does, the idea throbs. The idea kicks. The idea grows and on a glorious day, with the backdrop of the life being left behind, the entrepreneur registers that name, builds the website, opens the office, prints the cards, screams out loud and then hurtles straight off the cliff. Arms flapping wildly as they plummet.

You will fly. The siren sings.

The wings of your idea will carry you.

And so, Carnegie woke one fated night. It was the devil's hour. Past midnight when nothing good can come for the entrepreneur. He sat bolt upright. Something was there. Something? Yes something.

He slid out of his bed, careful not to wake his beautiful wife. And then he wrote.

He wrote and wrote. Scribbled jibberish. Diagrams across the paper. But the chords kept striking in his head. The words first. Then the numbers.

And then the business plan was formed, and Carnegie slumped in his creaking computer chair. He was very aware of the light coming in the office window. His mind buzzed. His friend between his legs ached and screamed and pushed higher than before. A metaphor for the birthing of the idea and the desire to release.

He had the urge to touch himself. To stroke his own ego hard enough that it spat at the world. Such was the pride and the passion of the entrepreneur.

The dark side. The desire to penetrate the womb of the world. To spring forth ideas that would change the environment and the world (for bad and good) and, in the meantime, give the entrepreneur the re-wards they seek, and the drugs that would rage through their body. Coursing. Sizzling.

Vanity of vanities.

Vexation of spirit, said the wise one.

Of course, argues back the entrepreneur.

We are the light of the world. We are the ones that give birth to change and progress. We are the ones that have the strength to harness Chaos and bring it into Order. Are we not Prometheus? The entrepreneurs' cry. *That brings fire. And harnesses for warmth in the cave. To cook the meat. To scare away the wolves. To cast light on the miracle babies.*

The dark side calls.

Vanity of vanities; vexation of spirit, repeats wise Solomon solemnly.

The entrepreneur refuses this argument.

All reasonable men and women are part of nature and adjust accordingly. Like sheep they lie quietly in the pastures not troubled nor worried; but content to be counted upon by nature and all of its forces and fray. But unreasonable men and women. The entrepreneurs. The goats. They do not.

So. The unreasonable is where progress comes from.

It's where the walls come from. The tools. The cart. The clothing. The cars. The computers.

Ah yes. Solomon nods, stroking his beard sagely.

And it is where the sword came from, the gun, the nuclear bombs, the pollution and social media.

Carnegie shook his head. These thoughts were troubling. But at least Solomon had removed his lust and replaced it with doubt. The dark side.

The dark side of entrepreneurism.

The Good Banker

Carnegie went to see the Good Banker. The Good Banker was known as the Good Banker because he was a Good Banker. He was a rare fellow with a stranger trait for a banker; empathy. The Good Banker was always hard to see and get an appointment with, because he had a large range of followers, fans and importantly clients. But because he was empathetic, and he was the Good Banker, he somehow always found time. Strangely enough, the Good Banker was also a Good Husband, a Good Friend and a Good Father.

As a result of all of this goodness, he was a Bad Sleeper. Somehow the lack of sleep didn't perturb him, and the Good Banker was always cheerful and upbeat finding solutions where even Einstein would struggle to find answers.

He loved to laugh and when his clients told him they were in a bad position and things were not going to work out – or when his colleagues told him a deal was impossible – he would love with those bright shiny teeth and say, 'Impossible. Is I'm Possible.' Or quote Martin Luther King.

This was a strange level of positivity for a Banker.

Carnegie sat in the hip Melbourne café and waited. He was early, having caught the early flight out of Sydney to Melbourne and survived yet another red eye flight.

Thankfully he had the art of flying early down pat. The combination turned out to be really simple, yet difficult to discover. Once Carnegie realised what it was he wrote it down neatly and carefully into his red notebook and memorised it. Even now he could close his eyes and see the list.

Check into the flight 24 hours beforehand
Pack all bags the night before
Lay out clothing
Set the alarm clock for exactly 3 hours sleep
Get up early and quietly
Go on auto pilot through the usual morning routine
Check list of items required
Drive to airport with an hour to spare
Check into airport lounge
Eat a light breakfast and read the paper
Respond to emails and update social status
Climb onto flight and fall asleep on take-off
Wake up (or be woken up) on descent
Drink 2 bottles of water

Carnegie smiled to himself. Life hacks.

He ordered a coffee and absentmindedly looked at his watch and phone. There was nothing there of course, but it was somehow a nervous tick that he developed. A sub-routine that occurred when he was by himself because he couldn't stand to be by himself. The phone clicked off and he looked around and wondered about all these Melbourne hipsters. It was a strange trend for Carnegie.

What was with all of the suspenders, short-sleeve checked shirt, 80s spectacles and short longs? Or were they long shorts?

They seemed to wander through life in a blatant manner, almost flipping the bird daily at modern society and trends. The beards were scraggly or trimmed. The hair slicked back in Brylcreem and the ladies just couldn't help carrying a 'fuck you' look on their faces.

Carnegie didn't get it.

Turns out he didn't get much and, if he had his time again, he would focus on communicating closer with computers. They acted far more rationally and logically. If only he could play the ball and not the man. But it was not the way.

'James!'

Carnegie's train of thought was interrupted.

The Good Banker had arrived.

He was a beautifully-skinned man, immaculately dressed and always energetic. Most people wouldn't have noticed, but the only thing that was even remotely out of place on the Good Banker was the dark rings around his eyes. A micro sign of the care and the worry he had for his clients or, as he would put it, his partners.

He was the only person who slept worse than Carnegie and seemed to appreciate the hours after midnight. Owl over Fowl but, in both their cases, they had become hybrid birds. Fowl and Owl or what they jokingly referred to as Foul Owls.

Carnegie smiled, the caffeine was working but, more importantly, the Good Banker was working.

'Hello, my dear friend,' Carnegie rose from the wooden polished bench. 'How are you?'

He gave the Good Banker a big bear hug – a common greeting that the two men shared with no hint of awkwardness.

Another thing they shared. Not the love of man, but man love.

The Good Banker pulled away and laughed. White teeth shining and dimples showing. 'Hope you haven't been waiting long, just had to make a few calls on the way.'

Carnegie smiled.

'Prepared to wait for a while for you mon ami,' he said with genuine feeling, really meaning it, unlike the pleasantries that are often shared at the beginning of these business meetings.

They sat down and ordered coffees. Carnegie was onto his third already, but it was just one of those things about travel; form goes out the window along with the routines of life.

'So ...' the Good Banker said, taking a sip from his double shot and stretching. 'What brings you down here to Melbourne? Surely whatever you want to talk about could have been done over the phone. It's unlike you Carnegie, to be so mysterious.'

'Haha,' Carnegie laughed. 'You're right. But I can tell you this type of shit has to be done face to face.'

Carnegie was right. When it came to life and death, it had to be done face to face. And he didn't want to unnerve the Good Banker by telling him the absolute dire straits his business was in.

It wasn't long after the GFC that Carnegie's business was hanging on by a thread. He had been forced to consolidate his business back to two offices and cut staff. This was the most depressing and cruel thing he had been forced into. Carnegie had no issue with terminating staff and team members when they had let the team down and performance was not right. However, he felt terrible sitting in front of people, that for no wrong of their own, were plunged into a dark pit of uncertainty; the hell of redundancy.

Carnegie's head knew it was right to cut off a leg to save a body.

But Carnegie's heart nearly stopped beating when he had to go through it for the first time.

He had been sacked for no reason before. And each time he had to do this to someone else, he lived their nightmare and his own nightmare, like a holiday repeat special of the Brady Bunch in a two-star motel in the middle of nowhere.

He drank. He smoked. He cried. He croaked.

Yet nothing but time could save him from the hell of putting an axe through people's lives. He was a serial killer in a different way. And he loathed himself.

And he couldn't share any of it. Especially with the Good Banker.

'What type of shit are we talking about?' asked the Good Banker enigmatically. 'The good shit or the bad shit?'

This was another important trait of the Good Banker. He had a way of adjusting his communications between client partners. Carnegie smiled when he said that – feeling that the Good Banker could have easily been at home in thongs and a tee shirt in outback Australia; or presenting a feasibility study on buying a throng of islands just off the coast of Latin America to the Queen.

'I would say a little bad and mostly good. But that is why I am here to see you.' Carnegie smiled.

'Ah well. Let's have it then. But first, how's things? How's business? The wife and kids?'

'The trouble and strife are well,' Carnegie lied. 'Business is good,' he lied again. 'And the kids are doing well.' Carnegie didn't lie, or at least he didn't think he did. The truth was he didn't really know.

'Good, good.' The Good Banker said smiling again.

'Thanks for meeting with me,' Carnegie said. 'I think there are some really good things we can do. I have some opportunities to discuss with you and the bank. I won't lie to you, it's been a tough, tough road over the last few months, but I'm guessing that you know that.' He gestured to the *Financial Review* sitting folded up next to him.

The Good Banker laughed. 'I know, I know. It's everywhere. Unless you are under a rock somewhere you will know that the economy and the business world is completely screwed.'

'Yup,' Carnegie grimaced. It was everywhere. 'The GFC is claiming scalps everywhere and who knows how long it is going to go on for. But there will be some winners, and I am determined we will be one of them. But we do know we need your help. And not the help of the last Banker you guys sent down to visit with us. You know the story of the rain, the umbrellas and banks. That meeting did not finish well.'

The Good Banker looked at Carnegie apologetically. 'Yes, you mentioned already and I'm sorry about that. I guess banking procedures are procedures that some of our colleagues follow almost too literally.' He shrugged and looked away for a second. 'Not my way of doing it, of course, but you have to understand we are really averse to risk right now.'

Carnegie smiled. 'I get it. Just difficult to digest when some random turns up all of a sudden and demands you open your books and then reduce your debt levels when you are already sustaining month after month losses.' He drank more coffee and continued. 'I really can't help the fact that my clients are closing down and there is nothing but cold hard negativity in the air.'

'Yes, it is tough on everyone right now,' the Good Banker said with feeling. 'I don't even know what is going to happen tomorrow or even if I will have a job. The bank is shutting down all sorts of lending and avenues for our traditional clients and it makes it even worse when I know we should be keeping the doors open for folks that are battling everywhere.'

'I know. But to my point there is winnings to be had right now. The pie is shrinking, and competition is going with it, but some of us can get a bigger slice if we have the courage and the support to stay positive and go after it.' Carnegie said from his heart, 'We've just got to do it.' He subconsciously clenched his fist under the table while gesturing with his right hand in the air.

'Where there is a will, there is a way,' the Good Banker said and smiled.

And that summed him up perfectly. The Good Banker believed. The Good Banker hoped. The Good Banker supported. His philosophy was in line with his good nature, diligence and his strong positive view on life.

After all, as Carnegie would find out later, the Good Banker's story was all about hope, belief, support and a will to find a way.

He was born on a small island in Fiji. It was so small that there was no English name for the island. But it could have been translated to 'The island in the middle of nowhere'. His family survived through sheer grit and the birth of their six weeks premature baby. When all had given up on his entry into this life, his parents had not.

They laboured heavily to keep him alive and keep him sustained until one day, the little tacker, like in life, had a burst of life and the grim reaper decided to look for other souls to collect.

From that time onwards, he and his family went on a journey. The journey was rough and horrible on all scales, but it led them to Australia. Where there was a will, there was a way. And the emblem of this family was a little life that refused to give up, even in the direst of circumstances. He was their good luck charm and the heartbeat of their family.

Despite racism, setbacks, lack of resources, they fought on and sort out a new life for their little son who had proven himself time and time again. That infectious smile that brought hope today to so many strugglers, brought hope to his parents.

Away from their heritage, they found a place in Melbourne and made it their own. And. like a good son, the Good Banker never complained at the frequent challenges, but worked hard through his education and then his career. Where there was a will, there was a way.

Carnegie was inspired.

Not at the story. Because, at that moment, he didn't know it nor the detail. But the Good Banker said it with absolute conviction. He believed it and embodied it and it was infectious.

'Are you sure you should be working for a bank?' Carnegie said, smiling his own broad smile with the heart just beating a little faster.

The Good Banker just laughed. 'It's not that bad. There is a place for all of us and a reason for the banks. They just sometimes don't handle things well and certainly don't always find themselves in a pleasant spotlight. And, let's be honest, it's always easy to bash banks.'

The Good Banker was loyal.

'I agree with you,' said Carnegie, remembering his own short time working with a financial institution. 'Most people don't see their side of the story. Let's face it, this sort of disastrous event was going to happen anyway and, to be fair, it's not like all banks and all bank employees are doing the dirty. They aren't all Gordon Geckos.'

'I'm glad you are philosophical about it James,' said the Good Banker. 'Now what have you got on your mind?'

Carnegie nodded. It was time to get down to business. He reached into his satchel and pulled out his laptop. It booted up after a while and he unveiled his plans to the Good Banker. It was challenging, it was close, it was not easy, it would be rough. But the plans made sense.

Carnegie finished twenty-five minutes later with a flourish. He was unaware of the layer of perspiration that had built up under his checked shirt. But it hit him now. This was critical. This was a pivotal moment. Without the Good Banker's support and being able to make it happen, it was likely over. Without an extension on their facilities and a line of credit, he was unable to keep the doors open. There was too much bad debt from customers unable to pay and Carnegie had exhausted all of his options from his accounts and a few friends and family members that he was willing to go to and ask for help.

For a moment there was silence.

The silence was almost violence for Carnegie. In his positive, challenge accepting, never say die mindset, he never thought he would end up here. A place of crossroads. The last roll of the dice. The last hand to play, against superior immovable forces, where the cards were stacked against his.

It seemed like an eternity.

But then the Good Banker smiled.

'I like it,' he said. 'I like it a lot. And I believe I can make it happen.'

Carnegie held his breath and then slowly let it out. His hands were shaking. The enormity of the situation was pounding his head like a sledge hammer on hard rock.

He believed. He could make it happen. The Good Banker was behind him.

Carnegie smiled, 'Thank you so much. I'm sure there are lots of questions and comments on this plan. I'm absolutely happy to share any details you want.' He rambled on for a bit more, trying to buy himself some time to calm down.

'It's okay,' the Good Banker reassured him. 'Send me what you have, and I'll work on it. If anything comes up I will be in touch immediately.'

'Thank you again,' Carnegie said, feeling slightly embarrassed at his reaction. 'I really appreciate it.'

And he did. From that time on he realised a number of things. The impact was so heavy on his mind he immediately sat down after the meeting in a shaded park and wrote them down in his red notebook.

Where there is a Will, there is a Way
Nobody is Self-Made

You cannot Control Most Things
Life can change on the Spin of a Dime

Carnegie smoked heavily when writing this down. His nerves were stretched thin and he was euphoric to the point of wanting to yell out and stick his head in the waters of a well-sculptured fountain that sat across him in the park. Belief, from another, is belief beyond belief.

And so, the Good Banker delivered. Delivered in spades. Delivered beyond reasonable expectations.

What Carnegie had hoped for as a result in raising finance that would help them survive, the Good Banker doubled down. It was hard to fathom. There was a bank that delivered umbrellas when it was raining! Carnegie could scarcely believe his luck.

It wasn't going to be easy and Carnegie knew it was an uphill battle, but this changed everything. Suddenly he had a lifeline. The Good Banker had faith – a rarity for a financier.

His vibe attracted a tribe and though few, the tribe was there if you had the courage to go and look. And the Good Banker was part of that tribe.

It took months for the Good Banker to deliver. And just when Carnegie was on his last few cents and his heart in his mouth, the Good Banker rang.

'It's done. You will receive finance as soon as you sign the paperwork.'

More euphoria.

Carnegie had cried that day. He wept in his office quietly. And then quickly disappeared to the nearby park and wept a whole lot more. When there were no tears to cry he went to his office, washed his face, sent some important emails to reassure some critical stakeholders and then immediately went home to collapse.

And finally sleep. And sleep he did. A whole twelve hours. A rarity for Carnegie. There were no demons or disasters invading his dreams. He simply just slept. And for the first time he kissed his wife goodbye without any shakes, took his children to school and let the mask dissolve.

And boy did the mask come off. And the smiles were real.

And Carnegie never stopped thanking the Good Banker.

From that time on, the business never looked back. It kept climbing and climbing. But somehow and somewhere along that steep climb, something in Carnegie was lost.

Like all soldiers of war. When the war turns and peace looms. A small part of the animal that was made for violence clings on. Eating and eroding away. Finding chaos. Seeking highs. Chasing risks.

Entrepreneurs. Escape artists. Soldiers of Fortune.

Conspiracy Theories

Hong Kong >

Carnegie finished a long chat with Heyloon and felt exhausted. Heyloon was his usual professional self and Carnegie was a shadow of the person that was the successful business man. He was in complete meltdown; throwing money away and abusing himself in every possible fashion he was capable of. It was not long after the scotch glass and sleeping pill incident that he found himself mournfully talking to Heyloon about Kennedy. It made him feel ten times worse and unfortunately, he could neither talk to the Waitress with the Kind Eyes nor the shrink who spoke in gentle tones. He was stuck in Hong Kong by himself with a horde of blank and uncaring faces.

Heyloon had told him he missed him and asked if he was ready to return, as apparently everyone was missing him. Carnegie was highly sceptical about this. After all, his companies were running well without him and he doubted his friends required another schmuck to drink with and talk nonsense to. And he doubted his wife and kids very much missed him. They were better off without his glum self-moping about the house and pretending to be interested in what the school was doing and when soccer practice was on.

He walked to the balcony and thought about his friend Kennedy. Kennedy and the Conspiracy Theories. It sounded like a bad 80s soft rock band. The amusing thought brought no relief.

< Sydney

No one knew it was coming. They were horrified when they heard the news. The network of friends and colleagues were stunned. Carnegie wept with guilt and despair. Why hadn't he done something about it? Why didn't he fucking know about it!

Kennedy was fond of the herb. And that was being mild about it. The truth was Kennedy was a pot hound. No one thought anything about it except for commenting on a regular basis to Kennedy to get off the marijuana.

Heyloon told him in his professional clipped tone, 'You might want to lower the dosage friend.'

Bruce said chuckling, 'Fuck me! You are like an epic chimney, Kennedy. Get off the gas!'

DJ: 'Your memory will go mate. Don't lose it; you may want to use it.'

Cassandra would hug Kennedy, tell him about the art of Zen and get on his back to dump the drugs and find inner peace.

The Pharmacist would also tut tut Kennedy and remind him that the herb was not a legal form of medicine and he had to read the label for side effects.

But for Kennedy, he wasn't interested in side effects. He wanted affects. He wanted to lose the anxiety that encompassed him and constantly grabbed at his throat, causing him to suffocate.

He told everyone to go and get jagged and he continued to suck down the calming smoke. It made him think clearer and get on with the job of surviving life.

'They are everywhere James,' he would whisper to Carnegie, his pale blue eyes wandering from side to side on constant alert.

'Who is everywhere?' Carnegie was aware of this game. The 'everywhere game' he would call it.

'You know. I've tried to tell you so many times before.' For a moment Kennedy looked desperate.

'The inter-governmental agencies. They are everywhere. They are probably watching us right now!' He looked sideways again and rubbed his eyes for a moment; shadowing over the top of his tiredness.

'Oh, those guys. Why the hell would they be interested in us?' Carnegie couldn't work out why some secretive intelligence agency group combined with other international groups would give two flying fucks about him and the group.

'Oh, believe me they are interested. Especially when we are together!' Kennedy looked at Carnegie with his sad dog eyes and reached out to pat him on the arm in a loving and patronisingly way. 'You see, we are a danger to them and their weapons of mass propaganda.'

Carnegie laughed. 'How are we a danger to them?' He couldn't see the combined forces of Carnegie, Kennedy et al being a danger to anyone. It was laughable.

'Because of here.' Kennedy tapped his forehead. 'We think. We read through the lines. We spot the fake. We translate the miscommunication and notice the lies on a daily basis. And I can prove it.'

Carnegie was a little surprised. This was the first time Kennedy was worked up enough to make an emphatic statement. 'What's your proof? What are we talking about? Roswell? JFK? The moon landing? What can you prove?'

'See. All of those so-called conspiracy theories are just plants to steer away from what is really going on. Money. Sex. Power. This is what lies at the heart of it all.'

He continued looking deadly serious while he fiddled with his phone. 'Social media is just there to control and herd the masses. They are all interested, and they want us to be locked down. Don't be surprised if you find yourself locked in a mental institution someday. That's what they do to thinkers like us. The lock us away and declare us madmen. It's simple and effective. The patriarch demigods are in control and they won't be shifted from their marble pedestals.'

'Here's my proof. If you have all the money, sex and power in the world, why would you give it up? What dictator has gone willingly and abdicated? Why do only a few people in Russia control the entire nation and its wealth? Because dictators rise up and grasp the power and then solidify it and take out all that oppose them.'

Carnegie had to admit, if nothing else, it was stimulating.

Kennedy looked incredibly sad. 'There are a few dynasties in the US that control power through all forms of government and organisations. And their power of misdirection is incredible. 9-11. Simply a gateway to war in the middle east to consolidate power and to take eyes away from a seemingly great country, rotting at its core. And our dissent and unwillingness to suck on their propaganda gas makes us most wanted.'

'This small group of dictators control our media and thus our mind space and thought processes. You can read all about it on the internet. They pump us full of fear of catastrophe that we turn to the thing we should be fearing the most. Hitler did it by burning down the Reichstag. Instead of destroying the devil in their midst, they saluted him and lay their heads on his feet – saluting the golden hero that would make all well. Think James, think!'

Carnegie was starting to get lost. The US. Hitler. Media. It somehow connected in Kennedy's mind, but he wasn't sure he was following. 'So, we are all sheep being led on a wild goose chase. I think I have seen that movie.' He didn't know if Kennedy, in his state, would detect the sarcasm. He sipped on his coke.

'Oh, we are sheep. But we don't have to be. Throw out the Murdoch controlled press. Burn down Fairfax. Make your own decisions and decipher what is being said. The government says war on terror. Point away. Classic misdirection! The governments talked about ending poverty, but more than the fair share of aid ends up in the hands of their cronies and puppet governments. The government talks about health, education and other such standard diets for our fellow citizens and yet it doesn't want us educated or healthy. We are here to maintain our routines and pay taxes, so a small group of demigods can remain in power, generate wealth and fuck all night long to Barry White, Bryan Adams or Lady Gaga.'

'Hollywood and the music industry are the greatest tools of propaganda, along with menacing religion that builds all the time to generate fear and self-loathing. Why? So we can turn to the very thing we should be turning away from. Do you really thing that God gives a rat's ass about the size of statues or buildings? Does God even know we exist?'

Carnegie couldn't think of an answer, so he sat and listened.

'James, it is like this. You are either taking the swill on or not. If you are not, then they are out to get you. Phone calls are recorded. Databases trawl the internet and social media, collecting data and building an optimised pattern to keep you docile and drugged up on day to day life. Hollywood pounds you full of mythology and goodwill to keep you enchanted and rooted in this life we call life. It's more like a slow death.'

'And so free thinkers and the awakened on this Earth are constantly assassinated, discredited or committed to asylums to avoid the truth getting out there and opening people's eyes. From the moment people wake up to the moment they sleep, their lives are packed so full of influence and the sense of activity that no one thinks anything through. The alarm goes off and then the radio and then the family, phone and so forth, so people's lives are so damn busy that they can't see the few almighty men that sit at the top of tree crapping on everyone below them.'

Carnegie considered the case before him and came up with the only logical response. 'Are you sure you aren't just being paranoid?'

Kennedy laughed bitterly and turned away. 'You too James? I thought better of you.'

He turned around abruptly in fury. 'Were those predicting the Global Financial Crisis paranoid? Was Julian Assange paranoid? Maybe if a few more people in this world were 'paranoid' as you put it, the world would be a better and more honest place! Perhaps Martin Luther King should have been paranoid? What about Harold Holt? Maybe if he had a healthy fear of being disappeared? No one really thinks he just walked into the ocean and drowned!'

Carnegie was stunned at the level of angst and anger in Kennedy. He wondered what he could say to his stirred-up friend and he secretly worried for his sanity. He just patted him on the back in the end, because he felt totally adequate. The Shrink with Gentle Tones would have been handy in this situation, but Carnegie hadn't yet made his acquaintance.

Kennedy, unsurprisingly, wasn't comforted by Carnegie's limp gesture of camaraderie.

He stood up abruptly and wiped at his face. He briefly looked at Carnegie with a despairing look of disappointment. Kennedy left his drink and slowly, sadly walked out on Carnegie.

Carnegie felt a gripping sadness and loneliness that crept into his heart. Had he inadvertently betrayed his friend? What should have he said or done differently?

After moments of contemplation, Carnegie jumped up and rushed out of the townhouse they had been gathering at. He burst out the front door, but Kennedy was nowhere to be seen.

'Kennedy!' Carnegie called out.

He jumped off the porch and nearly went flying on the slippery wet lawn.

'Shit,' he cursed. He ran to the front street and stood under the glow of the street light.

'Kennedy!' Carnegie called out again and spun around, hoping to see his friend shuffling away in the darkness. But Kennedy was nowhere to be seen.

Perhaps he had gone out the back. Carnegie ran back into the house and to the backyard. Heyloon, Bruce and the Pharmacist sat out the back around a dirty wooden table playing Texas Hold Em poker. The smoke from two cigars billowed out, irritating the mosquitoes who were hoping for some easy pickings – even if the supper was tainted by blue label scotch.

'You guys seen Kennedy?'

Heyloon looked up from his cards and passed the growing stack of his chips. 'He hasn't come out here James. What's up?'

Bruce made a comment under his breath about stoners and turned back to his poker mathematics.

'He left quickly and looked upset!'

Bruce made another comment and looked irritable. Clearly, he was not on the right side of the ledger.

The Pharmacist waved away the smoke billowing out of the chunky glass ashtray and put down his cards. 'Fold! I will go look for him with Carnegie.'

'Wait up. You can't leave the game now,' Bruce protested.

'I'll be back and then you can try and win a few hands.' The Pharmacist chuckled. It was an odd, guttural noise.

'Come on Carnegie.' The Pharmacist pushed Carnegie back through the door.

They spent the next hour combing the streets in the Pharmacist's sensible, classic Volvo – but to no avail. Their text messages and calls went unanswered, until Carnegie heard his phone vibrate through the thick denim of his designer jeans.

He dug it out anxiously. The message was from Kennedy.

'I'M HOME. AND ALONE. AND WANT TO STAY THAT WAY!'

Carnegie was relieved that his friend was ok, but he was a bit put off by the harsh message. As he woke up the next day, he was still trying to figure out what he had said wrong; and what he could say to make things right.

Hong Kong >

Carnegie sighed. Why the fuck didn't he do something!? Why couldn't he see what the hell was going on? He looked around the bar he was drinking at irritably. His head hurt like a bitch. The alcohol had no effect and all he could think about was the Waitress with Kind Eyes and his family. And how damn guilty he felt when it came to his beautiful wife and kids. What made him run from his so-called fabulous life? Why couldn't he be content with the lot he had been served with? Why had he lost his faith? Why had he lost his drive?

Why had he lost his friend?

< Sydney

Four weeks after the conspiracy episode, Carnegie stood at the door of Kennedy's apartment. A nasty stain stood below him that looked eerily like blood or red wine or both. Kennedy lived in a run-down block of flats in western Sydney. The stairwell had an awfully strong smell of stale madras curry and below, he could hear a couple arguing – trying in vain to hide their fighting with the TV on full bore.

Knock. Knock. Knock.

Carnegie was excited. He had the perfect remedy for Kennedy's malaise. A boys' trip to the Gold Coast. It was a ripper of an idea and Carnegie had put it together – dragging all the lads along, with Cassandra coming as well; just to add a female touch and kick the guys into shape. Kennedy would be able to get some sun and take his mind off solving whatever problems he thought the world had.

Knock. Knock. Knock.

'Kennedy! Hello!' Carnegie tried to stare through the peephole and realised how foolish it looked.

Knock. Knock. Knock.

Carnegie swore and fumbled for his phone. He dialled, but got Kennedy's voicemail.

'Thank you for calling. You have this number because you are a confidante. Leave no detail. Just say your name and your number. I may call back.'

Carnegie left his message and then immediately dialled Kennedy again. Same result. So he texted Kennedy. He thought he heard a phone beep inside Kennedy's flat, but he dismissed the thought as imagination.

Frustrated, Carnegie turned to leave. Bloody Kennedy!

He was halfway down the stairs when he heard the apartment door creak open. He turned around and Kennedy's pale face was peering through a slight opening in the doorway. Carnegie was shocked. Kennedy's eyes were encircled with terribly dark rings. He looked like he hadn't slept in days and a reddish-brown beard had sprouted from his hollow face like an old rug that nobody had bothered to throw out.

'James,' Kennedy croaked.

'Kennedy.' Carnegie leaped up the stairs, three at a time, and gave his friend a forceful hug. 'What's happening to you man?' He stared at his mate.

Kennedy stared back with a blank look and then slowly motioned him into the lounge. The place looked like a bomb had gone off. Junk food wrappings lay on the dirty vanilla carpet. Two bottles of bourbon lay empty on the coffee table along with a stained bong. The flat screen beamed out images of Asian lesbian vampire porn that Carnegie desperately didn't want to look at but couldn't help staring as a long-fanged woman licked the length of a stiletto shoe.

'What the fuck, Kennedy?'

Kennedy mumbled a reply and sank into a bean bag. He fumbled with the remote and finally shut off the show that was playing.

Carnegie perched on the arm of the leather couch carefully, making sure he didn't get too close to the debris that lay on the couch. The place smelt like booze, pot and semen.

'What's happening mate?' Carnegie asked him.

'Just life. Just life.' Kennedy shrugged and rubbed his eyes.

'You want a drink?' he asked apathetically.

'Ah no,' Carnegie replied, still trying to adjust to the once immaculate apartment that was now resembling an urban rubbish dump. 'You need some fresh air, mate. Let's get out of here.'

Kennedy looked off into the distance vaguely and sniffed. 'Nah, all good.'

'Well at least let's go and get some food. My shout.' Carnegie hoped to entice his friend out of the place.

'Well we can order delivery. What do you want? Pizza?' Kennedy looked remotely interested for a section and then slumped when he didn't see an equal interest from Carnegie.

'What about Thai? You love green curry, right?' Carnegie did his best sell.

Kennedy sat there slumped and tacitly agreed to go for some Thai. He changed out of his dirty Lee jeans and crumpled Nirvana shirt as Carnegie cleaned up and let in some sunlight and fresh air.

Later, they sat over some delicious Thai fare and Carnegie saw his friend's mood visibly lift. They were sitting in the dark auspices of a restaurant named Thai

Me Up. It was a cheeky chic inner Sydney restaurant with terrible service but extremely tasty food. The waitresses buzzed around seemingly ignoring everyone's pointed looks with emotionless faces. Carnegie had often wondered what they were thinking as they motored about wearing their blank masks.

Did they think about getting off their shifts and eating alternate foods?

Were they worried about their families wherever they were?

Perhaps they were thinking about some enormously difficult mathematical challenge?

Did they ponder the meaning of life as they carried servings of Pad Thai and Cashew Chicken?

Did they wonder if their boyfriends were at home masturbating to blonde cheerleaders?

Or perhaps they were thinking about the next bag they were going to purchase?

'What do you think they think about with their stony faces and dextrous movements?' Carnegie asked Kennedy, secretly wondering what he was thinking about.

Kennedy shrugged and sloshed his Iced Tea around in its glass. 'Maybe they don't think at all. Maybe they are just the lucky ones that the mind shuts down when surrounded by menial tasks.' He took a sip of his Iced Tea and sighed.

'What do you think about Kennedy?' Carnegie asked.

'I try not to James. I try not to. But when I do, I think about angels and demons. Saints and sinners. Heroes and villains.' Kennedy narrowed his eyes enigmatically.

Carnegie started to reply but got interrupted by a petite Thai girl with a cute bob haircut. 'You like to order?' she asked in a bored fashion.

They put in their order and she scribbled something down, with disdain, in a fading notebook.

Carnegie smiled and thanked her.

'They do that on purpose Carnegie.' Kennedy said with a conspirator's hushed tone.

'What do you mean?'

'They like to treat you mean to keep you keen. It's an age-old tactic. You desperately want to come back again and hope that one day they will smile at you and be nice to you and you just might fall in love.' Kennedy smiled sadly.

'What? You mean they give you crap service, so you keep coming back? Perhaps the food is that good they just don't give a damn. You will keep coming back for the spices and that perfect laksa.'

'Hahaha. Don't be so naïve. You think we go to places just for the food? Westerners go for the experience. And being treated with disdain is the perfect way to guarantee follow up.'

Carnegie was confused. Wasn't good service a reason to go back?

Kennedy stared his dark eyes back at Carnegie. 'You know, and I know, that if a woman you really like treats you like shit you just want to keeping trying until you break through. Right? Well this is no different. Secretly in all of us there is a desire to be loved, admired, desired, cared for; especially by the opposite sex who, like good mothers, take care of their children and nurse them until they are asleep on their bosoms.'

'What do you do every night? Whether it is working, drinking, fucking, gambling, playing, writing or whatever you do, you always curl up next to your wife and go off to sleep gently and peacefully. When you don't get that, you long for it. When we don't get that nurturing female care, especially when it comes to the caveman instinct of being provided for and fed, we long for it terribly and keep coming back for more.'

Carnegie shook his head. He was keeping up with this classic Kennedy ramble.

He decided to change topics. 'Kennedy, I want you to come with us on a boys' trip. It's about time the gang got back together and had a few days out. We are going to the Gold Coast for some sun and fun. Interested?'

Kennedy snapped a prawn cracker in two and bit into the half in his left hand. 'Can't afford it. Besides, I am not one for the sun,' he said poetically through a mouthful of prawn cracker.

Carnegie chewed on his own prawn cracker for a while and said, 'I will pay for you mate. Don't sweat it and you know we will be mostly sleeping through the day.' He laughed.

Kennedy half smiled. 'Nah it's all good. You go with the boys and have fun.' He suddenly looked very sad and alone.

'You are coming. And that's final.' Carnegie patted his friend on the arm before grabbing it. 'I won't take no for an answer.'

Kennedy groaned. 'I hate it when you do that.'

'So, you will come?' Carnegie smiled a devilish smile.

'I'll think about it.'

'Don't think about it; just come. Or we can't go. It won't be the same without ole Kennedy.'

'Who is going?'

'The gang. Bruce. Heyloon. The Pharmacist. Agro. Cassandra. You. Me.'

'Cassandra is going?' Kennedy looked interested.

'Yes, of course. Wait. You don't ...' Carnegie began to grin.

'No. No. No. It's just that she talks to me and seems to know what I am talking about.' Kennedy blushed under his unkempt beard.

'Come on. Cassandra is hot. She is single. She is magic. Have a crack mate.'

Kennedy looked horrified. 'No way. I couldn't.' He looked nervous and twitched.

'Come on mate. It's okay. You're a bloke. And she is a girl. Just be natural and talk to her.'

Carnegie began to understand the malaise Kennedy had sunk into. It was always the drug that brought you the lowest. The drug called love.

< Sydney

Carnegie scowled when he recalled the Thai restaurant. Love. He had learned to hate it. It burned up lives and spat them out continually. It was the most powerful poison. It all started with a smile. A look. A way of walking. The movement on a dancefloor. The accent. The tone. Stage one of love was a hideous thing. It invaded your mind. It invaded your thoughts. He remembered the Waitress with the Kind Eyes. The kind smiles. That one look. The Spanish music in the background. The light. And ultimately, the depression.

He remembered his wife. The first time he had met her. She was a delightful creature full of energy and zest. And not available. Carnegie hated that. He hated the way she invaded his mind while he was relentless pursuing his career. He hated how she had walked past him and turned and smiled at him.

And then, one night when he was plotting his next move to get her out to dinner and talk to her, she had bounced up to him and asked him out. He had acted like a silly school boy and stammered out a response while trying to be cool.

Love. Poison. Drugs.

He had been infatuated and the day of the date he had tried on several outfits and done his hair multiple times. He had wondered about cologne and what he was going to talk about. Where should he take her? What was she interested in?

He had cursed himself for behaving like a moron. After all, she was just another woman. But that smile. Goddammit that smile. The way she moved. The way she held herself when all others seemed so mundane. The way they had spent hours over wine and Italian food. The stories she told and the precious laughter that made Carnegie feel like he was the only man in the world.

Love the drug.

And he was high on drugs. He had bounced around and behaved stupidly; sending text messages during meetings and turning up late to presentations. He spent the early hours of the night chatting to her online and then waking early to pick her up, so she could ride with him to the office. He was tired. Drugged. Exhausted. High.

The sex came soon after and Carnegie felt a strange sensation. He did not want to fulfil all the lusts of the flesh. He wanted to make love to her. Passionately. Softly. Lovingly. He massaged her back and her shoulders. Then her feet, her legs; working like a demon and a possessed servant. He wanted to die next to her. Life couldn't be any better.

Love. Poison!

Then, inevitably, the drug took its course through marriage, honeymoon, kids, houses, super funds, wills. And, suddenly, one day, the drug wore off. No matter how Carnegie chose to pursue the drug, he couldn't get the high again. Sex had no pay off. Expensive holidays and renovations brought nothing. Sure, he loved his wife and his kids but he missed the high. It was a desperate feeling.

And then the drug struck him again; but it wasn't with his wife. It was another girl. And when he discreetly went about injecting himself, snorting down, smoking in the love; he realised that it was headed to the same place. Sober. Bored. Desperately seeking another high.

So, Carnegie quickly untangled himself from his affair and penitently bowed at his wife's feet – doing everything he could to wash away the guilt and the sin he felt while suffering from the dreaded hangover from the horrible all-consuming chemical imbalance.

Love. Drugs. Highs. Lows.

< Gold Coast

The merry band of men climbed into the coach – adrenalin pumping through their veins. They chatted merrily, recalling drunken tales, sexual conquests and sporting memoirs. They lounged in their padded seats on the bus and generally annoyed their fellow passengers who were on their way to more sensible pursuits of rest and relaxation, business and endeavours. But they didn't notice their surroundings. They were caught up in escapism, hope and excitement of the days and especially the nights to come.

Carnegie sat through the whole trip from the airport to the hotel feeling very pleased with himself. He had arranged an event and brought along his chums for a weekend of adventure and vice with no thought for the past or the future. He looked around at his mates.

Cassandra was stirring up Agro, who was responding largely with curse words and waving his hands about excitedly.

The Pharmacist was deep in conversation with Kennedy over some abstract story about pharmaceutical companies and their practices in Africa. Kennedy was earnestly responding while taking sidelong glances at Cassandra.

Bruce and Heyloon were staring at a video game running on DJ's phone and laughing while DJ desperately tried to improve his score as the phone bleated out sounds to match his button smashing.

The gang was in town and boy was it going to be fun.

Shortly after they checked into the penthouse they had rented on the 80th floor, they sprawled out in the living room; admiring the view and sucking down Corona's. DJ's setup was being put together and they were dead keen on some beats to match their thirst.

In the meantime, the gigantic flat screen TV pumped out tunes with Lady Gaga singing about a bad romance. DJ looked irritated as his continued his setup and Carnegie knew his thoughts about commercial music; but decided against another debate on the music market and what it meant to be a true muso and artist.

'Carnegie.'

He turned around to see Cassandra smiling at him with a bowl full of freshly chopped up lime.

'Care for some lime?' she said, offering him the supplement to all good Coronas.

'Sure.' He took a piece and jammed in the mouth of his bottle before taking an awesome swig to match Cassandra's. They chinked glasses and winked before cheering each other.

The air was cool and filled with the noise of music and chatter. Shortly after, DJ was pounding out some trance tunes that echoed off the floorings, walls and ceiling. Carnegie wondered how long before a phone call or a knock on the door came. Party poopers were always not too far away; lurking around the corner with self-mandated fun fascism as their mantra.

They steadily got inebriated before decided to run for some food on the Friday afternoon. An intense argument ensued before hunger eventually won out and the closest restaurant was filled with their laughter and consumption of red wine. The proprietor was a jolly fellow with a fondness of hubris and Sambuca.

He wandered between tables speaking a mixture of Italian and English while gesturing madly at the staff. He was a justification for stereotypes in all sense of the word with his zany behaviour and ability to snap into a docile state as soon as his plump wife bustled out of the kitchen and poked him in the chest.

They ate well and entered into the next stage of drunkenness – cheering each other and laughing at life in general. There was a sense of innocence mixed into the wine and pasta. A carefree aura that belonged to teenagers and those with the richness of life ahead of them.

They were soon back at the apartment and swearing friendship for life. The cigar smoke mixed with their wishes and desires and dreams of greater things.

Agro sidled up to Carnegie, who was sipping foolishly on Greenfairy Absinthe.

'Cigarette?' he asked, snapping the zippo lighter open to light the Marlboro that dangled out of his mouth in a rebellious way.

'No mate. Don't touch the things. But go ahead and kill yourself,' Carnegie joked.

Agro growled and punched him jokingly on the arm. 'You are such a fucking hypocrite.' He sucked in the smoke and exhaled smoke rings that vanished into the warm Queensland night.

Carnegie laughed and swallowed down his absinthe. 'Deadly shit this. Which dickhead brought this?' He giggled.

'Some fucking madman,' Agro growled. He sculled the rest of his scotch. 'Cassandra is shit hot tonight. What do you reckon? Are you going to bang her or am I going to have to?'

Carnegie smirked. 'Good luck mate. Besides Kennedy has got the hots for her.'

Agro snorted. 'The chances of him landing her are about the same chances that a pig could give birth to a Pope.'

Carnegie laughed at the stupid expression and then pointed. 'I don't know, they look pretty cosy?' Agro turned and looked and there, on the balcony, Cassandra sat listening intently to Kennedy as he smiled and talked through one his mad schemes or ideas.

'Well I'll be damned,' Agro said. 'Let me find out what he is banging on about.' Agro dodged the poker game and sidled up behind Kennedy; suggestively sticking his head in. Kennedy, deep in his own tale and wrapped up in the presence of Cassandra, did not notice Agro carrying on like a fool behind him.

Cassandra giggled and laughed at Agro's antics. Kennedy stopped, abruptly stood up and turned around. 'What the fuck?' He looked back at Cassandra who was giggling into her vodka.

Agro poked Kennedy in the chest. 'Stop boring her with your bullshit Kennedy!'

All of a sudden, everyone became interested. A trance tracked played away in the distance and DJ didn't stop from his deck.

Kennedy looked angry and uncertain of himself. He turned back to Cassandra who stood sipping on her vodka. 'Just ignore him Ken …'

'Yeah just ignore me doper.' Agro turned around. 'He's a pussy anyway,' he said drunkenly to the Pharmacist, Bruce and Heyloon.

'Pussy? Pussy!' Kennedy said softly and dangerously.

He quietly turned back to the table and picked up his bourbon glass. Everything seemed to happen in slow motion. He stepped forward a few steps and smashed the glass against the side of Agro's face. Blood spurted out and Agro screamed. He crashed into the balcony floor, clutching his ear and the side of his face.

Shouts rang out as the friends jumped to Agro's help. Bruce grabbed Kennedy and slammed him into balcony. 'What the fuck Kennedy!' He stood nose to nose, his imposing bulk against Kennedy's thinning body.

They gathered around Agro who was screaming.

The Pharmacist held his soft keyboard hands up against Agro's neck. 'Oh! He might have cut through an artery! Call an ambulance. We might lose him!'

Carnegie was in shock as he crouched besides Agro's body that started convulsing. Agro was screaming out. He turned to look at Kennedy who was in shock; looking at the blood running down the sides of his hands.

Cassandra looked up from Agro and said to Kennedy, 'What have you done?' She spoke with sadness.

Kennedy looked at her and back at his hands. 'Blood on my hands,' he said quietly, to no one in particular. He looked back at Cassandra and a single tear ran down his face. He mouthed something to her and, before anyone could react, he climbed up the balcony rail and jumped.

Carnegie froze.

On the Run

> Hong Kong

Carnegie awoke with a pounding headache. He looked around and shuddered. He had no idea where he was. A couch. It was a definitely a couch he was lying on. A vinyl one at that. A little more rustling around and he worked out that he still had a body, and his legs were attached, but they felt like hell. What had he done? He closed his eyes and in vain tried to block out the angry thudding in his head. His mouth tasted like ashes and he felt the heartburn all through his chest.

Where was he? What had happened?

He thought long and hard and then remembered something about a Hong Kong nightclub and a bunch of English guys. Wait. There were some Hong Kong girls as well.

Oh shit.

The memories flowed back.

He had been drunkenly dancing in a leather booth with a Korean girl with dyed red hair. She wasn't a classic beauty but a wild cutie that was very out there. What the fuck happened to her?

Carnegie flushed with shame. He had been very drunk. Not that he cared but somehow he still felt embarrassed by his devil may care, 'consume as much tequila

219

as possible', attitude. He pulled the blanket over his head and only then realised he was buck naked. He groaned. This was getting worse.

He was a married man and since Kennedy had died he had lost the plot.

Hammond had put it another way. 'You are fucked up mate and need help.'

Carnegie didn't believe that. The Shrink with the Gentle Tones wasn't going to get him any help any time soon and he just needed time to to get over the tragedy himself.

And, besides, he was in the game of self-help – not this other business of being a cot case and depending on everyone else.

He peered over the edge of the couch and got a nasty shock. Lying in all her natural glory was the Korean girl with the red hair; snoring comfortably on the fading red carpet. Her snake tattoo, that brought back debauched memories, rippled away across her tummy and chest as her regular breathing continued in a systematic manner.

Fuck!

Carnegie rolled back in fright. What the hell had gone down? What was the last thing he could remember?

He strained away and remembered something about pouring champagne down the girl's chest, so another unnamed girl could suck and lick it off her. He shuddered. How much had he had to drink?

His mind went off in another direction. What was the girl's name? He tried to think. Lydia? Lena? Laura? None of them sounded right in his head. But it was something like that. Had they had sex? Given the naked state they were both in there must have been some type of intercourse but why the hell couldn't he remember it?

He had been close to being unfaithful to his wife all his life, but this would strongly appear like he had finally crossed the line. He swore under his breath. Alcohol. Kennedy. A dangerous cocktail. He was angry with himself and also horrified with the thought of consequences of his actions. Would life ever be the same now he had stepped over the threshold?

The thought of his wife came to his head. And his children. He closed his eyes again and sighed.

Eventually Carnegie opened his eyes and tried to clear his mind of the negative thoughts. He knew he had to extract himself from the current situation, but that required at the very least the reuniting with his trousers and hopefully the rest of his clothes.

He sat up holding the blanket self-consciously around his groin and took a bleary look at his surroundings. It wasn't a hotel but a small apartment that must have been the Korean girl's pad. It was Spartan with a few unique items like the wall poster of Jason and the Argonauts, a full-length Japanese calligraphy artwork and a statue of a Greek goddess with a bountiful bosom.

He continued surveying the tiny apartment and then located a pile of his clothes. Unfortunately for him, they lay in the far corner next to a pile of empty Soju containers. A pair of red boyleg briefs hung from the corner of the chair next to the matching bra.

Carnegie groaned. He could only imagine the wild night that had gone on before. The air conditioner throbbed away but couldn't quite sift the smell of sex, booze and cigarettes from the air. *That explains the sore throat*, he thought grimly, especially when he saw a glass ash tray chocked full of white butts.

He slowly rolled to the side and gently put a foot down on the floor and then another. He tied the blanket around his waist and tiptoed past Lena/Lydia/Korean Girl. Within a few minutes he felt a lot better with his boxers on and his jeans.

What now? He had no idea where he was. Instinctively he patted his pockets. Something was there. The content revealed his wallet, cigarettes and his room key. Thank heavens!

How did he exit this scene, he wondered? He quietly padded over to the door, careful not to awake the slumbering girl. He was about to exit the apartment when his sense of chivalry got the better of him. He couldn't just leave her there; for all he knew she may have played the perfect host. He looked around for something to write on, but nothing came to mind.

He did spot one of those magnetic markers on the fridge. He tiptoed over to the kitchenette. He extracted a $50 Hong Kong note from his pocket and scribbled on it.

'What an epic night. You really know how to show a guy a good time. Ignore the dollar bill as I didn't have anything to write on. :)'

He pinned it under a magnetic that showed a whale rising majestically out of the water. He thought about the message for a second and added a couple of xx's and oo's just for the sake of being complete.

He was halfway padding across the living area when his hostess gave a snuffle and rolled over. Carnegie froze. Oh God don't let this happen. He stood there stiff.

Thankfully the sounds of her sleep returned, and he sighed with relief. On the way out, he grabbed his shoes and socks before quietly closing the door behind him. It was at that point of time he released, exposed to the rest of the world, he would have looked a mess. His greying hair must have been standing on end all over the place. His breath reeked of zombie's ass and he was positive at least ten other things were out of place.

He squinted into a metal panel and got a vague picture of what he looked like. Jim Carrey would have been perfectly happy with the makeup – he could play a perfect goofball addict. He desperately tried to flatten his hair and make himself look presently.

His head pounded as he walked down the corridor. A middle-aged Chinese lady hurried past, deliberately not looking at him. Carnegie never felt sicker and more self-conscious. He was lucky he was still well and truly inebriated because he wasn't sure he could do this hangover sober.

He banged on the elevator door and realised he was still carrying his shoes and socks. He sat in the waiting area and fumbled away, eventually getting them on. His feet started to complain, and he wandered in vain about how long he had been on the dancefloor.

'Big night ha?''

Carnegie looked up. It was an old man with a dubious moustache smiling at him with a gold tooth standing out predominantly.

'Umm yes.'

'You come to fuck Asian girls ha?'

Carnegie went red. 'No, No. No.' He protested.

'Hehe, I joke with you. Ha.' The old man giggled to himself before poking the elevator button again. 'This lift shit. Ha.' He grumbled.

Carnegie could have laughed. Such a surreal experience. He climbed off the floor and stood to the side, hoping to not provoke anything more out of this imp.

'Asian girls very good. Not just for fucking. Ha?' The old man chuckled. 'You take one back to your country? Many to choose from. Ha?'

Carnegie self-consciously touched his wedding ring. 'No. I'm already mar …' he trailed off, feeling horrible.

'Ha.' The old boy caught his drift. 'No matter. You have one already. You have another or maybe two more. If you have money you can have ten. Just don't let them meet each other ha!' He giggled.

He swore in Cantonese and belted the elevator button.

Carnegie said nothing.

'Old Chen here. He fucked up. Ha. Beauty wife. Very hot, horny young mistress.

Very, very good life. Drive cab. Make money. Two kids. Then wife find mistress and old Chen have nothing now. Stupid man ha.' Old Chen coughed.

'You stupid man too? Ha.'

Carnegie groaned. 'Yes.' It was the only thing to say and he figured it didn't matter.

'No matter. You young. You change. Ha?' Old Chen looked at him with his watery blue eyes.

'Change?' Carnegie was surprised.

Before anything could be said, the elevator made a distorted ding and the doors grinded slowly opened. Carnegie followed old Chen into the lift and nearly gagged. The smell of some exotic herbs or soup or something nearly knocked him over. 'Ohhhh.' Carnegie hoped he could withstand the lift going down the 60 floors …

< Sydney

The smell of roses, mingled with Cassandra's perfume, struck Carnegie in the surreal moment. He was standing next to Cassandra with his wife arms around both of them, as they all silently wept together. The tears rolled down past the sunglasses and tasted salty.

It was a small and intimate funeral, as Kennedy was a loner essentially and did a lot to avoid friends and fellowship in general. Perhaps he thought he was weird and avoided people.

'Or perhaps he just smoked too much pot?' said Hammond.

'Too early, too early,' Bruce replied, as the Pharmacist scowled.

Hammond shrugged. He was pissed off that he wasn't there and took the high-minded view he could have saved Kennedy's life. But that was classic Hammond. He took the alternate view and when it worked, it really worked. When it didn't, people wanted to see him get his weaner stuck in a drawer.

Carnegie sighed. Why had he organised the trip? And if he had, why had he organised a high rise? Why did he encourage Kennedy about Cassandra? Why did Agro come?

The questions kept coming and Carnegie sunk lower.

The service was simple and over quickly. The black suits and dresses flocked around the grave like bees around a flower before dispersing. Each sadly walking away knowing that they left a friend behind and took guilt, pain and sorry away with them. A life cut short. A life cut off.

The living gathered in the car park, mourning, desperately clinging on to each other hoping that somehow the contact would erase the sorrow and despair. But eventually the contact was pulled apart and the sorrow left to cling like a bad perfume.

'What now?' the Pharmacist mumbled, unable to provide a medical solution to the problem.

But they were soon medicated up to the eyeballs in an Irish Pub. The medicine was alcohol and it was being poured in double doses.

After a polite white wine, Carnegie's wife gently touched him on the elbow and tapped her Seksi watch. 'You coming?' she said in her gentle and hopeful tones.

Carnegie knew about the kids. He knew what the right thing to do was. But, he chose to let her go and keep drinking. Marital dysfunction could wait for another season. Carnegie's wife smiled her sad smile and patted him on the back before hurriedly leaving – searching through her large black designer bag for her keys.

'You okay?' Cassandra asked after a moment.

Carnegie turned. Her black eyeliner was running but Cassandra didn't give a fuck. She smelled like cigarettes and whiskey, which smelled pretty good to Carnegie.

'Fine,' he almost grunted. 'Cigarette?' He turned to make sure his wife was out of sight before trundling past his friends at the bar.

They were soon out in the beer garden, puffing away on Cassandra's cigarettes and draining scotch. Carnegie felt sick in the stomach and couldn't shake the final image of Kennedy leaping off the building. 'Fuck, Fuck, Fuck,' he mumbled. Carnegie slammed the last of his scotch down before shuffling out for a refill.

Soon they were back at it. Drinking. Smoking. Unable to say much but the occasional profanity and the basic of human gestures patting each other on the arm and holding hands.

'What are you going to do now?' Carnegie managed to string together some positive words.

Cassandra thought for a while.

'Well I'm going to quit smoking, working like a demon bitch and then get my 4th dan.'

Before Carnegie could respond, she added, 'But before then, I am going to drink until I drop and the walk the hangover off in the morning.'

Carnegie nodded. A great idea.

And then he saw it. A walk. A long walk.

He smiled and patted Cassandra again before stubbing out his half-finished cigarette.

'Where are you going?' Cassandra asked concerned.

'A walk.'

< Sydney

And walk he did. Carnegie went home and stuffed three pairs of clothes and a pot of Vaseline in his bag. He kissed his children goodbye, grabbed his phone charger and walked out the door.

His wife stared at him sadly as he strode off into the night.

< Country NSW

Nine hours later he stopped. He had long sobered up. But he kept walking. Walking through the night, the anger, the guilt, the frustration, the sense of being trapped, the feeling of resentment, the rage and the deadly combination of other emotions that threatened him with the foetal position and a river of tears. He did not stop walking until he came to the outskirts of Sydney and the highway opened up.

He was chafed, dehydrated and profoundly wet from the sweat that had been pouring out of his body. Carnegie looked around and booked into a roadside motel of dubious background. The bed was old and uncomfortable and there was definitely something in the roof. But Carnegie couldn't give a rat's ass and collapsed, clothes and all, into the bed with the grace of a pole-axed sow.

His sleep was long and horrible. Kennedy visited him frequently that night and even though he was exhausted physically, his mind wouldn't give him a moment's peace. His late friend floated around his bed non-stop talking about all of his conspiracy theories; only occasionally stopping to look at Carnegie with his sad red eyes.

Carnegie tossed and turned and swore. He tried sleeping under the covers and then on top of the covers, but nothing seemed to work. He got up and hobbled over to the small bathroom and drank from the tap. The scrabbling in the roof didn't help. With what little strength he had, he hurled a shoe at the roof when he couldn't take it any longer. He wept and laughed maniacally and stuffed the decaying pillow over his head. Nothing gave him solace and every time exhaustion took over and brought him into a brief slumber he would awaken again with the scrabbler running around in the ceiling; or Kennedy mumbling to himself about the moon landing or something inane.

In the end, Carnegie stuffed his headphones into his ears and turned Jack Johnson up full bore – staring wearily at the moisture-stained ceiling. The tracks went on and on until finally the sun rose and Kennedy decided to end his torment. Even the scrabbler had found somewhere to fall asleep and left Carnegie to his sleep.

He awoke somewhat recharged but with a pounding head and a sandpaper mouth. He tried for a while to wet his mouth and find some saliva but after a hoarse few minutes he decided to endure the hell and walk the few metres to the smelly bathroom.

He gulped down the water until his stomach felt bloated. Resting on the toilet, he rubbed his dry and dark eyes. 'Oh God,' he moaned. He wasn't sure where he was, but he knew he was somewhere awhile from home, as his blister-ridden feet told him. Every part of his legs hurt in a different fashion. He tried rubbing his legs, but it hurt and the angle he sat on the toilet did his back no favours.

Eventually, even the king has to rise from the throne, so Carnegie struggled off the toilet groaning and swearing. His eyes felt terribly dry and his greying hair was unkempt. He stared into the mirror and couldn't even find the energy to choose an expression that befitted his mood.

And then it hit him. He had to keep going. Despite the exhaustion, despite the guilt, despite the hatred against himself and his behaviour; he had to keep going.

The thought energised him. He hobbled into the bedroom and picked up his phone. Soon Queen was pumping while he scrubbed himself in the shower. He washed his clothes and hung them up to dry, before stretching and charging up his phone.

The phone kept beeping away, alerting him to missed calls and text messages. He ignored them and kept Freddy Mercury up loud – blow-drying his clothes until they were a combination of sodden and dry. He had to find some more provisions if he was going to make it to where he needed to go.

It was a small country town with a pub and a Post Office that Carnegie was tracked down by Agro. Accompanying him was a casually-dressed Asian in his middle ages, with a huge smile painted on his face.

Carnegie wanted nothing to do with Agro. Nor the smiling Asian. But his exhaustion and the fact they confronted him in the small pub, with intrigued locals hanging about, made him stop and sit down to sip on cold beers.

'Carnegie, mate, I'm glad I found you. I have been worried sick.' This was a different Agro, Carnegie mused. He was softer and soberer.

'Who's this then?' Carnegie asked, gesturing somewhat rudely to Agro's smiling companion.

'His name is Shing,' Agro spoke with an uncommon calmness. 'He is my meditation teacher, I wanted you to meet him. He has helped me very much in coping with the tragedy.'

'Meditation!' Carnegie was shocked. 'You, Agro, are doing meditation!'

'Yes James.' Agro gave him the universal meditation pose with this thumbs and forefingers touched together.

'Nice to meet you James,' Shing said gently; reaching out and shaking Carnegie's hand with both of his soft hands. 'Namaste.'

Carnegie awkwardly responded and turned back to Agro. 'You haven't gotten all kooky and mad on me, have you?' He was genuinely puzzled at what was an unbelievable set of events.

'No, not mad. Calm. I want you to understand that I am very sorry for my actions and, through Master Shing's help, I have been studying meditation and working to achieve consciousness.'

Carnegie grunted. 'Good luck with that,' he said somewhat bitterly.

'I understand James. Listen. I know what you are feeling. Let us talk about it together and heal together. I'm really sad and want to help.'

Carnegie gestured at the beer. 'This is what helps. This and walking into oblivion.' He felt incredibly sad.

Shing just watched him with a gentle smile.

And that was Carnegie done. He rudely shoved some dollars onto the table and swatted Agro aside when he stood up to confront him. There was no way he was getting into kooky nonsense.

Hong Kong >

Carnegie smiled as he watched two Chinese barter over some seafood. The reverie he had been in was very profound for him. The walk he had been on was a mixture of emotions and reminders of exorcising the pain he had felt. It hadn't cured him, and his depression had returned, but at least he had done something. The feeling of being trapped was a terrible one. The Shrink with the Gentle Tones had talked about this and actions to take; but he had not found out what to do and where to go and how to deal with life. Instead, he found himself on a small island in the middle of Asian slowly going crazy.

He flipped his phone out of his pocked and turned it on; waiting for the inevitable alerts and messages. Nothing. Carnegie felt disappointed. He ignored everyone but was pleased by the attention. It was an odd feeling. He knew he had serious mental problems when he wanted something but didn't want to reciprocate.

Absent-mindedly, he flipped through Facebook – looking sadly at the pictures of happier and simpler times. He opened Pandora's Box and was now playing a complicated game with his mind. And he wasn't winning.

He remembered why he had opened the door in the first place.

< Melbourne

The familiar sight of Tullamarine airport brought a raft of confusing emotions to Carnegie. He had finished his walk and spent three nights in a Melbourne hotel, rolling about in agony and slowly recovering from sheer exhaustion. Luckily, Dr Google had provided an amazing source of information to help him recover. And recover he did. On day three he had been able to walk again and sleep with the help of some pills he had bought. They had even banished Kennedy from his dreams, leaving him waking up with a clearer mind and a small sense of purpose.

He stood in the airport with fresh luggage and clothes, wondering about his next destination. Carnegie had performed the per functory tasks of advising his family of his whereabouts and had spent some chatting with his kids. He always felt so inadequate in explaining to his children where Dad was and where Dad was going. The conversations always left him guilty and helpless. Even his best efforts of conveying his love left him despondent and hurting inside. He wondered on a daily basis why beautiful people couldn't have children and fuckups like himself could reproduce almost at a whim.

Carnegie brushed off the thoughts and steeled himself. He looked up at the departure boards and instantly he knew where he had to go.

He sighed and walked to the sales counter.

A short time later, he was perched at a café – staring vacantly at a newspaper and sipping on a latte. The coffee tasted strong and delicious. He realised that he been off caffeine during his long walk and the coffee had instant impact. He felt awake and his senses tingled in anticipation off what was to happen next.

'James?'

Carnegie startled and looked up. The Zen Master stood in front of him in simple, loose-fitting clothes wearing a benign smile.

'Mr Irzai!' Carnegie shook his soft hand, instantly feeling the strength in the grip. 'What are you doing here?'

'I came down to see a relative.' The Zen Master smiled and slid his knapsack off his shoulder.

'Please join me if you have time?' Carnegie was pleasantly surprised. He admired the Zen Master and his sense of purpose in a complicated and complex world.

The Zen Master sat down opposite him on the creaky chair in a fluid motion.

'Coffee?' Carnegie stood up, ready to order for the martial arts expert.

'No. I don't take coffee. Just water if you would be so kind.'

'No problem.' Carnegie filled up two large glasses of water at the counter; smiling at the pretty young barista.

'So where are you travelling to James?' the Zen Master asked in his Middle Eastern accent.

'I'm going ...' Carnegie trailed off as the Zen Master looked at him with those patient, all knowing eyes.

He looked about. 'I'm not sure where I'm going,' he finally admitted.

The Zen Master looked at him kindly; interpreting the response in the correct matter. 'The journey is ahead of all us my friend. The important thing is to keep looking.' He smiled again and patted James's hand in a very paternal manner.

Carnegie choked back tears and looked away. In such a short interaction, the Zen Master had got to the root of the matter and touched him in the core.

'I ... Mr Irzai. I'm lost.' And then it spilled out of him. He let it all out and the minutes passed by.

The Zen Master sat; his water untouched. His face blank apart from a half smile that he wore in a benevolent manner.

He let Carnegie finishes his story before patting him again.

'To lose is part of nature. The cycle continues. What is important is not lose one's self. And if we do, we must find it.'

Carnegie nodded. He knew no matter what, he had to find the key to the cage he was locked in. No matter how much wealth he accumulated. No matter what he achieved. No matter how he looked to others, the pain inside had to be healed.

'I'm a bad person,' he stated, then sighed; aware of his own self-pity.

The Zen Master smiled. 'There is no bad, nor good. There is only ourselves. Find your code. Find your self-discipline. Heal and therein lies the balance of life. You cannot live for others if you cannot live for yourself.'

It was so plain to Carnegie and made so much sense, but there was something that he couldn't quite touch. It was like a revelation that his fingers could brush but sat at just the right distance away that he could not reach out and grasp it and hold it tight.

He sat there contemplating.

Abstractly, he said the first thing that sprung into his mind. 'I'm going to go to hell for what I have done.'

The Zen Master didn't say anything.

Then, finally, with the thought hanging in the air, the spritely man hopped up from the chair and shook Carnegie's hand before walking past him.

He turned at the last moment.

'James.'

'Yes?'

'You are not going to hell. You are going through hell. Hell is on Earth and we choose to live in it. If you are going through hell, keep going.'

Without further discussion, the Zen Master strode off leaving Carnegie to ponder the discourse.

Blood Bath

< Flying

Carnegie sat in his seat – grateful for the empty flight and the emergency exit seat. He stacked his newspapers and magazines in the empty chair and gratefully accepted the warm cloth from the carefully-groomed steward, who smiled at him pleasantly and welcomed him to the Singapore Airlines flight direct to Hong Kong.

Carnegie sighed and stretched out with a myriad of thoughts pounding his head. The Zen Master had touched on a central point within himself. He vowed to go and find himself and do the journey. He vowed to heal himself. He vowed to find a way to make things right with his family and friends.

The new purpose within himself started buzzing away. The feeling of euphoria crept over his body and he smiled with the thought of all the possibilities and hopes.

He was staring out the window, still bearing his foolish dreamer's grin, when something out of the corner of his eye caught his attention. Turning, he saw the shapely figure of a flight attendant leaning over to assist an elderly gentleman with his seat buckle.

'It's okay Sir, these can get quite complicated,' she said in a fabulously unique accent that commanded Carnegie's full attention instantly. The old gentleman smiled and immediately relaxed.

Carnegie was touched by her gentle manner and wondered what she looked like and what her story was. She turned and, in a sudden, Carnegie was drawn. He felt flushed and guilty but couldn't pull his gaze away. She was an exotic creature with full lips and eyes that could tell a million stories if only the transparent fortress surrounding her soul could be broken down.

She spotted his intense gaze and smiled. Carnegie grinned like an idiot and felt subconscious as the plane began to shrink in size. 'Oh God,' he muttered to himself as he looked away.

He forced himself to stare out the window. What was wrong with him? From the state of happiness and euphoria to a new buzz. Somehow, he knew he was deeply flawed; a broken human being.

He watched the ground crew still in a daze. They buzzed around on their tiny carts laden with the baggage of many a traveller. He wondered how many bags came in and out of Melbourne every day. How many travellers arrived and left? What were all of their hopes and inspirations? Did they leave for a better place? Did the return to a happy home and happy family? Or did they come back from burying someone to a tiny flat to sit lonely over a cheap box of noodles and tea?

He fiddled with his phone and sent through a few messages; particularly to Cassandra.

'Bumped into Zen Master in Melbourne. What a champion!'

He was pleased to get an instant response.

'Maybe you should join the program when you get back?'

He took a while and then responded.

'Let's see. Au revoir.'

Carnegie switched off his phone as the final announcement came over the plane's speakers. He checked his buckle and wondered why he bothered. If fate meant the journey ended on a plane over the Pacific, so be it. He thought about taking his seat belt off in a small act of defiance but it felt silly, so he left it tightly buckled over his hips and picked up a newspaper.

He wished the media was more honest in their news presentation. It should really be classified as bad newspaper because all they fucking talked about was bad news.

Death.

Injuries.

Rape.

Accidents.

Explosions.

Corruption.

And the list went on and on and on.

He soon lost the desire to read about the extremities of humanity and his own dark desires to read about the misfortunes of others. He tossed the paper in its dishevelled state on the vacant chair next to him before stretching out again.

'Excuse me, Sir.'

Carnegie looked up. Good heavens. It was the flight attendant who he had been staring at previously. She smiled at him again and sat down opposite in the folding seat and strapped in.

This could be awkward, Carnegie thought to himself. He smiled back at her and subconsciously folded his legs up under his chair, creating more space between them.

'Hi,' he finally managed.

'Hello Sir,' she said, smiling again.

What was that accent? Carnegie cursed himself. It sounded European, but where? He looked out the window and then grabbed the newspaper again; suddenly interested in having a physical object between himself and her mystery.

French. It must be French, he thought to himself. He replayed her words in his head. It was French.

He glanced up. She had coffee-coloured skin and Asian eyes but a full body and full lips. He started working the clues out in his head.

'Sir. Stop that.'

Carnegie's head snapped up. He flushed.

'Ah. Stop what?' he said in false bravado.

'You know. These thoughts or whatever is going in your head.' She smiled. 'It's uncomfortable for me.'

Holy Fuck. Was this girl a mind reader? Perhaps men did that with her. What was her secret?

'Okay, I admit it. I am curious. French accent. Asian heritage. Mysterious eyes. Singapore Airlines. I'm simply trying to get a read.'

She laughed.

He felt his skin cool down slightly and inwardly he sighed.

'So, how did you know I was trying to figure you out?' Carnegie chuckled despite himself.

'It wasn't too hard. I saw you and your intense, almost hypnotic eyes before.

Then the awkward body movements. The furtive glances. The pretence of the paper. Very obvious.' She smiled again – her pearly white teeth somehow standing out from her flawless, immaculate face.

Carnegie laughed. 'So, it was that obvious.'

They sat in silence.

The plane began to take off. The flight attendant locked her hands over each other and Carnegie noticed white knuckles and an intensity in her posture.

Impulsively, Carnegie reached forward and offered his hand. 'I'm James.'

She shook his hand, offering a perfectly manicured hand. She seemed to be grateful for the distraction.

'I'm ...'

'Wait.' Carnegie put his hand up. 'Seeing as you can read me. Let me guess your name.'

The flight attendant smiled, somewhat amused. 'Okay.'

She looked around at the passengers in their state of inhabitancy as the plane began to climb over the state of Victoria.

'So, let me see.' Carnegie took on the form of a curious detective, propping up his chin with enveloped fingers.

'You speak with a French accent, but you have Asian heritage. Not Chinese, Japanese or Korean. Your skin colour means you are from somewhere like Philippines, Malaysia or Thailand. But you have exotic features, so you must be some form of mix, right?' He searched her face for clues. But she was giving nothing away.

'Your accent is reasonably strong, so I presume you grew up in France, Switzerland or somewhere that French is the main language.'

She chuckled. 'And I thought you were guessing my name.'

'Wait, I'm getting there.'

He paused and pretended to think dramatically.

'You carry yourself very confidently and are an experienced flight attendant and are probably in your mid-twenties. That means you probably have been on the international circuit for a while.'

'I'm guessing you are second or third generation in Europe just from your mannerisms. That means your parents likely would have given you a more European name to integrate closer to your home nation. So ...'

He paused again for effect.

'I'm going to have three guesses: Melanie, Juliette or Marion.'

The flight attendant's face showed surprise. Her eyes widened.

And then she started laughing.

Carnegie's small moment of victory was brought crashing down. She kept laughing.

'Okay. Okay. Have your fun.' Clearly his attempt at playing Sherlock had failed miserably.

She finally stopped her laughter and then said, 'Those are three names of popular French actresses. Melanie Laurent, Juliette Binoche and Marion Cotillard.'

She giggled. 'Actually, you weren't too bad. I'm originally from Laos but my parents moved to Switzerland just before I was born. Yes, I speak French and I'm mid-twenties.'

'So, what is your name?'

'Alaula.'

'Oh, so I wasn't even close. What does that mean?'

Alaula got up from her seat as the plane levelled out. 'Light of Dawn.'

Carnegie sat there, just staring straight ahead. Hopefully it was a good omen.

After a few vodkas Carnegie became playful. He kept sneaking in doubles thanks to Alaula's fantastic job. He wasn't sure if she wanted him to be merry or simply have enough booze to fall asleep and stop annoying her. She was a difficult one to read.

In the end, he got into a bit of mischief with a few other passengers before Alaula came back to give him a talking to.

'Sir. You might want to sit down and keep the volume down a bit.' She frowned at him while, at the same time, the corner of her mouth twitched to reveal some inner amusement.

Carnegie gave her a fine salute. 'Oui mademoiselle,' he said in his best French accent.

He sat down with a silly grin on his face. He could feel the booze and didn't care. He was over life and was glad to be in a merry mood. Suddenly he felt thirsty again and thought another vodka or scotch might do the trick. He reached up and flicked on the service light again. (For a third time.)

Alaula eventually turned up.

'Sir what now?' She looked slightly cross this time.

Carnegie instantly felt foolish. Maybe he was getting a little carried away.

'Um. Another drink perhaps?' he said sheepishly.

She looked at him. 'Really? Perhaps you've had enough.'

Carnegie felt his face go red. There was only one other time he had been denied service and he wasn't even an adult then.

'One more will be fine,' he said, trying to maintain the bravado.

'One more and that's it Sir,' she said in a determined voice before walking past.

Carnegie looked out the window at the clouds and tried not to meet any passengers' gaze. Perhaps he was being a little foolish. All of sudden he felt very sober.

When the drink came, it was surrounded by a few packets of peanuts. Carnegie took the meaning and didn't meet her gaze.

He switched on a movie by folding out the screen and sticking his headphones on. Retreating sometimes was the better part of valour, he reminded himself.

After watching Batman once again outwit the villains, Carnegie packed up with the plane in descent mode. He had sobered up after the dozen drinks he had consumed. He felt a bit ashamed at his larrikin behaviour. He wasn't sure what came over him.

He hoped the beautiful flight attendant wouldn't think too badly about him.

As they got closer to the ground, Alaula sat down in front of him. Carnegie deliberately ignored her, feeling silly. The intensity and tension were back again. Right now, he could have used one of his friends sitting next to him to defuse the situation or at least be less of a pain in the ass. But alas Agro, Hammand, Heyloon, Bruce, Cassandra, the Pharmacist or Kennedy was not there to be with him.

The thought of Kennedy brought Carnegie down again and he sat staring out the window in sadness. He wasn't sure what Hong Kong could do for him; but at least loud music and booze awaited to drown his sorrows out.

'James.'

Carnegie looked up and the gorgeous creature was smiling at him.

'Are you okay?' she asked, this time in hushed tones.

'You are not cross at me?' he said somewhat bluntly.

'What do you mean? You were just a little rowdy.'

Carnegie smiled. She didn't hate him. For some reason he looked down and observed her gripping the armchair tightly again.

'What's going on with the white knuckles?' he said pointing to her hands.

'Oh. It's nothing.' She crossed her arms and looked out the window.

'Now you are deflecting. Go on, tell me what's happening.' Carnegie asked, gently studying her rigid posture.

'I …' She looked back at him, intensely trying to read him again.

Carnegie sat there in quiet compassion. And then it hit him. She had some deep wound. Some scar that she felt deeply. Had she lost someone? Had something terrible happened recently?

'I lost someone recently. He was a pilot. A close friend from my days in Paris. He died in a plane crash.' She sat there with her intense gaze. 'Jeez I don't know even why I am telling you this.'

She looked out the window and tensed again.

Carnegie wanted to touch her, hug her, reach out and hold her and tell her he had lost someone close to him too. But somehow, he couldn't find the words.

He just sat dumbly, before stupidly saying, 'I'm sure you will be okay.'

She didn't acknowledge his words, so he slapped himself mentally and summed up some courage.

'Alaula.'

She looked at him again.

'I know how you feel. I lost my friend recently and this is why I am on this plane. I am miserable and running away from my problems because I am probably deeply depressed.' He didn't know why he added the last part and began to feel extremely stupid.

'Thank you, James. The problem is, I have a fear of flying, which is why I tense up on taking off and landing. It's silly, especially as this is my profession, but this stupid fear and sad memories come back whenever I am not busy.' She looked angry at herself.

Carnegie tried his luck at some black humour. 'So, you are a flight attendant afraid of flying.' He smiled. 'That's a great one.'

She looked at him and then saw his genuine attempt to lighten the mood and she laughed. 'Yes, it is a weird one isn't it.'

Carnegie felt pleased with himself. She had relaxed a little and let out that pretty laughter.

They sat back and smiled. The tension was gone, and comfort returned. Nothing more was said but they couldn't help meeting eye contact and smiling. A connection was made.

< Hong Kong

Carnegie stood at the Hong Kong baggage delivery system feeling lighter and happier. He had enjoyed the interaction with Alaula and it took his mind off his problems. He wondered if he would ever see her again.

He smiled at that thought. *Not bloody likely*. And, besides, a beautiful woman like that would already be taken; not to mention he had his own relationship to concern himself with.

He looked up at the large baggage delivery sign. He was in the right place but there were damned delays. He was desperate to check in and get out of the clothes he had worn for the better part of a day.

Someone pushed him in the back. Carnegie turned around ready to react but there was Alaula with a mischievous grin on her face.

'Hello again James.'

'Ah hello. What are you doing here?' Carnegie was surprised and pleased.

Alaula pointed at the carousel. 'Waiting for my bags, why else would I be?' she said teasingly.

'Oh. I thought you guys got special delivery or express service or something like that,' Carnegie said facetiously.

'No. We just get our bags out first. That's why you never see us waiting except for this fucking delay.'

Carnegie liked how she cursed. It was very French.

They stood there awkwardly until Alaula asked Carnegie, 'So, what are you going to do in Hong Kong now you have run away from your problems?'

'Check in to a hotel. Smoke like a chimney. Drink like a fish. Dance like a daredevil,' Carnegie said with a little flourish at the end.

'Really. Should the women be worried?' She teased him again.

Carnegie winked but didn't say anything – instantly feeling guilty about his marital problems.

'You shouldn't smoke either. Even though I am French I don't like the habit. It is smelly and kills people.'

Carnegie laughed bitterly. He felt the same until recently, when the horror of everything got too much and he had let himself go.

'I hope to die long before these bitches kill me,' he said, pulling a pack of Marlboro's out of his pocket.

'Tsk, Tsk,' she said, before striding forward to grab her bag.

Carnegie's sense of chivalry leaped into action and he went forward to help her. His hand brushed her hand and he felt his pulse quicken.

'I'm okay. Really, I'm okay.' She lifted the large bag off the carousel and slid the handle up as a professional would.

Carnegie stepped back, slightly hurt.

'Goodbye James. Bon Voyage!' she said and turned to leave.

Carnegie thought he saw something in her eyes. He took a step forward.

'Wait. Would you like to get a drink with me?' he said, holding his breath.

She stopped and looked at him and he thought she said something.

'So, is that a yes or no?' he asked, sounding firmer than he intended.

There was a slight change in her expression. 'No,' she said in a firm voice and turned and left.

Carnegie felt his face go red again. This damn woman had that effect on him all the time. He felt a longing for her company and also a frustration of her way of easily disabling him.

'Careful buddy, she is with me,' a male voice said from behind him.

Carnegie turned to see who the speaker was. He was a clean-shaven Englishman with slicked back hair and a 'go fuck yourself' grin.

'Bite me.' Carnegie turned back to look at the carousel and instantly felt all eyes on him. He looked around. The poker-faced Asian men and women looked at him with no emotion, but he knew what they were thinking.

And he was rightly humiliated.

Hong Kong >

Carnegie smiled bitterly at the memory of Alaula's public rejection. He had deserved it. He was a cocky schmuck who had deserved to be put in his place. He wondered what the flight attendant who was afraid of flying was doing right now. He glanced at the watch he bought spontaneously. 12.45.

As usual, the streets of Hong Kong were packed with people on their way to their next destination.

Carnegie was jealous. They all had purpose. He had none except to exit this world; and he couldn't even muster the courage to take that step. He was spineless. A self-pitying cockroach that didn't even have the decency to behave like a cockroach.

He wallowed in his misery a little longer before slouching his way into a bar and ordering a beer with a tequila chaser. The alcohol added to alcohol and soon he was compounding his misery.

The next two bars provided no relief or distraction, so he slumped into a bus shelter and lit another cigarette. He was sadly listening to James Blunt when he decided to check his email.

He froze as he read the subject of an email from his wife.

IT'S OVER.

His fingers shook as he finally mustered the courage to open the email. It was short and to the point.

James,

I can't do this any longer. I know it is over. I have tried being patient. I have tried to be understanding but enough is enough. Come back home for your kids and to work out how we can separate in the best possible way. You can then get on with destroying yourself, but I can't live like this any longer.

I thought you just needed time but now I realise you are lost to me.

Please come home so we can deal with this. I know you need help. You need professional help.

Please let me know if you need one of the family or friends to come and get you. Take care.

He visibly slumped and lurch wildly into the dirty park bench with his head in his hands.

The shock came first and then there was paralysis. What he knew deep down was happening had happened, despite his undead denial. He felt like vomiting. His hands shook violently, and he sucked down the cigarette smoke deep into his lungs before exhaling violently.

He read the email again. And again. Again.

Finally, as the moment seemed to last forever, he rose up and punched the wall. The pain that sprung from his knuckles did nothing for him. Onlookers looked alarmed as they walked past. Carnegie look away ashamed and in pain and walked away.

He couldn't walk too far. Carnegie dry wretched into a bin full of disgusting left-over shell fish and burned out cigarettes. He could feel his stomach turning again and doubled over. Finally, he could make the short stumbling walk to the nearest bench. The old lady sitting quietly saw him coming up and, in a very dignified manner, rose up and politely walked away. Carnegie sat down breathless and ran his sweating hands through this greying hair.

Brutal imagery filled his mind.

The birth of his children. The joy of the first bath. The little hands holding on to his little finger. The pure joy and paradise lost.

Dancing with his wife on their wedding day.

His wife crying when he came home. The way she quickly wiped them away when he drunkenly lurched in late at night.

The look on his children's face when he sat staring vacantly into the distance from the balcony.

'No. No. No. No,' Carnegie moaned.

He instantly stiffened up when a concerned passerby nearly stopped to ask him if he was okay. Carnegie was humiliated but pride still lived somewhere in the shell of a person.

He sucked the last of the cigarette down and hurled it into the gutter. His hands shook, and he felt frozen in time.

It started to rain but Carnegie didn't care. The beats from a nearby night club pounded him. And the drops of rain intensified.

Carnegie didn't move and then a calm set into him. A dangerous calm.

He shuffled off to his hotel, stopping at a late-night liquor store. He pushed the door in, nearly falling over a stacked-up collection of shopping baskets. He ambled up to the counter.

'What's your most expensive liquor?'

The Asian lady behind the counter looked him up and down. 'What you mean?'

'You know, your most expensive bottle of booze.' He gestured in a silly matter, knowing it probably confused the matter more.

The Asian lady shouted out something in Cantonese and a young boy sprang from behind a door. Carnegie didn't even see in his drunken haze. The little kid held a Nintendo and looked grumpy.

'What you want?' he said while desperately trying to pause his game.

Carnegie repeated himself. Speaking slowly while steadying himself with a hand on the cluttered counter.

The little man said something impatiently to the lady behind the counter.

'Ah,' she said. 'You come here.'

He wandered through a back room with the lady and she pointed to an ornate bottle of scotch whiskey – Carnegie didn't recognise the brand.

'Four thousand Hong Kong dollar,' she stated. 'You want?'

'Yes. Yes.' Carnegie said, impatiently fiddling for his Platinum American Express.

With the package under his hand he exited the shop once again – nearly falling over the red plastic shopping baskets.

'Fuck!' he swore loudly, as he tumbled out of the store and up to his hotel.

Eventually he made it to the hotel and brushed past the doorman. The lights in the elevator were too bright. He shielded his eyes and waited impatiently until the box climbed to his floor. Thankfully he was alone. He checked his watch again. 2.00am.

He clenched his jaw as he remembered a famous line from Blade Runner.

He ripped open the door to his hotel room. Everything was so neat and tidy.

He stripped himself naked; leaving his clothes at the door and carrying the scotch to the kitchenette bench. Soon he was standing on the balcony in his birthday suit – sipping on a fine scotch and drunkenly glaring at the world. He looked over the balcony at the little people walking around.

Carnegie blew out smoke and said to himself, 'Nope.'

He grabbed the bottle of scotch and his Marlboro's and stumbled into the bathroom – pouring a bath and slopping it full of bubbles.

While it was pouring, he collected some items: the steak knife from the block in the kitchenette, an ashtray from the balcony and the gun hidden in his closet. He dragged a stool and propped it up next to the bath before arranging the gun, knife, cigarettes and bottle neatly on top of the stool.

He plunged into the bath and swore loudly as it burned his feet and body. Where he would normally have leaped out, he allowed the pain to come.

He let out a guttural roar as the pain kept coming and coming. His skin began to turn an angry red, but he stayed and finally the amazing coping mechanism of the human body kicked into gear – stabilising the temperature of his body.

'Fuck you, life.'

He lay there, sipping on his scotch and thinking about his life. Eventually, the memories came to a halt as he realised he was in a hotel bath in Hong Kong alone. He checked the time again. It was 3.33am.

Carnegie narrowed his eyes bitterly and lit a cigarette contemptuously – inhaling deeply. He coughed several times and laughed at the irony. The bitches didn't kill him.

Carnegie reached out and grabbed the knife. It felt the right thing to do. He closed his eyes and inhaled again. Enough was enough.

He flicked the cigarette at the bathroom sink and drew the blade over his left wrist. The water turned red and Carnegie sighed.

His last thought came in typical Hollywood style, courtesy of Blade Runner.

'Wake up! Time to Die!'

Pyscho

Hong Kong >

The angels came for him. They were dressed in white. Carnegie lay there in a state. As they approached, he was surprised. They were Asian. They were both Asian. And one of them had a familiar face.

He just lay there. He couldn't feel anything, and he smiled. He was happy. For some reason he hadn't ended up in hell. He couldn't understand why but he didn't care; he just floated along. He couldn't understand what the angels were saying but they stood next to him and hurried him along to what he thought was the gates of heaven. He tried to get up, but something restrained him. Perhaps his body was still in a coffin, so he couldn't get upright until the next event happened.

He smiled and lolled back and then blackness overcame him.

Bright light sprung forth, shaking Carnegie into a vision. This time there were four more angels and they were looking over him. And they were all Asian again. Carnegie wondered if heaven was full of Asian people because he died in Hong Kong. It was a silly thought to him. He wondered how he would manage the diet in this Asian heaven but figured there might be some of those wonderful dumplings he loved eating.

Blackness came again.

'James,' said a faint voice that was familiar.

He concentrated in the darkness. This wasn't his perception of heaven.

'James.' The voice had a familiar gentle tone to it. Somewhere in his mind he recalled where he had heard it. The Shrink with the Gentle Tones.

What was he doing here in heaven? Did shrinks even believe in heaven?

Slap.

Carnegie forced his eyes open. Urggghhhh. With the bright light attacking his brain, he managed to focus on what was in front of him. It was his therapist's face, standing over him and looking deeply concerned.

'Errr,' Carnegie slurred. He looked around and got a shock. He wasn't in heaven, he was alive. He registered that he was in a hospital and, judging by all of the oriental people, he was still in Hong Kong.

He looked down at his left wrist and saw the heavy bandages.

'Nooooo,' he moaned. He was alive.

'How are you feeling James?' his therapist asked him, smiling with his little moustache twitching away.

Carnegie closed his eyes and did not reply. A million emotions hit him hard. He couldn't do anything other than cry. And he sobbed. He wept for his wife and children; for the Man who Couldn't Die; his friends and the loves that he had in his life. He couldn't stop thinking about how he had failed in being a failure.

'There, there.' The Shrink with the Gentle Tones patted his shoulder and perched on his bed.

After what seemed like an eternity, Carnegie eventually stopped weeping. There were no more tears to cry. He had nothing left to say or do. He was at ground zero.

'Whatever you want doc,' he said feebly.

'Say again James.' The shrink leaned towards him and Carnegie smelled his faint aftershave.

'I'm on the program, whatever you want,' he said hoarsely. He had lost everything, and everything was lost, so there was no point in fighting.

'It's okay James. You were very lucky.'

Carnegie disagreed with him entirely but was too weak to voice an opinion.

'As for a plan; I'm going to get you back to Australia but first you need some good therapy. There is an excellent centre here that treats people and rehabilitates them back in health. I recommend it. Especially after what you have just gone through.'

Carnegie thought for a while, an exhausting process. 'That sounds fair but one favour please.'

'What's that James?'

'No friends or family. I am alone and want to stay that way.'

'Are you sure?' his therapist offered half-heartedly.

'I'm sure.'

'Okay, you rest now.' He patted Carnegie's arm again and was ready to move out when Carnegie lethargically grabbed him.

'Yes James.'

'Thanks for coming over to Hong Kong for me doc. I really appreciate it. But why didn't I die?' he asked tiredly, with sorrow building up tears in his eyes.

'Two reasons. Because life is like that; sometimes you get a second chance. And the other more practical reason is you set the smoke alarm off and the hotel staff got to you in time.'

He smiled and patted James again before leaving.

Carnegie was in shock and tried to shake his head at the irony. Cigarettes had saved his life. He vowed never to touch the goddam fags again.

The centre was appropriately named 'The Alain Bertrand Centre for Mindfulness and The Next Phase'. But Carnegie didn't like the name. In fact, he hated it. He couldn't understand why people had to complicate and create fancy names. It should have read 'The Nuthouse for Clinical Fuck Ups'. That would be a more honest approach.

The stereotypical poker-faced orderlies checked him in before an annoyingly positive woman named Beatrice took his details down. The Shrink with the Kindly Tones had explained the set-up but wasn't able to be there due to an urgent family matter in Sydney. He apologised profusely but Carnegie had waved him away. He already had guilt dripping off his arms, shoulders, head and more importantly his heart. He didn't want to add to his long list of debts to society.

They led him to his room like a lamb to a slaughter. He was numb at the surreal sights of the mental institute. It was a small, cell-like room with jasmine walls and a little white bathroom neatly built into the room. Carnegie sat on the edge of his bed and, with the cocktail of drugs flowing through this blood stream, he just sat staring distantly through the wall and through the edges of time. The air moved around him. Tiny little barely-visible fairy dots circled at the edge of his sights. He was familiar with these little dancing spirits. They usually visited him shortly after his hangovers started disappearing.

But these little fellows were more benign and less troubling.

It was a long time of staring at the dancing clear pixies in his peripheral vision, before he realised a head was poking through the door staring at him. He turned to see the chubby face of a Chinese man with an absent smile on this face.

'Yes,' Carnegie said, simply looking back with his own vague and absent smile.

'Oink,' replied the man and the head disappeared.

Carnegie shook his head and rubbed his face. Had he imagined what had just happened? He leaped to his feet and looked out the door way. A little chubby man was waddling away quickly.

He shook his head again. He had seen a lot of films like *One Flew Over the Cuckoo's Nest* and *It's Kind of a Funny Story* but he was hoping the stereotype wasn't true.

'Don't worry about Piggy,' said a small voice to his side. He spun around to see a little woman sitting there in a wheelchair. She was prematurely grey in her mid-twenties with a red bandanna pinning up her hair. 'He wouldn't hurt a fly.'

'Umm,' Carnegie said slowly. 'I wasn't worried he was just staring at me. And I kind of worried that I was seeing something.'

'Hehe,' she giggled. 'Them drugs will do that to you. They will fuck you up more than you are fucked up yourself.'

She rolled forward and put out her hand. 'I'm Dora.'

'Oh. Hi. I'm James,' he said shaking her hand; surprised to feel the roughness of her palms.

'Dora like the Explorer, huh.' Carnegie remembered the countless videos he had watched with his little girl. 'I suppose I should say Ola!' he said with a poor attempt at humour.

'Ha. I get that all the time. Ola me Dora!' she said with a fake Latin accent.

'So, what's your problem?' she asked.

'Ah. Well it's a long story,' he said, trying to deflect the question.

'Yup. But we have time for it. I'll give you the abridged version, because you will be wondering why,' she rolled past him into the room.

Carnegie was surprised at her forwardness but mutely followed her into the small room he was to call home.

He plonked down on the bed waiting for her to continue.

'You see it's the damn legs of mine,' she prodded her legs. 'They stopped working one day and it drove me crazy. I was a marathon runner and next thing your pins don't work. It kind of screws you up. So, I tried to throw myself off a balcony. I couldn't even manage that,' she snorted. 'So, they put me on drugs and in a wheelchair and here I am!'

Carnegie was surprised but felt he shouldn't be. Of course, there would be others here who had tried to take their lives. But he wasn't in a mood for a confessional, so he asked another question.

'So, why can't you get out?' He thought for a while. 'And why don't your legs work?'

'Great questions. I've been asking them for a while myself. They don't know why my legs don't work. They think it's my brain, but they don't know anything else and they have tried everything including throwing me into a pool to see if I could instinctively swim.'

Carnegie was horrified. How could you throw a wheelchair-bound person into a pool of water? What was this place!

'Don't worry,' Dora said, seeing his expression. 'It was just some sort of radical treatment like hitting someone over the head after they have been hit over the head.'

'Why would you hit someone over the head that has been hit over the head?' Carnegie asked in amazement.

'I don't know,' Dora replied bluntly. 'Doctors can be awfully fucking weird at times. And don't get me started on shrinks.'

'Hahaha.' Carnegie laughed. 'Yep they are a bunch of odd balls themselves.'

'So, why can't you get out?' he asked again.

'I don't know. They won't let me out. They say it's because I have nowhere to go and it's safer for me. I might try and roll in front of a train or something like that. But I've kind of got used to being on wheels. Of course, I miss sex and running but you are what you are, and depression doesn't last forever. Especially when you are ripped up on chemicals!'

She was about to say something further, but a bell rang.

'Come on James. Let's eat!' she said, spinning around and rolling out.

'Urr. Lunch right. I don't feel like eating anything.'

She looked over her shoulder and pushed back a greying lock. 'You had better come, or they will force you to come. We all have to live by the rules and the food is quite good since that French chef started volunteering on weekends. And today is Saturday, right?'

Carnegie's brow furrowed. He wasn't sure what day it was and since they had taken his watch and phone he wasn't really sure about much anymore.

But one word resonated. One precious word.

Volunteer.

He sat there. Slowly slurping a hot tomato soup and dipping his bread stick. His mouth was numb but curiously, he wanted to eat.

Dora was right – it wasn't too bad, and he was glad it was only soup.

'Gollum.'

Carnegie looked up to see a thin and very tall man offering a giant hand to him. 'James,' he said, wondering what Gollum meant. They shook hands. Gollum's hand was chillingly ice cold.

The giant beanstalk of a man sat down opposite of him and started eating in silence. He had dark ringing eyes and a neat bald patch at the crown of his head.

Carnegie shook his head. Was this the Gollum from the Lord of the Rings or the Jewish legendary figure who came to scare kids and rise up and destroy enemies? He didn't want to meet either version.

They ate lunch in silence, apart from the loud chewing of Piggy on the other table who seemed to get a great kick out of slurping, burping, crunching and munching at the highest possible volume.

Volunteer.

The word sprang around. His head. Echoing away. He didn't know what it meant, so he kept looking around the room for more clues as to why this errant and interesting thought began to occupy his mind.

The cafeteria was a decent size for the mid-sized group of people in place. It was clean and hygienic and reminded Carnegie of a hospital ward. But then he was in a hospital, he mused to himself. Clearly his mind wasn't working very well.

Surprisingly, there was a lot of young people in their twenties and thirties. They didn't look too different to the average joe walking on the streets. He spotted a man with an odd beanie, a girl with a tattooed face and old man that looked like IP Man sitting calmly and delicately picking away at his lunch.

Volunteer.

Volunteer + French chef.

His mushy mind was not making much progress. He was about to stand up when an eerie shadow cast down on this plate and table. Carnegie turned and looked up.

A middle-aged Japanese fellow with an expansive goatee stood over him. 'You are a dirty motherfucker,' he said, pointing at his face. 'How are you shithead?' He bowed politely.

Carnegie was taken aback. Instinctively, he started to stand up. Somewhere in his drug-addled state the defensive part of him rose up to challenge this new comer.

'Easy friend,' said Gollum. 'He means no offense. He has a disorder. He is like that to everyone.' He put a giant paw on Carnegie's arm as Carnegie sank back into his seat.

'Yeah sorry mate,' said the swearer as he sat down next to Carnegie. 'I can't help you are a miserable wanker.' He tilted his head politely towards him, swore again in Japanese and started to eat his lunch quickly. For some strange reason, Swearer looked perfectly happy. And perfectly bonkers.

Did the two go together?

Maybe the only rational response to this life is controlled insanity?

Carnegie blinked twice and took a deep breath. This place might take a bit of getting used to.

Volunteer

Later that afternoon, he had another visitor. The man who walked backwards. *What the fuck is this place?* Carnegie thought to himself as a greying old timer walked in backwards, sat with his back to him and started talking.

Carnegie just listened to him rant and rave about the condition of the air conditioning before he walked backwards out the door and on to the next listener. He didn't know his name, nor did he ask Carnegie's name.

Carnegie shook his head again and lay down on the bed. He was fucked up. But these people were really fucked up!

He wondered if they had a good counsellor like the Shrink with the Gentle Tones. Somehow, he doubted it. He scratched at his stubble, painfully aware of the bandage on his wrist and its dull throbbing.

Then it hit him again. Volunteer.

Wait a sec, he said to himself. Who in their right mind would volunteer here? Especially a French chef. That made no sense.

He rose out of bed. He had to find this volunteer and try to find out what was going on.

Carnegie quietly walked down the hallway until he found a somewhat friendly orderly who spoke in tones almost as soft and gentle as the Shrink with Gentle Tones. It turned out his name was Lee Lee. Carnegie immediately wanted to make a sarcastic joke about Lee's parents' lack of imagination, but something held him back.

'Lee.'

'Yes, Mr Carnegie,' Lee said putting his clipboard down and smiling with perfect white teeth.

'Ah, this is going to sound stupid, however …' Carnegie paused. 'Do you happen to know if there is a French chef that volunteers here?'

Lee smiled. 'Yes, you mean Alaula.'

Carnegie shrugged; the name not resonating with him. 'I guess so, if that is his name.'

Lee chuckled. 'It's a she not a he.' He laughed a little more.

'Oh. Sorry.' Carnegie shrugged again. The name didn't seem to have an obvious gender attached to it.

'Why do you ask?' Lee raised an eyebrow playfully and clicked his pen a few times.

'Um. I have this thing about.' He coughed. 'Well it's odd but is she really a volunteer?'

'Yes. Why do you ask?'

'Here?' Carnegie gestured to the floor with an exaggerated point.

'Yes.' Lee paused. He saw the look on Carnegies face. 'Ah I get it. You are wondering why she isn't making lots of money in a fancy restaurant downtown?'

Carnegie nodded. He got the volunteering. Just not the French chef part. At least in his addled mind, something didn't add up.

'Well if you need to know, you can ask her. I'm not sure it's my place to tell her story.'

Carnegie nodded again. 'Where is she?' Something sparked in his head. He flushed and felt self-conscious. He absentmindedly rubbed his bandage. And then put it behind his back wishing the ground would swallow him. The bravado was gone. And something had come.

Lee didn't seem to notice or care. He just said simply, 'Well find her in the kitchen. She will be serving dinner soon before going away for a week.'

Carnegie smiled. What luck. He could find this Alaula and ask her about this volunteering thing.

Off he went with a purpose. A simple quest. Or the beginning of a quest. An old flicker of excitement burst forth. Carnegie felt it but wasn't sure it was a good thing. He was determined to leave a new man or not at all.

He saw her. His jaw dropped. His eyes widened. And then it came back at once. It was Alaula: the lovely flight attendant he met on the way to Hong Kong. He smiled and then he stopped.

It was Alaula with the handsome pilot boyfriend.

And then another thought.

It was Alaula who rejected him directly and publicly.

The 'No' reverberated across the ages and smacked him in the head. His pride seized up his throat and his walk turned to ducking behind a column. His mind was a toxic whirlpool of emotions.

What the fuck was going on!

What in the almighty was she doing here?

Wait a sec. Carnegie started to breathe. *This has to be some sort of trick*, he reasoned with himself. Was it a trick of the centre? The trick of the Shrink! He felt anger. Maybe his mind was tricking him. He rubbed his eyes. Then he slapped himself on the face without making too much noise.

Taking a deep breath, he slowly peered out from behind the column. There she was. She was instructing some kitchen hands in preparing some food.

He sniffed. More soup. French onion? No, too obvious. Probably something exotic like she was. He could hear her talking away in a firm but not bossy manner. *Oh God*, Carnegie thought to himself. *That accent!*

He was behaving like a silly teenager, he told himself.

Then he remembered. *Volunteer.*

Right. Volunteer.

He wrestled his pride back into its place and slowly walked over to the serving area.

She spotted him coming and he was pleased. He thought. Then her eyes widened slightly. But he was displeased when she demanded of him why he was there.

'I remember you. You were the flirty Australian going to Hong Kong.' She didn't look pleased.

'Ummm.' Carnegie put his hands together in front of him, clasping them nervously.

'Wait.' She looked him up and down. 'Oh,' she said gently.

There was silence. Then she turned around and ordered the kitchen hands back to their duties. They had stopped and stared at the pair.

Carnegie finally found his mouth and his sense.

'Yes. I'm here. And sorry about the behaviour in the plane and the airport. I guess I was a bit forward and I didn't realise you had a boyfriend,' he smiled ruefully.

Alaula smiled a little. 'Don't worry about it. He's gone in any case. Off with another flight attendant I expect. But that's men.' She shrugged and scrunched up her face.

'Not all men ...' Carnegie began to say but then realised he was an idiot, a hypocrite and the great sinner. For he had long ago missed the mark.

Alaula pretended not to hear him or notice his embarrassment.

'So,' she said sharply and pointed at his hidden wrist behind his back. 'Are you going to tell me or not?'

She was direct.

Carnegie wasn't sure if he liked that or not. But Alaula reminded him of Cassandra and he felt he could trust her. As long as he didn't look into her eyes for too long. Then he wouldn't be able to trust himself.

'Yes.' Carnegie looked down feeling stupid and foolish. And old. Too old and too stupid and too foolish. He could hear his father's booming voice echoing through this mind: 'THERE'S NO FOOL LIKE AN OLD FOOL.'

'Well ...' Alaula grabbed hold of him, sensing his vulnerability and weakness. She led him to the nearest table, managing an imperious flick of the wrist at the staff which roughly translated to –

1) *Get on with your job*
2) *Stop eavesdropping*
3) *I'm busy*

They sat down on the not-too-uncomfortable benches.

He looked at her with tears in his eyes.

It was his first interaction with a friend or someone that knew him from before (was she a friend or did she know him) apart from the Shrink with the Gentle Tones.

She softened and offered a corner of her apron that wasn't splattered with soup, meat juice or melted cheese.

It was a surreal moment. Carnegie couldn't resist a giggle. Alaula responded with a giggle as well.

So, he told her his story. And he summarised. Because he was blatantly aware that he was interrupting her schedule. But she didn't seem to mind and, in the end, there were tears streaking down her coffee-coloured face.

'Oh, I am sorry,' Carnegie said automatically touching her shoulder.

'No, it's okay,' She sobbed a little and looked for a corner of the apron. But there was none, so Carnegie pulled out his shirt and offered her a space for her tears. She wiped her face with his shirt and they had another laugh.

'My brother committed suicide,' she cried a little more. Carnegie couldn't help but hold on to her and hug her tightly. 'That's why I volunteer here between my flight roster.'

Ah, Carnegie thought. *There it is.* Somebody who had risen above and had a purpose and was giving their services to help the needy. A volunteer. He felt light. This was no strange circumstance. This was not sleight of hand or trick of the mind. This was a leading lady right there with him.

Suddenly, he was aware he was holding this beautiful lady. And he had no right to.

He slowly eased away from Alaula and patted her again.

'I'm so sorry about your brother,' Carnegie said in a manner that was a little stunted. All of a sudden, he felt terrible. He was a reminder of her brother's suicide.

He felt sick and nauseous. And ashamed.

Alaula wiped her face again and firmed up. 'That's okay James.' She stood up. Time had flown. Carnegie always got mad at the universe and its maddening ability to speed up the good times and slow down the bad times!

'Wait,' he said. 'What should I do?' He instantly regretted asking her. Or rather asking anyone. Entrepreneurs always had the vision. Always had the answers. Had he lost the madness and the magic.

She turned and, before she could proffer any advice, he said quickly, almost stammering, 'What I meant to say. You are doing good and bad has been visited upon. I have done bad, so it would seem I should do a LOT of good.' He was instantly confused. But she got it. Boy did she get it.

'James. You need to sort yourself out. You are no good to anyone like you are. You need to reconcile yourself. What is that word? Ermmm.' She swore in French, looking for the word.

Her swearing in French made him smile and feel a bit weak in the stomach. He couldn't think of the word either and contented himself in smiling like a schoolboy.

'Ah Salvacion!' She smiled at herself. And swore again.

'Salvation?' Carnegie was confused. He grimaced. That sounded like religion.

'I didn't pick you as a religious person,' he said, trying to keep the disappointed tone out of his voice. *God*, he said ironically to himself, *I am not going back here again.*

Her eyes flashed a little too dangerously and she stepped back towards him, arching her slender neck up at him. Carnegie almost stood back. The wings of the butterfly causing a tornado.

'We should not disrespect people's beliefs, hopes and choices. Their faith. But I mean salvation in the terms of being saved.' She looked at him with saucer eyes, somewhat staring into his soul.

'Saved from what though?' he asked puzzled.

She stared at him. Red passionate mouth slightly agape. The silence.

Then she laughed. And it was genuine. The sound of tinkling crystal echoing through the caverns of the centre. Her workers stopped serving the food into the large containers. Carnegie stared and then he laughed as well.

Fool! Idiot!

Of course, he understood. He laughed as well.

He needed saving. He was a sinner. He had fallen short of the mark. The arrow had missed its mark. He had entered the underworld and was roaming lost. Seeking the peace of death.

He had been saved from bankruptcy. He had been saved from death. He had been saved from lost potential. He had been saved from ruin.

He laughed harder. Longer. The tears ran down.

Carnegie sank to his knees, stunned by the realisation. Of course, he needed salvation. He was his salvation. And this little exotic angelic creature had rescued him from hell. Unlike the failed man that was Morpheus, Beatrice had come and pulled him from the dark world of hell. The scales fell from his eyes. The darkness cleared away.

There was no one but he.

Work out your own salvation. The words hit him hard from his Christian upbringing.

He reached out and held her hand, impulsively touching his forehead to her hand.

'James,' she said in embarrassed tones. Once again, she flicked her wrist at the workers and quickly and quietly, with smiles on their faces, they set about their activities; buzzing away like bees.

He held her tight. And then finally he rose again.

'Thank you.' It came out choked and hoarse. The fire raged through his heart. This was not love; this was more. This was love for himself. A love for the world. A love for this angel. A love for Salvation.

He hugged Alaula tightly and took control of himself.

'Merci. Merci beaucoup cherie.' He bowed low to her with no form of mockery or puppetry but bending his body to her felt like the only thing he could do. And in that moment, Carnegie bowed to the world.

They embraced one more time. A lingering smile between them that promised one more day. But more importantly, they smiled for the sinner. And they smiled for salvation.

Because he had fallen short of the glory. However, like all beautiful tales of the human spirit, death did not take him but rather it built him. The phoenix rises. From the ashes. One tear drop in genuine love touches the tongue of the parched soul and life begins again.

But not an old life. The hero does not rise from the grave. The soul does.

Inmates

Hong Kong >

Fourteen days later – or was it fifteen – the Shrink with the Gentle Tones came to visit Carnegie in his room. Carnegie sat there listening to him speak about his schedule and his apologies before tiredly waving him away again.

'It's ok doc and I'm doing fine,' he rubbed his numb face and stared blankly at his therapist.

Carnegie had spent the previous fortnight in a chemical and emotional state. He had dutifully taken the pills that were doled out. They calmed his mind and helped him to stop crying and stop being paralysed by thoughts of the past, present and future. He kept Alaula's face in his mind but did not dwell on her as a romantic interest; instead a Joan D'arc symbol of a just cause and a heroic quest.

There was something there. But he couldn't figure it out. The epiphany was tantalisingly close but every time he reached out in his mind it would allude him. So, after a while he let go of it. And just spent time with the folk and their madness.

It was both entertaining and saddening and a tiny but maddening. He felt his soul being aroused but impotent in doing anything with it.

'So how do you feel?' his therapist asked him.

'Drugged and bewildered but otherwise okay.' Carnegie replied, not sure what to say or how to articulate his current state of mind.

'Do you want to get out of here? Do you want visitors? Can I do anything for you?' the Shrink with the Gentle Tones asked, smiling benignly.

Carnegie thought for a while. 'Look doc. I tried to kill myself. I'm not sure I am ready for the world again. Just make sure my kids are okay and everything else is in order as best as it can be. And no, don't ask anyone to come and see me like this,' he said very directly. He muttered sorry as an afterthought, maybe it was rude of him to put it like that.

'Okay, okay.' The Shrink with the Gentle Tones rubbed his little moustache. 'I can tell you everyone is fine. The kids want to see their dad, but your wife has the situation managed. Also, the business is fine, you have a great group of managers that have picked up the slack.'

'Good, good,' Carnegie said, staring off into the distance.

'Do you know what you want to do?'

'What do you mean want to do?' Carnegie asked.

'Well you can't stay in here forever. You have the rest of your life.'

Carnegie snorted. 'I should be dead right now, so I don't know what to do.'

'What about business, your friends and family?'

'Yes, I know. But I don't feel ready yet. And I don't feel interested in anything much anymore. I don't want to go back to the old version of myself. I am content to just sit here and wait for something to come to me. I mean, there is something. But I can't put my finger on it.'

His therapist looked at him and smiled. 'Sometimes in life you have to go looking for the next step as it won't always come to you. But take your time, you should never rush recovery.'

Carnegie nodded. That was clear to him.

The Shrink with the Gentle Tones smiled at him. 'Tell me more about this thing, or thought, you can't put your finger on.'

'Well if I could put my finger on it I could tell you.' Carnegie coughed and shrugged. 'I mean, it's there but it isn't making itself known to me. And when I chase it, it seems even further away.'

'Ah,' said the Shrink with the Gentle Tones. 'Ah.'

He wrote some notes in his notebook, leaned back in his chair and smiled that smile that used to drive Carnegie crazy. Now it just made Carnegie shrug.

'Hmmmm,' the Shrink said again. He wrote again in his notebook. He leaned in with hand propped under his chin that gave off a dramatic effect.

'When did this thought or feeling appear?' he asked, looking at Carnegie in great interest.

'Well I don't know,' Carnegie paused and tried to think. 'Maybe after I met Alaula. Yes! After Alaula.' He smiled when speaking her name for the first time since he met her.

'Oh, you mean the French chef.' The Shrink with the Gentle Tones smiled. 'She's a beauty that's for sure.' He said this deliberately with provocation, knowing his patient's attraction to females particularly of the exotic descent.

'No,' Carnegie said firmly. 'Not like that. I mean yes, she is beautiful, but no not in that way.' He felt slightly disappointed that his therapist had leaped to a conclusion that was in line with his previous life.

The Shrink with the Gentle Tones chuckled and said in impossibly gentle tones, 'Just teasing James. Glad to see you haven't defaulted to your previous mode of operating.' He smiled again. 'So, what is it then, if it isn't attraction of that sort?'

Carnegie managed a bit of a smile. 'Well she seems lovely and amazing in the way she is volunteering for others. Wait! That's it. Volunteer!' He said it with emphasis. It hit him again. 'Volunteer.'

'Go on James.'

'Well I can't get that off my mind. The word; volunteer! I mean it's serving others, right? Giving time up to help those who are needy and require assistance. I mean, she could be anything and she is hear with us crazies.'

He stood up, unable to sit down any more. Something had jolted him out of his stupor.

'Well, what do you think it means to you James?' the Shrink with the Gentle Tones asked him, trying not to smile.

Carnegie paced.

'Well helping others is what I have done through donations. But volunteering is something I never had time for and seemed to be a waste of my time and talents.' Carnegie immediately regretted the last part of his sentence.

'Sorry doc that sounded arrogant.' He sat down with a thud and ran his hand through his hair very aware of the scars on his wrist.

'No, I understood what you meant. But where is this going for you? Do you want to volunteer? Do you want to help others?'

'Ah.' Carnegie began and then closed his mouth shut. Did he? He rubbed his forehead and a million ideas and thoughts hit him. A voice spoke to him in the silence. Yes. And then another said No. What right did he have in helping others or anybody? He couldn't even help himself.

There was silence. The Shrink with the Gentle Tones somehow knew the conversation that was playing out in Carnegie's head.

'What's appealing about volunteering?' he finally asked Carnegie, writing the word volunteer in his notebook and circling it three times for good measure.

'Well it's not sexy and it's not that appealing but …' Carnegie stopped. Maybe that was it. Maybe he had been chasing the wrong things in life?

The thought puzzled him, and the voices stopped debating in his head.

'Why don't you give it a try?' the Shrink with the Gentle Tones said, softly opening his arms wide.

Carnegie paced for a while. 'I don't understand it.'

'Maybe that's the point, James. Maybe you should just go with it and try to feel it rather than understand it? Not everything can be rationalised down to numbers, business plans or logic. Sometimes our meaning and our purpose is felt here,' he gestured to his heart, 'and not here,' he pointed to his head.

Carnegie scowled for a second. 'The mind is for solving things doc. The heart is for feeling things and I haven't had a good track record operating at the emotional level.'

The Shrink smiled gently. 'Just let it sit there James. Give it a few days.'

Carnegie thought a lot about that over the next few days and decided the Shrink with the Gentle Tones was right. It was a tough bridge to climb over. But if nothing else, he realised he had nothing to lose. His brain had taken him only so far. His mind and materialistic approach had put him in the crazy bank. Plenty of money but zero meaning. He no longer had a Why. So, the who, how, where and what seemed completely irrelevant. He had nothing to lose and the damn word volunteer didn't go away.

From that time onwards, he offered to help out everywhere – except the kitchen, as he didn't want to see Alaula again. Well, he very much did want to see her, but he felt he wasn't able to see her until he had found this salvation that they talked of. Something was rising in him and he wanted to keep it away from anyone who resonated with him in such a heavy way.

Carnegie mopped the floors.

He cleaned out the bins.

He gave out hugs willingly and genuinely.

He helped with the exercises and spent a lot of time inspiring others by getting super lean and super fit.

He packed boxes away and cleaned up messes.

He joined a meditation class and then began to help with the instructions.

He talked at length with Gollum, Piggy and the backwards man.

He wheeled Dora around the grounds and entertained her with books that he found in the library. They read Dostoevsky, Campbell, Joyce, Dickens and at times when the head hurt, plenty of Dan Brown and JK Rowling.

He didn't know what to say or do but Carnegie found that listening helped his fellow inmates. And strangely enough, they seemed brighter and happier. Even though he had no revelations, ideas, helpful thoughts or cures.

Gollum seemed less severe and stopped.

Piggy started to lose weight and ate a little more gentile.

The backwards man turned around twice in one day!

And then the miracle happened. Dora.

'James,' she said one day when they were discussing Joseph Campbell's thoughts on universal mythology.

'Yes Dora,' he said, turning to look at her. 'What's up?' He smiled.

'You're a lot better,' she said smiling.

'Me?' Carnegie was surprised. 'Me?' he questioned. He hadn't really noticed. He had been more just focusing on a routine and following the volunteer quest.

'Yes you!' Dora spun around in the wheelchair and poked him in the chest. 'You have more colour, you have put on weight and you seem to be at peace. You even smile.'

Carnegie raised his eyebrows and looked at the garden around them. 'Well I suppose. Wait.' He looked at the garden. What was this? The flowers seemed so vibrant. My God! He whispered under the breath.

'Excuse me Dora,' Carnegie got up and went over to the beautifully blossoming roses. Woah! The colours were incredible. He smelled the sweet fragrance. Wow! He hadn't seen anything this beautiful for a long time. He was in a trance. It was vivid. Crystal clear. Sharp.

He took a sharp intake of breath. What was this? It seemed like he had entered the garden of Eden. 'Wow,' he said out loud. He touched the flower, gently caressing it as if it was made out of designer crystal. 'Wow!'

He couldn't stop smiling.

It seemed like an eternity had passed. Never had he felt this enchanted and so present with time and nature. The head was clear. His mouth was parted.

And before he could be in any further awe a beautiful golden bee floated through the sky and landed on the flower. It seemed like a giant in Carnegie's mind and eyes. Plant and animal and human seemed explicitly connected. Carnegie almost stopped breathing.

The bee was being.

The flower was being.

James Andrew Carnegie had stop doing and started being.

He didn't know how long he stood there for, but a voice interrupted his reverie.

'James.' He felt a hand at his back.

He turned around slowly, and Dora was there patting him on the back.

'Oh my God Dora. I have not seen anything so beautiful. Look.'

So, they stood there, the four of them. The rose blooming magnificently and the tiny little bee exploring away. And then it hit Carnegie.

'Dora. What the fuck!' he said impulsively, staring at her with a pale face. Wild eyes.

'I know James.' She wept. 'I don't know how. But I can walk again.'

No one could believe their eyes. No one could explain it. But there were tears everywhere. Dora was the centre of attention. She was studied by scientists, interviewed by journalists and visited by friends and family. Carnegie just sat there behind the scenes, offering coffee to people with a dopey smile on this face. He swore blindly he had nothing to with it but told people the feeling he had and the story of the Rose and the Bee.

He hugged Dora a lot. She was of course scheduled to leave after a period of observation. Her legs improved from the weird shuffling gait after hours of physical therapy. Carnegie just couldn't help smiling. He had nothing to say about it at all. He couldn't think it through. But it felt right and that was good enough for him.

The Shrink with the Gentle Tones talked with him a day later when he was scheduled to come in. He was beaming.

'I know doc.' Carnegie beamed. 'Can you believe Dora?'

The Shrink laughed. 'Amazing. But have a look at this.' He handed over a report. 'How are you feeling? You look great James.'

Carnegie smiled and simply nodded. 'What's this report then doc?' He saw numbers and words but didn't really understand the report or care to understand it, such was his state of being.

'Well your blood levels and all markers are exceptionally strong. You are in amazing shape.' He teasingly squeezed Carnegie's biceps that had become bigger and stronger through hours of fitness and training at the centre.

Carnegie smiled. 'Yes, I feel great – I can't remember the last time I was this fit.'

'Yes, yes.' The Shrink with the Gentle Tones smiled, 'But look at this.' He pointed to a range of numbers at the bottom of the report.

'And … Come on doc.' Carnegie prodded his therapist in his round belly.

'Well it means you haven't been on chemicals for two weeks. And you look great.' He smiled again.

'You mean?'

'Yes James, they have been giving you placebos. You are completely standing on your own feet.' He smiled and shook Carnegie's hand warmly.

'Well …' Carnegie was lost for words. He had put down his calm Zen-like state to the drugs kicking in and really working. But it was something else. Out of impulse, he hugged The Shrink with Gentle Tones.

The hug lasted long and was tender.

In that moment, the patient realised he had been with the patient.

He had needed genuine caring and had been with someone who had been genuine in the caring.

In that moment he promised to pay it forward seventy times seventy.

They talked about the plans going forward and then without much further ado, Carnegie shook hands with the Counsellor with the Gentle Tones and promised to meet him the following week back in Australia.

He stood and walked out to go and find Dora.

He left behind a middle-aged man, tired and looking at a huge file on James Andrew Carnegie. The last page had a picture of a Rose and a Bee. The Counsellor smiled and gently let his tears crash into the paper, smudging the blue ink. If he had looked closer, he would have seen the blue ink run down the page.

The mixture of art, ink and tears formed a beautiful symbol. A Bleeding Rose and a Sitting Bee.

For Others

Hong Kong >

A few days later, Dora left smiling and happy – promising to see Carnegie in Australia as soon as she could make it. Carnegie smiled and promised he would find her again and go for a very long run with her. They even agreed to retrace Carnegie's long dark walk from Sydney to Melbourne and this time, do it properly.

With Dora gone, the centre went back to its usual routine. Carnegie helped out as usual, glad for the peaceful surroundings and even gladder for the new-found peace in his heart, mind and soul.

He wrote a diary every day finishing it with the words:

I couldn't help myself, so I helped others and that was the help I needed for myself.

It pleased him to be reminded of his purpose and his great revelation.

Eventually he was given a discharge notice, so he said his goodbyes promising to return. He sat down and wrote a series of letters to his friends and family knowing that he would be going home but just not yet. There was something left to do on this island that had been both his hell and his heaven. And somewhere in between.

And then in a blur of time, he was standing under the sign that had once greeting him ominously. He felt calm despite the traffic and hustle and bustle.

Before he could hail a taxi, a familiar face hollered at him across the road. It was Agro and the ever smiling Shing.

'James!' Agro shouted at him. He had a broad smile on his face and looked five years younger. Smiling Shing smiled even broader. They hurried across the road while Carnegie smiled in a silly state.

They shared hugs and then Agro insisted they go for a coffee, refusing to take no for an answer.

'Where are you headed old boy?' Agro said with his arm around Carnegie. For Carnegie it was all surreal, being outdoors with Agro and Shing, his old friends.

'Um.' Carnegie coughed. 'I've got to go back somewhere and resolve some matters.' Agro enthusiastically clapped his hands. 'Wonderful!' Agro exclaimed. 'We'll come with you.'

Shing grabbed his arm gently. 'Yes, let's go together James.' His touch was cool and calm.

Carnegie spoke softly and in a reconciled tone, 'No thanks guys, I appreciate it, but I have to do this alone.'

He expected the usual rebuttal from Agro, but Agro just nodded sagely and then gestured to the coffee house. He ordered green tea for them, with no sense of irony, and proceeded to calmly tell Carnegie what was new among the usual gang of friends and family.

Carnegie listened numbly to the news and talked away the morning with the two companions.

Shing eventually interrupted the news reel with a wise look at Carnegie. 'James you know you can talk about it.' Carnegie was stunned out of his reverie. 'Talk about what?' he responded blandly.

Shing smiled and put his hand on Carnegie's wrist gently. 'Anything James, anything. But you have been through a lot and maybe sometimes it's good to share your journey.'

There was something bewitching about the gentle Asian's face. It reminded him of the Shrink with the Gentle Tones.

The calmness that he felt in Shing's presence, made Carnegie finally understand Shing. He had it. He smiled off in the distance. Then he realised it that Agro had it too.

The realisation made his eyes widen. He looked at Agro. Who got it, as he usually did. But this time he got it in the right and correct way. He smiled back at Carnegie and nodded.

'Yep,' he said without saying anything further nor having to say anything further.

Carnegie drank his tea and they sat there for a while in quiet calm silence.

He started to talk and then stopped. A flood of tears began. 'I don't know how to say ...' His voice trailed away.

Agro and Shing exchanged knowing glances and looked back at their friend.

Honourable Shing finally spoke.

'Go inwards James.' He smiled again. 'Go inwards.'

He looked at both of them.

Agro smiled. A serene smile eerily similar to Shing's. Nothing like the Agro of old who was a passionate raging beast of a man, kind to a fault and flawed beyond belief.

Carnegie shook his head. How things had changed.

He tried to explain his journey, but it was disjointed, and the feelings and words poured out like a volcano. Then he stopped. How could he explain it if he couldn't piece it together himself?

Normally Carnegie, the born storyteller, with natural ability of the entrepreneur, was able to explain and articulate anything – even subject matter that was foreign to him and he knew little about.

But it wasn't coming to him.

So, he simply said, 'Once I was lost, now I am found.' He could hear the soul aching tunes and words of *Amazing Grace*. Maybe he had found salvation, he thought to himself.

And in that simple thought; in the simple environment of a coffee house with two smiling old faithful souls, it happened.

That moment of enlightenment.

A coursing fire shook through his body.

Like a lot of developing heroes, he knew he had faced a literal death instead of the metaphorical death of the mid-life. The mid-life crisis. The hero's journey. The turning point.

The answers lay within. Not without. It was consciousness not rational thought.

Joseph Campbell echoed in his mind:

Those who say they know; don't know. Those who say they don't know; know.

And he knew.

It did not lie in riches. It did not lie in consumerism. It did not lie in materialism.

It did not lie in the treasures of the earth. Names on buildings. Racing cars. Nubile women. Mind-altering substances.

He had been on the fool's journey. He had chased the gold at the end of the rainbow and found it. But it was fool's gold. Holding it in his hands it had melted away. The gold had rusted. The water was rank, dank and stank.

Shing had said it.

Carnegie closed his eyes and the tears streamed down his face. It was joy. It was shame.

Agro reached out and took one of his hands. Shing took another.

'You are going to be okay,' Shing said softly.

'Now you will see,' Agro said, patting Carnegie's hand.

And he knew they were right. His heart raced, and an immense joy ran through his body. He wanted to live. More than ever. And for the purpose he had found. That precious meaning. But he now knew the past was there for a reason. To learn and to learn to let go.

They closed their eyes. An old friend. A new friend. But connected through a collective consciousness brought on, not by perfection, but the overcoming of failures and fears. The true grit that belonged not to the talented or the princes of the world but of those who were overcome and then overcame at the end of time.

Those who go inwards and draw on the source of the eternal water springing up not by outward substances but the everlasting joy of enlightenment.

The thoughts pounded at him. He knew he had to write them down. So, he promised to tell his tale. But just not now. Because there was something he had to do first. Somewhere he had to go.

He left his friends and hailed a taxi, with the promise of returning to Australia together. He immediately caught a taxi to his old hotel.

There was a dragon waiting for him. But he wasn't going to run from it anymore. The hotel loomed ahead.

This was the place of his self-destruction, his inner agony and his demons. He knew he had to go back and confront them or there would always be a landmark of fear looming in his mind, stunting his new life.

He felt nervous as the taxi pulled in to the hotel. Familiar memories flooded

Carnegie's mind. Stumbling into the foyer. Standing outside chain smoking. Hating and loving this place at the same time.

Carnegie's hands shook, and he felt desperately in need of some chemicals; nicotine, alcohol or anything to take the feeling away.

Then he remembered his purpose and breathed deeply, practising his meditation. A minute passed and so did the memories. Carnegie felt the calmness return.

He paid the driver, giving him a generous tip, and stepped out of the taxi.

He smiled at the porter who greeted him. For a second the mask dropped as the porter recognised Carnegie. He looked at Carnegie's left arm and then quickly looked away; the mask returning with its hospitable smile.

'It's okay,' Carnegie said patting him on the arm. 'I'm alive and I'm sorry for the mess I caused.'

He walked into the perfumed foyer, calmly heading towards the reception desk. Before he could get to the front counter an arm shot out and grabbed him.

Carnegie turned to see the smiling Barry welcome him. 'Mr Carnegie. So good to see you again. I trust you are feeling fine.'

Carnegie smiled back. Barry the ultimate professional knew just how to handle an odd circumstance.

'I'm good Barry. And I'm sorry for all the trouble I caused,' Carnegie said with genuine remorse. He had been a pest and a problem.

'Nooooo problem Mr Carnegie. We all have our own troubles. You are most welcome back. Let me take care of things. Would you like a different room this time?'

'No. The same room will be fine,' Carnegie said firmly. A sense of destiny had taken hold of him.

'You sure Mr Carnegie?' said Barry, his kindly face taking on a frown.

'Most definitely. Thank you Barry.' He smiled reassuringly at the caring man.

And so, after the usual checking in and paperwork, Carnegie stood outside his old hotel room door.

He had an ominous feeling but shook it off; flourishing his room key with a false bravado. The plastic card filled naturally into the slot and the familiar click softly called out to him with a promise of an open portal awaiting him.

He pushed open the door and walked in – the familiar view greeting with him a mix of welcome and accusation. It felt very similar to the feeling of walking into his own house.

Carnegie rolled his Antler bag into the room and fought back the memories of his exodus in this tiny insignificant piece of Hong Kong real estate.

He lay back on his bed and stared at the ceiling as he had done so often before. In his sobriety it seemed so plain and clean and somewhat calming. Carnegie had stretched out for some time before he kicked off the fatigue and memories and made his way out to the balcony. The landscape remained the same, however, was somewhat dull and mundane. In that moment Carnegie wanted to be anywhere else but where he was. It felt like a prison. A lonely locked cage where men willingly climbed in and remained comatose. A place where liberty was a nightmare and imprisonment represented the Holy Grail for troubled and tortured souls.

Carnegie smiled at the thought. Had he been so fucked up that he willingly submitted himself to this fate for days and months. 'God,' he murmured to no one in particular with a sense of self-realisation. He shook his head as if to clear it and rubbed his palms on the black Levi jeans that had made it through the entire journey. It felt comfortable and dirty at the same time.

Somewhere on the streets below laughter rang out and the dull thudding of someone's bass system wafted through the air in a somewhat crude and tribal manner.

Carnegie smiled again and stood up. He stretched and felt tired. He had become accustomed to his midday power naps.

He respected fatigue now. He had become very aware of himself and his body and the desire to keep it in a healthy and healed state. And if that meant afternoon siestas, well that was what he was going to do. The centre and his retreat had brought him back some very simple lessons. He began to give the world, the earth, the nature and his own place in it more respect.

He respected the natural rising of the sun and the appearance of the moon and the wonderful desire to fall asleep and wake up again reborn, fresh, energised and a new man.

Whereas, in his purgatory state he had lived like a vampire, he now lived as a creature of the day, a disciple of the sun. It felt natural and calming to have a pull from the earth and nature.

Carnegie shucked off his shoes and lay down on the couch where he had often stumbled in drunk and passed out. He let himself go and drifted off to sleep.

He dreamed of a long journey. He dreamed of passing through gates along with strangers who were on the same journey. And then he was aware of someone with him. He turned in his dream and saw Kennedy. This startled him, but he couldn't take his eyes off his old friend. How he looked different. His greasy hair was clean and hung around his shoulders. He was dressed in a clean white kimono wearing clean dark sandals that hardly touched the dreamland they were walking on. His faced glowed and there were none of the usual droll expressions on his face. The puffy eyes and dark rings were gone. Kennedy had been transformed.

He wanted to say something. But strangely his dream mouth didn't work. His lips felt like they were sewn together. Kennedy just smiled and kept walking next to him. For how long he walked next to his old friend in the dream, he did not know. But did know it was going to be okay. Kennedy was at peace and was always with them. Walking together, not being able to communicate because of their separate realms, but being able to smile. And that was all that mattered.

He woke up with the sun still high in the sky, glowing through the grey clouds and sending shards of light down onto the earth.

Carnegie shook his head. The symbols were everywhere. Why hadn't he looked before?

He stood up. He was done with the place. It held no fear for him anymore. Suddenly he wanted to see Agro and share the vision he had just been witness to. He wanted to get home. He wanted to see his kids and tell them how sorry he was. He wanted to make things right with his wife whatever that meant.

He had so much to do. So much love to spread.

It was time. Time to live and prosper.

He decided to shower before leaving and, without thinking, wandered into the bathroom, toilet bag in hand. The small immaculate bathroom stood out as the memories crashed at him wave after wave. He had walked into what was meant to be his final resting point. The emotions came rolling in.

It must have been a solid ten minutes of standing there; fighting negativity, the feelings, the bitter memories and the impossibility of living.

Eventually his troubled mind calmed. The dragon was defeated.

And in that moment, he turned and looked at himself in the mirror. A small pure conscious thought emerged. An energy came into him like never before.

A smile came from within the man. The thought echoed again and again.

He thought of his children. He thought of the Good Wife. He thought of his friends. He thought of his fellow inmates at the gloriously named mental facility. He thought of all the people in his life. He thought of all the world and its humanity. And in that instant, he loved them all.

And looking at the man that stared back at him in the mirror; he realised he loved himself. His stupid smile. His dumb worrying about aging. The struggle to sleep. The failings. The successes. The foolish mistakes. The wonderful triumphs. The addictive personality. He loved it all.

He stood with purpose and smiled at the mirror. The man on the other side smiled back and the thought, precious and pure, brought tears to both of them.

If he couldn't die for himself, he could go on living for others.

~~The End.~~ The Beginning.

About the Author

Geoff Olds has been an avid writer and poet since early teenage years. Over the past 15 years, he has focused his energy on building technology businesses, speaking at events and working as a volunteer counsellor.

Break Up. Break Down. Break Through., Geoff's first published work, is a personal collection of poetry and writings on love and grief – each entirely raw and honest.

Death of an Entrepreneur is his first novel.

Geoff spends his spare time practising martial arts, writing, travelling and helping others, which he believes is the greatest way a person can live a meaningful life.

You can read more at www.geoffolds.com

About Godsforge

Godsforge is a creative agency and publishing business dedicated to artists all over the globe. Publishing your work in a very competitive and complex world is difficult, so Godsforge works hard to bring art to the eye of the public. Our motto is:

"We're better by creating together."

You can find out more by visiting www.godsforge.com

Twenty percent (20%) of all profits goes to The 360 Foundation which is dedicated to empowering individuals through technology, training and education in the Developing World.

You can read more about our foundation by visiting www.the360foundation.com